THE MEMORY KEEPERS

THE MEMORY KEEPERS

NATASHA NGAN

HOT
KEY
BOOKS

First published in Great Britain in 2014 by Hot Key Books
Northburgh House, 10 Northburgh Street, London EC1V 0AT

A CIP catalogue record for this book is available from the British Library.

ISBN: 978-1-4714-0154-1

1

This book is typeset in 10.5 Berling LT Std using Atomik ePublisher

Printed and bound by Clays Ltd, St Ives Plc

www.hotkeybooks.com

Hot Key Books is part of the Bonnier Publishing Group
www.bonnierpublishing.com

To Nicola,
for making it happen

'Memories warm you up from the inside.
But they also tear you apart.'

Haruki Murakami

2.30 a.m., Hyde Park Estate

Seven bit back a curse as his fingers slipped on the balcony ledge. One hand lost its grip and swung free, his body smacking against the building he was scaling (completely illegally, of course). He only just managed to cling on with the other. In front of him, the wall rushed down in a hard, shining waterfall of polished white. He was only three floors up. Land on lawn from this height and you'd get away with just a few broken bones. But this house was ringed by a marble patio –

One slip and he'd be a goner.

Sucking in a deep breath, Seven grabbed the edge of the balcony with both hands again and pulled himself up. His arms were aching by now. He'd already scaled the five-metre fence to get into Hyde Park Estate, and that was *before* starting the slow climb up the side of the house, which had annoyingly tall floors.

'Why the eff do rich people need such big houses?' he muttered through gritted teeth. Of course, if *he* had millions of pounds to his name, he would probably buy a house twenty times the size of this one, just because he could. But that wasn't the point.

The balcony was small, with twisted iron bars fashioned to resemble a rose bush and painted white to match the walls. Once he'd pulled himself safely up onto it, Seven crouched in the shadows. He caught his breath, pushing back the sleeves of his top and ruffling his messy black hair with one hand. He checked his worker boots were done up securely – undone laces were the downfall of many a skid-thief – with the ends of his slim blue trousers tucked in.

The glass doors which led out onto the balcony were dark, no lights on in the room beyond. Seven strained to see through the layers of net curtains drawn across the doors, but all he could make out was the shadowy depths of the room, the sense of space and height.

A few minutes passed as Seven waited.

Leaves rustled around him in the darkness. An owl hooted from somewhere nearby, and rabbits scampered in the bushes, but for the most part it was quiet. The private estate was set within the huge grounds of what had once been Hyde Park. There were only five houses scattered within. At this late hour, even the near-constant purr of traffic and building work in the city had faded away to a thick, sleepy silence.

Seven had been observing this house long enough to know its residents' rhythms. They should all be in bed by now, including the servants. Still, you could never be one hundred per cent certain, and it was better to be safe than sorry. Seven didn't *really* fancy his chances with the death penalty.

Finally confident no one was around, he took out a lock-pick from the utility belt slung round his hips. He slid it into the doors' keyhole and eased it round in the lock.

Seven's heart hammered. A tight, anxious feeling wound its way up his chest as he worried, like he did every time, that this wasn't going to work, before – exhale, relief – there was the softest of clicks and the lock released.

'Thank you, gods,' he whispered with a grin. Not that Seven believed in any gods, of course. If there *were* any, they'd clearly forgotten to look out for him so far. But prayers were free (unlike pretty much everything else in London).

Pushing open the door, Seven slipped inside.

The first thing that hit him, as it always did, was the smell of the room. Clean air, papery and musty from the books lining the shelves, and most definitely *not* containing any of the following scents: puke, piss, shit, garbage, cigarette smoke, factory fumes, hashish, weed, or any of the million other stinks that filled the streets near his block of flats back in South.

Stretching his arms above his head to ease the knots in his muscles, Seven breathed in deep. The pungent scent of flowers filled the air. As his eyes adjusted to the moonlit darkness, he saw whole bunches of them in vases throughout the room, overflowing in clouds of pearly white. He wrinkled his nose in disgust. That was another thing he hated about rich people; they were so arrogant with their money, they threw hundreds of pounds at things that not only smelled awful, but would only die a few days later.

Creak.

A sound from the landing beyond the room. Breathless, Seven pressed back against the wall, melting into the shadows. Sweat prickled his neck. Finally, when no further sounds came from the landing, he peeled away from the wall.

'Straight to business, then,' he mumbled.

Seven was so used to thieving jobs he usually took his time, browsing the shelves, running his fingers up and down the spines of books. He even helped himself to food when it was left out. But tonight he couldn't afford to go about it so casually.

This was Hyde Park Estate, the most expensive area in North.

This was the White family's residence.

The *White* family.

This was the home of the man who handed people like him straight into the arms of Death himself, and smiled while doing it.

Moving as lightly as he could, Seven went out into the hall, which disappeared at both ends into darkness. Directly ahead was a broad, curving sweep of stairs leading down three floors to the base of a huge entrance hall. A circular window painted with intricate swirls took up most of the wall above the tall front doors. Moonlight filtered through the glass, recreating the window's pattern across the marble floor, like a ghostly tangle of vines.

It was without doubt the grandest house Seven had ever been inside, but he wasn't the slightest bit impressed. Scowling at the view, he turned away and headed down the hall.

The room he was looking for – the memorium – was at the back of the east wing of the house, tucked away behind a secret doorway in the least used of the family's eight drawing rooms. Seven had learnt these details on his observation trips. Though the memorium didn't have any windows, so he couldn't be completely sure, he'd seen the same layout in other houses he'd stolen skids from. Plus, he'd spotted figures disappearing into the bookshelf on the far right of the room. Unless he was going mad (a possibility – it was a side effect of hunger), then that had to be where the Whites' memorium was hidden.

There was *always* a secret doorway. After all, memories were powerful things. You didn't want them getting into the wrong hands.

'And guess what *these* are?' Seven grinned, raising his hands and giving a little wave as he reached the drawing room.

He only had to scan the bookshelves lining the far wall once before spotting the edge of a doorway etched into the wood, moonlight catching on the ridge. He tiptoed over. Heart quickening as it always did in this moment – his second favourite part of a thieving job – Seven pressed his hands against the wood to one side of the shelves. For a few seconds, he hesitated. If the door was locked, he'd come all this way for nothing. But, reminding himself that Northers rarely locked their memoriums, he slid his fingers into the grooves of the hidden doorway and pushed.

It opened, its weight gently giving way under his hands.

Seven relaxed, a grin sneaking its way to his lips.

And then his stomach plummeted.

There was a light on in the room, a flickering lamp set on a desk, and the door swung wider to reveal a girl inside. Her glossy curtain of auburn hair rippled in the firelight as she turned towards him. He saw it all as though in slow motion; her pretty eyes widening, her mouth dropping open, hands balling into fists at her sides.

For some mad reason, Seven didn't run. He could have. He might just have made it out. Instead, he was rooted to the spot. All he could do was stare stupidly at the girl, his lips still twisted in a half-grin, thinking how annoying it was that this time he wouldn't get to experience his number one favourite moment of a skid-thieving trip –

Getting out of the house with the stolen memories, having not been caught.

ELEVEN HOURS EARLIER

1

SEVEN

It was the room at the back of the flat. Past the living room and kitchen, the three small bedrooms and the grimy bathroom (the flat *was* being rented by three grimy teenage boys, after all), and behind a door Seven always kept locked.

There was no sign on the door. Not one suggestion of what lay behind the peeling paint. Still, Seven liked to think you could feel the power of what the door hid, like a pulse, a heartbeat, a soft touch behind your eyeballs that made you pause as you walked past. He imagined his flatmates Sid and Kola wondering, *What the eff is in there?* whenever they went by. Then they'd probably forget all about it as soon as they looked away.

But Seven didn't need to wonder, and he never, ever forgot what he kept hidden inside the blue filing cabinets behind the door.

Sometimes, before he even went into the room, Seven knew exactly what he wanted from it. A few of the cabinet handles were smeared with his mucky fingerprints from being opened frequently over the years. And, though he wouldn't admit it, even if anyone did know about the room, on top of one of the cabinets was a broken mug in which he kept his favourite pieces of the collection. Those pieces were like friends to him; were his *only* friends, really. He knew them entirely, and they were always there whenever he needed them.

Other times – like today – Seven would simply walk into the room and ask it, 'Surprise me.'

The room was small and windowless. Blue metal filing cabinets lined each wall. Tucked into one corner was a strange-looking machine, tall and skinny, just like Seven. The place was nothing like the grand memoriums of the rich people's houses he stole from, all dark, polished wood and marbled floors, but it was his, and there weren't a lot of things he could say that about.

After locking the door with the key he wore on a thin chain round his neck, Seven stepped into the centre of the room. He swiped sweat off his forehead with the back of one hand. It was just as hot here as the rest of the flat. South was stifling in October, with its cramped streets and tall tower blocks and smoggy air choked with smoke from the factories. Thankfully, in just a few minutes, he'd be far away from here.

Closing his eyes, Seven flung open his arms and launched into a tight spin on the spot. Seven turns later (that was his little joke, though it always saddened him there was no one who knew about the room to appreciate it) he stopped, stumbling slightly with dizziness. He savoured the moment, eyes still shut, a deep, rushing excitement spiralling through him as he wondered what the room had to offer him today. Then he opened his eyes.

His outstretched arm was pointed at a cabinet labelled: *Fear, Desperation and General Wetting-your-pants Kind of Stuff*. Not the world's most sophisticated labelling system – the banks and memoriums went by date – but it worked for Seven. He knew instantly what he was going to get.

'Good choice,' he told the room, grinning. 'You want to give me a little adrenalin shot, huh? Or maybe I'm getting fat and you're trying to tell me to do some exercise?'

Seven looked down at himself. Through his faded grey shirt, he pinched the flesh that ringed his belly. It was barely enough to hold between his thumb and finger.

Nope. That definitely wasn't it.

Not that he minded being so scrawny. Thieving would be pretty hard with a great big belly getting stuck in every window he sneaked through. So Seven told himself that he was glad of his size, that he had to keep himself that way. He pushed away the thought that always hovered at the edge of his mind: *Still not eating enough*.

Besides, he'd learnt to feed himself with something other than food.

Opening a drawer of the filing cabinet at random, Seven rifled through the small square DSCs – Digital Storage Clips – inside. They rattled and clinked, their metal cool against his skin.

'Today's dish *du jour*', he announced to no one in particular, in a French accent he'd picked up from the fish-houses by the river, 'is a *petit* helping of heart-stopping terror, followed by a mouthful of *très* tasty pant-pooping.'

He pulled out a random DSC. Marked in red ink across its label were the words:

10.04.2143, R.L.S., 27 Radcliffe Court

Seven labelled his collection by the piece's date, owner's initials, and where he had stolen it, but he never said what its actual contents were. Apart from the DSCs in the mug, whose contents he knew by heart, he liked rediscovering pieces in his collection. That way he could almost believe they were his *own* memories, made so long ago he'd forgotten about them, and each time he came across one he'd surfed before it was like finding his way back to a home he never knew he had.

Clutching the DSC in his palm, Seven went over to the machine tucked in the corner of the room. Twists of cables curled round it like the ivy clinging to the concrete walls of his block of flats. At its top was a rounded cap of metal. This was Seven's pride and joy: a Memory Butler 3S. He had borrowed (well, stolen) the machine from a run-down skid-surfing emporium by the river years ago. It was an old model, not nearly as sophisticated as the ones in the banks and memoriums, but it did the job.

He powered up the machine and dragged it into the centre of the room. Sitting on a stool beside it, he strapped the wristbands dangling on cables to each arm – these controlled your heart-rate with electropulse technology to achieve the best conditions for skid-surfing – and placed a cap, also attached to the machine by cables, onto his head. It clipped itself in place with the blunt-ended pincers round its rim.

Seven winced. 'A pleasure as always, Butler.'

Next, he plugged the machine's feed cable into the DSC. He watched as the bar on the control screen filled, loading the contents of the clip. As soon as it was full he jabbed the *ACTIVATE* option. He held his breath as, for one moment of delicious excitement, he wondered just what it was he was about to experience, what new world he was about to discover.

What new person he was about to become.

At first, there was nothing. Just the continued hum of the machine's vibrations and its arrhythmic clicks. The muffled cooing and wing-beats of pigeons in the courtyard on the other side of the wall. Distant city sounds as London went about its afternoon. Then the machine's humming grew louder, joined by a sharp, high-pitched keening sound, and there was a sudden flash of light that made Seven screw his eyelids together and bite down on his lip –

'*MEMORY ACTIVATED,*' came a flat, robotic voice, echoing up from somewhere deep within his skull. '*EXPIRATION IN EIGHT MINUTES, THIRTY-ONE SECONDS.*'

Seven opened his eyes.

The world had turned black. Silent. Still. It was like floating in nothingness. He reached out a hand and felt the ripple of memory-air, its honeyed warmth tickling his skin.

'OK,' Seven muttered, rolling back his shoulders and looking round at the darkness, searching for a sign as to why this memory was filed under *Fear, Desperation and General Wetting-your-pants Kind of Stuff*. He grinned. 'Do your best, R.L.S., or I'm coming for a refund.'

15

2

ALBA

Afternoon lessons were the worst. Especially around four p.m. It was the hottest, stuffiest, muggiest time of day, when Alba's ears felt like they were blocked with cotton wool and it was physically painful to keep her eyes open. Four p.m. was a time for daydreaming and naps. Lazy walks around the grounds in Hyde Park Estate. Reading a novel in the overgrown meadowland that stretched along the northern curve of the Serpentine.

It was most certainly *not* a time for Modern History lessons with Professor Nightingale, which were to lessons what four p.m. was to afternoons –

The worst.

'Then, late in the twenty-first century, of course, was the Big Dip, where stock prices crashed and international relations were at their most tenuous. And of course, the EU's dissolution and the subsequent riots and mini-wars. And of course, the Warming had taken full effect on the world, with the British Isles' climate mutating and the instability of the seasons.

Temperatures were rising by an average of three degrees each decade. And of course . . .'

Alba propped her head in her hands as though listening intently, her face dutifully cast towards the front of the classroom even though her eyes (not to mention her brain) were half-closed.

Professor Nightingale was really not helping the situation, she thought. Practically everything about him was designed to make staying awake in his lessons even harder. His flat, droning voice and the way his face was shrivelled with wrinkles, as deep as the creases in his plaid suit. What was left of his hair clung to the top of his head in a wispy cloud.

Alba's eyes fluttered shut. Professor Nightingale was going on about something boring – no change there – and she felt herself drifting off on the current of his voice, a soft wave pulling her towards sleep. She sunk lower into her chair. The silk of her school-dress clung tightly to her skin, feeling as warm and cosy as her duvet back home, and she was just slipping away into dreams, when –

'Mistress White? Could you tell us the exact date of the Independence Governance Treaty signed by all eight of the proposed city-states here in the British Isles?'

Alba jerked awake. Professor Nightingale was staring right at her from the front of the classroom. His bug-like eyes wobbled behind round-framed spectacles. The room was silent, every student holding their breath (the mere mention of Alba's family name was enough to do that to a class).

Hurriedly, Alba straightened. 'The sixteenth of January, 2101, Professor,' she answered promptly.

That was an easy one. The date was a Bank Holiday for Londoners, set to commemorate the event. All North children were taught how the British Isles had dissolved into eight city-states at the start of the twenty-second century to be ruled independently by separate Lord Ministers. It was the result of decades of conflict, competition for overseas business, and social tensions, which had grown too much for the national government. The cities were still bound to national laws observed by a representative board of delegates from each city, but for the most part they functioned individually. London's current Lord Minister was a French-born man named Christian Burton-Lyon, elected mainly because of his connections with European traders.

Professor Nightingale nodded. 'Correct, Mistress White. Five-thirty p.m. to be exact. And could you also tell us the date of the subsequent Memory-Surfing and Trading Practices Summit, where the International Memory Laws were created?'

This was a tougher one. Alba glanced down at her schoolbook; its pages were empty.

'Oh, er . . .' she murmured, trying to look busy by fussing with her notebook, her mind scrambling for the answer.

They had not yet learnt the detailed history of memory-surfing. Alba knew roughly what had happened from Net programmes and articles, and brief overviews in their school textbooks. After neuroscientific breakthroughs in the late twenty-first century, the first memory-machines were created, right here in London. Though they had initially been used for medical research – diseases such as Alzheimer's and dementia were on the rise – after the collapse of the national government

18

the reduction in state funding meant the research companies turned to private investors. New consumer uses for memory-machines were developed, and with growing numbers of investors from overseas becoming involved, the technology was soon taken up by a number of other countries.

The concept of memory-surfing and trading was understandably popular. At the time, oil reserves were almost depleted, international relations had been strenuous for decades, and technology had become increasingly insular, people more used to screens than nature. The ability to explore the world from the comfort of a memory-machine fitted into that backdrop perfectly. It wasn't a cheap exercise, however. In London, with the divide between North and South, a culture of memory-surfing was cultivated in the North, while for Southers it was a luxury; often one they never got to experience.

But those were just the basics of what had happened. Alba knew little of the details, such as when the Memory-Surfing and Trading Practices Summit had been held.

She snuck a hopeful glance at Rosemary Dalton's book on the table next to hers, which (what a surprise) was positively *smothered* in notes, but Rosemary – a big blonde girl with a piggy face constantly trapped in a sneer – caught her looking and stamped her arm across the pages. Alba sighed. Twirling a loose curl of her thick red hair round one finger, she tried to look thoughtful.

'I – I think it was something like the twenty-third of March, 2138, Professor? Or was it 2137 . . .' She drifted off, cheeks reddening.

Professor Nightingale's sigh was so long and slow it almost sent Alba nodding off again. 'No, Mistress White,' he said, breaths whistling through his nose, 'it was neither of those dates. It was, of course, the second of May, 2138.'

'Of *course* it was,' muttered Alba beneath her breath.

Dolly was waiting for her outside the school gates when classes finished. Even though Knightsbridge Academy was only twenty minutes from her house, Alba wasn't allowed to walk home alone. Before Dolly had persuaded them to let Alba walk – with Dolly as a chaperone, of course – Alba's parents used to send her to school in one of their chauffeur-driven Bentleys with the family crest rising up in silver metal from the end of its hood. She had hated it, because it meant that every single person they passed on the street knew exactly who was inside.

Well, not that it was *Alba*, but that it was her family, and that was the problem.

Dolly was squinting in the late-afternoon sunshine, half-turned towards the road. She wore her servant's uniform of white silk pinafore, blouse and stockings, the White family's crest embroidered in black thread on her apron pocket. Her long purple hair was tied sleekly in two buns on top of her head.

Alba hurried across the schoolyard. In the playground, young children were shouting and laughing, their cries cutting through the thick, heat-choked air. The street beyond the gates was busy with traffic. The vibration of cars skimming down the road, smooth from their electric engines, rolled against Alba's skin like rippling waves in the air.

Dolly turned before Alba could sneak up on her and tickle her waist.

'Not this time,' she said in her bright, warm voice. Her

youthful face crinkled into a smile. She brushed a loose hair back from Alba's face and they started down the street. 'How was your day? I hope you learnt a lot.'

Alba snorted. 'Oh, *tons*,' she said, lacing an arm round Dolly's waist.

Alba loved how slim Dolly was. Dolly had the sort of body her mother called boyish but Alba thought was beautiful; tall and slender, soft muscles sliding over sharp bones. Alba wished she looked like Dolly. Instead, she was plump and short for her sixteen years. She was glad they at least had some similarities in their faces. Both of them had strong cheekbones, curved chins, and large, wide-set eyes, though Dolly's were blue and Alba's green.

Alba liked to imagine sometimes that Dolly was her sister. She didn't know any other of the Knightsbridge Academy girls who were as close to their handmaids (though she didn't really *know* any of the other Knightsbridge Academy girls in the first place. It was hard to make friends when she was only known for being Alastair White's daughter, and her parents never let her spend much time away from the house outside of school). Handmaids were traditionally paired with their charges at a young age to create a sisterly bond. Dolly had only been around nine when Alba was born, and she learnt her role by shadowing and aiding Alba's mother's handmaid, who looked after Alba until Dolly was old enough to take on the role fully. She was still young, in her mid-twenties now.

Alba had heard some of the other girls at school talking down about their handmaids. Even though a lot of servants were from the lesser families in North, many were from South, and there was always that divide running between families and their help. An invisible wall, a barrier slicing the two worlds neatly in half.

North.

South.

Light, and its shadow.

But there was none of that between Alba and Dolly. If anything, Alba felt as though Dolly were the only one with her on her side of the wall. Everything else in North was on the other side; detached, a façade of glittering glass and jewels and fake smiles. A world she never quite felt part of.

'Did you have Professor Nightingale again today, by any chance?' Dolly asked, grinning down at Alba.

She rolled her eyes. 'Why else do you think I've turned into a zombie?'

Dolly laughed, and it was a sound like bells, bright peals that drifted down around them, as soft and light as summer rain, and for the millionth time Alba wished that it was Dolly who could be her mother, her sister, her family, and take her far, far away from here.

3

SEVEN

'What an effing waste of time that was,' Seven grumbled to himself as he pulled off the metal cap and let it drop on its cables to the side of the memory-machine. He rubbed his temples where the pincers had dug. 'That's eight minutes and thirty-one seconds of my life I'm never getting back. You're going in the bin, R.L.S. And you!' He detached the wristbands from his arms and waggled a finger at the room. 'You better get your act together. Dunno why that skid was in that cabinet. It should've been filed under *So Boring Your Eyes Will Fall Out*.'

Grinning at his own joke, he glanced round the room, half-waiting for a laugh he knew wouldn't come. There was no cabinet under that name. Instead, he'd stuck the label to the bin behind the door.

Seven pushed the machine to the corner of the room, distracted now. How did that skid end up in the *Fear, Desperation and General Wetting-your-pants Kind of Stuff* cabinet? Every new memory he thieved was filed away after its first surf. There was

23

no way he'd have ever considered that one as anywhere near pant-wetting stuff. It was just a vast, empty space of blackness that seemed to have no end, and the low buzz of voices whose words he couldn't make out. He must have made a mistake when sorting it.

But as Seven slipped out of the room, locking the door quickly behind him, an unbidden thought fluttered at the corner of his mind: *I'm a skid-thief. I don't make mistakes.*

I can't afford to.

Seven had a few hours to kill before going to the skid-market that night, so he spent the rest of the afternoon on the roof of the flats where he lived. Because Butler often overheated, he was limited to just one or two surfs a day. If he didn't have to worry about breaking his memory-machine for good, Seven knew he'd be on it all the time. There wasn't much else to do around South.

The roof had become his private hang-out place. He told himself it was because he liked the view – which was true – but he ignored the other truth. That the group of big boys who hung in the courtyard, smoking and drinking cheap beer and vandalising every inanimate object in sight, saw Seven as an experiment to find the limits of how many punches a teenage boy can take and still stand (hint – not that many). So he'd learnt to stay well away whenever their voices echoed up from the courtyard.

Seven could hear them now from where he sat on the edge of the rooftop, thirty floors up. He was positioned facing the city towards North: the beautiful half of London, all glittering glass towers, green parks and immaculate homes. This view was one of the reasons he'd moved into this particular block of flats. The building was right on the upper edge of Vauxhall, next to the broad band of the River Thames, silver now under the blaze of the sun.

Watching North from high up here, Seven could pretend he was a part of its world. That he wasn't stuck on a pigeon-dirtied rooftop in South. That there weren't grimy, smog-choked streets stretching out behind his back like an ugly grey blanket. That all he had to do was open his arms and he'd fly out over the swollen curve of the river, and South would be a thing of the past.

(Seven would never admit it to anyone, not even himself – but once, a couple of years ago on his fifteenth birthday, after a particularly bad run-in with the courtyard boys, he had seriously considered opening his arms and jumping from the edge of the rooftop, knowing full well he wouldn't fly.)

Closing his eyes, Seven leant back on his arms, legs stretched out in front of him. Even though it was late afternoon the sun was still strong. A heavy, pressing tongue of heat. Sweat prickled his skin, sticking his thin shirt and slim blue trousers to his skin.

He tried not to think about what he'd be doing that night. Seven always felt nervous the day before a job. Excitement came when darkness fell, the whole city seeming to take on a different identity in the night, transforming into a world where anything was possible.

But this was no ordinary job. This was the White family's house. It was like looping a noose round your own effing neck and handing the rope to the devil.

'Hey, man.'

Seven jumped at the voice. Thinking it was the boys from the courtyard, he scrambled to his feet and spun round, but it was just one of his flatmates, Kola.

Kola was a tall, wiry Malaysian boy with handsome features and deep mahogany skin. He'd come to London when he was ten to escape the ethnic riots that had claimed the lives of his family. Though they got on OK, there was something about Kola that unsettled Seven. Maybe it was how quiet he was, sombre even, or the fact that Kola's eyes were so dark you felt as though you were falling into them when you looked straight at him.

The two of them stared at each other for a few seconds. Then, breaking his gaze, Kola strolled over and sat down beside Seven. He looked out at the city.

'So this is where you go every day.' He spoke slowly, every word turned in his thick Malaysian accent.

Seven shrugged. 'Nowhere else to go, really.'

'True.'

'And the view . . .'

'It *is* good,' said Kola, nodding. 'I come here too sometimes, though I don't often get to see it in the daylight.'

They fell silent. Seven thought this was probably the longest conversation they'd had since Kola answered his ad for a flatmate four years ago. Kola worked at the docks during the day and Seven was out thieving at night (not that Kola knew that – Seven told him he did night shifts at a construction site), so their paths rarely crossed.

'I thought I should warn you,' Kola said suddenly. 'The

boys who hang out in the courtyard. One of them said he saw you come up here. They were thinking about coming to look for you.'

Instinctively, Seven's body tensed. It was as though every inch of him remembered the feeling of the boys' knuckles, their heavy boots, and was trying to shrink away, hide from the memory of the pain.

The possibility of more.

He swallowed hard.

'Do you want to fight them?'

Seven snapped his head round. Kola was staring ahead, gaze still trained on North. His face was expressionless. Sunlight turned his dark eyes amber.

'Do I . . . *what?*' Seven spluttered.

Kola didn't turn. 'Do you want to fight them?' he repeated, voice flat. 'It's just that we're a bit outnumbered.'

A strangled laugh caught in Seven's throat. *Understatement of the effing century*, he thought. It took him a few seconds more to realise Kola had said *we*.

'Er, maybe next time.'

Kola nodded. He stood up, patting down his trousers. 'Well, they'll be here in a few minutes.' Before Seven could reply, he turned and walked back to the stairs leading down from the roof.

Seven waited a couple of minutes before hurrying down after him. By the time he got back to their flat on the twenty-third floor, the door to Kola's room was shut, the silence behind it sounding louder than it ever had before.

4

ALBA

The house was quiet when Alba and Dolly arrived home. They'd taken their time, going on a detour through the grounds of the estate, Alba telling Dolly all about stuck-up Rosemary Dalton and the two of them laughing as they planned increasingly outrageous ways to get revenge. But as soon as they walked through the tall front doors of the house, they fell silent.

Something was wrong.

Alba knew the rhythms of the house inside out. Late in the afternoon on a school day it should be filled with noises: voices drifting from the kitchens as the maids prepared dinner; cutlery clinking as the butlers set the dining table. Her mother would be in her parents' private quarters in the east wing, reading or listening to music, or talking on a tablet with another society wife.

But today the house was silent. Alba's heart began to flutter. Her mother must be having one of her bad turns.

She hadn't had one in a long while. She'd been kind, happy,

on the sunlit side of her coin. It was only a matter of time before she fell back into the darkness.

Dolly squeezed Alba's shoulder reassuringly. 'I'll find out what it is,' she whispered, before heading off towards the kitchens.

Alba waited. The silence was heavy, pressing in on her like a weight. *It'll pass, it'll pass*, she thought over and over, something she'd done since young to calm herself when bad things were about to happen.

It'll pass.

It'll pass.

When Dolly returned a few minutes later, Alba could tell straight away by the look on her face that things were *not* going to pass this time. Not for a long time.

And not without trouble.

'Straight to your room,' Dolly said quietly, clutching Alba's hand and leading her across the hall. It would have been quicker going up the curving flight of stairs that swept up one side, but that brought them too close to her parents' quarters. Too close to her mother. They went instead to the servants' staircase at the back of the house.

'What happened this time?' Alba murmured when they were inside the hidden passageway, the marble walls close around them as they started the tight circle upwards. Tiny lights like stars winked out of the walls. She could feel Dolly's heartbeat against her palm, smell the warm, woody scent of her handmaid's skin.

'A rumour about your mother has been going round. Something particularly nasty, by the sounds of it. Some of the women at a lunch she attended today snubbed her because of it.'

Of course, Alba thought. It was always to do with North society. As Alastair White's wife, her mother was one of the most powerful women in North, and therefore one of the most envied. Other women in North would kill for the privilege of being married to the city's lead criminal prosecutor (perhaps they had already tried. Alba wouldn't put it past them).

'Into your room and straight to bed,' Dolly said when they reached the second floor. She put a light kiss on Alba's forehead before turning to leave. 'I'll sneak you some food as soon as I can.'

Alba waited until she was alone in the quiet back-passage before drawing a deep breath. She stood tall, gathering her courage before opening the door and stepping out into the hall.

The walk round the corner to her bedroom felt as though it was miles and miles long, even though it only took a few seconds. Alba slipped inside and shut the door silently behind her. She didn't let out her puff of held breath until she was safely laid down on her large, wrought-iron bed, painted white with decorative flowers worked into the metal and purple silk sheets draped across the mattress. Squeezing her eyes shut, she pressed her face into the duvet.

It took a while for her heartbeats to slow.

Sometime later, Alba woke to a darkened room. She hadn't meant to doze off. Her mouth felt dry. Grey shadows stretched across the bleached floorboards, the barest hint of silver touching the edges of the furniture that filled the room.

She noticed straight away there was noise in the house

now; metallic clattering and footsteps, orchestral music floating beneath it all, the swell and fall of strings filling the air like spun threads of gold. Cooking smells rose from the kitchens below.

Alba pushed herself up, swinging her legs off the bed just as the door to her room opened.

Dolly smiled as she entered, though her face was tight. 'Oh good. You're awake. Your mother's mood has improved. She's decided she wants a big dinner ready by the time your father gets home.'

Alba rubbed her eyes. 'What time is it?'

'Just after eight.' Dolly sat at Alba's side and begun fussing with her hair, which was mussed from sleep. 'And we've only got fifteen minutes until dinner . . . so we're lucky you got a little extra beauty sleep.'

'Hey!' Laughing, Alba poked Dolly in the ribs.

Dolly worked fast. In just ten minutes, she'd transformed Alba's messy, after-school hair into an elegant bun at the nape of her neck – little flowers plucked from the gardens threaded through her curls – and dressed her in a pretty dress made of a shimmering, pearl-coloured silk. She had also washed Alba's face and dabbed a swirl of cream blusher on her cheeks and a pink tint for her lips.

Alba watched Dolly in the dressing-table mirror as her handmaid fastened a set of heavy gold necklaces round her neck.

'When will you show me how to dye my hair like yours?' she asked, eyeing the glossy swirls of Dolly's purple hair, still in their usual buns.

'You know how much your mother would hate that.'

'That's *exactly* why I want to do it.'

Dolly's lips tightened, but she didn't say anything. That was one of the (many) reasons Alba loved her. Dolly didn't patronise her with empty words about how dearly her mother cared for her, how cherished she was as a daughter even if she didn't always feel it.

Because, of course, she wasn't cherished. Any idiot could see that. Alba just wished that any idiot also knew not to try and convince her she was.

The worst part of it was, Alba wanted to believe them. When her mother was in one of her good moods, like she had been for the last few weeks, she could almost see it. Her mother's affection came out slowly, unfurling like a veil of gold smoke that turned her world glittery and beautiful. And then she'd snap, just like that, and the fall was all the worse because Alba had allowed herself to think once again that her mother really did care, that she *was* cherished above all else.

Dolly curled a hand round Alba's shoulder. 'Two more years and then you'll be studying English Literature at one of the world's top universities,' she said, smiling. 'Somewhere far away from here. What do you fancy? India? Switzerland? Or how about America? I've heard our relations with them are finally improving.'

'I want to go anywhere Professor Nightingale isn't,' replied Alba, and this got an immediate laugh from Dolly, though she fell silent just as quickly.

From downstairs, the dinner bell had rung.

5

SEVEN

He arrived at the ruins of Battersea Power Station just past eight. In October the sun set fast, and the huge building was pitch-black against the glittering riverside streets and promenades of North across the river. The only lights were the reflections licking the water, the headlights of river-taxis and container ships making their way along the Thames.

Seven always found it eerie here in the darkness, the sounds of water slapping against the walls of the flooded building and low groans as wind found its way in through the station's crumbling bricks and partially collapsed roof. Broken concrete slabs and discarded shells of old boats littered the muddy floor. The scurrying noises of rats, invisible in the dark, set him on edge.

Picking his way carefully over the uneven ground, Seven made his way to a hidden entrance round the north side of the building. Anyone who didn't know better would walk straight past its shadowy opening (not that they'd even be here in the first place, of course) without noticing what years of attending the skid-market here had taught him to look out for.

A light in the darkness of the tunnel.

Its flicker illuminated a sliver of the arched walls of the tunnel, moss glistening on the wet bricks. Seven stepped inside. The light danced back. He heard quick breaths in the shadows.

'I'm one of Carpenter's,' Seven announced, voice echoing off the dripping walls.

The light edged closer. A young boy emerged, outlined in the glow of the lamp he was carrying. Tattered clothes hung off his small frame.

'Let's see yer ID,' he growled, raising a gun.

Quickly, Seven yanked down the collar of his top, revealing the tattoo inked in black in the middle of his chest. It was the outline of a saw, pointing downwards: the sign of Carpenter's skid-thief crew. Each crew had its own mark designed around its leader's name. Carpenter was one of the most well-respected crew leaders, despite his relatively young age.

The boy nodded. 'Get in, then,' he said, stepping aside.

Shadows swallowed Seven as he headed deeper into the tunnel, the light from the boy's lamp quickly fading. The whole place stank of moss and stagnant water. For a while there was nothing apart from darkness and his own breaths; the soggy sound of his footsteps on the mud-slicked floor. Then a light appeared at the end of the tunnel. As he approached, walking faster in excitement, it expanded and swelled, bright, brighter, brighter, rushing him at once in a fireball burst of colour and sound and activity.

Squinting and shading his eyes, heart drumming with energy,

Seven stepped out into the enormous turbine hall of Battersea's B Station.

The place was crawling with people. Their elongated shadows licked across the towering steel frames of the hall as they moved. The size of the hall was overwhelming; walls stretched up to a shadowy roof. In the ceiling, the long, rectangular strip of glass was blacked out with paint and wooden boards. Scaffolding crisscrossed the interior of the hall like a metallic spider's web, and open balcony ledges ran round all four walls, remnants of the abandoned renovation work.

Seven knew London's black market had been lucky to get such a perfect venue for its biggest skid-market practically handed to it (before this, they'd used the sewers. He was pretty glad that'd been before his time). The power station had been badly damaged in the 2089 Thames flooding. Renovation works had been forced to a halt, and after years of subsequent floods the project was finally abandoned.

Voices echoed in the vast space. Lights were strung along the railings lining the balcony edges and hung from scaffolding, bathing everything in a yellow glow. Cooking smells drifted over from one side of the hall, where steam was rising from the portable cookers the hawker stalls had set up on the first floor, taking advantage of the busy trade.

'First things first,' Seven said, looking towards the unfurling clouds of steam. He patted his stomach, and it responded with a loud, rumbling growl. He grinned. 'Exactly what I was thinking.'

Seven's boots made soft sucking noises as he headed across the water-logged floor before climbing up the scaffolding to the first-level balcony ringing the hall. He was just stepping off, still clinging to the metal frame, when a blur at the corner of his vision made him flinch.

Whoosh.

Something small and round flew by, grazing the hairs on his cheek. It smacked into the scaffolding with a crunch.

'YOU!'

Seven spun round at the shout. He dropped to the floor just in time to duck as another apple (OK, so it wasn't a rock like he'd first thought, but apples are pretty hard things too) whizzed past him. Ahead, a girl was striding towards him between the plastic table and chairs surrounding the food stalls. Every inch of her face was etched with anger. Her mouth – a silver hoop looped through the bottom lip – was a taut line. Sharp, slanted eyes narrowed into dangerous slits.

Loe.

'Effing hell,' Seven muttered. 'What've I done *now*?'

Loe was dressed in a grey top and skinny black trousers, ripped at the knees, a skid-thief belt slung low on her bony hips. Below the tanned skin of her collarbones was the tattoo of a saw; the same one Seven had inked on his own chest. The tattoos were always covered in public, but here the marks were almost a badge of honour.

'You!' the girl snarled again. She whipped her arm back and threw another apple.

Seven only just managed to duck. 'Loe! What the hell?'

Luckily, he noticed with a sigh of relief, she finally seemed to be out of apples.

Loe crossed her arms, her scowl deepening. 'Oh, don't act

like you don't know.' Her cropped hair was messy around her face, dark strands sticking to her skin in the heat. She flicked her head to get her fringe out of her eyes. 'Carpenter just told me about the big job the two of you have been working on for weeks. Congrats, Seven. You must be honoured. Carpenter finally chose *you* for an important job over me. What d'you have to do for it?' She tilted her head, eyes as cutting as knife-blades. 'Promise to do all his dirty laundry, huh?' she said, smirking. 'Lick the mud off his boots?'

'Shut it, Loe,' Seven snapped.

His cheeks were burning. He wanted to throw a punch to wipe that smirk off her face, but of course he couldn't hit a girl (not that he could hit a boy, either – not before they got him first). Seven knew Loe was just jealous about Carpenter choosing him for the White family job. Loe and Seven had joined Carpenter's skid-stealing crew within a month of each other. They fought hard over every job.

Just as Seven was about to tell Loe just *where* she could stick her apples, a bright voice rang out over the noise of the hall.

'Loe! Loe! Loe!'

A girl in a red dress ran out from the crowd of food stalls. She was young, only five or six, with dark, burnt-almond skin. Her frizzy cloud of black hair was tied into a bun on the top of her head, sticking out like a bushy antenna. Reaching Loe, the girl started looping round her legs, her face glowing with delight.

'Look what I stole from the fat old Chinese lady's stall!' Her voice bubbled with glee. She thrust out her hands to show off a big steamed dumpling.

Loe sighed heavily. 'Mika,' she groaned, crouching down.

'What've I said a million times? When you steal something, you don't go shouting about it, 'cause then what happens is –'

'*There* she is!'

They all looked up to see a big Chinese woman in a dirty apron marching towards them, pointing a fat finger in their direction. Luckily, her size was impeding her process; her belly kept getting stuck in the tight clusters of tables and chairs.

Seven snorted. 'Who's the one in trouble now?' he said, smirking.

Loe glared at him. 'Oh, don't think I'm finished with you. We'll talk about this later.' Then, scooping Mika up into her arms, she hurried past him in the opposite direction of the stall-owner, towards the scaffolding.

Mika's large brown eyes turned to Seven as they passed. She waved a pudgy hand, the offending dumpling still clasped tightly in her fingers.

'Seven!' she cried, beaming. She waggled the dumpling, some of the filling spilling out. 'Look what I stole from the fat Chinese lady!'

He grinned. 'Nice one, Mika.'

As they disappeared down into the shadows below the scaffolding, Seven heard Loe's exasperated sigh.

'Mika! What did I *just* tell you?'

6

ALBA

'Little Alba,' her mother purred as Alba entered the dining hall. Her thick Ukrainian accent curled her words. She smiled across the room, green eyes glittering from under dark, make-up-smudged lids.

Alba bowed her head politely. A sick feeling in the pit of her stomach worked up into her throat, but she swallowed, pushing it back.

She knew that look in her mother's eyes. Her dark mood wasn't fully gone yet.

Fiddling with the hem of her dress, Alba followed one of the butlers to a seat at the end of the long oak table dominating the room. Orchestral music played from concealed speakers, filling the grand space with the rushing of keys and strings. She sat down opposite her mother, folding a napkin across her lap. Her hands trembled.

Oxana White was undoubtedly one of the most beautiful women in North. She had a face you couldn't help but stare at: a high forehead sloping down to a perfectly straight nose; smooth cheeks; defined cheekbones; full, rounded lips painted now a dark purple, and those *eyes* . . . eyes that were large and cat-like, the green of her irises even brighter than Alba's.

When she was younger, Alba had wanted so much to look like her mother. She wanted to dance in those wide, beautiful eyes. Fall asleep on the soft cushions of her lips. But this was before she discovered the darkness that lay beneath the surface of her mother's perfect features. This was before she learnt that beauty could be used as a mask.

Tonight, Oxana's blonde hair was swept up from her face. A midnight-blue dress clung to her curves. 'I'm so sorry about earlier, my darling,' she said, leaning forward on the table, her jewellery jangling. 'I didn't mean to upset the whole house like that. But the things some of the women were saying about me . . .' She paused. 'Can you forgive me, my darling?'

She was watching Alba intently, the same unreadable smile just touching the corners of her mouth. Lights twinkling down from the tall ceiling made her lipstick glitter, a starburst of diamonds on her lips.

The way she said it, it wasn't a question.

Oxana tilted her head when Alba didn't reply. 'Little Alba?'

Alba felt her hands shaking. She *hated* being called that. Forcing herself to smile, she nodded.

'Of course, Mother.'

Oxana clicked her tongue. 'I've told you before, darling. Being called Mother makes me feel old.'

And being called Little Alba makes me feel like a baby, Alba thought, biting back a scowl.

They stared at each other. Alba dared her mother to read in her eyes all the things she was thinking. It was always this way; her swinging between terrified and defiant, between a scared little girl and a rebellious teenager who couldn't care less what her parents thought. But no matter how much Alba wanted to stand up to her mother – really, truly, saying what she felt – she didn't have the courage to do it.

She was only that brave in her dreams.

'Madame White and Mistress Alba.'

A butler stepped into the dining room, breaking their silence. Like the maids, the male servants also wore uniforms of all-white. His shirt and trousers were crisp.

'Master White has arrived for dinner,' he announced, bowing.

'Finally,' sighed Oxana. She tapped her nails on the table and flashed a smile in Alba's direction. 'I'm so hungry I even considered eating my own daughter.'

The butler bowed again before leaving. A moment later, Alba's father strode in.

Alastair White was a tall man, as handsome as Oxana was beautiful. His black hair – speckled now with grey – was slicked back from his forehead, and he had small, dark eyes that glittered like cuts of black granite. A hard jaw and cheekbones edged his face. It looked as though he'd come straight from work. He was wearing the dark grey suit and black robes of his position as a criminal prosecutor, his robe fixed at his collarbones with a golden bulldog clasp.

The bulldog was the symbol of London, its teeth bared, snarling at the world. Alba always thought the clasp looked strange on her father. He was always so calm, so collected.

He never snarled at the world or bared his teeth in anger; he just handed out his sentences in a cool, detached manner. She guessed he was so used to it by now that he didn't give it much thought, didn't consider it might not be just.

Because it *was* just . . . wasn't it?

Alba hated the death penalty, but it was restricted only for the worst offences: murder; crimes against the London Guard; theft and illegal trading of memories. Perhaps it was important to make an example of these criminals to keep London in order.

To keep South in control.

To keep North safe.

A part of Alba hated that she felt that way, but what else could she think? She'd never met anyone from South to know otherwise, had only heard of the violence and squalor and crime that existed in the dark half of their city.

Kissing Oxana lightly on the top of her head as he passed, Alastair White took his seat at the top of the table. Flicking out a napkin, he laid it across his lap. He reached out and brushed Alba's hand, smiling, and Alba felt a swirl of happiness. Her father was often distant, preoccupied by work. She cherished every little moment of affection he gave her.

'I'm sorry I'm late, my dears,' he said, as butlers returned to take away the lids keeping their food warm. 'I hope you're not too hungry.'

The table was laden with all sorts of dishes. There were ginger and soy steamed fish, sautéed vegetables dripping in butter, minced meats, Spanish *tortillas* and Indian *roti* to dip into curry sauce. Though Oxana liked to try new foods from London's myriad of ethnicities, not once had she ever let a

Ukrainian dish anywhere near the table.

Alba knew her mother hated her home country. Oxana had never spoken in Ukrainian or talked about her life there. Alba wondered what secrets the country held for her mother; why she felt the need to carve away that part of her life from her world, wipe clean her past.

Alba picked at her food. She felt nervous about her mother's mood, and her father seemed distracted too. He ate quickly, eyes glazed as he stared down at his plate.

'How was work today, my darling?' Oxana asked. Fingernails clicked as she picked up her glass of wine, the red liquid so rich and dark it looked like blood.

'As busy as always.' Alastair White's voice was low, hard-edged. His cutlery clattered on the side of the plate as he set down his knife and fork. 'We've had a tip-off about an illegal memory-trading ring. Pearson is keen we move fast on the information.'

Alba leant forward, eager to hear more. Her father didn't often talk about work in front of her. 'An illegal memory-trading ring?' she said. 'What is that exactly, Father?'

Lacing his fingers into an arch, Alastair White set his elbows on the table. 'You understand how memory-trading works in the banks, my dear?'

'I think so. We're just starting to cover it in Economics and Business Theory.'

Her father nodded. 'Simply put, traders in banks facilitate the sale of memories between buyers and sellers, focusing on memories they believe can get them a high sale figure. The banks fight between themselves for access to the most valuable memories –'

'Really, Alastair,' interrupted Oxana, curling her fingers

round his arm. 'Is this really appropriate dinner conversation?'

He covered her hand with his. 'She needs to understand the way things work, my dear.' He paused. His voice softened. 'She needs to know why it is I do what I do.'

Alba watched her parents, feeling uncomfortable. She felt as though she were intruding on a private moment. Something flashed between their gazes, some spark of understanding beyond her reach. Before she could pinpoint the expression on their faces her father broke away.

'Illegal trading upsets this framework because it undermines the value of memories put up for trade,' he continued, turning back to her. 'A memory is worth more when it is unique, only one copy existing in the world. When a memory is stolen to sell on the black market, it forces the price of that particular memory down. Illegal memory-trading rings are organised systems that facilitate these kinds of trades.'

'Alba fiddled with the napkin in her lap. 'I understand. But – I mean, is any of that really bad enough to *execute* people over?'

Her father's expression darkened. 'Memories are the most intimate things a person has, my dear. We might share them, trade them, surf other peoples', but we alone choose which memories to let go, and which to keep to ourselves. Memory-thieves tear apart that most sacred of choices. They come into our homes, into our banks, and take the most precious moments from our pasts. They take what is most private to a person and treat it as a mere commodity, selling secrets and hidden pasts without caring whose lives they ruin in the process.' His voice lowered. 'It is the highest form of betrayal. Does it not therefore deserve the highest form of punishment?'

Alba bit her lip, looking away from her father's intense gaze. She could see how much he believed what he was saying, and she wanted to tell him that she agreed. But for some reason, his openness with her now only made her want to be honest with him, too.

'I don't think so, Father,' she said quietly.

A flash of surprise crossed Alastair White's face. He leant back in his chair.

'I mean,' Alba said hurriedly, 'don't the same things apply to the traders in the banks? They're just looking to make money from selling and buying memories too. And surely the Southers who steal memories are only doing it out of desperation. Perhaps if they had access to better jobs they wouldn't feel the need –'

'Don't presume to know a thing about what *those* people feel.'

Oxana spoke suddenly, her voice uncoiling with a snap.

Alba fell silent at once. She tightened up at the cold look in her mother's eyes, a prickly sensation crawling across her skin. Something wild and hot spiralled through her.

'But,' she tried, cheeks flushing, 'I only meant –'

'Alba! That's enough.' Her father pushed back, standing, dropping his napkin onto his empty plate. 'Your mother is right. Do not pretend to know about a world you don't understand.' With one final stern look at Alba, he brushed his lips to Oxana's forehead – 'I'll be working in the study, my dear,' – and left the room.

For one quick beat, nothing happened.

Then –

'Maybe I'd understand if either of you actually let me *see* something of the world.'

It was out before Alba could stop it.

The whole room seemed to suck in. Alba knew without looking that her mother's eyes were staring fiercely at her, their vivid green colour like a siren, a warning. The swell of the music playing in the background seemed to rise to a roar.

Alba swallowed, still staring down at the table. Her heart crashed against her ribcage. 'I – I'm sorry –'

Oxana swept round the head of the table so quickly Alba didn't have time to avoid her; the force of her mother's backhand into her cheek knocked her off her chair. She only just managed to put out a hand to catch herself, to stop her cheekbone from dashing into the polished marble. She felt her wrist crack as it snapped under her weight. Pain flashed up her arm.

Her mother hadn't hit her in a long time. Alba was so caught off-guard she just lay there, heaped on the floor in a tangle of limbs. Her chest heaved up and down as she raked in deep breaths. It'd been so long she had almost forgotten how this felt, crumpled on the floor as her mother stood over her, twin feelings of pain and shame flooding her veins.

'You want to see South?' Oxana hissed, bending over her. 'After your father and I do everything to protect you, provide for you, give you everything you need – *this* is how you thank us?'

She grabbed Alba's shoulder and yanked her roughly back. Alba's hair came undone, flowers scattering around her knees, falling from where Dolly had twined them so carefully. Their petals were soft on her skin.

'You're lucky your father didn't hear you.' Oxana's face was so close to Alba's she could smell the wine on her mother's breath.

'It'd break his heart if he thought you didn't care. Everything he does at work is to make London safer for us. For you.'

What's the point? Alba wanted to scream. *I'm barely ever let out of the house to see any of it!*

But she gritted her teeth and stayed silent. No matter how scared she was, how much pain or anger she felt, she refused to make a sound.

Her mother didn't deserve so much as a single sob.

Alba knew it was stupid to drag it out. Oxana always stopped if she cried. Alba didn't know whether it was because the sound made her mother feel remorse for what she'd done, or because she felt satisfied she'd done enough.

The sound of a metal lid clattering to the floor made them look up. A butler had come into the room to clear away the plates. He seemed to realise what was happening and bowed hurriedly, backing out of the doors, muttering apologies under his breath (to Oxana, of course, for interrupting).

Letting go of Alba, her mother straightened. She smoothed a hand down her dress. Her eyes were cold and final as she stared down.

'I'm done with you,' she said quietly, then stalked out of the room.

As soon as she was gone, Alba let herself drop to the floor, cradling her injured hand to her chest. Cold marble pressed into her cheek. Her ragged breaths were loud in the quiet of the hall, and she realised then that someone had finally turned off the music. There were footsteps around her as butlers came to clean the table, working around her in silence.

None of them said a word to Alba and, somehow, that hurt more than anything else.

47

7

SEVEN

Carpenter's makeshift den was on the third floor at the very back of the turbine hall. Corrugated iron sheets and draped cloths enclosed it from the rest of the market, muffled lights flickering from behind the tattered fabrics. The same saw design tattooed on both Seven and Loe's chests was painted onto one of the metal sheets in red.

Seven drummed his fingers on the railing lining the balcony. Low voices were drifting out from the den. He was waiting for his appointment with Carpenter, and according to the clock that hung from the middle of the hall, he was five minutes late.

'Effing Loe,' Seven muttered, toeing the underside of the railing with his boot.

When had saying Loe's name ever *not* been preceded by an *effing*? It felt as though she'd been put on this earth just to annoy him. Perhaps she was trying to tire him into an early heart attack so she could take over his skid-thieving jobs and become Carpenter's favourite.

He wouldn't put it past her.

Seven scanned the busy hall, but he couldn't spot Loe and Mika. They were probably hiding, waiting for the Chinese stall-owner's rampage to be over. One dumpling might seem a silly thing to get so upset over, but Seven (and his stomach) understood. Everyone in South was living like he was; day to day, breadcrumb to breadcrumb.

'Or should I say, dumpling to dumpling,' he murmured with a smirk.

Just then came the heavy flap of a burlap sheet being lifted. Seven turned to see another member of Carpenter's crew leaving the den.

Without waiting for an invitation, Seven ducked through. It was a big space, thieving gear stacked in haphazard piles across the floor, and in the middle was a large sheet of rusted metal propped up on crates to serve as a table. Candles and buzzing neon strips lit the room in lurid whites and soft yellows. The place smelled like the rest of the skid-market: a mixture of tangy metal, decaying water, the bite of chemicals sharp at the back of the tongue.

'S. You're late.'

Carpenter emerged from behind a cabinet in the far corner of the room, lifting a set of tools in his arms. He was tall, with thick, ropey muscles broad across his shoulders and chest. His dark blond hair was cropped close to his scalp. Sweat glistened across his torso, bare apart from the crawling tattoos covering every inch of his skin, all the way down to his low-slung khaki trousers.

'Loe and Mika,' Seven explained simply. He pulled out a wooden crate and sat down at the table.

Carpenter raised an eyebrow, a hint of a smile on his lips. 'Of course.'

He dropped the tools he was carrying onto the table and wiped his hands on his trousers. A scar ran through his left eyebrow, cutting it in half and pulling it up in the middle, making it seem to Seven as though he was constantly amused, always caught on the tail-end of some secret joke no one else had heard.

'Mac's appointment ran over anyway.' Carpenter's voice was hardened by a rough South accent. 'Stupid bastard almost got caught last night on a job. I'm thinking of dropping him.'

Seven felt the undercurrent of a threat in those words. He watched warily as Carpenter sat opposite him, slinging his legs onto the table, his boots making heavy *thunks* on the metal top. Carpenter was in his mid-twenties, the youngest of all South's skid-thief crew leaders, but he carried himself in a way that demanded authority.

Seven still remembered how intimidated he'd been when he'd first met Carpenter. He'd only been nine at the time. Carpenter had caught him stealing food from a market stall in Kennington, but instead of telling the stall-owner, he had invited Seven to try out for his skid-thief crew.

Carpenter crossed his arms. 'Well,' he said. 'Tonight.'

Seven nodded, glancing away. His insides squirmed.

Tonight. The word felt dangerous, a bullet dropping down at him through the air. For so long the White job had been weeks, days away. Now it was really here.

'Want to look at the plans of the house one more time?' Carpenter asked.

Seven shook his head. 'I know it.'

He always memorised the plans of the houses he was breaking into, but this one especially he'd gone over and over until he was absolutely certain, and he'd been on more observation trips than for any other job, just to make sure the plans he'd made were right. There was going to be an effing blueprint of the White house engraved in his mind for the rest of his life.

'Good,' said Carpenter. 'Now walk me through it.'

Seven straightened, rolling his shoulders back. 'I'll make my way to North the same way as usual,' he began, reciting the memorised list, 'crossing under the river using the old sewer tunnel. From the exit at Chelsea Harbour, it's a forty-minute walk up to Hyde Park Estate. Twenty if I run. There's a tree on the south side of the estate I can use to climb over the fence. It's far enough away from the main gate to avoid the guards.'

Carpenter nodded, blue eyes dark in the shadows cast by the light above.

'Then it's ten minutes across the grounds to the White family's house.' Seven ticked each thing off on his fingers as he went. 'The house itself is unguarded, but to be absolutely sure I'll approach from the south side, where there aren't any outfacing lights. I'll scale to the third floor from the east wing to avoid the servants' dormitories, in case any of them are still awake. To get inside, I'll pick the lock on the balcony doors of one of the drawing rooms. The house doesn't seem to have any security alarms . . . but I guess we'll soon find out.'

'Don't joke, S.'

Seven's grin faltered. 'Right. Sorry.' He coughed. 'So, inside. The memorium's in the east wing behind the eighth drawing

51

room. Should be easy enough to get to. And then it's the usual drill – get the memory and get out. Though you still haven't told me which skids to steal,' he added.

Carpenter reached into his trouser pocket and retrieved a folded piece of paper, holding it out. Without looking at it – Carpenter never liked to discuss the memories he wanted stolen – Seven slipped it into the thieving belt hung round his hips.

Carpenter swung his legs off the table. 'It's just the one skid. As always, memorise the note, then burn it. Now get your stuff. I'll buy you a meal before you head off. You need to be on your best tonight for this job, S.' His voice hardened as he fixed Seven with his cool, unreadable gaze, hands pressed into the metal table-top. 'It's not one you – *we* – can afford to mess up.'

8

ALBA

'I don't think it's broken, but it's definitely sprained. Hold on. Let me feel for fractures. This might hurt.'

'What have you done so far that *hasn't*?'

Alba and Dolly were on a bench at the back of the herb-house, a medi-kit open between them. Rows of plants filled the building in a rush of textured green. Moonlight glittered through the glass ceiling and walls, dappling the floor with shifting shadows. The air was heavy with the smell of plants; a clean, fresh scent that helped ease Alba's nausea at the pain of her injury.

Gently running her fingers along the skin of Alba's wrist, Dolly inspected the extent of the damage. Little needles of pain sprung up everywhere her handmaid touched, making Alba grit her teeth.

'It's only a sprain,' said Dolly, laying her hand on the bench as she spread some cooling gel from the medi-kit across her wrist. 'That's lucky.' She caught the look in Alba's eyes and said quickly, 'I didn't mean –'

Alba forced a smile. 'I know.'

Dolly got up and disappeared between the rows of plants. She returned a few minutes later with a pestle and mortar in one hand and a bunch of plants and herbs in the other. 'Northers underestimate the power of natural remedies,' she explained, 'but I was born in the country. I know how effective they can be.' She worked the leaves in the mortar, smudging the lumpy, pungent-smelling paste onto Alba's skin. 'Arnica, aloe and black seed for pain and inflammation.'

'If it looks as good as it smells,' said Alba, wrinkling her nose, 'then I'm definitely going to be cured.'

Dolly smiled. 'See? Sarcasm. You're feeling more like yourself already.'

When she was finished with the paste, she wiped her hands, her voice softening. 'Do you want to talk about it?'

Alba looked away. She took a shaky breath. 'What is there to say? My own mother hates me. She thinks I should be grateful to her and Father for keeping me in this cage, protecting me from the world. But they forget that it's trapping me too.'

'You'll get out soon,' Dolly said, lacing an arm round her shoulders. She pressed her cheek to the top of Alba's head. 'There's more for you than this, Alba. A lot more.'

Is *there*? Alba thought, but instead she smiled and said, 'I hope so.'

Dolly squeezed her. 'Well, I *know* so.'

That night, Alba lay awake for hours. Dolly's herbal mixture had helped with the pain and nausea, but without them to distract her she couldn't avoid thinking about what had happened earlier. She replayed the blow from her mother's back-hand over and over. She did this every time her mother hit her, making herself live through what had happened again and again, hoping perhaps to catch a lost opportunity or moment where she could have defended herself, or avoided it all in the first place.

But more than anything, Alba wanted to understand *why*.

What had she done to deserve this? Why did her mother turn into this monster, when other times she could be so kind and loving it almost made Alba forget about when she wasn't?

Sighing, Alba rolled onto her side. Dolly's outline was dark against the bleached boards where she lay asleep on the floor. She'd insisted on staying with Alba that night in case she needed anything, even though Alba had promised her she was fine.

Tears pricked Alba's eyes. She couldn't imagine what she would do without Dolly. It terrified her to think what her life would have been like if Dolly hadn't taken a job with the Whites.

Then she felt a slap of self-disgust. *How selfish can you be?* she thought. It's not as though Dolly had never experienced Oxana's anger for herself.

Alba wondered sometimes why Dolly didn't leave. Was it the same reason none of the other servants left? Fear for their reputation, of not finding another job to provide for their families? But Dolly didn't have a family. She didn't even have a boyfriend (despite half the male servants in the house being hopelessly in love with her). Alba didn't like to admit it, because it made her feel horribly guilty, but she knew the truth.

That Dolly stayed for *her*.

Too restless to stay in bed, Alba got up, stepping carefully around her handmaid's sleeping figure. She padded barefoot across her room and opened the door to the hall, cradling her bandaged wrist to her chest.

The landing was thick with that special past-midnight silence Alba loved. This time of night always felt magical to her, as though another world had settled on top of her usual one, making everything silver-edged and new. Starlight spun through the hushed air. She went down the hall towards the main staircase and headed upstairs.

The top floor of the house had beautiful views over the grounds of Hyde Park Estate. On nights like this when she couldn't sleep, Alba loved to sit in an armchair by the window in the drawing room at the very back of the house and read a book by candlelight. She'd gaze out at the view, and it helped remind her that her life wasn't so bad. *Look at all you've got*, she'd tell herself. *You have no right to feel unhappy.*

She'd imagine the teenagers living in South. Many of them probably had parents far worse than hers, *and* they lived in South. She was lucky, she'd remind herself. Luckier than most.

Tonight, however, nothing seemed to be helping. She had lit a candle in a glass lamp, set it down on the table beside the comfy armchair she was curled up in, book open in her lap. Usually she'd be feeling better by now. But not tonight. For some reason, today's incident felt different to the ones before: worse, somehow.

And suddenly, in a flash, Alba realised what it was.

I'm done with you.

She heard the words as though her mother were right

here whispering them into her ear. Not the most hurtful or threatening words she'd ever spoken to her, but powerful in their simplicity. Alba felt flung aside like a piece of trash. Was she really so unwanted? Did she really mean that little to her mother?

Feeling sick, she dropped her book and scrambled up, pacing restlessly round the room.

I'm done with you.

Alba couldn't escape those four little words. They followed her, a shadow, a coldness creeping at her back. The fear, the hurt she felt started to boil into anger (it always did in the end). She ran the fingers of her uninjured hand along the spines of the books in the tall shelves lining the walls.

I'm done with you.

Then just leave me alone! Alba wanted to shout. A hot, red fury was taking over her body, burning every vein. She moved quicker, pressing her fingers harder against the books. *That'll be just fine with me. I don't need you. I'm sick of this cage you and Father have trapped me in. If I really mean that little to you, then why don't the both of you just SET ME FREE!*

In her anger, she slammed her hand against the bookcase she was striding past –

And it gave way, a panel opening up under her fist.

Alba froze, shocked still, waiting to see if anyone had heard the sound of her hand slamming into the bookcase. Nothing happened. She relaxed a little, though her heart was still thrumming, as quick as an insect's wing-beats. Running her hand along the edge of the bookcase, she realised with a stomach-flip of excitement just what it was she'd uncovered.

A doorway.

Sixteen years Alba had lived in this house. She thought she knew everything about it. But here was a secret, hidden doorway, like something out of a book or a dream.

Alba pushed the panel in the bookshelf open further. It opened into shadows and darkness. Crossing back to the armchair where she'd been reading, she snatched up her lamp. The wet flame of the candle licked across the room as she hurried back to the doorway, held the light out in front of her and went inside.

'A memorium,' she breathed, knowing immediately what the hidden room was.

Memoriums were people's own private memory rooms. Alba had never been allowed anything to do with memory-surfing. Her parents said that until she was eighteen and a legal adult, she hadn't earnt the privilege to try it herself: just another of their ways to keep her from experiencing the world. Heavens forbid she see anything that made her question the life they'd created (*curated*, more like) for her in North. They kept Alba away from the boutiques and memory-houses in North offering sessions with memory-machines to its customers, and she'd only once caught a glimpse on a school trip years ago of one of the plush rooms the banks had for their customers to sample memories.

This secret room was big and windowless, and smelled of old wood. Grand mahogany cabinets lined the walls. In the centre of the room was a desk. Instead of a normal seat behind it though, there was a large, sleek-looking metal thing –

A memory-machine.

Alba shut the door behind her. Feathers of excitement tracing her spine, she set her lamp on the desk to inspect the machine.

It was open at the front with a cushioned seat built into it, made from a soft, spongy material that moulded round her hand when she pressed it. Clasps stuck out of the armrests. At the top was a rounded cap on an adjustable slide. A logo was printed on the back of the machine – a pair of black wings, spread wide as if in flight – and there was writing underneath:

SONY LIFE-FLIGHT v7.8.

Alba was just reaching out to touch the logo when a noise behind her made her heart stop.

9

SEVEN

The girl turned slowly, as if in a daydream. Her mouth fell open and her hands curled into fists at her sides, but apart from that she looked surprisingly *unsurprised* to see Seven standing there. In fact, he thought, she even looked a little guilty herself.

Seven decided he disliked her immediately. He'd seen the girl before on observation trips to the house, but up close she was far too pretty. Rich and beautiful and well fed (she was chubby – you didn't get that way without plenty of food).

Some people had it so *easy*.

Scowling, he took in her pink cheeks, her cascade of dark red hair. The white nightdress she wore shimmered in the low light, skimming across her milky skin, which was as soft and pale as moonlight.

Seven wondered why he wasn't running away. Instead, he was just standing there dumbly. They were *both* just standing there dumbly, staring at each other.

Perhaps if she had been an adult he'd have tried to escape.

But this girl looked not much younger than him, and utterly harmless. She seemed like the kind of girl who was weak, soft, and more likely to huddle up and cry if you annoyed her than throw apples at you.

Eventually, the silence made Seven so uncomfortable he had to say something.

'Er . . .' he began. He rubbed the back of his neck and attempted a grin. 'Well. This has never happened before.'

The girl blinked. She had wide green eyes, deep and soft, the same colour as fresh grass or the water of the Thames at sunrise. They flitted to the door behind Seven, which was still half-open.

She's gonna scream, he realised, heart thudding, fear at being discovered finally hitting him as the shock of finding her in the room wore off.

Carpenter's voice sounded in his head.

You need to be on your best tonight for this job, S. It's not one you – we – can afford to mess up.

The girl glanced at the door again. Suddenly she spoke in a rush of tumbling words, her voice clipped with the poshest North accent he'd ever heard. 'If you're not planning to rape or kill me, could you please just shut the door?'

Seven stared. He had to have misheard her.

'Oh,' she breathed when he didn't move. She shut her eyes and stepped back, grasping the table behind her, letting out a little puff of air. 'You *are* planning to rape or kill me –'

'What?' Seven gasped. 'No!'

Without really knowing why (he could have closed the door with himself on the *other* side of it, surely?), he pushed the

61

door shut. The girl watched him, head tipped low, a curtain of hair fallen over her shoulder and half-covering her face.

'What *are* you here for, then?' she asked, jutting up her chin and pushing off the table. A steely undercurrent sharpened her voice. 'I've had a bad enough day without having to deal with you too, so if you could just get whatever you're planning over with and leave me in peace, that'd be wonderful. Thank you very much,' she added, as though remembering her manners.

Seven gestured round the memorium. 'Well, I kinda need to use this room.'

'You need to use this room?' she said warily. 'Why?'

'To steal something.'

The words were out of his mouth before he could stop them. But then again it was pretty obvious what he was here for, him being a complete stranger and having broken into her house in the middle of the night.

He coughed. 'So what are you doing here?'

'Excuse me?'

'I said, what're *you* doing here?'

The girl's nose wrinkled. She took a quick huff of breath. 'You don't ask someone why they're doing something in their *own house*.'

Seven shrugged. 'Just seems kinda odd, you being here in the middle of the night. Getting me to shut the door 'cause you're scared someone in the house will hear us and find you here.' He forced down a grin. He kind of wished Loe was here to high-five him. She would have appreciated that.

The girl looked guilty again for a moment, before rearranging her expression into anger. 'Oh, I could tell on you. Don't think

62

I won't. My father certainly won't be very happy to see you here. Do you know who he is?'

Just like that, Seven's heart began hammering away again.

'I'll give you a clue,' she went on. 'His last name begins with a W.'

Seven eyed the girl, wondering whether he could bring himself to punch her. If he could just knock her out, he'd be able to steal the skid and go. But she was a *girl*. It wouldn't be right to hit her. Besides, she'd seen his face: she'd be able to tell her father exactly what he looked like.

He ran a shaking hand through his hair. The way he saw it, he had two choices. Either he ran away and hoped to effing hell Alastair White couldn't be bothered to dirty his shoes in South to find him, or he told his daughter exactly why he was here.

The girl pursed her lips. 'Well? Shall I call for Father? I should warn you – he will *not* be happy being woken at this hour.'

Seven scowled, doing a quick mental calculation. Face the girl's father? Certain death. Face the girl . . . living was a decent probability.

He'd take those odds.

'I'm a skid-thief,' he told her, 'and I've come to steal one of your father's memories.'

10

ALBA

Throughout their exchange, Alba had been convinced someone in the house would hear them. The whole time she'd been imagining what her parents would do if they found her here in their memorium, and with a boy, no less.

It wouldn't be pretty.

Somehow, she'd managed to fudge confidence and bluff well enough to convince the boy she might call for her father (if only he knew). It was all rather ridiculous, Alba thought. He was the one who'd broken into *her* house, but it was *her* that was in the real danger.

Now she knew what the boy was here for, a strange sense of peace filled her. All he wanted was some stupid memory.

Let him have it, she thought. Anger flared in her chest. *Good riddance. I wish he could go into my mind and take away some of* my *memories, too.*

'Which one are you here to take?' Alba asked, fiddling with the hem of her nightdress, trying – unsuccessfully – to tug it lower over her legs. She was really regretting her decision not to wear a dressing gown. The boy's eyes kept drifting to where the dress skimmed the top of her thighs.

'Like I said – one of your dad's,' said the boy.

Alba was too busy studying him to take this in at first. His features had an exotic edge to them that she couldn't place. Perhaps he was part Japanese? Dark, messy hair fell into slim grey eyes. His mouth was small, and he spoke with it twisted up at one side. He was certainly weird looking (he was so tall and lanky Alba felt like a hippopotamus just being in the same room as him) but there was something strangely attractive about him too. Perhaps it was his smooth, tanned skin, or how he smelled of mint and sweat and *boy*, an enticing, sweet mixture of scents she'd never come across before.

Alba blinked, dragging her thoughts back to the moment. 'What do you want with my father's memories?' she said warily.

The boy shrugged. 'Dunno. My crew leader wants it.'

'Crew leader?'

'All skid-thieves are part of a crew,' he said with an impatient huff, as though she were an idiot for not knowing. 'The leader's the one that organises our jobs, what skids we're gonna steal. That sorta thing.'

Alba frowned. 'You keep saying *skid*.'

A lopsided grin flashed across the boy's face. 'You haven't heard of memories being called skids before?' Laughter teased his words. 'It's after skid-marks. You know, when you go to the loo and –'

'Yes!' she said hurriedly. 'I've got it now, thank you very much.'

Alba's cheeks were hot. She couldn't believe she was here,

talking to a boy about *toilets*. It was strange enough to be talking to a boy in the first place; the Knightsbridge Academy only encouraged male and female students to mix at social events. It was unheard of to be talking to one in the middle of the night in her family's secret memorium (*about toilets*).

'So that's your job?' she asked. 'Memory-thieving?'

He smiled proudly. 'Yep.'

Alba didn't know how to respond. The boy didn't seem to care that his job was a crime punishable by death. Despite his casual attitude, she felt a shiver of unease. This boy was a criminal. The type of person her father sent to their death every day. Memory-thieving was the highest form of betrayal, her father had said at dinner. And here she was talking to a memory-thief as though they'd just bumped into each other in the street!

The irony was that Alba was more afraid of her parents finding her here with this boy than she was of the boy himself. She couldn't let them discover him. He'd be arrested in a heartbeat. She would send him to his death, and sentence herself to a life even more caged than it was now. If her parents knew a memory-thief had been in their house – had even come into contact with their own daughter – they'd never let her out of their sight again.

None of it was fair, and thinking about her parents made Alba angry more than anything. This boy seemed so *free*. He came and went into people's houses and lives and memories as he pleased. How wonderful it must feel to be able to slip away from your own life whenever you got sick of being you.

Alba bit her lip. 'What do you do with the memories you've stolen?'

'Well, the skids go to my crew leader, and he trades them on the black market.'

'Do you ever . . . ever surf them first?'

The boy laughed. 'Yeah. Course. Every time.'

He didn't have to say it; Alba could just see it in the way his grey eyes were shining. Surfing memories was clearly what he lived for.

Suddenly it seemed as though all of today's events had been leading to this. Why had Alba discovered the memorium tonight? After sixteen years of living in this house, she just happened to be here at the very same time this boy came to steal a memory.

She and this boy were destined to meet. She was sure of it.

Alba drew a shaky breath. 'Can you show me how to do it?' she asked, touching the curving back of the Sony Life-Flight. Excitement sparked through her. 'Show me how to memory-surf, and I'll let you steal the memory you came for without my father ever knowing you were here.'

'Now? With that?' The boy pointed at the machine, scowling. 'No way. I wanna get out of here as soon as possible. And the Life-Flights keep a record of every session. I'm not leaving behind any clues I was ever here.'

That was her opportunity to back down. But Alba wasn't ready to give up on the promise of freedom yet. Not when this boy who could give it to her had walked right into her life as though sent from a god, on the very night she needed him most.

She stepped towards him and looked straight into his eyes, fiercely, daring him to object. 'Then take me back with you,' she said. 'Take me surfing on *your* memory-machine.'

11

SEVEN

He woke late the next day from a dream about pirates and an endless ocean. Loe had been there, laughing as they'd jumped off the side of a ship into glittering, sun-drenched water. It had been a good dream (not because Loe was in it, he might add). Seven just liked dreaming of the sea. All that open water made him feel clean and free; two things he never felt living in South.

Eyes still closed, Seven lay in his bed, content. Warm sunlight fell across his blankets. For a while, his mind wandered with bland, everyday thoughts. And then he remembered –

The girl.

Last night.

What he'd promised her for *this* night.

'Oh, effing hell!' Seven groaned, swinging upright.

Last night's events came back to him in a flash of images: the White girl's fingers curling into fists as she turned; the way her pretty green eyes widened as she saw him; her silk and lace nightdress (and what was – barely – underneath).

How she'd stepped closer to him, the sweet, floral smell of her skin unfurling in the air, and said fiercely, *Then take me back with you. Take me surfing on* your *memory-machine.*

What could he have said? No effing way? Seven wasn't really in a position to argue, what with the girl's father being, oh, you know, just *Alastair White*.

Anyway, one skid-surf seemed a small price to pay for getting away with the job. It was too much of an important one to mess up. Carpenter never had to know it hadn't gone quite as smoothly as they'd planned. He'd have his memory. That was all that mattered.

But still. It was *insane*.

The trip to Hyde Park Estate felt like one long, crazy dream. Surely, Seven was about to wake up again any second. He couldn't have made a promise to take that stuck-up North princess back to his flat for her to try out Butler.

He *couldn't* have.

'Well, you *did*, you complete idiot,' he groaned, dropping back onto the mattress and covering his head in his hands.

12

ALBA

School finished early on Saturdays, which was both good and bad for Alba. Good, as it meant, well, less school, obviously. But bad, because it also meant more time in the house, and more opportunities to incite her mother. After yesterday's events, Alba actually found herself wishing her last lesson would never end.

This time, she didn't run to meet Dolly outside the school gates when classes finished.

'Hi,' she said sullenly, slipping her uninjured hand through her handmaid's arm.

Dolly smiled. 'How were your lessons today?' Her face turned serious as she noticed Alba's mood. 'And how is your wrist feeling?' She lifted her arm and inspected her wrist, which she'd bandaged afresh this morning before school. 'Still painful?'

'Not even a bit,' Alba replied, forcing a smile.

She felt a guilty twinge as she lied, and not just about the pain. About the fact that she had said she'd slept well when

Dolly asked her this morning, instead of telling her the truth about the boy and the memorium. She hated lying to Dolly, the one person she felt she could truly trust and confide in. But this might be just a bit too much. Alba couldn't think of a way to explain what had happened without sounding like a total lunatic.

Oh, well, last night while you were sleeping I made a complete stranger – from South, no less – promise he'd take me back to his home tonight to surf memories he's illegally obtained. I do hope that's all right.

None of it felt real. Alba wished she'd thought to ask the boy his name, something to anchor him to her reality so he didn't feel so much like a half-remembered dream, or a ghost slipping away in the night.

Dolly touched her arm, the corners of her lips tucking up into a proud smile. 'That's my little fighter.'

Little liar, *more like*, Alba thought grimly.

But no matter how bad she felt about keeping all of this from Dolly, she couldn't ignore the excitement that had been racing through her all day. It was truly terrifying, the thought of leaving her house in the middle of the night with a boy she hardly knew the slightest thing about, especially as the things she *did* know – that he was from South, that he was a memory-thief – weren't exactly reassuring. And she didn't even want to imagine what would happen if her parents caught her. Yet alongside the fear was a giddy, rebellious thrill.

Alba had finally found a way to defy her parents. For the first time in her life she was clasping her hands round the metal bars they'd built around her, years and years of towering walls, and was pushing them apart.

13

SEVEN

He headed along the riverside path towards the pub where he was meeting Carpenter to give him the White memory. It was another sunny, cloud-blushed day, the afternoon air thick and claggy, making Seven sweat in his trousers and faded T-shirt. Overhead, birds circled in noisy clusters. Their keening caws cut through the air as they darted down to snap at the dead fish washed up on the bank (South's, of course – North's riverside was pristine, cleaned twice a day by South workers).

The path curved along the Thames up towards Vauxhall and Lambeth, shunted in on one side by the river and by grimy buildings on the other. Across the river – busy that afternoon with water-taxis, ferries and huge container ships from the factories – North's promenades and glass-fronted offices shone golden in the sunlight.

As he neared a bridge, Seven's heart began to thud a little faster. Traffic was at a standstill on the bridge, vehicles waiting for the London Guardmen in their red jackets to check their passes. This was the only way to cross between the two halves of the city (the only *legal* way, anyway). Southers had to have a pass for work or personal reasons, signed off by officials, but Northers' IDs allowed them to move across the border in both directions without question.

Sweat pricked Seven's palms. Even though they had no reason to stop him, he still felt as though the London Guardmen knew what he'd done. As though his boots were leaving behind glowing footprints on the dirty pavement, revealing somehow where he'd been last night.

Seven hated the London Guard, the men who ruled the city under the Lord Minister's control. He hated everything they stood for, running the city as though their only job was to keep North protected from South scum like him. But he also feared them, and hating and fearing were pretty much the same thing in his world.

Just then, one of the guards turned.

He had a hand raised to shade his eyes from the glare of the sun. His gaze caught Seven's, something snapping between them before Seven dragged his eyes away, heart stuttering. He stumbled on, not realising he'd been holding his breath, until he reached the pub and let out a hard puff of air.

The Bespectacled Wizard was a dark, stuffy place smelling of river-water and rotting wood. It slumped low on the bank beside the water, clinging to the underside of a small bridge. The river rushed by just metres away. Despite the blazing sun, the wide, low-ceilinged interior was grey with shadows, the windows so grimy they barely let any light through.

Seven moved further in, looking for Carpenter. He spotted

73

him in a corner, sloped in a seat set into a bay window, looking out at the river. The cut through Carpenter's eyebrow was more pronounced in the murky light of the pub. Today it made his expression seem a little threatening, as though the secret joke that usually amused him had turned sour.

Carpenter looked round as Seven sat down.

'S,' he said. He pushed a glass of beer at him, honeyed liquid slopping onto the already-sticky surface of the table.

'Thanks,' Seven muttered, though he didn't touch it. Beer reminded him of the boys from his block of flats, the reek of cheap alcohol on their breath as they cornered him, goaded him, laughed and shouted into his face. It was the taste of their punches and kicks.

Carpenter leant back, one arm slung across the back of his seat. 'So. You got it?'

Seven glanced nervously over his shoulder. 'I got it.'

The pub was full, their voices swallowed under a rolling tide of rough voices and laughter, but Seven was still tense. He was just about to get out the DSC on which he'd copied Alastair White's skid last night when the door to the pub slammed open, the crack of the old wood smashing into the wall like a gunshot ricocheting through the noisy room.

At once, the place fell silent.

Seven swallowed. He didn't need to look round to know who'd just entered. There was only one thing that could quieten a busy South pub so quickly –

The London Guard.

'IDs out,' growled voices from the doorway.

Boots, heavy footsteps sounded as the guards moved deeper inside.

Of all the times for them to be doing an ID check, Seven thought, *it's now, when I've got a stolen skid from Alastair effing White tucked down the front of my pants.*

He must have been acting as skittish as he felt, because Carpenter leant across the table. 'Easy now, S,' he said quietly, before swiping up his glass and leaning back, taking a long drag.

Seven didn't know how he did it. Carpenter made everything he did seem as though it were the most natural thing in the world. Picking up his own pint, Seven took a sip, then slammed it back down a second later, coughing as the liquid went down the wrong way.

'IDs,' came a voice behind him.

Seven had been coughing so loudly he hadn't noticed the thud of boots drawing closer. Jumping at the voice, he dug into his trouser pocket, scrambling for his identification card, while Carpenter calmly handed his card over. There was a high-pitched beep as the London Guardman swiped it through one of their checking devices, indicating it as valid.

The guard tossed Carpenter's card back. 'Now yours.'

Seven started again at the guard's voice. This was why he loved night-time, why he loved thieving: it was just him and the darkness. At night, he felt like the master of the world.

In the daytime, he just felt exposed.

'Oh, er, yeah,' he spluttered. 'Here –'

He was cut off as the guard grabbed his card the second he'd raised it.

A heartbeat moment of terror. Then –

Beep.

Seven sagged in relief, taking his card back as the guard

moved off to check others. The card was a fake one Carpenter had organised for him when he'd first joined his crew, with a false name, address and work details. It hadn't ever failed him (yet). He slipped it back into his pocket.

'You need to work on that, S,' Carpenter said, raising an eyebrow. 'Act suspiciously and they'll think you've got something to hide.'

Seven grinned shakily. 'Don't know what you're talking about.' He pointed at himself. 'I'm the *king* of not-suspicious. The *model* of calm.'

'And the master of bullshit,' Carpenter added.

Seven laughed, but he didn't relax until the London Guardmen left the pub a few minutes later, the noise and chatter rising up again. He waited a while longer to be sure the guards weren't coming back before pulling out the DSC from its hiding place in his pants and handing it to Carpenter under the table.

As it left his fingers, Seven hesitated. He felt a strange pang of unease, as though there was something terrible inside they should have left buried in the darkness of White's memorium.

'You know I keep my crew safe, S,' Carpenter said, sitting back, the DSC already hidden somewhere on him.

Seven nodded. 'Yeah, I know.'

And he did. He wasn't lying about that. The trouble was, he also knew that nothing Carpenter did to look after the members of his thieving crew mattered if the London Guard found just the slightest break in their protection. They were criminals – the lowest even of those – and if Seven was caught, no amount of prayers to non-existent gods would save him.

Almost every skid-thief he'd seen caught over the years had been convicted through fast trials. Fast trials were only used if the prosecution obtained memories explicitly showing the suspect as guilty. Half the time these skids were confessions, freely given by the suspects. Well, not freely given exactly. Seven didn't want to know what prosecutors like White did to obtain them.

There was only one outcome of fast trials: a guilty verdict. And there was only one outcome of a guilty verdict for a crime like skid-thieving.

Execution.

14

ALBA

Once again Dolly and Alba took the long way home from Knightsbridge Academy. Veering off the path to the house that led up through Hyde Park Estate, they wandered instead through fuzzy, sun-blushed fields towards the Serpentine, the lake at the heart of the estate. Long grass tickled their legs. High above, the sun was bright and hazy, washing the world in golden light.

When they got to the sloping bank of the Serpentine, Dolly laid out a blanket under the shade of a mulberry tree. The lake spread before them in a vast pool of pure, crystalline blue, spotted in places by floating islands of algae. Insects buzzed, hidden in the green blades surrounding them. The low growl of a lawnmower sounded in the distance.

Sitting down on the blanket and stretching out her legs, Alba gazed at the grounds of the estate. Everything was touched with a silvery fire from the sunshine. She wondered if it was moments like this that people kept in their memoriums; it's what *she'd* choose to record. A never-ending supply of peaceful moments to dip into, when the world seemed to turn with such a simple, perfect elegance, everything calm and steady and right, and all the bad things slipped away, shadows melting under the sunlight.

'Alba,' Dolly said suddenly. 'I need to tell you something.'

And just like that, the shadows were back.

Alba knew something was wrong from the tone of Dolly's voice. Despite the heat, she felt as though she'd been dunked into ice water. Every muscle in her body went taut. She turned to Dolly and saw the sadness in her eyes.

'It's – it's about you going to university.' Dolly was speaking slowly, as though the words were sticking to her tongue.

'Don't,' Alba whispered.

'Your mother –'

'*Don't*. Please.'

She knew immediately what Dolly was trying to tell her. She felt it like a stone dropped into her chest. It was something that had always been a possibility, but that Alba had hid from her mind for as long as she could –

Her parents had found her a suitor.

They were going to marry her off.

Dolly's lips tightened. 'It's not decided yet,' she said fiercely. 'I'll find a way to make her change her mind. We'll get you out of here, Alba. I promise.'

But Alba just shook her head. A hollow feeling opened up in her stomach. She'd clung to the knowledge that in two years' time she'd be out of here. That no matter how bad it got, however much her parents tried to keep her within their cold, gold cage, each day that passed pulled her one bit closer to freedom.

Now they'd snuffed out her one tiny flame of hope.

'How do you know?' she asked quietly.

'Your mother invited a matchmaker to dine with her today at the house. Mrs Archibald, from Fulham Grove. She works for many of North's prominent families. She has . . . found you a suitor.'

The word *suitor* shivered down Alba's back. She'd seen girls leaving Knightsbridge Academy only to be married away to boys (or even men) from North's most powerful bloodlines, to ensure that the future of the city lay within the hands of the North's elite. But up till now Alba's parents had not mentioned marriage or brought suitors round for her to meet.

She hoped that they knew how much she wanted to go to university. Her father *had* to; they'd talked about it so many times. He wouldn't do this to her. He wouldn't snatch away her dreams.

No, Alba realised. He *would*, because her mother had made him. She must have convinced him this was the best path for their daughter, and Alastair White couldn't say no to his wife. He did everything for her.

For her. Not for me, Alba thought, tears pricking her eyes.

Alba stared out at the lake. She wondered dimly how long it took to drown. If it hurt. She almost laughed – as if she had no experience of pain! – then put her hand over her mouth, tears blurring her vision.

She felt as though she were already sinking.

'Your mother made all of us leave before they could discuss it properly,' Dolly continued, 'so I don't know who your suitor is. I imagine it's a good offer though. Your mother was in such a favourable mood after the meeting.'

Alba swiped at her eyes. She was furious with herself. How could she have not seen this coming?

'I shouldn't have told you,' Dolly said, sounding pained.

Alba shook her head. 'No. I'd rather find out from you.' She snorted, though it came out as a half-choked sob. 'I bet dear *Mother* wouldn't have told me until the night before the wedding. Once she'd got me safely in handcuffs, of course, so I couldn't run away.'

'It might fall through.' Dolly reached for her hand again, their fingers twining together. 'We'll try and find a way to get you out of here.'

Alba screwed her eyes shut. She felt like screaming. She knew Dolly would try – she knew Dolly would do anything for her – but she also knew her mother would never give in. This must have been what she'd planned for her all along.

In a few years' time, Alba would be in a different kind of prison. The walls would look different but they'd still be there, black and towering and holding out the rest of the world as much as they held her in. Because, more than anything, by being married off Alba would never have the choice to define who she became. And Dolly would be taken from her and she'd be given a new handmaid, one who hadn't brought her up like her own daughter or sister, who hadn't held her hand and wiped her tears away and sneaked her food from the kitchens in the middle of the night, and always always always was there for her, every minute, every day.

No.

Her parents had controlled too much of her life already. Alba would not give them her future as well.

81

15

SEVEN

The house looked the same as it had the night before when Seven arrived, just before midnight, slinking through the shadowy row of elms to the west of the building. The marble façade glittered against the darkness of the grounds.

Seven stopped beneath the tree closest to the house. He looked out, imagining the girl inside her room, waiting for the clock to tick midnight to slip from her bed and come outside.

'As if she has the balls,' he murmured with a snort. Because of course she didn't.

The White girl was rich and pampered. She'd never had a reason to be brave. Not like him. Seven had had to fight, claw, scrape for every single thing in his life. When had she ever needed to work for anything herself?

He was so sure the girl wasn't going to show that when he saw the servants' side door opening and her slipping out of the house, that cascade of thick red hair unmistakable in the bright starlight, he didn't let himself believe it.

Then –

'Crap,' Seven said, scowling.

He hated being proved wrong.

16

ALBA

She'd waited until the house was dark and silent before getting out of bed. She had dressed in an emerald-green sweater Dolly had given her for her sixteenth birthday, plain black trousers that hugged her legs, and a pair of old plimsolls. After making sure she had the key to the servants' door tucked safely in the pocket of her trousers – Dolly had given Alba a copy years ago to allow her to slip in and out of the house quietly – she'd left her room and headed down the hidden staircase.

When she pushed open the door and went out into the grounds, Alba felt as though she were stepping into another world.

It was a cool night, a fresh breeze stirring the grass and filling the air with a papery rustling. Wind-teased strands of hair danced round her face. She brushed them aside, squinting into the darkness, her eyes roaming the shadows below the line of Dutch elms just beyond this side of the house across the flat, silver-tipped lawn. Moonlight made everything look icy, crystallised.

Alba's entire body felt alive and alert. She wanted to laugh, or cry, or run across the estate with her hands spread at her sides until she was going so fast she could have lifted off the earth and danced into the air.

Everything she'd been feeling that day had fallen away as soon as she left the house. Gone was the image of her mother's sly smile over dinner; Oxana hadn't mentioned the visit from the matchmaker, though Alba saw the secret brightening her eyes. All Alba felt now was exhilaration at the small act of rebellion she was about to make.

She breathed in deeply, savouring the green scent of the grounds, the freshness of the midnight air. Her stomach gave an excited swoop as she spotted the boy from last night, hiding under the elms. He motioned for her to join him. There was only the slightest second of hesitation before she nodded to herself (*He won't hurt you – he's too afraid of what Father would do*) and went over to him.

'Hello,' Alba said, avoiding his eyes.

She hugged her arms across her chest, feeling suddenly self-conscious. Just like last night, everywhere the boy looked at her made her skin feel hot, as though his gaze were a touch, soft fingers brushing her body and face.

'Hey.'

His voice was husky. He was leaning against the tree, wearing the same blue trousers, work boots and grey shirt as yesterday. Reaching up an arm to scratch the back of his neck, he flashed a wide, lopsided grin.

'Almost didn't recognise you with so many clothes on.'

Alba blushed furiously. She rolled her eyes. 'Well, are we going to go, or not?'

The boy laughed. 'Right this way, Princess.' He stepped aside, bowing and twirling out an arm. Teasing eyes glittered from under his flop of dark hair. 'Unless her majesty would like to use me as her steed?'

'No,' Alba snapped, stalking past him. 'Her majesty most certainly would *not*.'

The boy, who was called Seven (Alba only just managed to remember her manners, stopping herself from asking why he had such a strange name), led her to the edge of the estate. The five-metre wrought-iron fence loomed dark against the row of houses opposite.

'Over?' Alba whispered in disbelief, wrinkling her nose. Wary of the estate guards, she kept her voice low. 'You want me to go *over* it?' She clutched the hem of her jumper and tugged it down, cheeks flushing as she imagined her bottom wobbling in Seven's face.

It was obvious he didn't like her. She didn't need to give him any more bait for snide remarks.

Seven smirked. 'You're welcome to dig your way under it if you'd prefer.' When Alba only glared at him in reply, he shrugged and headed up to the fence. 'Come on. It's not that hard. Anyway, it's the only way past the guards.'

After fumbling around in the darkness at the base of the railing, he stepped back, pulling a rope that tightened as he moved away, revealing its end tied round the tree on the other side. One if its branches skimmed the top of the fence.

Seven held out the rope. 'You go first. So I can make sure you get over OK.'

Steeling herself, Alba took the rope. She tugged on it until it was pulled tight, then braced herself against the fence, one foot pressed against the iron columns, the other still on the ground. She drew a deep breath. Then, clinging to the rope so tightly her fingers already felt numb, she pushed off the ground and placed a second foot on the fence.

Her plimsolls slipped. Before she could slide back down, Alba pulled harder on the rope and took another step. Then another. It was hard going, the painted metal of the railings slippery beneath her weight, but she kept climbing, determined to make it, despite the stinging bite of the rope against her palms and the pain screaming in her injured wrist.

Besides, Alba could feel Seven's eyes on her as he waited below. More than anything, she wanted to quickly get up and over the fence so he'd *please* stop staring at her bottom.

17

SEVEN

He had to admit, he was a little disappointed when the girl finally reached the top. He'd been kind of enjoying the view.

It took longer than usual to get to Chelsea Harbour because Alba kept stopping on the way, gasping at every little thing. It was as though she'd never seen the city before. Or maybe it was just the city at night, Seven thought, with its starlit streets, everything brushed in the soft glow of the streetlights. There *was* a kind of magic to it. He didn't think a stuck-up North princess like her would have cared, but maybe there were certain kinds of magic in this world that everyone couldn't help but notice.

'Isn't it beautiful!' the girl whispered, gazing round at the North streets as they headed for the river.

Seven smirked and muttered under his breath, 'Just wait till you see South.'

He didn't tell her how they were going to cross the border

until they arrived at the harbour. They perched at the end of one of the jetties overlooking the Thames. The river glittered under sparkling riverside lights, water-taxis and sleek, modern cruisers bobbing at their moorings in the harbour. Along the jetty-front behind them the restaurants and bars were still busy, the chinks of glasses and bursts of laughter filling the area with noise.

Alba bent down and peered into the shadows of the tunnel entrance to the old sewer carved into the side of the jetty. This particular part of the sewer system had been disused for years, but it still carried the smell of stagnant water and rotting things. River-water splashed up over its lip.

'This takes us under the Thames?' she asked, her voice stuffy-sounding.

Seven guessed she was holding her nose. He snorted. *Effing hell. How is she gonna manage when we get to* South?

'Yup,' he said. 'Come on.'

Before she could protest, he grabbed the rim of the entrance and ducked, swinging his legs inside. A few moments later the rusted metal beneath his feet clanged as the girl came in after him, landing heavily.

'The *smell*!' she moaned. There was a pause. 'I think I'm going to be sick.'

'Well, don't. It smells bad enough without you adding to it.'

Moving forward in a crouch, Seven found the lamp he'd hidden. He fumbled with a match. A moment later the lamp's flame flickered into life, casting amber light on the curving walls of the tunnel. Holding it out before him, he led Alba deeper into the shadows, their shoes squelching in the stagnant water.

There was a yelp behind him. Seven smirked. The girl must

have spotted the rotting fox corpse half-buried under the mucky brown water.

She groaned. 'I almost wish you'd left us in the dark.'

An hour later, they arrived at his flat in Vauxhall. Since South residents worked all hours, its streets were not nearly as quiet as most of North's had been, even at this time of night. Seven had to take a longer route home to avoid drawing any unwanted attention. Not only was Alba a girl – and a stupidly pretty one at that, a fact which still very much annoyed him – but her clothes gave her away as a Norther. She may as well walk through the streets with a flashing light on top of her head, shouting, 'Here I am, boys! I'm rich. Come and get me!'

Seven couldn't risk Alba being seen. The boys in his block of flats had already proven that if it came down to a fight, he would most certainly *not* be on the winning side.

To be honest, Seven didn't really know why he cared. If the girl was taken from him it was unlikely she'd ever be found (alive, that is). The knowledge that he'd broken into her house to steal a memory would die with her. He'd be safe.

But actually, Seven didn't like to think of Alba dying. He didn't like to think of what a bunch of rough South boys would do to her. For some inexplicable reason, he felt a strange pressure to protect her from harm. Maybe it had something to do with how pale her skin was, like a clean, unbroken canvas, or the sky just before sunrise. It seemed criminal to spoil it.

Though wasn't that what he was? A criminal?

'Well.' Seven waved a hand at the door to his flat. 'Here it is. *Chez* Seven.'

He took in its familiar red paint, faded and peeling, the broken number plate. A pile of rubbish had been dumped outside. A straggly cat with mangy fur slunk up to them, and when Alba went to stroke it the animal hissed and darted away.

Seven laughed humourlessly. 'Welcome to South.'

Now they were here, embarrassment knotted his stomach. He remembered the clean, musty smell of the Whites' house. How everything shone and glittered. He cringed.

There was a long beat of tense silence. Then Alba broke it, a cheerful smile on her face.

'It's . . . lovely,' she said.

Seven looked sideways at her, eyebrows raised. A second later they burst into laughter. Even though he didn't like to admit it, it felt weirdly nice to be laughing with her.

He was so used to laughing alone.

'I'm sorry,' Alba said, clasping a hand to her chest. She forced down her smile. 'I don't mean to be laughing at your home.'

He rolled his eyes. 'Oh, come on. It's a complete dump. And you haven't even seen inside yet.' He laughed again, but the girl didn't join in.

'Have you lived here all your life?' she asked quietly, her cheeks flushed (man, was she pretty when she blushed).

'Nah. Just seven years.'

'With your parents?'

He shook his head, voice turning bitter. 'Don't have any. They abandoned me when I was just a kid.'

The words were out before he could stop them. Now it was Seven's turn to flush red. Only Carpenter knew Seven's history; that he'd been abandoned as a child and had grown up on the

91

streets. Seven hadn't planned to tell Alba, but somehow her questions had caught him off-guard. And when she looked at him like that, all soft pink cheeks and glittering eyes, he felt himself opening, unfurling towards her, the lies that usually lay on his tongue falling away to let the truth rise gently up.

Seven coughed, rubbing the back of his neck. 'Anyway, I like it. I get to live by my rules. No parents telling me what to do.'

There was a pause.

'You're lucky,' Alba said quietly, and it was the first time anyone had ever spoken those words to Seven.

18

ALBA

She had expected his flat to be cluttered and dirty, all unwashed crockery and clothes and mess, as you'd anticipate from three teenage South boys living together. Instead, it was bare. The front door opened up into a small living room with a tattered brown sofa and a cheap-looking plastic table.

As his flatmates were home – Alba could hear one of them snoring from behind a door with the name *Sid* scrawled across it in Biro – Seven bundled her quickly through the flat. She didn't see much of it, but the impression she got was one of emptiness. She wondered whether it was because that's how they liked it or simply because they couldn't afford many things.

The thought it might be the latter filled Alba with guilt. Her room at home was full of beautiful, expensive things. Their whole house was.

The whole of *North* was.

Seven led her to a small room at the back of the flat, locking the door behind them as they went in.

He waved a hand. 'So. My memorium. I know it's nothing like yours,' he added quickly, catching her eyes as she looked round.

She shook her head. 'No. It's – it's lovely.'

This time, Alba didn't have to lie. There was something special about the room; she could feel it. Though the memories were hidden away, they seemed to hum from within the blue filing cabinets lining the walls, filling the air with a shimmering, magical quality. The room thrummed with the promise of hundreds of possibilities, hundreds of worlds just a heartbeat away.

Seven leant against a cabinet. 'What d'you wanna surf, then? I've got over 300 skids.' There was a touch of pride in his voice.

Alba walked slowly around the room, fingers trailing the cool metal fronts of the cabinets. 'All these are memories you've stolen?'

'Yup,' he said, grinning.

Alba couldn't help it: she was impressed. She was less impressed, however, with his labelling system. Seven did use some . . . interesting phrases. The *Fear, Desperation and General Wetting-your-pants Kind of Stuff* cabinet, for example. Wetting her pants wasn't exactly something she wanted to be thinking about in front of a boy. Or at all, for that matter.

Another cabinet's label caught her eye: *BORING BORING NOTHING TO SEE HERE.*

Alba's curiosity was instantly stirred. She moved closer. The label was peeling at the edges. 'There's another label underneath this one,' she said, lifting her fingers to prise it back, but in a flash Seven was pushing her away.

'Nah, you don't want those,' he said hurriedly, throwing out his arms to hide the cabinet. The tips of his ears turned pink.

Alba stepped back, reddening herself. She had an inkling

just what sort of memories might be in that cabinet. Once, Dolly had taken her to Soho for a rare shopping trip, the two of them taking the opportunity while Alba's parents were away on business. They'd gotten lost in its tangle of narrow backstreets and come across a woman in a tight dress standing in a neon-lit shop entrance under a sign flashing the words: *PORN-SURFING*. The pink light had glazed her exposed flesh.

At the time, Alba had been too young to understand what the sign meant, and Dolly had ushered her away before she could take a closer look. It was the only time Alba had seen her handmaid blush.

Now, Seven was the one who was blushing.

'Maybe you should try one of those,' he said, voice unnaturally high. He nodded to a cabinet across the room, labelled: *Get the Effing Hell Outta Here*.

'Are they memories about travelling?' Alba asked, interested.

Seven nodded. He peeled away from the cabinet he'd been hiding and dragged a strange-looking machine out from one corner of the room. 'From all over the world.'

Excitement fluttered through Alba. 'So I can just pick where I want to go from the places you have in the selection?'

'Well, not exactly. I don't say what's in the skids.'

'But how do you know what's in them? Won't it always be a surprise?'

Seven grinned, his smile crinkling his eyes and dimpling his cheeks in a way that made Alba feel a strange flush of something hot in her belly.

'That's what makes it so fun. Now, come on.' He patted the machine. 'Butler's waiting.'

19

SEVEN

He couldn't help it. There was something so exciting about introducing someone to skid-surfing that Seven didn't even mind it was *this* girl, of all people. A girl he should have left to die in the stinking tunnels of the sewer deep under the Thames, but was instead letting her use Butler, not to mention his small, precious allowance of electricity.

Maybe it was about power. This was something he had over the girl, after all. She was relying on him to help her, to show her how to surf. She was putting her trust in him.

Not many people did that.

And maybe that was it: the fact that she *was* trusting him, even though everything she knew would have taught her to do the complete opposite.

Seven finished fixing the wrist-straps to Alba's arms and stepped back, grinning at how funny she looked, all wired up to Butler. Though even the metal cap pinching onto the top of her head couldn't take away from how pretty she was. It was annoying. He plugged the feed cable into the DSC she had picked at random from the travel cabinet.

'Ready?' he asked.

The girl swallowed. Her green eyes flickered with something that took Seven a second to place –

Fear.

'I'm . . . I'm scared,' she said, biting her lip and glancing away.

Seven could have laughed. He could have thrown a snide comment or made fun of her. He could have ignored her, because what was the effing problem? She'd dragged her own stupid ass into this so there was no point complaining now.

But instead he said, 'Don't worry. You'll have a great time,' and in the brief moment after he pressed the *ACTIVATE* option on the screen and before Alba dipped away into the memory, their eyes met and they shared a smile.

20

ALBA

'*MEMORY ACTIVATED*,' came a flat, robotic voice, echoing up from somewhere deep within her skull. '*EXPIRATION IN TWENTY-ONE MINUTES, SEVENTEEN SECONDS.*'

Alba opened her eyes and let out a cry of wonder.

The world had turned green and golden. Gone was Seven's memorium, the blue metal cabinets and old memory-machine and swirls of dust. Instead, sunlight filtered in through the canopy above her head, where huge, twisted trees arced into the sky. All around came the rustling of leaves and animals nosing through the undergrowth. From unseen depths sounded the cackling of monkeys – *monkeys!* – and a rushing, watery noise came from up ahead, beyond the thick tangle of vegetation.

Alba could scarcely believe her eyes. And not just her eyes: *every* one of her senses had come alive. Sounds, smells, even the taste of greenness in the air and the feel of the heat on her skin.

It wasn't like a dream where you were slightly detached, numb from it all. It wasn't even like a memory. It was like a moment, a string of moments, and you were right *there* in it, living it as it happened, everything vivid and real and –

'Oh!'

Without meaning to move, Alba started forward, as though something was pulling her. She slipped on the leafy ground. Regaining her balance, she began to walk, falling into a steady rhythm, feeling a strange need to be moving in this direction. A light pressure at her back pushed her on.

'I'm in a memory,' she said out loud to herself, laughing with amazement. 'I'm in someone else's memory! And I'm walking because that's what they did!'

It didn't feel restrictive. It felt simple. Instinctual.

As Alba walked on, the rushing sound grew louder. After a few minutes it soared into a roar, and then with a suddenness that drew her breath away, the forest opened into an enormous clearing, a huge, tiered waterfall cascading down in a shining white-blue torrent.

'Oh lords,' she breathed, coming to a stop.

The view was incredible. Golden sunlight filled the clearing, the sky above such a pure, clean blue it seemed to be made of glass. The river poured down through the centre. Each of the waterfall's tiers had a wide basin where the water pooled, gurgling and splashing in and over itself. Rocks lining the edges glistened with moss.

A need grew inside Alba. A hot, playful feeling that teased a grin onto her lips and made her heart start to race. All of a sudden, there was nothing more she wanted to do than to be *in* the waterfall.

To *jump*.

Alba ran. Steady at first, then picking up speed, breaking into a sprint towards the lip of the cliff, running and running until she was at the edge, pushing off with one foot and leaping into the sky.

I'm flying! she thought, heart soaring. *I'm* flying.

Then the water burst open as she slammed down into the middle pool of the waterfall, going under so hard and quick she didn't even have time to be scared.

Alba gasped as her head broke the surface moments later. The rush of the water cascading in from above roared in her ears, but apart from a slow, tugging current that was trying to pull her towards the edge of the basin, the water was gentle here. Treading to keep herself afloat, she swiped a hand across her forehead, pushing back the hair glued to her skin. Her clothes were heavy. Following another instinctive urge, she swam to the side of the basin where the cliff ran down alongside the waterfall, and climbed out. Tugging her jumper and trousers off her body, she threw her soaked clothes to the ground, not even caring that she was naked and might be seen at any moment.

Because how could she care, when she felt like this? So weightless. So free.

Alba realised that, for the first time ever, she *was* free.

It was the absolute best feeling in the world.

She slid back into the pool. The water was silk on her body. Sighing, she eased down until she was submerged up to her neck, and closed her eyes. Sunlight poured over her face.

She never wanted it to end. The memory was glorious. It was a million times better than anything she could have imagined. The sounds of the water and the rainforest pulsed in her ears, raw and beautiful and so *alive* it made her want to cry.

And she did. Floating there in the middle of a waterfall in a place that must have been miles and miles away from her home, and possibly years and years away from her present, Alba cried, and for the first time in her life it was from joy.

21

SEVEN

They barely spoke on the way back to North. Seven didn't mind; Alba was less annoying when she didn't talk. And it was a weird kind of nice, walking quietly through the darkness with someone at his side, their footsteps falling in time. It felt almost as though they were friends.

The night was at its deepest when they arrived back at Alba's house, shadows swallowing the estate and making them stumble on the uneven ground. Above, the sky was a hard edge of black. The moon had disappeared. The wind that had earlier been refreshing now had a biting edge: winter was on its way.

Alba squeezed her arms around her chest as they stood at the edge of the cluster of elm trees. The house was white and silent before them. She stared at it, biting her lip. Something about that movement gave Seven a funny, twisty feeling in his stomach. He realised yet again how pretty she was, then scowled, angry with her for making him think it.

'Soooo . . .' he said, rubbing the back of his neck. He grinned.

'Your first time in South. Bet you're wishing you were born on the other side of the river now, huh?'

Alba didn't reply, still staring at the house.

Seven's grin faded. Annoyance buzzed through him. Sure, he'd only done it to stop her telling her father about him, but he'd taken her skid-surfing, for eff's sake. He'd shown her the most precious thing to him – his memorium – and she couldn't even say thank you.

He was just about to leave (what did he think was gonna happen? That this stuck-up North princess would show her gratitude by rewarding him with all the riches he could have ever dreamed of? That there was any other way for this weird situation to end other than her walking back into her golden North life, and him crawling back to South?) when Alba spoke.

'Will you take me memory-surfing again?'

Seven blinked, shocked.

'I – I know you've kept your side of the deal,' she went on, 'and I won't tell my father about you breaking in, or any of this. I promise. But . . . I really enjoyed memory-surfing. I'd like to do it again with you. If you don't mind,' she added in a whisper.

As if I could say I do, Seven thought, on the verge of scowling, but (much to his surprise – and pride) something warm in him was unfurling at the thought of seeing her again, at how she'd said *with you.*

At the thought that maybe, maybe this was what it was like to make a friend.

Letting out a heavy sigh, he shrugged. 'Sure. Whatever. We should probably leave it a week, though. You know. Don't want to make it too obvious or anything.'

Alba's smile was as bright as sunshine. 'Oh!' she cried happily. 'Yes! Yes, of course!' And before he knew what was happening, she lurched forward and threw her arms around his neck.

Seven froze.

For one long, long moment, neither of them moved. Alba stood stiffly against his body, her fingers only just meeting at the base of his neck, her face pressed into his chest. Every inch of Seven was still apart from the shuddering of his heartbeat, quick and fast, racing against his ribcage.

He'd never hugged anyone before. No one had even touched him in any way that wasn't trying to cause pain. Well, Mika hugged him all the time, but she was so small she could only wrap her arms round his legs, so he wasn't sure that counted.

Now Alba's body was pressed up against him, their hearts thudding together, the wind whipping around them, and Seven had no idea what in the effing world to do. He was so stunned he couldn't even think of a joke.

That had to be a first.

22

ALBA

What in heaven's name was she doing! One minute she'd been looking at the polished white façade of her house, thinking about cages and walls and the taste of freedom she'd had that night, and the next her arms were looped round Seven's neck, her senses filled with the sweet, minty smell lacing his skin and his hard body against her.

Never in her life had Alba been this close to a boy. Oh my word: she was *touching* him. No, not just touching, grasping, *embracing* him, their bodies pressed together, not an inch of space separating them. Alba couldn't breathe. She could barely think –

Something moved near the house.

Footsteps.

Then a voice.

'Pearson. What's so important it couldn't wait until morning?'

Alba jerked away from Seven, her eyes flashing wide. Seven was still frozen to the spot, arms hanging stiffly at his sides, but his eyes were wide too, and she saw the fear in them, the same fear that had suddenly clutched her own heart.

That voice.

It was her *father*.

Luckily they were still hidden in the deep shadows under the elm. Instinctively they shrank back, pressing against the thick trunk of the tree. Alba's heart thudded. She craned her head to look out under the dancing leaves and saw the tall silhouette of her father crossing the lawn. There was someone with him: a stocky figure.

It was impossible to tell who it was in the moonless darkness of the night, but her father had called him Pearson. It must be Russmund Pearson, Head of the London Guard.

Her breath hitched in her throat. Her father and Russmund Pearson! Just metres away; the last two people in the world she'd want to come across Seven.

'I won't be long,' said Pearson. 'My driver is waiting round the front. But there is something we need to talk about, Alastair. Privately.'

Their two figures stopped just short of the elms.

'You know my house is devoid of surveillance for this very purpose. What is it we need to discuss?'

'TMK.'

The letters shivered in the air like spun silk. Alba bit her lip, her heart speeding up.

'What happened?' asked her father.

'Two of our TMK Candidates died during Phase Nine training this week. Neuro-haemorrhages while surfing. That leaves us with just one Candidate in training.'

'So the active TMK total is down to just three.'

'Yes. And with a rate of fifteen surfs on average before neuro-haemorrhage, we need new Candidates within a month. Or else –'

'I understand. Speak to Vallez – the current system is unsustainable. His Science team need to sort it out, and fast. In the meantime I will let Recruitment know we need a higher intake of Candidates.'

Pearson said, 'It's getting more and more difficult to keep this quiet, Alastair.'

'Things will be even more difficult for us if we don't.'

There was a long, tense pause. Then Pearson nodded, turning away, his footsteps muffled on the grass as he headed round towards the front of the house. Alba's father followed him a few moments later.

When they'd been alone in the quiet grounds long enough to be sure both men were gone, Alba and Seven peeled away from the tree.

'What the eff was *that* about?' Seven whispered.

Alba shook her head. 'I don't know,' she said, not adding what she was thinking –

But I don't like the sound of it.

Not one bit.

23

SEVEN

'What're you looking so smug for?'

Seven scowled. 'Always nice to see you too, Loe.'

He was slouched on the ground in a corner of the market, back resting against one of the wrought-iron pillars dotting the tall, arched hall. There had been a skid-thief crew leader's arrest the day before: Murray, a tall, bony man with a shaven head Seven had never spoken to, who had been caught during a thieving job. Carpenter and the other remaining skid-thief crew leaders had decided to avoid Battersea Power Station in case its location had been compromised.

This week's meeting was taking place instead in Borough Market, a domed glass and metal structure set on a busy South street near the river. It was open at both ends. Hawker stalls and market booths clustered amid rows of benches, everything painted an ugly shade of green.

By day, the market was one of the busiest in South, selling fresh meat, fish and vegetables, but it was also a hive of activity late into the night as a popular meeting place. By eleven this evening, the hall was packed. Over the chatter and raucous laughter, a Screen fixed high in the middle of the market blared its news, bathing the hall in a shifting sea of colours.

Seven had been watching the crowds for hours, lost in thoughts.

It had been six days since he'd taken Alba to his flat to skid-surf, though it felt more like six years. Time seemed to move even slower that week than it normally did, as though some laughing god above kept turning the world's clock-hands back, just to watch Seven suffer. The worst part was, Carpenter hadn't gotten in touch with any more thieving jobs, so there was nothing to distract Seven from thoughts of Alba (and there were a lot of those. An awful lot more than he'd like to admit).

He wondered whether she was also finding it hard to adjust to everyday life again after their secret meeting. Whether the magic of skid-surfing for the first time had changed *her* world too, the way it had for him.

And, of course, whether she was still wondering what the eff her father had been talking about with that man outside their house.

Nothing about Seven's life had felt properly real since that night. Everything seemed a little faded, the colours not quite right. And at the same time it felt as though that night with Alba never happened. The world would make much more sense if it hadn't. A criminal from South and a stuck-up North princess couldn't ever be friends . . .

Could they?

'You're doing it again.'

109

Seven started, looking round to find Loe staring at him from beneath her choppy bob, a knowing glint in her eyes. She crouched beside him. She was wearing a tattered T-shirt and ripped black jeans, tight on her scrawny body.

'Doing what?'

'Smiling.'

Seven rolled his eyes. 'Just because *you're* angry all the time doesn't mean the rest of the world has to be.'

'Ooh!' Loe smirked. 'Someone's on their period.'

Yeah – you, he wanted to say, but he bit his tongue. You had to pick your fights with Loe (which basically meant don't try and fight at all).

'Where's Mika?' he asked instead. 'I haven't seen her yet.'

'Carpenter's teaching her how to steal properly. Said she'll need to start now if she's ever gonna be a skid-thief like us.'

Seven raised an eyebrow. 'Is that what you want her to be?'

'What d'you mean?' Loe shot him a hard look. 'What *else* is there for her?'

She was right, of course. What future was there for a young South orphan, and a female one at that? Seven knew Mika was lucky to have been taken in by Loe. There were worse things she could do to earn money than skid-thieving.

No one knew what had happened to Mika's family. Why she'd been wandering the riverside streets near Loe's place in Bankside two years ago, just a toddler, barely able to walk. Loe had never told anyone. She'd just turned up with the girl at the skid-market one day and glared at anyone who looked as though they were even thinking about asking.

'Anyway.' Loe elbowed Seven in the ribs. 'What d'you think

110

about the whole Murray business?'

'Oh, just overjoyed, of course.'

'Seriously, you idiot. Do you think Carpenter'll be next?'

'No way,' Seven said quickly. 'He's smarter than the other crew leaders. He won't let himself – or any of us – get caught.'

Loe looked away, tongue playing with the loop through her lip. Her guard had slipped for a moment, and Seven could see how worried she was. He felt a warm flash of affection for her, then inwardly grimaced.

His brain must be malfunctioning. First Alba, and now Loe? He was going soft.

'You really think that?' she asked quietly.

'Yeah. When has Carpenter ever let us down?'

Before she could answer, a shrill voice danced towards them, bursting with excitement.

'Loe! Loe! Loe! Seven! Seven! Seven!'

Loe rolled her eyes. 'I swear, that girl has a tracker on me or something.' But her face softened all the same as Mika ran into view, a bush of fuzzy black hair weaving in and out of legs and tables. Loe pushed off the floor and mussed Mika's hair. 'What *now*?'

Mika jiggled on the spot. 'Carpenter wants you,' she said to Seven. She giggled. 'Maybe he wants to teach *you* how to steal, too.'

Loe sighed heavily. 'What d'you think we all do for a living, Mika?'

'I know what *you* do.' Mika hid behind Loe's legs. She pointed at Seven and sang gleefully, 'Your job is fancying *him* –'

'MIKA!'

Loe's roar was so loud her voice cut through the noise of the market crowds, practically cleaving the air in two.

'Oops!' screeched Mika, and she threw her hands in the air and ran back into the crowds, her giggles floating around her like a cloud of technicolour bubbles.

There was a heartbeat of tense silence. Then, throwing Seven a thunderous look that practically hissed *Don't you even* dare, Loe stormed off after Mika, her cheeks flushed so dark they were almost purple.

'How was that *my* fault?' he shouted after her.

In his head, he took back his earlier affection for Loe. He might be going mad, letting himself care about a stuck-up North girl like Alba, but to feel anything other than anger and annoyance towards Loe, Seven would have to go *completely* insane.

24

ALBA

It had been the longest week of her life. Not even a million lessons with Professor Nightingale could have felt longer (not that she'd care to try it to find out). Alba spun through minutes like Alice floating down the rabbit hole – Carroll's *Wonderland* books were her favourites – drifting in a current separate to the rest of the world, things slipping by, unable to touch her. And the worst part of it was, it wasn't over yet.

One more day!

She didn't know how she'd manage.

Whenever she thought of Seven, Alba saw him in the dusky, night-time places of last Saturday: walking towards her under the shadows of the elms in her garden, or a flame-lit figure ahead of her in that awful sewer tunnel, his outline yellow and glowing. How he'd frozen as she'd asked him if he'd take her surfing again and she'd thought for a split-second he was going to say no, and the fast, spiralling feeling that had wound through her chest then, a rush of emotions she couldn't quite place.

Seven had only let her surf the one memory that night, worried about getting her back to North before it got light. One memory wasn't nearly enough. Alba wanted more. Hundreds more. She wanted to surf his entire collection, and even then it wouldn't be enough.

She'd been to a tropical rainforest, swam naked in the azure water of its pools, while her parents and Dolly and everyone else in her house had been here, just sleeping. They might have been dreaming, but dreaming was nothing like memory-surfing. Surfing was so much *more*. It was like living moments from the most beautiful, sparkling life.

And there was the problem. Now Alba had had a taste of freedom, she couldn't bear the thought of it being taken away.

Dolly was getting Alba ready for bed when there was a knock on the door. It opened before they could answer, Oxana stepping into the room in a cloud of too-sweet perfume and bustling silks.

'Mistress White!' Dolly gave a polite bow, still holding the brush she'd been using to comb through Alba's hair.

Alba pulled her silk dressing gown tighter around her, face paling. Even though it had been a week since the night her mother had hit her, the memory of it still felt fresh. Raw. She had spent the week avoiding looking into her mother's eyes because every time she did, there it was again: the snap of her wrist; coldness of the marble floor against her cheek; wine on her mother's breath; the ugly look on her face as she'd said, *I'm done with you*.

For the past few days, it'd seemed Oxana was keeping to

her words. Apart from dinner every night and their weekly Sunday church visit, Alba hadn't seen her mother, and even when they were together her mother hadn't pressed her to talk.

Now she was here in her bedroom, and there was nowhere Alba could escape to.

'Dolly,' Oxana said, smiling, clasping her hands in front of her. She was still wearing her dinner outfit from earlier. The long green dress skated over her curves like a dark emerald waterfall, picking out the colour of her eyes. Her blonde hair was slicked back in a sleek ponytail. 'May I have a few moments alone with my daughter?'

'Of course, Mistress White.' Giving Alba an encouraging smile, Dolly squeezed her shoulder and left the room.

Alba stared down at her lap, fiddling with the tie of her dressing gown. Her stomach flipped dizzily. For one terrible moment she could barely breathe, because she truly thought her mother was about to tell her she knew what had happened last week.

That she knew about Seven.

It was strange, but the two nights Alba had shared with that weird, awkward boy from South seemed more binding than if they'd grown up together, spending years in each other's company. She felt as though they were tethered together now. Tethered by their shared secrets, yes, and what they'd overheard between her father and Pearson, but also bound by the gift that Seven had given her.

Because that's what it felt like to Alba; a gift. And she had no idea what she'd done to deserve it.

Then her mother said in a gentle voice, 'I want to apologise for the other night, my darling,' and all Alba's fears suddenly spun away.

She jerked her head up. Before she could say anything, her mother walked over and took her hands, leading her from the dressing table to the bed.

Oxana let out a slow huff of breath as they sat on the edge of the mattress. 'I'm so sorry for what happened, my darling. I really am. It was abhorrent of me. I never should have said those things, or acted the way I did.' She stopped, mouth tightening, and reached out to tuck a stray lock of hair behind Alba's ear. 'I have felt horrible about it all week,' she went on. 'But your father and I – we need you to understand the truth about South. It is a dark place, Little Alba. Darker than you can imagine.'

Alba swallowed, looking away. She thought of Seven, how he'd told her not to worry when she'd admitted she was nervous before memory-surfing, and the soft look then in his eyes.

'No,' she said.

Her mother's hand stiffened in hers. There was a long, heavy pause.

'What do you mean, my darling?' Oxana asked eventually, a hard thread running under her words.

Alba took a deep breath. 'I mean no.' All of a sudden, her words fell out in a rush. 'I know what you're trying to tell me, Mother. What you and Father were saying the other night. But it's not right. It's not fair. Even if South *is* dark, that doesn't mean all the people who live there are too. We shouldn't judge them that way, when we don't know anything about their lives or what they think and feel –'

Alba bit her lip, falling abruptly silent. She'd been so close to mentioning Seven then. How she knew what he did was wrong,

116

but he did it because he had no choice. Because memories were the only thing that made him feel free (they were the only thing that had ever made *her* feel free, too).

Her mother let go of her hands. 'But we *do* know,' she said quietly, though her voice was icy. 'Southers are dangerous.'

'And Northers aren't?'

It came out sharper than Alba had meant it to. She saw her mother's eyes click to her left wrist. It wasn't in a bandage any more, and the pain had subsided, but there was a ring of purple bruising across the skin where the sprain had been. She knew her mother was thinking of the night when she'd hit her.

Alba felt a surge of guilt, even though, as always, she knew she'd done nothing to deserve it. 'I – I didn't mean . . .'

Oxana clicked her tongue. She waved a hand, not quite meeting Alba's eyes, and just like that Alba felt herself dismissed, and her mother hardening again.

'It's getting late. I should let you get to bed.'

Standing, her mother smoothed down her dress. For a moment she watched Alba, some unreadable emotion passing across her face. Then she looked away.

'We are trying to teach you about the world,' Oxana said coolly. 'So you don't have to learn for yourself, the hard way. It is important you understand your place – and everyone else's – in this society.' She moved to leave the room, then paused at the door, turning back to Alba. 'One day, my darling, if things go as planned, the world will look to you for guidance and wisdom. And you must be ready to show them the right path.'

It was only after the door clicked shut that Alba took in her mother's parting words. Her mind was spinning. What on earth was her mother talking about?

'One day the whole world will look to *me* for guidance and wisdom?' she murmured to herself. It sounded so ridiculous, but a shudder ran down her spine.

Just *who* did her mother think she would become?

25

SEVEN

Carpenter was conducting his meetings in Borough Market in a dimly lit corner of the hall. A row of stalls, their shutters locked for the night, hid them from the main crowds, though people were still milling by. Their voices put Seven on edge. He kept looking over his shoulder every time someone passed, wary they were listening.

'Relax, S. They can't hear us.'

Carpenter was his usual calm self, sitting opposite Seven at one of the round tables, one leg propped up on his seat. His khaki-coloured shirt was rolled back at the elbows and open low down the front, revealing the dense forest of tattoos twined across his skin. There was a saw in there somewhere, Carpenter had once said – the same design that Seven and the rest of the crew had inked on their chests – but Seven had never been able to locate it (urgh. Maybe it was somewhere he didn't *want* to locate).

Seven picked at a piece of gum stuck to the table. 'It's just hard to relax after Murray and everything.'

'I know.'

'Everyone's worried it'll be them next.'

'I know.'

Seven sighed, running a hand through his hair. It was impossible to read Carpenter.

A laughing group of men sauntered by. He glanced over to watch them pass when Carpenter spoke suddenly, making him turn back.

'S. Listen to me.'

Carpenter's voice had changed. It was sharp now, an edge to his words.

'The White memory. Did you surf it?'

Seven's cheeks flushed. 'What d'you mean? I don't –'

'I know you copy all the skids you steal,' Carpenter interrupted, 'so don't waste time telling me you haven't. Just answer me. Have you surfed it yet?'

'But –'

'I don't give a bloody *toss* about you copying them, Seven!'

He slammed a fist on the table so hard it shook, but it was the use of his full name that really got Seven's attention.

'All my crew do it,' Carpenter said. '*I* do it. I wouldn't expect anything less from a skid-thief. I just need to know about the White memory.'

Twisting his hands in his lap, Seven shook his head. 'Not yet,' he answered.

The truth was, he'd completely forgotten about Alastair White's memory after everything that had happened with Alba. Seven had used Butler every day, but only to surf the memory she'd chosen that night, over and over, feeling each time as though he could somehow sense her in it, the ghost of her body imprinted in the memory-space, wanting to know how she'd felt when she'd been in the lush rainforest with its cascading waterfall, what she'd been thinking as her body plunged into the blue.

Carpenter nodded and looked away. 'I believe you.' Then, speaking so quietly Seven almost couldn't hear, he muttered, 'I thought it would protect us. That *I* could protect us by having it. Use it as blackmail, if it ever came to it. Something to keep that White pig away. And after Murray . . . But it's bigger than that. I should've left it alone.'

Seven watched him warily. 'What're you talking about, Carpenter?'

His crew leader's eyes snapped back to him. In one sudden move, Carpenter dropped his leg down and leant across the table. His features were edged with panic. A muscle was twitching in his temple: a quick, frantic beat that made Seven's own heart speed up.

'S. This is important. This is your *life* we're talking about.'

There was a pulse of noise from deep in the hall. Seven broke Carpenter's gaze, turning to look over his shoulder. Something seemed to be rousing the crowd. Shouts echoed off the domed roof.

'What's going on?' he muttered, distracted.

'S, listen to me!' Carpenter's voice was a growl, barely audible over the growing sea of noise behind them. 'The White memory. *Do not* surf it.'

Seven looked back round.

'Promise me you'll destroy it,' Carpenter urged. 'No one can ever find it, or know that you had it.'

The panicky edge in his voice worried Seven.

Carpenter was scared.

He was *never* scared.

A tentative grin snuck across Seven's lips. 'Come on, Carpenter . . . you're weirding me out.'

'FOR FUCK'S SAKE!'

With a roar of frustration, Carpenter swung back, pushing up from the table so he was towering over Seven, his face a twisted shadow in the glow of the lights above.

'This is important! Stop being a complete idiot and just fucking *promise* me –'

Something whistled past Seven's ear. A second later, Carpenter let out a soft hiss of breath. Surprise flitted across his features. He raised a hand to his neck then drew his fingers back. They were slick. Wet. Red.

'Fuck,' he muttered, blood bubbling up over his lip.

And then Seven saw it –

The dark hole in the side of his neck.

Carpenter's eyes swivelled, focusing on Seven. 'The memory, S. Destroy it.'

His eyes unfocused. A wave of sadness flushed his face, and it made him look young, as young as a child, lost and alone and scared of the darkness. Scared of the sounds in the night.

'S-sorry.' Carpenter forced the word out, voice thick and gurgling.

More blood filled his mouth. His teeth were *black* with it.

Seven couldn't move, couldn't think. All he could do was whisper, 'C-Carpenter?'

But his crew leader didn't respond. His eyes just rolled up in their sockets, his face softening, and then he fell straight back with a thud to the floor.

Before Seven had a chance to do anything – even *think* anything – the roar of the crowds swelled louder and suddenly there were people everywhere, a tide surging through the hall, bodies breaking against him in the rush, and above it all the hard, angry studs of gunfire, and screams, as more bullets found their mark.

26

ALBA

Voices stirred her from sleep.

Alba woke, disorientated, so twisted up in her duvet and sheets, pillows scattered around her, that she felt a rising thrum of panic. She was trapped. Trapped as she'd been in her dream. It took her a few moments to realise where she was.

The voices were coming from outside her room, scratching in the night-time silence. Easing out of the tangle of sheets, she padded across the room and opened the door.

There were lights on in a room down the corridor. On this floor, that end of the house was Alba's parents' private wing, a part she was forbidden to enter unless invited by one of them, which was rare. The lights were on now in her father's office. Their yellow glow spilled out into the hallway, shifting shadows thrown across the floor as figures moved inside.

The voices were male, gruff, tense. Alba couldn't make out what they were saying from here; their sentences were shapeless, only noises. Then she heard a single word that made her body run cold –

Memory-thief.

'Seven,' she breathed.

Heart thudding, Alba tiptoed down the hall. She kept close to the wall, touching her fingertips to the velvety wallpaper engraved with soft, swirling patterns lost in the darkness. She stopped a short way from the open door to the office, close enough now to hear snatches of conversations inside.

'. . . the raid . . .'

'. . . Borough Market . . .'

'. . . ten dead, and at least thirty more injured . . .'

'. . . unconfirmed . . .'

'. . . escaped . . .'

The men were talking over one another. It sounded like there'd been some sort of raid by the London Guard on a memory-thief meet-up. Alba remembered Seven mentioning something about these big events where all the thieving crews got together to do business.

'The London Guard have been placed on high alert for suspected memory-thieves that might have escaped the raid.'

Her father's voice cut above the busy chatter. At once, the room fell silent. There was the rustling of suits, a chink of a glass being set down as the men gave Alastair White their full attention.

'They have identified some of the tattoos marking out the different crews, and will be searching both South and North for people carrying those signifiers. Without any strong evidence or confessions, however, we are unable to ascertain how many memory-thieves have gone unapprehended.'

There were jeers.

'Give Interrogations a few hours. They'll have those confessions in no time.'

'South scum. What did they think – that they could keep taking our memories without any repercussions?'

'Let's see how they like a bullet in the head.'

'Men. A little dignity, please.' Her father's voice quietened the room again. His tone was smug. 'Remember, we *are* in North.'

The room burst into laughter.

Alba dashed back to her room. She'd heard enough. Pressing her back to the inside of her door she heaved in deep, shaky breaths, listening to the footsteps of the men passing as they left a few minutes later. She stood there long after they'd gone, the slam of the grand front doors too loud in the stillness of the house, quiet now despite the storm of thoughts inside her mind.

Raid.

The London Guard.

Memory-thieves.

Interrogations.

Bullets –

Alba stuffed a hand over her mouth. She felt sick. How could those men – how could her *father* – talk so flippantly, so smugly, about the loss of lives? They'd even laughed about it. *Laughed*.

Alba let the anger overtake her, let it rip through her in a roar of red, because the alternative was worse. Utter sadness over what was happening to those poor skid-thieves right now, and the horrible, sick fear that Seven might be one of them.

27

SEVEN

He only just escaped, only just made it out alive.

The market had turned into a wave, a chaotic, churning, surging swell of bodies, all straining to reach the shore where the hope of safety waited outside the glass-roofed hall, just metres but miles and whole lifetimes away.

Seven was swept up along with the crowds. When it came to fighting, his scrawniness had always been a disadvantage; tonight it saved his life. He used elbows, bones, limbs to battle his way out of the crush of bodies, stop himself from going under. He slipped through gaps. He ran, crawled over others where he had to.

And he had to, to live.

Because he wanted to live. So badly. He might wonder why the hell he bothered most of the time, but right at this minute, on this night, after seeing one single bullet fell Carpenter like a chainsaw to a tree, Seven *had* to live.

Death roared around him and he fought his way from it.

It felt like he was running for hours. He only let himself slow when he realised he couldn't hear gunshots any more, that he was alone on a dimly lit street, gulping for air.

Seven looked blearily around. He had no idea where he was. He hadn't even noticed where he'd run, just that it was in the direction the men and their guns weren't. Staggering into the shadows of a nearby alley, he slumped to the ground, letting himself relax for the first time since leaving the market (well, not relax. This was *nothing* like relaxing, this heart-still-pounding, mind-still-a-bloody-mess kind of state).

'The London Guard,' Seven gasped, choking on the words.

Of course that's who the attackers were. Who else would know to raid a night-market in South where a secret skid-thieving ring just so happened to be doing business? Who else would come in with guns first, questions later, only for the ones they caught alive? Who else would have shot Carpenter in the neck, shot him dead –

Dead.

It couldn't be real. Not Carpenter. He was sturdy, strong, built of muscle and grit. He was clever and sharp. It didn't seem possible that he'd been hit. Seven wouldn't have been surprised if his crew leader had calmly plucked the bullet from his neck and went on as though nothing had happened.

If anyone should've died, it was him. Seven could barely lace his own boots without falling over himself, for gods' sake. He should have died. His body should be back there in the market, piled with the others.

Except it wasn't.

He was alive.

Seven tipped his head back against the wall behind him, closing his eyes. They felt strange. Wet. A moment later, he realised why: he was *crying*. Effing *crying*. He stuffed his hands into his eyes and ground his knuckles against them until the tears stopped.

All he could keep thinking was, *I'm alive*. But it didn't feel good. It didn't feel like relief.

For some reason, it felt like the worst thing in the world.

28

ALBA

The raid was all anyone could talk about the next morning at school. Alba didn't think it was because the girls were that interested in London politics; it was more because of the thrill of it. Guns and death; these sorts of things felt a world away from the plush lives of the Knightsbridge Academy students. Something exciting, a different world entirely. Like going to the zoo to stare at caged animals, or how some of the girls from Alba's class would walk along the bridges crossing the Thames, just to get a close-up glimpse of South and its residents (another type of caged animal, she supposed).

But to Alba, the consequences of the raid felt very real. She couldn't stop thinking about Seven. How had he felt during it all? Had he even been there when it happened?

She hoped he hadn't.

Just a few more hours, she kept telling herself as the morning's lessons dragged on. *He'll come tonight, and then it'll all be fine. He'll come, and you'll know he's alive.*

He will *come.*

Alba didn't let herself imagine what it'd be like if he didn't.

Perhaps she only cared so much because Seven was her link to memory-surfing. That he had helped her escape, at the very time she needed it most.

But perhaps it was more than that.

Perhaps it was also because this strange South boy had given her a gift, opened up a whole new world to her, when he hadn't even known how much it would mean to her. Apart from Dolly, no one had done something like that for her.

Alba felt connected to Seven now. She felt as though she owed him. And how could she ever repay him if he was . . . if he was *dead*?

A compulsory broadcast about the raid was being shown on the main news Net channel at midday. Unlike South, there weren't any public Screens in North displaying news at all hours, so when it was time for the announcement the students filed out of their classrooms to the assembly hall, where a large screen slid down from the ceiling to hang above the stage.

The hall was grand, with dark, carved wooden walls and an elaborate chandelier dominating the ceiling. Its crystal embellishments threw sparkling shards of light across the room. Ornate gilded frames lined the walls, painted portraits of past headmasters and headmistresses staring blankly down. As Alba took one of the seats filling the hall, Rosemary Dalton sat down in front of her.

'I hope all of the memory-thief scum they captured are executed live on the Net,' Rosemary said, tossing a blonde curl over her shoulder. 'Serves them right, thinking they can take memories for free from people who've worked hard to get to where they are. *And* sell them on for a profit.'

Alba bristled. She leant forward and clutched the back of Rosemary's chair. 'Did you ever think they might not have to steal if we didn't make things so hard for Southers in the first place? Maybe *we're* the ones who have been stealing.'

An image of Seven flashed into her mind: him spreading his arms to gesture round at the blue filing cabinets of his little memorium, unable to hide his pride, even though the place was dirty and dingy, and in a block of flats so horrible Alba's mother would probably rather die than set foot in it. He needed those memories as much as Alba needed them now.

To escape reality. Escape the truth of his life.

Seven stole to *survive*.

Of course, he hadn't said so to Alba, but she could tell. It was obvious by the way his eyes lit up every time he talked about memory-surfing. How he had patted Butler like he was a real person. The excitement in his voice as he'd told her about his life as a memory-thief on the way to South that night.

Rosemary looked over her shoulder, her piggish face scrunched in disgust. 'Who'd have thought it? Alba White, a liberal.' She let out a whiny laugh, and a couple of the girls nearby joined in.

Alba scowled. 'At least *I* don't get excited about watching people die live on the Net.'

'What *does* excite you?' Rosemary sneered. 'Dirty South men? Like mother, like daughter, huh?'

The words were a slap in the face.

Alba couldn't help it; her mouth dropped open in surprise. Her cheeks flushed. Around her, the hall started spinning, everything whirling into a colourless blur.

'What did you say?'

Rosemary smirked. 'You heard me.'

Alba realised that the students nearby were watching her. Some of their faces were painted with the same disgust Rosemary was wearing, but some looked scared or shocked.

No one spoke to Alastair White's daughter the way Rosemary just had.

Before Alba could think of an appropriate response that wasn't to launch herself at Rosemary and claw out her hair (and her mother said it was only *Southers* that were dangerous), a gong rang out. The hall fell into an expectant hush. Everyone turned to the stage as the school's headmistress walked out.

Headmistress Fortescue was a tall, sharp-boned woman, her greying cloud of mousey hair the only soft thing about her. The ridge of her collarbones stuck out through her blouse. As she did for all assemblies, she wore a sweeping black robe with dappled purple-and-white fur trim. It swirled around her heels as she walked to the front of the stage.

'Girls,' she began in a high, nasal voice. 'As you are aware, there is a compulsory broadcast on the Net today dealing with the raid on an illegal memory-trading ring last night. As London's future leaders and wives of leaders, it is of the utmost importance that you all take an active interest in our city's politics. A Knightsbridge Academy young woman must understand the rules of our society, and the necessity of abiding by and maintaining those rules for the health of the city at large.'

Headmistress Fortescue looked round the hall, her gaze seeming to sweep a cold wind wherever it moved. When the gong sounded again, she gave a curt nod.

'The broadcast is about to begin. Girls, may I remind you that this is not a football stadium or public square in South. You are all young ladies of the highest breeding. There will be no cheering or shouts during the broadcast, no matter how pleasing it may be.'

Alba could have slapped her.

Heels clacking on the wooden floorboards, the headmistress took her place with the rest of the teachers on a raised ledge to one side of the hall, and a few moments later the screen suspended across the stage flared into life.

A roar of colour and sound flooded the hall. Alba squirmed in her seat as the familiar face of her father appeared. He always seemed different somehow on broadcasts to how she thought of him. Colder. Hard-edged. But after overhearing him last night, she saw that perhaps *she* was the one who had the wrong image of him. The breeze lifted his cape as he walked out of the courthouse, the doors of the Old Bailey behind him pulled shut by two suited workers.

Camera lights flashed. Reporters hidden off-screen shouted out, but Alastair White ignored them.

'We can confirm that last night a raid was undertaken by the London Guard on an illegal memory-trading ring in Borough Market in South,' he announced in his flat, detached voice. 'Eleven Southers were killed, and twenty-nine more injured. Eighteen memory-thieves have been taken into custody for questioning. Official footage of the scene of the raid will now be shown. Please be aware it contains graphic images.'

The screen cut to black. For the split-second before the footage came on, Alba willed her eyes to close. She didn't want to see this. She *didn't*.

But her eyes wouldn't shut.

Her heart jumped when the screen lit back up and images of the aftermath of the raid flashed across it in a lurid display. Bloodied bodies littered the floor of the market, some half-hidden under tables and chairs; arms and legs flung wide; close-ups of eerie white faces, mouths gaping.

Alba was frozen, terrified she was about to see Seven's face like that any second, ghostly and pale, his eyes staring blankly out.

When the footage stopped and the broadcast cut back to her father on the steps of the Old Bailey, his voice echoing around the hall, Alba's eyes finally squeezed shut. But no matter how relieved she was that she hadn't seen Seven in the footage, she couldn't escape the sick feeling all the images of the other dead Southers had brought, and the thought of their families being forced to watch.

And, worst of all, the way her father had just carried on talking as though nothing, nothing at all, had happened.

29

SEVEN

'Fucking joke!'

'Cold bastards.'

'Showing off people's deaths to the world like it's a bloody party.'

Anger rippled through the crowd gathered at Clapham Arches. Seven, watching from the back of the crowd the Screen that hung inside one of the archways under Clapham Bridge, let himself be pushed and shunted, people jostling to get out. His eyes were still focused on the Screen. He felt hollow. Carved open. Even though he didn't know any of the dead faces he'd seen on the footage, he couldn't help imagining himself in their place, or Loe, or Mika.

He felt sick to his stomach.

After Alastair White finished his speech, a sombre-looking reporter came on. She stood outside the market. London Guardmen patrolled the perimeter behind her, red jackets flashing in the midday sun. The tall entranceway was covered with a crime-scene sheet of black fabric.

'The London Guard are asking those with information on the whereabouts of the escaped memory-thieves to come forward,' the reporter was saying. 'A monetary reward is being offered for those whose information successfully leads to a conviction.'

Some of the people who'd been turning to leave the archway hesitated, glancing back. Seven felt a new feeling ripple through those gathered there; eagerness. Everyone was suddenly alert.

The mention of money did that in South.

'They have released visuals of tattoo markers they believe the different memory-thieving crews use as identifiers,' the reporter continued. 'If you see anyone with these markers, the London Guard urge you to report them immediately. We ask you all to familiarise yourselves with the following images, which we suspect to be the crew signifiers.'

The screen changed to show a series of black patterns. With each one, shivers of unease ran up and down Seven's spine. He knew them all.

The outline of a tennis racket: that was Murray's crew.

A rose: that was Timothy Rose's.

A lightning bolt: Abel Potter's.

A saw –

Seven's heart flew into his throat.

It was the exact same image as the one inked beneath his collarbones. The tattoo was hidden today under his grey shirt, but he still clutched at the collar, sure somehow the mark shone brightly enough for the whole world to see. How did the London Guard know about their tattoos? Had they found them on the bodies of the skid-thieves their guns had brought down, or the ones they'd captured alive?

What about Carpenter's sign? Carpenter's skin was a riddle of tattoos. It was impossible to know what was what.

Or else . . .

'No,' Seven said out loud. He didn't want to even *think* about the possibility that someone in his crew had been captured or killed. Mika and Loe; he'd go to their house now, prove to himself that they were OK.

They had to be OK.

As Seven pushed his way through the crowd another thought hit him, so strongly it made him stagger.

The girl.

Alba.

Alba *White*.

No. She wouldn't have.

Would she?

Her annoyingly pretty face came to mind. Thick red hair, dark and glossy, soft curls brushing pink cheeks. Bright green eyes. He remembered the way she'd looked after surfing; vulnerable and sad and happy all at once. She'd seemed so *grateful*. It had made Seven feel as though he'd given her something. A gift, a tiny piece of treasure worth more than the hundreds of expensive things lavished on her back home.

He'd thought that gift was the joy of surfing for the first time. After all, he remembered exactly how *he'd* felt after his first skid-surf, when he'd known the world wouldn't ever be the same for him. But what if he was wrong? What if he'd given Alba the gift of something else entirely, and she'd just been delighted about having it to use against him, to pass it on to her father.

Information.

The truth.

Seven had told her things about his life as a skid-thief. Things no Souther would have ever told a Norther. He'd been stupidly open, answered her questions honestly, because . . . because she made him feel as though he *could*. As though he could trust her with anything.

You humongous bloody idiot! Seven thought, gritting his teeth hard to stop himself from shouting. He was so angry he could punch himself. He'd been a complete fool to trust that stuck-up North bitch.

Seven curled his hands into fists, shoving his way through the noisy crowd.

So he'd given Alba a gift, had he? Wrapped up all the details about the life of skid-thieves with a neat effing little bow for her? Well, now it was time for *him* to take something back in return.

An eye for an eye, that was the rule, wasn't it? Alba had ruined his life. Now Seven would ruin hers.

30

ALBA

Dolly's voice reached her from the en-suite over the sound of running water. 'Bath's ready! Hurry up or the water'll go cold.'

Alba sighed. The last thing she wanted was a soak but Dolly had insisted, saying that Alba had been restless all day and this would calm her (no doubt she'd laced the water with herbal sedatives, just to be sure).

Twisting her hair into a bun and sweeping away a few loose strands, Alba padded to the bathroom. A haze of steam filled the air, woody smells of sandalwood and sage enveloping her. The bathroom was almost as big as her bedroom, white and gold tiles covering the floor. In the centre was a large, claw-footed tub with a gilded rim. Candles bathed the room in a comforting glow.

The taps squeaked as Dolly twisted them off. The bathroom fell into a secretive hush, the only sound the popping of the bubbles in the tub and the patter of raindrops on the window.

'Come on then.' Dolly went over to Alba and took off her

bathrobe, folding it on a chair by the sink. 'You'll feel better after an hour in here.'

Alba climbed over the side of the tub. She slid in slowly, the water – a perfect temperature, warm and golden – rising to her neck. Bubbles hid her body from view. Straight away, she felt calmer. She tipped her head back to rest it on the edge of the tub and gave Dolly a small smile.

'You know, I feel a little better already.'

But as soon as she said it, Alba thought guiltily of Seven. She thought of the skid-thieves lying dead on the floor of the market. The ones who had been captured by the London Guard, and were now enduring whatever horrible processes were involved in their interrogations.

How could she relax after everything that had happened? When she didn't even know if Seven was alive?

Her face must have fallen, because Dolly stepped over and crouched down. 'What is it? I know something's wrong. You're keeping something from me, and I'm worried, because if you don't feel like you can tell me about it then it must be bad.'

Alba dropped her gaze. 'It's nothing,' she murmured.

'Alba . . . are you hiding something?'

'No, I –'

'Is it your mother?' Dolly's voice was sharp. Her eyes narrowed. 'Has she hurt you again?'

Alba bit her lip. Hating herself, really hating herself then, she looked down and nodded. 'I don't think I can take it much longer, Dolly.'

'Alba Philippa Darcy White,' said Dolly sternly, and Alba jerked her eyes up at the sound of her full name.

Dolly cupped Alba's face with both hands. 'Now, you listen to me. Your mother might not always know how to show it, but *I* know just how special you are. You are strong and brave and honest and good. Work hard at school to get your grades and prove to your parents that there is more for you than this arranged marriage, and in two years' time you will go to a university far away from London, just as we've always dreamed. And I will come with you, and you will succeed and make yourself proud, and *you*, Alba Philippa Darcy White, will forge your own future. Do you hear me?'

Dolly fell silent, and Alba felt her eyes welling up. She stared into her handmaid's brilliant blue gaze, too humbled and grateful to say anything.

'If you were *my* daughter,' finished Dolly quietly, 'I would never stop telling the world how proud I am of you.'

Alba laced her arms round Dolly's neck. Tears tracked her cheeks. They clung to each other, neither one of them caring that Dolly's clothes were soaked from Alba's wet skin, or that bathwater had spilled over the side of the tub. Alba realised properly then that she did have a family that loved and cared for her, and it was Dolly, this incredible woman holding her.

'I'll come back in an hour to get you ready for bed,' Dolly said when they pulled apart. She stood, a soft smile lighting her face as she brushed down her uniform and left the room, pulling the door shut behind her.

Alba wiped away her tears with the back of one hand. Was it possible, the future Dolly had promised for them? She didn't dare believe it was. Everything good in her life was eventually ruined. Why would this be any different?

Just as she closed her eyes, sinking back down into the perfumed water, the door opened again.

'Dolly?' she murmured, sitting up and turning, expecting to see her handmaid in the doorway.

But it wasn't Dolly –

It was *Seven*.

31

SEVEN

Holy effing hell, she's naked!

32

ALBA

Oh almighty god, I am naked!

33

SEVEN

Alba's face flushed so red, a tomato might have mistaken her for one of its own. Even through the dewy haze of the bathroom it was *that* red. She splashed down in the bath, fragranced water slopping everywhere, the tub squeaking as her body – her *naked* body – slid along its smooth ceramic curves. She dipped low, her mouth just above the water's surface. Hair loosened from the messy bun she'd piled on the top of her head, red curls framing her cheeks.

'What on earth are you doing here!' she gasped. Her eyes travelled over his wet hair and clothes, drenched from the walk here in the storm. 'How did you get in?'

Seven's anger had rolled away the instant he saw Alba in the bath (his mind had been too full of the thought of her naked right here before him to have space for anything else). Now it gnawed its way back.

Who cares what she looks like? This North bitch is the reason Carpenter's dead.

'How d'you think I got in?' he snapped. 'I break into houses for a living.'

Seven tried to keep calm, remembering the reason he'd come in the first place – revenge, an eye for an eye and all that – but he couldn't help the grimace of a grin twisting his lips, the way his cheeks flushed with anger and embarrassment. He ran a hand through his rain-slicked hair, trying for a cool, *I don't care* gesture. Instead, his fingers got tangled and he spent the next minute tugging them out.

'You shouldn't be here,' Alba whispered.

He glared. Of course she'd think that. He was just a Souther to her. What made him think he could just come strolling into North?

'Don't worry,' he said coldly. 'I'll be gone soon.'

She shook her head fiercely, the motion causing more water to lap over the side of the tub. 'Of *course* you shouldn't be here, after last night! If they find you –'

'I know exactly what'll happen. I'm not an idiot.'

'I wasn't saying you were.'

'You were thinking it.'

'No!'

'Look, just stop with your lies, all right? I know what you did!'

It came out as a shout. Alba's eyes widened. When Seven stepped towards her she shrank back, shifting to the other side of the tub as though scared of him.

'I dunno why I ever thought I could trust you,' he said, voice rising with each word. He gestured wildly round the room and gave a barking laugh. 'Look at this! It's not like you've ever had to struggle for anything in your life. You have no idea what it's like. I hate all you Northers, lounging here in your fancy houses and splashing money around and killing Southers like we're *rats* –'

'Little Alba.'

From the bedroom there was a knock on the door, then the sound of it opening.

One second.

That's all the time Seven had to react. One tiny second.

Running forward, skidding on the spilled bathwater, he dived round the back of the tub, pressing as flat against its curving side as possible.

There was the click of heels as someone entered the bathroom.

'I thought I heard voices.'

The voice was a woman's, its letters curled with an Eastern European accent.

'Just – just me here, Mother.'

Seven's eyes widened. He'd seen Alba's mother before when observing the house. She was blonde, icily beautiful, as though her features were carved from stone; it was strange to think of Alba as her daughter. He held his breath, heart thundering in his ears.

'Did you want something, Mother?'

Alba sounded terrified. Her voice was faint and trembling.

Why is she scared? Seven wondered. *Why isn't she giving me away? She should be* glad *to have me trapped.*

'Please, darling. How many times do I have to tell you to stop calling me that?'

The snap of heels on the ceramic tiles drew closer and Seven shrank back, pressing his back so hard against the tub it hurt his spine.

'What's that awful smell?'

For a second, Seven thought Alba's mother meant *him*.

'Herbs,' Alba murmured. 'Dolly mixed them into the bathwater. It's supposed to be nice.'

'Well, it's not. What remedy is she concocting now? Trying to help slim you down before the Winter-turn Ball?' A pause. 'That's not a bad idea.'

'Yes.'

Alba's voice was so small it crushed Seven. It hit him then just how wrong he'd had it. She hadn't told her parents about him, or given them the information leading to the raid last night. Otherwise she'd have told her mother he was here by now.

A memory came to him of Alba standing outside his flat, her voice quiet as she'd said, *You're lucky*.

Lucky wasn't a word Seven would associate with himself (hah! As if). He'd thought Alba had been trying to make him feel better about living in his dump of a flat. But now it was clear she'd actually meant it. She envied him, because she wished she could escape *her* parents, too.

Alba envied *him*.

He'd never imagined someone from North could envy a Souther.

'It's getting late,' Alba's mother said, breaking the tense silence. 'Don't be too long. I don't want you to be tired at church tomorrow.'

'Yes, Mother.'

'And one more thing. Perhaps you *should* try and lose weight before the Winter-turn Ball. We've got an important announcement to make on the night, and I want my daughter looking her best.'

The bathroom door clicked. Heeled footsteps on the wooden boards of Alba's bedroom grew faint as her mother left, the room falling silent once more.

34

ALBA

She would have liked the silence to have stretched on forever so she could try and convince herself the last few minutes of her life had never happened, thank you very much. But of course Seven had to say something.

'Well . . .'

He drew out the word. She heard him get up from round the back of the tub, cracking his joints as he went.

'I can see where you get your lovely personality from. Your mum is a real treat.'

Alba closed her eyes. 'Just don't.'

She didn't want to look at him. It was utterly humiliating. Her mother had been cruel to her before in front of the servants and Dolly, but somehow this was worse. This was a boy from South who barely had a thing to his name.

Now he'd seen that it was actually *her* who was the one who had nothing.

'I'm joking, Alba,' Seven said.

'Well, I'm not in the mood for jokes.'

'Are you ever?'

'Seven! Will you please just *get* out and leave me alone!'

It came out louder than she'd meant it to, but Alba didn't care. Her insides writhed with anger and shame. She waited for him to leave. Her shoulders and the top of her back were exposed, and she imagined his eyes travelling over her pale skin. Had he noticed the freckles sprinkled across her back? *How can he* not *have?* she thought. *You'd be able to spot them from space.*

The fact that she'd gone through all this while being naked was beyond humiliating.

And Seven was *still* here.

'Oh, *why* have you not gone yet!' Alba cried, finally spinning round to face him. Bathwater slopped over the lip of the tub. She hugged her knees, squeezing her arms around them to hide her body. 'You said you hated me a minute ago. So just leave! God forbid you have to spend another second in my presence if it disgusts you that much.'

Seven's face twisted. He stood there, frozen to the spot, drenched clothes clinging to his skinny body. His hair was plastered to his forehead. He looked hurt, mad, confused and frustrated all in one.

It was clear to Alba then that this was the last time she'd ever see him, and she felt horrible that this was the way they'd remember each other: angry, cruel words thrown between them. Aside from Dolly, he was the only friend she'd ever made.

Or at least, she'd *thought* she'd made.

Some unreadable emotion passed across Seven's eyes before he jerked suddenly round, walking quickly past her and shutting the door without so much as a backwards glance.

There weren't even any tears. Alba just lay back in the bath, looking up at the ceiling, tiny lights scattered across it to mimic the constellations outside. She tried to remove every memory of Seven, of memory-surfing, and of the friendship they might have shared from her mind.

They should have machines to erase *the past*, Alba thought. *Not preserve it.*

Some memories were too unbearable to keep.

When Dolly came to get her ready for bed, Alba put on her biggest smile, her happiest face. She didn't want Dolly to know her bath had had the opposite effect she'd desired, making her feel far worse instead of better.

Once Alba was changed into her nightdress, her hair dried and left loose around her face, Dolly sat with her on the edge of the bed. Outside, the rain drummed harder. It filled the room with a watery rushing sound, which made Alba think of the waterfall memory she'd experienced last week in Seven's flat. She'd been hoping to surf it again tonight.

No, she reminded herself. *Erase*.

'I meant what I said earlier,' Dolly said. She looked serious and hard, no hint of the tears that had overwhelmed her earlier. 'We'll find a way to make it happen. You don't have to give up on your dreams. I'll get you out of here. I promise.'

Alba wanted to believe her so badly. She rested her cheek on her handmaid's shoulder, and they stayed that way for a while before Dolly pulled away.

'Bed now. It's almost midnight.'

Alba flinched. Midnight. That's when she had meant to meet Seven to go memory-surfing.

No, she thought. *Erase.*

After Dolly left, Alba took her time getting to bed. She stood in the dark at the windows, watching the growing storm outside. Raindrops rolled down the glass in winding streams. Wind lashed the trees, whipping their branches sideways.

She should have been getting ready to sneak out to meet Seven right about now. She wouldn't have cared about the storm. All she would have been feeling was excitement at seeing him again, safe after the raid, and the call of the memories waiting for her back at his flat.

No.

Erase, erase, erase.

Alba padded over to her bed and climbed inside. The mattress was warm from the heat-stone Dolly had placed there. Yawning, her eyes fluttering shut, she slid an arm under her pillow –

And froze.

There was something under it.

Scrambling back, she threw the pillow aside and saw a piece of paper folded in half. On the top side was her name written in a messy scrawl:

Alber

Her stomach flipped.

'You misspelled it, you idiot . . .' she whispered, unable to stop a disbelieving laugh escaping her lips. She snatched the note and unfolded it.

We said same time, same place, right?

She let out another laugh. In an instant, everything that had passed between them earlier fell away. Alba knew exactly what Seven was trying to tell her, even though he'd put it in his weird, awkward, stupidly wonderful way. She could practically hear him speaking to her as her eyes scanned his words once more.

Midnight. Outside.

I'm waiting for you in the rain, so hurry up, you stupid effing idiot.

(I'm sorry.)

35

SEVEN

The rain was driving down so hard, and the darkness so thick
– apart from flashes of lightning illuminating everything in a
ghostly, silvery glow – that he didn't see or hear Alba coming.
One minute he was staring at the house, the next he was
jumping back as a figure appeared, grabbing the collar of his
shirt and pulling him into a tight hug.

Seven stiffened, arms hanging at his sides.

Not again! he thought, groaning inwardly. He really wished
Alba would stop impulsively embracing him like this. Now
she was pressed up against his body and, just like the last time,
he had no idea what to do.

When she finally pulled away, Seven grinned shakily. 'You
got my note then,' he said, running a hand through his rain-
matted hair.

They were under the patchy shade of the elm grove near
the house, but rain was still finding its way through the thick
canopy of leaves. Alba was already soaked. Her usually full,

bouncy hair was plastered to her face. Raindrops clung to her lips. Only her clothes were dry, hidden underneath the camel raincoat buttoned up to her throat.

'Yes,' she said. 'Though I could barely read it. Your handwriting is terrible.'

Seven scowled. 'Well, no one ever taught me how, did they? Didn't go to Fancy McFancy-Pants School for North Princesses like you.'

'Oh. I'm sorry. I didn't think.'

'Neither do I, most of the time.'

Alba laughed, but her face soon turned serious. 'The raid last night. I thought . . .' she trailed off, letting out a huff of breath. 'I was so worried. What happened?'

An image of Carpenter falling, eyes rolling back in his head. Blood splattering the tables and floor.

Screams cutting the night apart.

Gunshots, gunshots *everywhere*.

Seven swallowed down a rush of nausea. 'They got my crew leader. Some other skid-thieves I know got out OK, though.'

He'd gone to Loe's home earlier to check on her and Mika. Seven hadn't realised until he saw them alive just how worried he'd been. Mika almost bowled him over, jumping on him the second he appeared. Loe had just scowled and grumbled something about keeping them waiting, but that was practically affectionate for her.

Perhaps Seven *did* have more friends than he thought.

Alba shook her head. 'All those people they killed. I thought . . .' Lightning flashed, lighting her eyes. 'I thought you might have been one of them.'

He grinned. 'As if they could ever get me. I'm way too fast for those London Guard idiots.'

'Seven.'

'All right,' he snapped. 'It was effing horrible. Is that what you want to hear?'

Alba's mouth tightened. Then, slowly, hesitantly, she took his hands in hers.

A jolt ran through Seven at the feel of her touch. Her hands were wet but warm, and he felt her pulse on his own skin, as though a butterfly was trapped between their palms.

'You don't have to talk about it if you don't want to,' she said.

Of course *I don't wanna talk about it*, he thought. Not that there were words to describe it, even if he did.

How could he convey the horror of seeing someone shot down in front of him? The bubbling rasp of Carpenter's voice as he'd tried to speak with a great big bloody bullet hole in his throat? The senseless panic of a crowd rushing to live? Or – worst of all – the guilt Seven had felt when he finally came to a stop on some lonely street miles from the market and realised he was alive, and wondered why that was when so many others were dead?

The storm picked up around them. Seven felt like howling into it when he thought of all the things that had been taken from him in just one night.

Alba was watching him with concerned eyes. Her hands were trembling. He'd half-forgotten they were holding hands. Part of him wanted to yank his away, but another part didn't ever want to let go. He felt strangely stronger with her hand in his, as though she was anchoring him to this world that felt as if it were crumbling down around him.

This is it, Seven realised. *This is your chance to let her in. Let her be your friend.*

Gods know you could use some of those.

But the weight of last night's events was crushing down on him, and despite what he knew, despite how he felt, Alba was still a girl from North whose father was most probably one of the people responsible for the raid last night. Seven looked at her and saw everything that had been taken from him.

Well, if he was honest, he also saw a girl he found annoyingly attractive, but he pushed those thoughts down. Alba could never be his friend, let alone anything more. And besides, stolen memories were all he had to offer her. What point would there be, him letting her in, trying to win her over? In the end, some stuck-up North prince was bound to come along with the whole world in his arms, and what girl would give that up for a few stolen skids?

Seven cleared his throat. 'Look. You and me – we're never gonna be friends.'

Alba stared at him. After a pause she asked quietly, 'Why not?'

He gave a strangled laugh. 'Come on! You're from North. I'm a Souther.'

'So? What does it matter, really?'

'Course it matters. Don't be stupid –'

'Don't call me stupid.'

'I'm not –'

'I don't care about North or South, Seven.'

'Look –'

'I said, I don't *care*. Why can't we be friends if we want –?'

'Alba, don't be so effing naive!'

Seven's shout was swallowed by the storm, the lash of the rain. He dropped Alba's hands and stepped back.

'We both know what this is, all right?' he said roughly. 'You wanna skid-surf. I don't wanna get handed over to the London Guard. That's it. You use me, I use you. That's how life goes, no?'

Alba glared at him. She seemed frozen to the spot despite the whip of the wind and the rush of the rain. Lightning flashed, turning her eyes into two discs of white gold. For some reason, seeing her like that made something in Seven's stomach twist, almost painfully.

He'd hurt her. She was trying to care, to be kind, and he was throwing it back in her face.

'I was never going to tell my parents you stole a memory from them,' Alba said softly. 'Just so you know.'

Seven's face twisted. 'What does it matter? Tell them if you want. It's not like I've got anything left to lose.'

(That was both a lie and not a lie.)

He coughed, tearing his eyes away. 'So come have your surf, Princess, and then we never have to see each other again. Thank *gods*.'

Seven grabbed Alba's arm and pushed her forward. With every step, he forced himself not to look at her, or think about everything he didn't have, yet might have just lost.

36

ALBA

The storm had died down a bit by the time they got to Seven's memorium, the rain a distant rush on the walls outside.

They hadn't spoken a word during the journey here. This was partly because for most of it, the rain had been beating down in driving, wind-whipped sheets, thunder growling across the sky. But it was also because of the things they'd just said to each other. Words that were pressed between them like a physical weight in the air, keeping them apart.

Now, in the hushed quiet of the memorium, Alba felt the coldness between her and Seven even more. She was hurt, but also angry with him too; some of the things he'd said were unnecessarily cruel. She couldn't wait to get away from here and lose herself in a memory. And – though it made her feel a little guilty – she was already feeling the pull of the hundreds of memories calling for her from behind their blue cages.

If this is my last time memory-surfing, she thought, *I'm going to make the most of it.*

Alba unbuttoned her coat and laid it on top of one of the cabinets. Her plum-coloured jumper, black trousers and boots were all water-logged, her supposedly rain-proof coat beaten by the strength of the storm. She wrung the hem of her jumper out; water splattered onto the floor.

Leaning against the door, Seven stuffed his hands in the pockets of his trousers and stuck his elbows out.

'Go on, then, Princess,' he said, sighing, and ducked his head, sweeping out an arm.

Alba didn't need telling twice. She spun on the spot, looking round at the cabinets, trying to decide what type of memory she wanted to surf tonight (the problem was, she wanted them all). Then her eyes caught a broken mug on top of one of the cabinets. Inside were a few of the small metal clips the memories were recorded on.

'What are these?' she asked, reaching out.

But before she could touch the mug, Seven had rushed over and grabbed it, cradling it to his chest. The tips of his ears were pink.

'These are – these are private,' he said, avoiding her eyes.

Alba stepped back. 'Oh. I'm sorry.' Feeling awkward, she dropped her eyes, and noticed one of the metal clips on the floor. She picked it up. 'Here. One fell out.'

As she held it out to him, she noticed the writing on the label:

24.10.2128, A.W, the White family's house (Hyde Park Estate)

'Is this . . . is this my *father's* memory?' she asked in a whisper.

A thrill of something – anticipation? Fear? – ran down her spine. Before she met Seven, Alba had never really thought of her father as someone who had secrets. Of course, she understood his job was difficult, and he had to *do* difficult things for it, but after overhearing his secret meeting with Pearson outside their house and his words on the night of the raid, she realised there were so many things she didn't know about her father.

Holding one of his own memories in her hand made Alba feel sick. What dark things were buried in his past?

Did she *want* to know?

Alba looked up. 'Have you surfed it?' she asked Seven.

He shook his head. 'I put it there to remind myself to sort it, but I forgot about it 'cause of everything that happened after –'

He stopped abruptly. For a second, Seven's face was blank. And then it twisted. His eyes were wide. He was staring at the object in her hand as though it were a bomb, about to explode and shatter the world any second.

Alba frowned. 'What's the matter?'

'That skid,' Seven croaked. He took a step back (now Alba really *did* feel like she was holding a bomb), and ran a shaking hand through his tangled hair. 'That's what Carpenter was trying to warn me about before he – before he was shot.'

37

SEVEN

Seven had been so caught up in escaping the raid and the horror of Carpenter's death, then wanting to confront Alba, that he'd forgotten all about Alastair White's skid and Carpenter's warning.

He stared at the DSC in Alba's hand, stomach churning. What was so terrible about that memory that had made Carpenter – Carpenter, who never got scared – beg him to destroy it?

I thought it would protect us. That I could protect us by having it. Use it as blackmail, if it ever came to it. Something to keep that White pig away. And after Murray . . . But it's bigger than that. I should've left it alone.

'What is it?' Alba asked, stepping towards him. Her eyes were wide with concern. 'What's wrong?'

But Seven barely registered her words. He was back in the night before, back at Borough Market, the noise of the crowd swelling around him, the stink of fish-blood and rotten vegetables so strong he felt like being sick, and a gunshot –

A gunshot that seemed to tear right through the very fabric of the world and split it into two.

The memory, S. Destroy it.

Blood spilling from Carpenter's lip.

S-sorry.

Seven snapped back to the present. Before he could worry about the consequences of what he was about to do, he ran to Butler and powered up the machine. He sat down on the stool so heavily it skidded on the floor. His hands shook as he closed the wrist-straps round his arms, fixed the metal cap to his head.

'Seven!' Alba cried. 'What are you doing?' But her voice sounded distant, calling to him as though from another place, another world.

In the fraction of a moment when the DSC had loaded and he hit the *ACTIVATE* option, Seven wondered whether he was making a mistake. He'd told Carpenter he wouldn't surf this memory. He'd made a promise to a dying man. What was he thinking, breaking a promise like that?

But then there was a rising, piercing sound and the flash of light like a million cameras going off, and it was too late to turn back.

'*MEMORY ACTIVATED. EXPIRATION IN FORTY-NINE MINUTES, TWO SECONDS.*'

Swallowing nervously, Seven opened his eyes.

He was in a small room, bare and clinical. Strips of white light beat down from overhead. An electric hum filled the air. Through the honey-like warmth of the memory-air, Seven felt a coolness on his skin. Cold air was pumping from a hidden air-con unit.

'Mr White?'

He turned.

A short, greying man with soft brown eyes and a brush of speckled stubble was walking towards him. He wore a white lab coat over a brown suit and plaid shirt. Round his neck hung a nametag: *Dr Merriweather, TMK Division, Chief Science Co-ordinator.*

Seven's heart thudded hard. TMK! That's what Alba's father had been talking to Pearson about that night outside her house.

'Merriweather.'

Seven cringed as his voice came out in Alastair White's cool, deep growl: it still weirded him out every time he spoke in skids as someone else. But he had to resist the urge to fight it. He had to let the instincts of the memory take control if he was going to experience it exactly as White had.

Merriweather fiddled with his hands. 'Sorry, ah, about the delay. A technical hiccup. The team are ready for you now. It's just this way.'

'A technical hiccup?' Seven asked as they went out into a narrow corridor, more tubes of light fixed to the ceiling. They passed a series of identical doors. 'I do not expect *any* hiccups in this process, Merriweather. Especially not after what happened with the last intake.'

'Of course, sir. Of course. Just that the cerebral cortex nerves are delicate things. Especially in, ah, Candidates as young as ours. And then with the introduction of a foreign object . . . swelling and breakages are to be expected.'

'Indeed. But this is the nineteenth intake since TMK was initiated. I would have expected your team to have addressed these issues by now.'

166

'Yes, sir. We hope to have done so with this intake, sir.'

Merriweather stopped outside the door at the end of the corridor. Above it, a red light was lit. A label beneath the light read: *LAB 32*.

As the doctor bent to grasp the handle, Seven noticed a placard in the centre of the door, only just catching the last word before they went through:

KEEPERS

Keepers? he wondered. *Keepers of* what?

At first, the darkness of the lab blinded him. All he could make out were glaring spots of light, spaced throughout the ceiling, and a sense of space. When his eyes adjusted, Seven saw that they were in a glass atrium overlooking a large, chamber-like room. The whole place was kept in near-blackness. Strange flickers of light from machinery glowed like small thunderstorms amid a sea of dark clouds.

Merriweather bustled round him, moving to a door at the right end of the atrium. 'This way, sir.'

A metal staircase led down to the hall. The lab was cold, pricking goosebumps across Seven's skin. A soft whirring noise filled the space, along with erratic clicks and beeps of machinery. There were incubators spaced evenly throughout the room: around twenty or so, a person in a lab-coat stationed at each one, bent down to adjust something or stood making notes on a tablet.

Merriweather led Seven to the nearest incubator. It was nestled in sleek machinery, wires feeding into the clear curve of its shell and blinking displays showing complex sets of numbers and graphs. A round light hanging over the incubator gave off a comforting blue glow.

As they approached, the woman standing beside the incubator stood straighter, shifting her lab-coat into place. She bowed, smiling.

'This is Misaki,' said Merriweather. 'She's in charge of Candidate One –'

Something quick, like a flash of electricity, shot through Seven. *Did he just say Candidate One?*

'– who is doing well. Very well indeed. Misaki?'

'Oh, yes, she's a fighter, all right.' The woman stroked the plastic curve of the incubator tenderly. 'Candidate One has had fifteen bleeding incidents as a result of dislocation of the Controller implant after attachment, but has survived them all. Currently she's in Phase Three, attachment having been stable for at least one month. Her vitals have been steady thirteen days now, though her blood pressure is still a touch higher than we'd like. However, her cerebral cortex seems to be adapting well to the Controller. We expect her to progress to Phase Four soon, when we will begin cognitive testing.'

Seven longed to look down and see what was in the incubator, but White seemed to have no similar urge, and he was letting the memory's full instincts take over, still determined to experience this exactly as White had.

'Thank you,' he said brusquely. 'The next Candidate, then, Merriweather.'

It went on like this for five more incubators. Then the moment came that Seven had been waiting for.

'On to Candidate Seven, then, sir.'

Seven's blood turned to ice, but his focus didn't waver.

'I've heard of this one,' he said in White's cold, curt voice. He stopped before they reached the incubator.

Merriweather nodded, shifting uncomfortably. 'Ah, yes. Of course. The incident last week.'

'I need your promise it won't happen again.'

'Most certainly not, sir.'

'Because if it does, and word gets out about TMK . . .'

The doctor twisted the hem of his lab-coat. Even in the strange, womb-like darkness of the lab, Seven could see the fear etched in the man's features; he'd recognised the threat in White's voice.

'Understood, sir. Now, ah, please. Candidate Seven.'

The man tending the incubator turned at the sound of their footsteps and nodded in greeting.

'Sirs. Seven is stable after a stroke eighteen days ago and a prolonged period of cranial fluid leakage. He has currently had stable attachment of the Controller implant for two days. Vitals are within acceptable range. We anticipate he will progress safely to Phase Three.'

White nodded. 'Good,' he said, and then he bent over to look at the incubator and Seven was finally able to see what was inside.

His breath hitched in his throat.

It was a baby.

Candidate Seven couldn't have been much older than six months; his head was still larger than proportionate, with narrow grey eyes and ears that stuck out a little. His eyes were wide, his fingers podgy. Wires crawled all over his body, some connected to a cap on his head, flickering with multi-coloured dots. A tiny heart-shaped birthmark was printed like a kiss on the sole of one foot.

Meeting his eyes, the baby smiled, and for the first time in this memory Seven felt as though someone had actually seen past his appearance as Alastair White to him inside.

But, as White, he didn't return the baby's smile.

'Very well,' he said, straightening. 'On to the next.'

It took just under half an hour to finish the rest of the visits. Once they had finished, Merriweather led him back up to the glass atrium at the front of the lab. The doctor hesitated by the exit.

'So, ah, I trust you are pleased with the progress, sir? Sixteen out of twenty Candidates stable. Our best intake yet.'

'It is promising,' Seven replied in White's cool voice. 'But we have been at this stage before. I want to see progression to Phase Five, Merriweather. So far, only six Candidates have passed Phase Four successfully. I want to know the Controller implant can work on higher numbers, and that the TMK project is not a waste of resources.'

'Of course, sir. I have high hopes for this intake.'

'I do not deal in hopes, Merriweather. I deal in results.' White's voice was a purr of a growl, a soft coat hiding a body of blades. 'I will be back in a month for a further update.'

He said something more, but his words were drowned out by a high-pitched whine, growing steadily louder. There was a flash of light –

A falling feeling –

Seven opened his eyes to blue filing cabinets and the rushing sound of rain. He blinked, disorientated. His eyes adjusted slowly after the darkness of the lab. Nearby, Alba was sitting on the floor against a cabinet, her eyes closed. She must have fallen asleep while he'd been in the memory.

Fingers shaking, Seven unclipped himself from Butler. He drew in a long breath before untying his right boot and slipping off his sock. He hesitated then, staring down at the top of his foot.

'Just do it, you wimp,' he muttered.

Steeling himself, Seven pulled up his foot and twisted it round to examine the skin of his sole.

His breath caught in his throat.

There it was. A small, heart-shaped birthmark in the middle of his foot. No bigger than a thumbprint, no darker than the lipstick-echo of lips left on the rim of a glass.

38

ALBA

She was silent for a long time after Seven finished recounting what he'd seen in her father's memory. The sound of the rain driving down again in the night filled the memorium, and a gutter somewhere outside was dripping incessantly. But it all felt distant, as though this small room was another world. A world where North and South collided. A world where pasts were turned inside out and secrets unfurled themselves like thorned vines, winding menacingly out of the darkness.

Alba could practically feel Seven silently screaming at her to say something, and she let out a slow breath.

'So that's why you're called Seven.'

'Seriously?' He finally stopped pacing – which was a relief as it had been making her dizzy – and glared down at her. 'After everything I just told you, that's all you've got to say?'

'Well, I *had* been wondering why you've got such a strange name . . .'

Seven made a strangled noise in the back of his throat.

'Unbelievable,' he muttered, dropping his eyes back to the floor and resuming his pacing.

'I just don't know what to say.' Alba tucked her legs underneath her to one side. She fiddled with the hem of her trousers, which were still damp from earlier. 'I'm so sorry about what you saw in the memory. What it might mean.'

'You've got nothing to do with it.'

'But my father . . .'

He snorted. 'Bet you're so *proud* to have a parent like him.'

Alba flinched.

'Sorry,' Seven said quickly, his eyes softening. 'I didn't mean –'

She shook her head. 'It's fine. You're angry. And I don't blame you, after what you've just seen.' She lowered her voice and looked away. 'What I *am* surprised about is that you chose to tell me.'

After everything Seven had said earlier, outside her house, Alba didn't think he'd have wanted to share something as personal as this with her. *Perhaps*, she thought, *he* does *want to be my friend after all.*

And then he said, 'Well, I thought you might wanna know. Anyway, I just needed to talk about it,' and she realised she was wrong.

Of course she was. She, the daughter of the very man who had the power to take Seven's life, was the last person on earth he'd want to be friends with.

'Can I surf the memory?' Alba asked after a long, tense pause. 'I'd like to see for myself what was going on.'

Seven pointed to his memory-machine. 'Butler would have a heart attack. Look. He's halfway there already.'

He was right. The machine was still shaking, making wobbly, whiny noises, like a dog whimpering.

'All right,' Alba said, sitting up straighter. She tucked her hair behind her ears. 'Run me through it again, then. There was a laboratory filled with babies in incubators who were having some kind of experiment done on them. And this Dr Merriweather person showed Father around, getting updates about each baby, which they referred to as . . . Candidates, was it?'

'Yup,' Seven said, letting out a grunting laugh and pointing at himself. 'One of which is right here, ladies and gents.'

She ignored him. Her brow furrowed. 'Candidates – that's what Father and Pearson were talking about the other day. Do you remember what they said? It sounded like these Candidates are having some kind of medical problem that is causing them to die from neuro-haemorrhages during memory-surfing.' She nodded to herself, then looked up. 'Was there anything else you noticed in the memory?'

'Just what I already told you – your dad and the doc kept referring to TMK,' Seven said.

Alba bit her lip. 'Do you have any idea what TMK stands for?'

Seven raised his eyebrows. 'I don't have a clue what *any* of this is about, Alba.' He kicked the floor absent-mindedly. 'Oh, and there was a sign on the lab. All I got to see was the last bit – *KEEPERS*.'

'Keepers? Keepers of what?'

'No idea.' Seven thrust his hands in his pockets. 'But what I really don't get is that the Candidates are just surfing memories. Do you remember what that guy said to your dad?

The Candidates were involved in Phase Nine training – but it sounded like that was just skid-surfing. What's so special about that? Why all this secrecy if that's all they're doing?'

'And why do they keep dying because of it?' Alba went on. 'People do it all the time.'

Seven stopped suddenly. 'Maybe – maybe they're not *just* surfing.'

'What do you mean?'

'Well, if they're dying during surfing,' he explained, 'then maybe that's not all they're doing in the skids. Maybe they – *we* – can do something else in memories.'

Alba took a deep breath. Her eyes were wide. '*Can* you do anything else in memories?'

Seven shrugged. 'Dunno. I just surf how I surf, and you do it your way. We can't go into a skid together to see if I'm doing it any different.'

They fell silent at that.

'Seven . . .' Alba started tentatively after a while. 'If you *are* a Candidate, then how come you're here? How come you're free? TMK is all so secret, and from what we overheard the other night it sounds as though there is a shortage of Candidates. So if you really *are* one, then why did they let you go?'

Seven stopped pacing. 'I don't know.' He rubbed the back of his neck. 'You're right. It doesn't make sense. They're trying so hard to keep it a secret – your dad practically threatened to kill Merriweather if there was another incident which might expose the whole thing.'

'And it's not like my father to just let someone walk free,' Alba added quietly.

She remembered her father's cold laugh the night before. His mocking tone as he'd talked about the raid. How he'd discussed Candidates dying as though it were nothing, as though their lives being lost didn't bother him in the slightest. He sentenced people to death every day but she hadn't ever thought badly of him for it because she thought it was about justice, that he was protecting London – protecting her – from criminals.

Alba didn't know who the criminals were any more.

A shiver of fear ran down her spine. Why *was* Seven here, being allowed to live, even though he'd been involved in such a top-secret project?

Had he somehow escaped? she wondered.

And if he had –

Was her father *looking* for him?

'Hey,' Seven said. 'What's the time? That was a pretty long memory.'

Alba scrambled up as she looked at her watch. 'Three thirty!' she groaned. 'I have to get back.' She grabbed her coat and hurriedly did up the buttons, then stopped just as suddenly.

Seven looked so lost, so broken, standing there in the middle of the room, his clothes rumpled and damp, his dark hair flopping into those strangely attractive eyes. Even though he'd told her they weren't friends, she felt guilty leaving him like this.

'Don't worry 'bout me,' he said, seeming to read her mind. He grinned, though it looked strained. 'Done all right without you all these years, haven't I? I'll manage just fine for a few more.'

Alba forced herself to ignore how much that comment stung. 'But don't you want to find out what all this is about?' she urged.

Seven rolled his eyes. 'Oh, yeah. Why don't you just waltz in

176

and ask dear *Daddy* what on earth TMK is, and why all these Candidates keep dying, and could he pretty please explain why I'm not still locked up in some lab being forced to surf until my brain fries, thank you very much?' His voice was hard and cold. 'That's how things work in your world, isn't it? All you have to do is ask, and everything gets handed to you on an effing silver plate.'

Lips tightening, Alba glared at him. *No wonder he has no friends*, she thought acidly. *Every time I try to be nice, he throws something like that back in my face.*

Well, let's see how he likes it when someone throws back.

'Yes,' she said coolly, tossing her hair back from her face. 'That's *exactly* what happens, Seven. *That's* why I've never been allowed to memory-surf, or make proper friends, or do anything that my parents haven't approved first. *That's* why I'm being married off to someone of their choosing and will probably spend the rest of my life stuck in North pretending to be happy next to some horrible man, even though really I'm dying inside. *That's* why I was so grateful to finally meet someone who actually did something nice for me for once, and just perhaps might want to be my friend. Of course, I see how wrong about that I was now,' she finished icily.

Everything went silent. Even the noise of the storm outside seemed muffled. Alba's face was flushed, and she could feel her hands trembling at her sides where she'd curled them into fists.

Seven blinked. 'You're getting married?'

Alba gave a frustrated sigh.

'What? It's kinda big news!' He let out a huff of air. 'Congratulations, I guess.'

'*Seven!*'

'All right!' he half shouted, throwing out his hands. 'What d'you want me to say? *I'm so sorry to hear that? Come here, let's hold hands and talk about our feelings over a cup of tea?* I'm no good at all this – this *friends* stuff.'

Alba blushed, something warm flaring inside of her.

He'd said *friends*.

'Look, this TMK crap has just thrown me,' Seven went on. 'After last night, I didn't think things could get any worse. Then this happened.'

His eyes dropped to the floor. For once, there wasn't a trace of sarcasm on his features, no mocking expression on his lips. His face was just soft. Open.

Alba knew exactly how he was feeling because it was how *she* felt too: that they'd lost control of their own lives. Though perhaps neither of them had any to begin with.

But here was a chance for them to take that control back.

'We need to find out what TMK is,' she said firmly.

Seven looked up. 'How?'

'Well, you're a skid-thief, aren't you?' Alba's eyes flashed. 'Maybe it's time you stole another memory.'

39

SEVEN

It wasn't going to be easy. Thieving jobs usually took weeks of planning, and that was *with* Carpenter's direction (Seven still couldn't get over the fact that his crew leader wasn't around any more). And after the raid, the London Guard was on higher alert. It would be even more dangerous than usual. But it's not like he had any other ideas, and what Alba suggested did make a lot of sense. Stealing memories was what Seven *did*. It was pretty much the only thing he was good at.

There was just one big problem –

How did you find a memory when you didn't even know if it existed in the first place?

Seven and Alba arranged to meet again in a week to give him enough time to hunt down a skid about TMK.

So far, Seven had wasted a day panicking and grumbling and moaning about how the eff he was gonna do it. He'd wasted a further day catching up on sleep; meaning, he collapsed from exhaustion and was pretty much dead to the world for twenty-four hours. But once he'd had some rest he was able to come up with a plan.

Even though Carpenter had been the one who'd handled the trading and planning side of things, Seven had a few contacts of his own from his years working as part of Carpenter's crew. It took him two days to track down Mac, one of the skid-thieves from another crew he'd chatted to a few times who seemed friendly enough to give help, then another day before Mac's crew leader Finch agreed to meet with him. In exchange for five skids, Finch arranged a meeting for Seven with the Librarian the next day.

Seven had never met the Librarian before, never even caught a glimpse of him. He was like some kind of mythical creature or god. The crew leaders were usually the only ones who had any contact with the Librarian, and their relationships with him were one of the most important aspects of their jobs. Seven had seen crews fall apart because their leader had fallen out of his favour.

He wasn't sure how exactly the Librarian did it, or how he'd been doing it this long without getting caught (Carpenter had mentioned something about him being so skilled at hacking he could access the data of every single memory-machine in the world). All he knew was that the Librarian was exactly what his name suggested: a catalogue, a directory of every skid that had ever been recorded.

If there was another memory about TMK somewhere out there, he'd be the one who could find it.

* * *

Seven stepped out into the dusky grey morning. The sun was only just rising behind the thick bank of clouds, and the South streets were pooled with litter-filled water from the previous night's rain. The air bit with the chill of oncoming winter. Shivering, he rolled down the sleeves of his shirt and hurried towards the river. It was going to be a long walk. He may as well enjoy the view of North as he went.

Finch had given Seven directions to the Librarian's base in Richmond. Seven had never gone so far west before. The city was mostly urban farms and energy plants out that way, and he had been wondering how the Librarian was living in such a London Guard-controlled area when he arrived three hours later at an overgrown marshland close to the river and realised where he was.

Like Battersea Power Station, Kew Gardens was another renovation project North had abandoned after the floods. Too close to the river to develop into useful land, the gardens were now a sprawling expanse of tangled vegetation and water-logged forest. Derelict buildings hid among the greenery, wreathed in vines and broken apart by the burrowing roots and trunks of trees.

Following Finch's directions, Seven headed across the grounds towards a large, glass-shelled building. It was mid-morning by now; the sun glinted out from behind shifting clouds, catching on the glass, flashes of purple and amber lighting the broken panes covering the greenhouse. Birds flitted across the sky. Their sharp cries cut through the clicks and buzz of insects that filled the abandoned gardens with a constant hum.

'Effing bugs,' Seven muttered, swatting dancing clouds of

gnats away (of all the things to be attracted to his face. This was probably as close to kissing as he'd ever get).

By the time he reached the greenhouse his skin itched raw with bites. His boots were soaked, trousers soggy to the knees from squelching through the mud. Leafy trees towered high above, broken through the building's casing. Seven peered through one of the broken panes of glass into the steamy, shadowy (and extremely smelly) interior. The place was bursting with greenery: ferns with leaves the size of his head; fragrant lilies; twisted vines like rope winding round the steel pillars of the building's frame.

'Er . . . hello?' he called.

No answer.

Feeling stupid, Seven knocked on a pane of glass, but again there was no answer.

Annoyed now – it had been a long walk, and he was tired and fed up of being a walking lunchbox for the insects – he made his way inside, flinging aside the leaves blocking his path. Sweat slicked his forehead; the greenhouse was muggy with steam.

'I'm here to see the Librarian!' Seven shouted. 'We've got a meeting – *argh*!'

He let out a strangled cry as the floor gave way underneath him.

Seven plunged face-first into a hidden pond. Stinking, stagnant water closed around him. It went up his nose, filled his mouth as he gasped for air. Kicking frantically, he threw out his arms, feeling vines and roots hidden in the depths of the murky water. They twisted round his limbs. The more he thrashed the tighter they became, until Seven realised he was going to die here in the rotten water (of *course* this was the way he'd go, the most effing undignified death there ever was), and for some mad reason Alba's face came to him then and he wondered if she'd miss him, if she'd even notice he was gone –

There was a tug as something hooked round his waist. Seven let out a grunt as he was yanked upwards. Seconds later he broke the surface of the water, spluttering and retching, and was dragged up onto muddy ground.

'Well, you certainly know how to make an entrance.'

The voice was gruff and wheezy. Swiping a hand across his face to clear the mucky water from his eyes, Seven looked up into a pale, lined face with chapped lips and long white beard plaited with coloured ribbons. The man was tall, his dirty brown shirt – at least five sizes too big for him – hanging off a willowy frame. Thick glasses magnified his intense blue eyes.

So *this* was the Librarian. Seven wondered why he'd been so intimidated at the thought of meeting him. The man was even more of a mess than *he* was.

'Didn't you hear me knock?' grumbled Seven with a scowl. He stumbled onto his feet, untangling himself from the metal hook round his waist.

The Librarian's smile was wide. 'Course I did. But this was so much more fun. Now, come on. Show me your marking.'

It was pretty much visible through his wet shirt already, but Seven unbuttoned his top anyway to reveal the saw tattoo on his chest. The man's smile widened. He reached out and traced its outline with a long, dirty fingernail.

'So *you're* Carpenter's boy.'

Seven flinched away from his touch. 'Yeah,' he said, buttoning his shirt back up.

'Sad news, that. He was always my favourite. He had such beautiful arms.' The Librarian let out a puff of air, eyes glittering. 'So, boy. Finch said you were after a skid. Let's see if we can find it.'

He moved surprisingly fast for an old man. Seven stumbled after him through the dense foliage. He swatted the blade-like leaves of a fern out of his way: they slapped back into his face with a snap.

'So how does this work?' he called, words almost lost under the incessant buzzing of the mosquitos.

'You tell me the skid you want. I find it. In exchange for something *I* want too, of course.'

'Which is?'

'I haven't decided yet.'

They reached the far side of the greenhouse and stopped by a cluster of towering palms.

Seven doubled over, spitting out a fly that had flown into his mouth. 'I kind of expected there to be computers or something,' he said, and when he straightened back up the Librarian was grinning at him, crouched beside an open trap-door in the floor that revealed a set of steps disappearing into a cool, blue glow.

'What? Like the ones that are down here?' He let out a croaking laugh. 'I'd have thought a skid-thief would know how deceiving looks can be. Now get in and close that pretty mouth of yours before another fly decides it looks inviting.'

Throwing the Librarian another scowl, Seven hurried down the steps, hearing the thud of the trap-door shutting behind them. Instantly, the frantic noise of the greenhouse was silenced. The air was cool here, filled with a low, electric hum. Everything was bathed in blue light. The steps were steep, and it took a while to get to the bottom. When they did, Seven bit his lip, not wanting to give the Librarian another chance to gloat, but he couldn't help but be impressed.

They were in a large, underground room filled with computers and sleek machinery. Blue lines of text scrolled dizzyingly fast across the black screens of the computers, making the room flicker as though they were underwater. Wires crawled over the floors and walls in organised tracks. To one side of the room was a small bed and kitchen; the only messy part of the space. A row of memory-machines were lined up against the opposite wall.

Seven's heart started beating excitedly just at the sight of them.

'Go on, boy. You can admit it. Pretty slick, huh?'

The Librarian walked past, chuckling. Wheeling out a leather-backed chair, he rolled over to one of the computers.

Seven shrugged. 'It's all right.'

The man smirked. 'Stubborn, aren't you? Just like Carpenter. Well, tell me.' He stroked the keyboard, long nails clicking. 'What're we looking for?'

Seven hesitated before answering. Could he really trust this weirdo? But then he thought of Carpenter, the only person he'd ever truly trusted (before Alba, that was, though he still wasn't one hundred per cent certain about her, even if something in his gut made him want to be). If Carpenter had trusted the Librarian, so could he.

'There's this thing we –' Seven stopped abruptly. 'This thing *I've* found out about. I dunno much except it's called

185

TMK and it's got something to do with these people known as Candidates.'

He searched the Librarian's face for any signs of recognition, but the man's face was unreadable.

'You don't like to give much away, do you?' said the Librarian. 'You really *are* like Carpenter. No matter. Just so happens I don't need much to go on.' He ran a hand down his beard and winked. 'I'm *that* good.'

Turning back to the computer, he started typing. His fingers danced across the keyboard. As Seven watched, his stomach kept doing uneasy flips. *This is it*, he thought. *If nothing comes up, I'm screwed. There's nothing more we can do.*

Given his luck, he wasn't hopeful.

Alba would no doubt be just fine living without knowing the truth about TMK – she was only really affected because her father was involved – but Seven didn't know how he could go on being aware he was a Candidate but never understanding what that actually meant. He felt as though his whole life had been stolen from him. Past, present and future, all taken away in the space of a few weeks. A world he'd thought he knew (even if it wasn't one he liked) crushed to nothing.

And then the clattering of typing fell silent, the Librarian turning round and smiling toothily at Seven.

'Good news, boy,' he said. 'We have a match.'

40

ALBA

She could tell it had gone well as soon as she saw him. Even in the pitch black of the stormy night – she really should thank Mother Nature for making these night-time trips such a *pleasant* experience – with rain lashing the trees, leaves whipped into the air by the wind, Seven's grin was so wide and bright it was as though it'd been cut from a piece of the moon.

'You found one!' Alba cried, letting out a small laugh that was part relief, part happiness at seeing him again. She'd run the short distance from the house to where he was waiting under the line of elms, but already her raincoat and black trousers were soaked through. She flicked her wet hair out of her eyes. 'Another memory about TMK. You actually *found* one!'

Seven cocked his head. 'Come on, Princess. You know you didn't doubt me for a second.'

Alba smiled, holding back the truth that she'd worried sick about him all week. Stealing a memory about TMK seemed ridiculously dangerous, especially since the raid, and even though memory-thieving was his job she still couldn't quite marry the picture of the awkward, gangly boy she knew with one of a sleek, stealthy thief. Every night at dinner she'd asked her father for news on whether the London Guard had made more arrests.

Her parents were delighted, of course. They no doubt thought she was finally starting to appreciate the severity of the crimes of memory-thieves. If only they knew she was friends with a boy she was *helping* to steal memories.

'How did you find it?'

Alba almost had to shout as she followed Seven through the dark grounds of Hyde Park Estate, bent against the wind and driving rain. Their boots squelched in the mud. They were huddled together, and whenever one of them stumbled on the uneven ground they'd bump into each other, sending an electric pulse through her body, and she'd forget for a moment how to breathe.

'There's this man.' Seven gave a strangled laugh. 'The Librarian.'

'What's funny?'

'Nothing. Well, actually, kind of everything. He's a right weirdo. Anyway, he can hack into memory-machines and banks and stuff and get all their data. He found two skids about TMK. One was your father's, so we already know about that one.'

Excitement fluttered through Alba. She licked her lips; they were wet with raindrops. 'And the other?'

'It was just in some flat in South.' Pride touched Seven's voice. 'I've stolen skids from the poshest houses in North. Compared to them, stealing it was a breeze.'

'Have you surfed it yet?' Alba asked eagerly.

He didn't reply for a few moments. 'Er . . . well, I kinda thought you'd wanna be there when I did,' he said eventually, in an odd voice, and somehow it was that more than anything that made her feel as though Seven was *finally* allowing her in.

Alba smiled into the darkness.

When they were almost at the fence, a thought hit her.

'Seven?'

'Yeah?'

'What did the Librarian man want in exchange for giving you the location of the memory?'

'You know, that was what's so weird. He said I could have it for free,' Seven said, glancing at her, 'as long as I use it to find out the truth about TMK.'

They squeezed out their rain-drenched clothes in the quiet of his memorium, making puddles on the floor. Alba's teeth chattered. She hugged her arms across her chest, trying to keep herself warm in her jumper, which was so wet the moss colour was almost black. They didn't speak as Seven brought his memory-machine into the centre of the room and powered it up, its humming and ticking filling the air.

'What do you think the memory will be about?' Alba asked as she watched him strapping himself in.

Seven shrugged. 'The Librarian said the skid was coded in such a way the data corrupted when he tried to download it. Apparently the other TMK skid was like that too.'

'It sounds as though whatever TMK is,' she said, 'it's big.'

He threw her a wide grin. 'Nothing I can't handle, Princess,' he said, but in the split-second before the memory took hold and his lids fluttered shut, Alba saw fear flash in his eyes.

She waited a few more minutes until certain Seven was deep in the memory before reaching for his hand. Tentatively, feeling breathless, she twined her fingers with his.

'I know,' she whispered. 'I'm scared too.'

41

SEVEN

'MEMORY ACTIVATED. EXPIRATION IN SIX MINUTES, FORTY-ONE SECONDS.'

Seven entered the skid running.

He was breathless already, chest aching, a stitch digging deep into his side. Everything around him was a blur of darkness and spots of stark white light. The wail of a siren screamed through the air. He swerved down endless narrow corridors: the person whose memory it was seemed to know their way around whatever building he was in. Their pace didn't let up.

'Shh. Hey, it's OK!' he shouted, his voice coming out older, deeper.

Seven wondered why on earth the man whose memory he was in was talking to the siren that way. And then he realised with a jolt –

He was talking to something else.

Someone else.

Looking down, he saw the baby cradled in his arms.

It was crying, its contorted face stained with the glaring neon-white of the lights. A blanket swaddled its body. One of its hands had worked up out of its binding and was waving around, grasping at the air.

Seven focused back on where he was going, confused thoughts swirling through his head as he ran on. What on earth was happening?

Ahead, the corridor ended in a door. Keeping hold of the baby with one hand, he held out the other, swiping a card across the door's access panel. It beeped and he crashed through into a stairwell, still not slowing as he started up the stairs, taking two at a time.

'Eddie!'

A door slammed open a few flights above. Seven craned his neck and saw a woman leaning over the railing, motioning frantically.

'Hurry! They're here –'

She disappeared as the sound of a gunshot tore through the air.

From higher up in the stairwell came the pounding of boots. Seven thought the woman had been hit, and his heart stopped, thinking of Carpenter and the night of the raid – *No, not again, please no* – but then she reappeared, pulling out a gun and arcing her arm up to fire returning shots.

Seven stumbled up the remaining stairs, jumping the last few to meet her. She stopped shooting to kick open the door behind her. A blast of chill night air hit him.

'Get the baby out of here!' she yelled.

More gunshots studded the air.

Nodding a quick thanks to the woman, Seven ducked,

running through the door and out into the rain-flecked night.

He was in a wide North street. Glittering high-rises towered around him like a forest of steel and glass. Clusters of people stood on the pavement, staring with wide eyes. Behind him, the wail of the siren spilled out of the building.

'Eddie! Get in!'

There was a car parked on the pavement, engine growling, headlights dazzling in the dark. A man leant out, door thrown wide. Seven started towards him when he felt something punch into the back of his leg.

He was knocked to the ground. He rolled as he fell, using his body to shield the baby from harm. Pain like fire tore through him. He tried to stand and cried out; he'd been shot right through his kneecap. Blood was already pooling on the polished pavement. Gritting his teeth, he struggled to his feet –

Someone collided into him.

Seven fell back down. Twisting round, he saw a huge man in the red jacket of the London Guard scramble on top of him. The guard raised a gun to his face.

'Wait!' Seven cried in Eddie's deep voice.

He thrust the baby between them. It was just long enough to make the guard hesitate, giving Seven time to buck, pushing him off. Scrambling to his feet, he stumbled the short distance to the car and fell inside.

Gunshots crunched on its metal casing as the car swerved away. The baby was taken from him and Seven sprawled on the leather seat, panting, clutching his injured leg with wet, bloody hands.

'We got him,' the woman beside him gasped, cradling the baby. 'Candidate Seven. We fucking *got him*.'

42

ALBA

She hadn't realised the memory would be so short. When Seven's eyes began to flutter, Alba quickly let go of his hand. She twisted her fingers through her hair and smiled shakily.

'Welcome back.'

He glanced at her but didn't say anything. There was something hard and wild about the look in his eyes. Panting, he unstrapped himself clumsily from Butler, then stumbled off the stool, clutching his head in his hands.

Alba frowned. 'Seven? What happened? What did you see?'

'Me,' he croaked.

She bit her lip, watching him nervously as he paced the room.

'It was back in the labs, or some place like it,' he explained breathlessly. The sounds of his footsteps mingled with the rushing of the rain still driving down hard outside. 'I was running, carrying a baby in my arms, trying to escape. There were London Guards. They shot me, but I managed to escape. There was a car waiting outside and I got in and they took the baby from me, and they called it – they called it Candidate Seven.'

'The baby was *you*?' breathed Alba.

'It was important we got the baby out,' Seven went on. 'I could tell. That was the whole point of the mission. I had an access card, so I must have been working in the labs. The whole thing was planned, Alba.'

She shook her head, dizzy with confusion. 'By who?'

'Dunno. It's not like I had time to ask for a business card.'

'But did they say why?'

Seven let out a strangled cry. 'No, they *didn't* effing say why!'

With a movement so sudden it made Alba flinch, he lunged forward and ripped the DSC from the feed cable connecting it to the memory-machine, throwing it to the floor and grinding it under his boot.

'Seven!' she cried. She ran towards him, but he flung his arms out, glaring at her.

'Don't you get it, Alba? I don't *wanna* know. This was a stupid, stupid idea. Who gives a crap what happened to me in the past? Obviously no one cared enough about me or they'd still be here!' He gave a harsh, barking laugh, his eyes wild. 'Where are they now, huh? Where're all these people who fought so hard to free me from TMK, then just dropped me like the piece of crap I am?'

Seven fell silent, chest heaving as he raked in heavy breaths. The grin twisting his lips looked painful. Alba realised with a jolt that his eyes were wet.

She was close to tears herself. As he dropped his head, arms going limp at his sides, she took a tentative step towards him.

When she was confident he wasn't going to lash out at her again, she reached out, fingers curling round his arm.

He flinched under her touch, but she held on.

'Don't *ever* think that's what you are,' Alba said sternly. 'I don't know what happened with those people, but I'm sure that if they were fighting so hard to free you they wouldn't have just let you go afterwards.'

'Then why am I alone?'

Seven's voice was so small it broke her heart.

'*I'm* here,' she whispered.

And for the first time since they'd met, it was Seven who opened his arms and pulled Alba against him, his heartbeat fast where her ear pressed to his chest, the smell of mint lacing his skin and his strange, beautiful scent of boy closing round her like a kiss.

43

SEVEN

They said goodbye as usual under the elms outside her house. Starlight touched their faces: the storm had finally cleared. They were both soaked through, and Seven tried to avoid looking at all the places where Alba's clothes clung tightly to her body – which was difficult, as they were practically flashing at him with signs saying, *LOOK AT ME*.

Alba smiled up at him through thick lashes. 'Tomorrow, then,' she said simply.

Seven loved how it wasn't a question.

So *this* was what it was like having friends.

He grinned. 'Wouldn't miss it for the world.'

44

ALBA

Sunday service at St Paul's was more of a social event than a religious one, though of course none of the attendees would admit it. The cathedral's breathtaking interior, with its gilded domes and carved columns and velvet sheets draped over white stone walls, were just a backdrop for the finery of North's most prominent families, decked in their Sunday best.

'What on earth was Hilary Goodwin thinking when she got dressed this morning?'

'Heavens knows. She looks like an overstuffed pumpkin. That shade of orange belongs only on a child's Halloween costume.'

'Well, that dress could certainly pass for one.'

Alba resisted an eye-roll as she passed rows of gossiping women to the high-backed wooden pew at the front of the nave. She didn't think she could cope with all the bitchiness and social strutting that came with Sunday service today. Her life in North was feeling ever more like some faded dream; one she couldn't wake from until she ran out into the moonlit grounds of the estate and saw Seven waiting for her under the elms.

'Watch your dress,' her mother muttered as they took their seats. Oxana slipped out of her fur coat and folded the delicate chiffon of her dark red dress around her. Her hair was pulled up into a sleek bun. A flick of black liner defined her eyes. She gave Alba a sharp look. 'Chartreuse creases easily, and I don't want people to think we employ incompetent servants. Though it often feels like it.'

Not wanting to give her mother any reason to become angry with her, Alba rearranged her dress so the fabric wasn't crumpled. She stifled a yawn. Earlier this morning – and just hours after she'd got back from South – Dolly chose a beautiful yellow dress for her to wear. It fitted snugly around her waist before spreading out in a structured fan-like effect over her legs, stopping just past her knees. Tiny jewels were sewn into the fabric like drops of dew on sunflower petals.

Despite everything the dress stood for, Alba couldn't help but feel pretty wearing it. It hid her plumpness and elongated her figure. She also liked how Dolly had done her hair in a twisted braid wound over her head, a few soft curls falling free around her cheeks.

I wonder whether Seven would like me in this, she thought. Then she sighed, giving a little shake of her head. What was wrong with her? Seven probably wouldn't even notice if she was wearing a bin bag right now. His whole world was tipping sideways, everything he knew – his job, his security, his past – slipping out of reach.

Alba snuck a glance at her father. He was sitting on her mother's other side, head bowed as he talked to the person beside him. The low rumble of his voice cut under the noise of the hall, like a threat lurking, waiting to break free.

What are you doing? she wondered. *What secret are you hiding in Lab 32? What's TMK?*

And what is Seven's *part in it all?*

Alba was so lost in thought she didn't notice the boy who had sat down next to her until he spoke.

'What a bore, don't you agree? I'd still be asleep if I had my way. But we must keep up appearances, I suppose.'

She looked round, mouth falling open when she saw who it was.

Thierry Burton-Lyon.

As in, *the* Thierry Burton-Lyon, son of the city's Lord Minister, Christian Burton-Lyon, who had ruled London for the past twelve years.

Thierry looked much like his father. He had a round, unattractive face with squashed features: dark beady eyes and a large, flat nose. The shiny olive suit he was wearing turned his flushed complexion a sickly shade. His brown hair was smoothed back over his head, the comb-lines still evident. Unlike his father, however, he was tall and strong-looking, the hint of muscles under a suit a size too tight.

Thierry's lips stretched in a lazy smile as she met his eyes.

'Miss White.' A French accent curled his words. He reached out and brushed her cheek with the back of his fingers. 'I am so pleased to finally meet you.'

Finally meet me?

The phrasing seemed odd. Alba didn't know how to respond.

'Oh, um . . .' She forced a smile. 'Thank you. I – I haven't seen you at Sunday service before . . .'

Thierry clicked his tongue. It was a sound she associated with her mother, and did nothing to help her warm to him.

'Religion. A mode of practice for those too poor and spineless to afford their own sense of self. I have no time for it.' He shrugged, breaking eye contact to scan the room. 'My parents wanted to debut my return to London, and it seems this is where high society goes to show off their children. After all,' he added, smiling again as he turned back to her, 'look at *you*.'

For what seemed far too long a time to be decent in public, Thierry's eyes crawled down the front of Alba's dress. It was as though his gaze had somehow forced apart the fabric stretched over her chest and he'd pushed his way inside, careless fingers crawling over her flesh. She felt violated.

'Return?' Alba asked, resisting the urge to punch him straight in the face (which would not be seemly of a young North lady, least of all because they were in a holy place). 'Where have you been?'

'France – I've been attending boarding school in Paris, studying at my father's old school. But now I'm nineteen I have returned to work with my father. And find a wife too, of course.'

God help the poor girl, thought Alba.

But she gave him what she hoped was a sweet smile and said, 'And have you found anyone yet?'

Thierry raised his eyebrows. He let out a chuckling laugh. 'At least my parents found me someone with a sense of humour.'

It took Alba a moment to take in his words. By that time, the vicar had stepped up to the great carved altar in front of them, the choir in the stalls beginning to sing as an organ flooded the cathedral with noise, and thankfully all attention was diverted from Alba, whose face was pale with shock at the prospect of marrying Thierry Burton-Lyon.

Her mother's fateful words came back to her, the meaning all too horribly clear now.

Because one day, if things go as planned, the whole world will care what you think.

Alba was to become the wife of the Lord Minister's son.

Throughout the service, Thierry kept a hand close to her on the pew, moving it occasionally to brush her hips or legs as though he'd already claimed her for his own. He snuck sideways glances, smiling in a way that made Alba's skin crawl. Every time his hand grazed her dress it made her want to be sick. Each time he looked at her it made her feel like screaming, like jumping up and running out of the cathedral.

Running out of her life.

Alba knew one thing for certain. There was no way on earth she was going to spend the rest of her life with this boy.

When the service ended, Oxana turned to her, a sly look in her cool blue eyes.

'My darling, I see you have met Master Burton-Lyon,' she said, leaning in, her voice low so Thierry couldn't hear. 'We're joining him and his parents for lunch. We thought it would be a wonderful opportunity for the both of you to get to know each other better. We're so hoping you'll get along.'

Oxana was smiling at Alba as though Thierry was some delicious treat she couldn't wait to give her. Her mother truly thought that Alba was going to be happy with her match.

It was so ironic Alba could laugh.

'Mrs White.'

Thierry leant past her and stretched out a hand to her mother. He raised her fingers to his lips. 'You are looking as beautiful as ever.'

Oxana's smile glittered. 'And you even handsomer than when I last saw you. You must tell me all about your recent adventures in Paris, Thierry. I do miss that city. Memory-surfing simply does not do it justice.'

She rose, Thierry standing with her. They started towards the end of the pew where crowds were moving down the centre of the hall, leaving the cathedral. Her mother glanced over her shoulder to make sure Alba was going to follow them before being swallowed up by the rush of colourful silk suits and sparkling dresses. Her father's seat was already empty; he always left as soon as the service finished.

Alba toyed with the idea of not following them. But it was never really an option. As much as it killed her to admit it, she wouldn't dare defy her mother in such an outright, bold way.

Though her secrets felt safe in the ink-blue shadows of the night, daylight exposed her, took her bravery away.

Brushing down her dress and swinging her coat over her shoulders, Alba followed the crowds out of St Paul's, the thought of what Seven would make of Thierry just enough to bring a small, sad smile to her face.

45

SEVEN

Despite everything that had happened, Seven felt weirdly happy that morning when he woke.

He didn't try convincing himself that last night had all been a dream. He didn't groan at the thought of having to see Alba again. He just stumbled out of bed, head groggy from tiredness, pulling on his tattered grey shirt and blue trousers before heading out of the flat, a twisted little smile dancing on his lips.

Yes, his life was a mess. But for the first time ever, he had someone to share that mess with.

Seven headed through Vauxhall to Clapham Road. The street was busy with traffic. Glaring grey light from the overcast day glanced off the metal shells of cars and motorbikes and lorries, the blare of their horns and grumbling engines loud in the fume-clogged air.

Digging in his trouser pocket, Seven pulled out the few coins he had. He bit back a curse. As always, it was less than he'd thought; even though he'd been poor his whole life, he still half hoped some sort of miracle would happen and he'd suddenly discover a giant pot of gold tucked down the front of his pants. But his last payment from Carpenter for stealing Alastair White's skid had gone almost entirely on rent, and there was barely any left.

Seven's stomach let out a growl.

'I know,' he said sadly, patting it. 'Trust me, I know.'

He followed the road towards the Overground track that cut through at Clapham North. Most of the old railway lines had been removed for new buildings, but like so much of South the regeneration work was often abandoned due to lack of government funding. Seven didn't mind though. As with the ancient Battersea Power Station, Southers had appropriated the space for their own use. He liked the market that had sprung up along the disused tracks here. It was busy and noisy: perfect conditions for thieving.

At the bridge over the tracks, Seven jumped the low brick wall and went down the grassy bank onto the railway line. Amid the tangled foliage that carpeted the metal tracks in greens and browns, hundreds of market stands and hawker stalls had been set up. They ran down the centre of the disused line in a colourful display of flapping awnings and signs. His stomach growled louder at the food smells wafting up from cookers in thick clouds of steam.

'Two for a pound,' called out a stall-owner, catching Seven eyeing her melons (the fruit kind, he might add).

Ducking his head, he moved on through the busy crowds.

The trouble with stealing from Southers was that they *expected* it. That's why Seven often took food from his skid-thieving jobs in North to keep him going. Northers left their food out, not a care in the world. In South you were considered a prince if you weren't so starving you could actually save food for later.

After a few minutes browsing the market, Seven found what he was looking for. A stall selling freshly made pastries and breads was wedged in on one side by a gnarled old oak. The tree's wide trunk protruded onto the path, creating a bottleneck outside the stall.

Seven slipped in with the crowd. He followed its flow, moving closer to the bakery stall. Even over the stink of the bodies pressed against him, he could smell fresh bread, and it made his mouth water.

He was right next to the stall now. He chanced a quick side-glance to see what was on offer; all of it looked delicious. Then, keeping his head down, he reached out a hand.

He was away with a handful of pastry before he'd even taken another breath. Seven allowed himself to be swallowed back up in the stream of people. He counted in his head as he moved away from the stall, waiting for a shout or cry of recognition.

One.

Nothing.

Two.

Nothing.

Three.

Still nothing.

Confident he'd got away with it, he looked at what he'd stolen. It was some sort of sweet pastry, sticky with a thick maple coating and braided with raisins.

'Well done, hands,' Seven muttered, grinning, then lifted the pastry to his lips. But before he could take a bite –

Crash!

Out of nowhere, something collided into him.

Cries flew up, the crowd scattering as Seven was bowled over, the back of his head smacking into the trampled grass. His eyes jammed shut as pain snapped down his spine, and then he was opening them, looking into the black-furred face of a dog.

A huge, effing *beast* of a dog.

Its front paws pressed down heavy on his stomach. Letting out a huff of hot, wet air into his face, it dipped its head down, going for the pastry clutched to Seven's chest. Its rough tongue scraped over his hands.

'Hey!' Seven cried. 'That's mine!'

Grabbing the dog's muzzle, he shoved it away.

The dog growled. Its ears snapped back. Baring its teeth, it lunged forward and grabbed the collar of his shirt. Teeth dug into his skin. The dog jerked its head from side to side and the sound of the fabric tearing was like a whip-crack through the air. When the dog finally pulled away, still snarling, a piece of Seven's tattered shirt hung from its muzzle.

Seven scrambled to his feet. He held up the sad, squashed remains of his pastry, debating whether or not to eat it. *So it has a little dog-dribble on it now*, he thought. *What doesn't?* Then he realised the crowd had gone silent, everyone staring at him.

His cheeks flamed.

'What?' Seven shouted, glaring at them.

It took him a few more seconds to realise what they were staring at.

The front of his ripped shirt had flapped open, and the tattoo on his chest – the outline of a saw, one of the marks the London Guard had shown on their broadcast about the raid, offering a monetary reward for information that led to any of the skid-thieves' capture – was now clear for everyone to see.

'Oh, crap,' Seven muttered.

Then he turned and ran.

46

ALBA

They had a table at Goldman's Grill, an expensive, brasserie-style restaurant in Paternoster Square. It was on the top floor of what used to be one of the world's premiere investment banks before America's triple recession at the end of the twenty-first century. A glass wall ran along one side of the restaurant. Low-hanging chandeliers lit everything in a crystalline glow. Waiters in black waistcoats and silver aprons moved carefully between the tables, trays balanced on their hands.

Alba was sat with her back to the window, though she wished she were facing it instead. The view over Paternoster Square with St Paul's' great spired dome would have been far more pleasant to look at than the faces of her parents, Thierry, and his mother and father.

She had been surprised they'd chosen such a busy restaurant for lunch. The Burton-Lyons were the most recognisable family in London. Security would be of the utmost importance. But towards the end of the meal, Alba noticed a couple of men in black suits standing just outside the entrance to the restaurant, scanning the room behind dark glasses; they must be the Burton-Lyons' guards.

'Don't worry,' Thierry said when he noticed her looking. He leant in close. 'They'll leave us alone whenever I ask.'

'Perfect,' she muttered.

They had been at lunch for almost two hours. The waiters had just brought dessert: rosewater crème brûlées and delicate vials of sweet wine. Though no one had brought up the specific subject of marriage yet, Alba knew it was coming. The Whites and the Burton-Lyons had never dined together alone before. There was a reason they were starting now.

Thierry's hand was hovering dangerously near her leg, and she was just wondering whether to slap it away or ignore it when there was a faint buzzing sound from somewhere under the table.

Thierry pulled out a small tablet from his trouser pocket. Despite herself, Alba couldn't help but be interested in the device. As well as limiting her watching the Net, her parents wouldn't allow her to have any tablets of her own.

A girl's face came up on the screen as the caller.

'A friend of yours?' asked Alba, trying to sound uninterested.

Thierry slid his finger over the screen to reject the call. 'Just a girl I met who will not stop hounding me,' he said, shrugging. 'It's unfortunate when girls take a few nights together as meaning something more. They need to understand that there is no time for love when you are preparing to run a country.' He put the tablet back in his pocket, and before she could stop him, placed a hand on Alba's thigh. 'Wouldn't you agree?'

Alba broke his gaze, cheeks burning with disgust. Thierry had effectively just told her he'd already slept with quite a few girls . . . and he had said it so casually, as though it were nothing. Was this really the sort of man she'd have to spend the rest of her years with?

And as for love? Alba didn't care what Thierry thought. She *certainly* had time for it (with someone other than him, of course). She wanted romance and passion. She wanted the butterflies-in-your-stomach and the head-in-the-clouds kind of love. The sort of love she read about in novels, where the heroes and heroines were prepared to die before they would ever give each other up.

She wanted –

'Seven.'

Alba nearly jumped out of her seat.

'What?' she blustered, looking round wildly at Thierry.

'I know,' he said, nodding at her expression. 'Seven families already asking my parents for my match with their daughters. There'll be more, I'm sure.'

Alba blinked.

His hand tightened on her leg. 'That's why my parents are in such a hurry to announce *our* match –'

'Are you whispering our secrets, Thierry?'

Thierry's father, Christian Burton-Lyon, smiled at them from across the table. There was something almost ridiculous about his appearance: his hair was set in little oily black curls on the top of his head, and a moustache twirled over his top lip. His neck and belly were wide with age.

'You've only been back in London less than a week.' Christian

Burton-Lyon's smooth voice was thick with a French accent. He twirled a glass in one hand, teeth glittering. 'At this rate, soon the entire city will know the details of our most intimate business.'

Thierry gave a brusque laugh. 'Apologies, Father. But how is a man to keep quiet when he is sitting next to such a beautiful woman?'

'Too right, my dear boy,' said Christian Burton-Lyon, smiling. 'Too right.'

'Oh, will you boys behave.'

Thierry's mother, Julia, smiled and shook her head. She was pretty, with a tall, slender frame and short brown hair cropped around her chin. Unlike her husband and son, her accent was that of a high-class Norther.

'Your mother is right,' Christian Burton-Lyon continued, after giving his wife a playful poke. 'No matter how eager we may be to share it, the news is not to go public until the Winter-turn Ball.'

'My lips are sealed, Father.'

'*Merveilleux*. Now, where were we . . .'

As the adults at the table fell back into conversation, Thierry leant close to Alba. She didn't hear a word of what he was saying, still reeling from the knowledge that their engagement would be announced at the Winter-turn Ball. That was just a couple of weeks away. It was far too soon.

Though a million *light-years* away was too soon when it came to Thierry.

Dolly had promised she'd find a way to save Alba from marriage. But what could she do in two weeks? And once the news of the engagement went public, Alba would never be able to escape it. Her name would be tied to Thierry's forever.

'What now?' Thierry growled suddenly, pulling his hand off her knee and sliding the tablet back out of his pocket.

'Another needy ex-girlfriend?' asked Alba coolly.

He didn't answer. He was holding the tablet in such a way she couldn't see the screen, so when he let out a booming laugh, she flinched.

'Wonderful news from the London Guard,' Thierry said loudly, cutting off the chatter around the table. 'They have just named another of the escaped memory-thieves from the raid at Borough Market. Apparently he was spotted in South an hour ago. The tattoo on his chest was recognised as belonging to one of the thieving crews. They've got his ID now. The ugly bastard will be caught in no time.'

Thierry set his tablet on the table. He pushed it forward so everyone could see the picture of the boy on its screen.

Alba's heart nearly flat-out stopped.

Before she'd even looked at the image she knew whose face it would be, but it still hit her with a force so strong it took her breath away. There he was, those small grey eyes and rumpled hair and beautiful, twisted grin looking up at her from the screen, and printed below them the words:

WANTED FOR IMMEDIATE ARREST

47

SEVEN

'You look terrible, man.'

Seven had forgotten Sunday was Kola's day off. As he crashed through the door to the flat, panting from running the whole way back from the market, he stumbled back in surprise to see Kola sitting on the sofa.

In the murky light, the sky outside thick with clouds, the flat was cast in shadows. A single light buzzed overhead. Kola was dressed in a slim brown shirt and black trousers. He had been reading from a newspaper folded open across his knees; an underground South publication from the look of it, the headline reading: *BLOODBATH AT BOROUGH MARKET*. He placed it on the table, eyes not straying from Seven as he took in his bloodied chest and ripped shirt.

'You look *really* terrible.'

Seven let out a disbelieving breath. 'Thanks for that,' he said through gritted teeth. He pushed the door shut behind him and sagged against it. 'I hadn't noticed.'

Kola stood. His eyes paused on the tattoo on Seven's chest before moving to look over the damage of the dog's bite below, where his flesh was raw and mangled.

'What happened?'

Seven scowled. 'An asshole of a dog happened, that's what.'

'Let me take a look.'

'It's OK.'

'You're injured,' Kola said patiently. 'I've tended to wounds on the other workers at the docks when they haven't been able to afford doctors. I might be able to help.'

Carefully, Seven lowered the hand grasping his wound. It came away slick with blood. Immediately the pain intensified, throbbing nauseatingly; it felt as though each movement was shifting the tears in his flesh. He hadn't noticed how bad the dog's bite had been at first. He'd just been concerned with getting as far away as possible. Now the adrenalin had died down, the pain was like a siren, screaming in his chest.

Kola gestured to the sofa. 'Take off your shirt so I can get to the wound. And keep your hand pressed against it.'

As Kola disappeared into the kitchen, Seven collapsed on the sofa. He tugged off what was left of his shirt and threw the bloodied fabric to the floor. He didn't even have space in his head to worry about the fact that one of the only shirts in his possession was now beyond repair. His mind was spinning, and not just from the pain.

What was he meant to do now? Some of the people at the market were bound to report him to the London Guard. They might even have done it by now. And then the London Guard would figure out who he was and where he lived, and then –

Panic whirred through Seven. This flat was his home. The memorium was his life's collection, everything he worked for. He couldn't lose all of that now because of one pastry and a stupid-ass dog.

'Right.' Kola walked back into the room with his hands full of medical supplies. 'Let's sort out this wound.'

Seven's eyes widened. 'Where the hell did you get all that?' There were strips of gauze, bandage fabric, antiseptic cream, a bottle of cleaning fluid and even a pair of sterile gloves.

Kola set the items down on the table. 'I thought it would be good to have some things in case of an emergency,' he said. 'I don't think the North doctors who pass through the docks will miss a few supplies here and there.'

Seven couldn't help grinning. So he wasn't the only thief in the flat. His smile soon disappeared when he noticed the needle in Kola's collection.

Kola followed his train of sight. 'I'm going to have to stitch the wound closed after I clean it,' he explained. 'Unfortunately, I don't have any anaesthetic for you to take.'

Seven closed his eyes. 'Of *course* you don't.'

Maybe it was the loss of blood or the sight of the needle, or just all the events of the last few crappy hours catching up with him, but he really was feeling very faint again now. He sagged into the sofa, letting out a hiss of breath. His chest felt as though a small star was bursting inside it.

'Seven?'

Kola was watching him, his handsome face with its straight nose and thin lips set into an expression that somehow managed to be both soft and firm at the same time.

His lips pulled into a small, tight smile. 'Don't worry. It won't hurt as much as you're thinking.'

Just like that afternoon on the rooftop of their block of flats a few weeks ago, when Kola had asked about fighting the boys who terrorised him, Seven felt a rush of gratitude towards this boy he barely knew. Kola was a lot like Alba, he thought (though, to be fair, *she'd* started their friendship with blackmail): ready to help out someone they had no need to.

Kindness wasn't something Seven was used to. After looking away, embarrassed, he turned back to meet Kola's eyes and nodded.

'I'm ready,' he said.

Kola nodded. Then, before Seven could do or say anything to stop him, Kola drew a hand back, closing his fingers into a fist, and the next thing Seven knew was the feel of Kola's knuckles smashing into the side of his jaw and his world snapped off into black.

48

ALBA

Voices whirled round her at the table, but she felt separated from it all.

Alba stared at Thierry's tablet and the image of Seven's face, wanting more than anything not to believe what she was seeing, but at the same time knowing in the pit of her stomach that it was horribly, horribly true. Her mind buzzed with questions. What was happening to Seven right now? Was he home? Was he safe? Or had the London Guard already found him?

Panic fluttered in her chest.

'It's despicable what those Southers think they can get away with.'

'And the worst part is how ungrateful they are.'

'I agree, Oxana,' said Thierry's father. 'We provide them with jobs and homes and safety, and this is how they repay us. Stealing our memories – it's the lowest form of betrayal. The one thing most private to any person, and they sell it on the black market as though it's worth nothing more than a pound of common tobacco.'

It was that which finally made Alba snap.

'People in North trade memories, too,' she said, looking up from the picture of Seven's face to glare instead at those round the table. 'Only we do it for leisure. For greed. For curiosity. Southers do it to experience just a moment of what their lives could be like if they weren't dirt poor. They do it to *live*.'

It was as though she'd slapped each and every one of them. Her parents' faces were blank, stunned. Beside her, Thierry took in a sharp breath. His mother Julia's jaw dropped open a little, revealing clumps of crème brûlée still stuck to her tongue, and Christian Burton-Lyon's gaze turned cold.

'Look at our city,' Alba went on into the shocked silence, her voice cresting with anger. 'All the things we have in North. The way we keep it to ourselves, locked in by the river and the London Guard and live executions of South criminals, trying to scare them so they'll never fight back. We only have ourselves to blame if Southers want to reclaim just one tiny piece of what we've taken from them. None of us would survive even one day if we had to live with the little they've got.'

Alba thought of Seven and his small memorium, of how much he needed those stolen memories to escape his life. She thought of the fear and anger she'd seen in his eyes after the raid, when what little he'd had in the world had been ripped from him.

'What did they do to deserve getting that kind of life,' she continued, 'other than be born on the wrong side of the river?'

'Little Alba.'

Her mother's voice was cool and calm, but icy underneath. Oxana spread her hands on the table. 'Darling, I think the fever you had a few days ago has returned. You're not sounding like yourself.'

'I'm perfectly well, Mother.'

Ignoring her, Oxana slid off her seat and swept over. She touched the back of her hand to Alba's forehead. 'My darling, you're burning.'

'You *do* look a little pale,' Thierry's mother offered sweetly.

Alba opened her mouth to protest but Oxana shushed her, pressing the back of her hand so hard against her forehead that the sharp diamonds of her mother's wedding band dug into her skin.

'We must get you home at once.' Oxana turned to her husband. 'She can take our car home, Alastair. We'll be fine with a cab back later.'

Thierry shook his head. 'But, Mrs White – you must ride with us in our car.'

Christian Burton-Lyon smiled. 'Yes, you must.' He took a sip of wine, his hand tight around the stem of the glass. 'We are all soon to be family, after all.'

Alba's skin crawled at his words.

'And we can all have a spot of afternoon tea back at our residence,' his wife added, her voice enthusiastic. 'We had the place refurbished last summer. Number Ten never looked so good.'

Oxana flashed a wide smile. 'Wonderful,' she said, looking genuinely relieved that the Burton-Lyons didn't appear to have been affected by her daughter's outburst. She gripped Alba's arms and pulled her up from her chair. 'Let's get you home, then, my darling.'

Alba knew better than to protest any more. At least this

way she was leaving lunch early and didn't have to spend a second more in Thierry's company.

Everyone at the table stood, inclining their heads.

'I look forward to seeing you again at the Ball,' Thierry murmured, taking Alba's hand and pressing it to his lips. 'I hope you are fully recovered by then, because we will have a lot of celebrating to do.'

Celebrating.

The word made her stomach squirm. What did she have to celebrate about her union with this creep? She'd have more fun at a funeral.

In fact, Alba realised, that's *exactly* what the Winter-turn Ball would be with her and Thierry's engagement announced on the night. The burial of her own future. Her own dreams.

She forced a smile. 'I look forward to it,' she said, as sweetly as she could muster.

Once Alba was in the car and Hans, the driver, was pulling out of Paternoster Square, she had an idea. A reckless one, of course. But it was her only way of knowing if Seven was safe.

She leant forward and tapped the dark screen that ran along the back of the front seats. A second later it drained away to clear glass. Hans's stubbled jawline shifted round slightly as his eyes in the rear-view mirror flicked up to meet hers.

'Mistress Alba?'

'Hans,' she said, smiling. 'You know, I'm *so* craving honey madeleines. There's a café in south Pimlico that makes the best ones in the city. On Grosvenor Road. Do you think you can take me there?'

'Your mother told me to take you straight home, miss,' he said. 'She said you weren't well.'

Alba waved a hand. 'My parents are going to Downing Street with the Burton-Lyons after lunch for afternoon tea. They're not going to be home for a few hours. It will only be a short detour . . . No one would ever know.'

Hans sighed. 'Very well, then, miss,' he said, reluctantly. 'As long as we're quick, I don't see what harm a small detour will do.'

49

SEVEN

When he regained consciousness, Seven felt the bandages tied round his chest before opening his eyes and seeing them. He blinked, dazed. His fingers brushed the smooth white fabric covering his wound.

For one horrible second just before Kola had hit him, he'd really thought that Kola was turning him in to the London Guard, and he had felt a sting of betrayal, even though Kola had no real ties to him. Now he realised Kola had just wanted to spare him the pain while he stitched his wound.

Seven had no idea how long he'd been unconscious for. He was lying on the sofa, a blanket draped over his body. The flat was dimly lit, full of shadows, but it wasn't dark enough to be night yet. The single bulb in the centre of the ceiling hummed noisily, lighting the room in a flickering glow.

Tucking his elbows beneath him, Seven started to push himself up, but a flash of pain ripped through his torso and he fell back with a curse.

'Hey, man. You're up.'

Kola walked in from the kitchen. He set down a glass of water and an oily package on the table before sliding an arm under Seven's shoulders, helping him sit up.

'Sorry I had to knock you out like that. I thought it would be preferable to experiencing all of that without anaesthetic.'

He handed Seven the glass of water and Seven drank gratefully. There was a bitter taste laced in with the water.

'Painkillers?' Seven asked, giving back the empty glass.

Kola nodded. 'That's all I have though, I'm afraid. Here.' He offered the warm newspaper-wrapped package. 'You need to eat something. This was the first thing I could find.'

Seven unwrapped the package, the grease soaking the paper instantly slicking his fingers in an oily coating. Inside was a battered sausage. The deep-fried smell made his mouth water.

'I'll pay you back for this,' he said gruffly, looking up. 'Honest. And for all the medical stuff, too.'

Kola gave him a tight smile. 'Don't worry about it. You were hurt. It was the least I could do.'

Not true, Seven thought. The *least* Kola could have done was ignore him, as he was sure his other flatmate Sid would have. Or worse: he could've reported him to the London Guard. Kola must have recognised the tattoo on his chest by now, and he would know from all the media coverage about the monetary reward for turning Seven in.

As if reading his mind, Kola said, 'I'm not going to tell the London Guard you're here. But you should finish eating and decide what you're going to do before Sid comes home. I can't say he'll do the same.'

Nodding, Seven bit into the battered sausage. Life instantly coursed back into his limbs with each oily mouthful, his energy levels rising from *about as energetic as a zombie* to somewhere more in the region of *could just about curtsey if the Queen walked by*. He still felt horrendous, and the agonising ache in his chest was only somewhat dimmed by the painkillers. But at least he didn't feel completely hopeless any more.

'Think you're able to get dressed now?' Kola asked when he'd finished.

Seven grimaced. 'Just about.'

Kola waited outside his bedroom while he changed. It was difficult. The ache in his torso filled Seven's entire body, a heavy, draining pain that turned his muscles to lead and made him want to vomit every time he shifted and it rolled up inside his flesh like a giant black wave.

Stripped down to his underwear, he looked over himself for the blood he'd been covered in earlier, but he was clean. He realised Kola must have washed it off while he was unconscious. How embarrassing. Biting back the pain, Seven pulled on a pair of slim black jeans – the only pair of trousers he owned besides the blue ones the dog had pawed all over today – and a thin maroon jumper that fitted snugly over his bandaged chest.

He sat on the edge of the bed when he was finished and called for Kola.

'So,' Seven said, grinning. 'How do I look?'

A small smile touched Kola's lips. 'Good. Better than before, anyway.'

Seven looked away. He could feel his ears pinking. 'Look, Kola,' he muttered. 'I'm grateful for your help, I really am. I

225

just – I don't get why you're doing it.' He looked back up and gave a cold laugh. 'Most Southers would've just turned me in and claimed their reward.'

Kola pushed his hands into the pockets of his trousers. He was silent for a long while. When he next spoke, his voice was cool and clear.

'I left Malaysia all those years ago to escape death. In my own country, people had turned on each other. Forgetting the things that unite us, they instead chose to kill their fellow countrymen because of their differences. Race, religion, beliefs . . . they thought these things divided us. I hoped to come to a country where I could escape all of that. But even here in the British Isles, in London, a city where the streets are supposed to be paved with gold, there are people who walk on those gold streets and people who are on their hands and knees, scrubbing them. And what is important to remember is that it is those who scrub the streets who are the ones making it shine.'

Kola fell quiet, silence wrapping the flat. Seven felt as though he was trying to tell him something important (though to be honest, he didn't have a clue what the hell he was going on about).

'We will win in our own way, man,' Kola said, quiet but firm. 'No matter how many times people trample dirt into the streets, I will keep scrubbing them. I will continue to make my patch as golden as it can be.'

Seven stared, wondering how to respond. But before he could say anything, there was a knock on the front door.

He froze.

The knocking came again, louder, insistent.

Kola frowned, peering round the bedroom door. 'Should I answer it?'

Seven shook his head frantically. 'What if it's them?' he croaked. His heart beat fast, spiralling up through his chest into his mouth. His words stumbled in his panic. 'What if it's the London Guard and they're here to take me away? They're gonna arrest me! They're gonna throw me in prison and –'

The knocking stopped.

Seven screwed his eyes shut. He tensed, readying himself for the sound of the door crashing open, the London Guard forcing their way in, and thought, heart breaking –

So this *is how it ends.*

He wasn't ready.

Then a muffled shout came from behind the door.

'Seven! If you're in there, let me in before I die of the effing stink out here!'

50

ALBA

She rushed inside the moment the door opened. Barely noticing the boy who'd let her in, she headed straight to Seven, her whole body thrumming with relief at the sight of him here, safe, alive. He was leaning against the back of the sofa, holding one arm awkwardly to his chest. His face was tight and paler than usual.

Then he flashed her a wide grin, his eyes crinkling at the edges, and Alba melted, forgetting everything in that instant, just falling into the beauty of his smile.

'You should watch your language, Princess. That's no way for a lady to speak.'

Alba rolled her eyes, just able to hold back a smile. 'I wonder where I learnt it from.' She moved closer, frowning. 'I was so worried, Seven. I didn't know if you'd still be here. The report said –'

'The report?'

A voice from behind made her jump. Alba spun round, noticing properly for the first time the boy who'd let her into the flat. He was tall and handsome, with a dark, serious face

228

and smooth mahogany skin, his black hair cropped short. A simple shirt and trousers clung to his slim frame.

'What report?' he asked again, taking a step towards her.

She shrank back at his agitated tone.

'Don't worry,' Seven said, seeming to sense her unease. 'This is my flatmate, Kola. We can trust him. Kola, this is Alba. The A stands for annoying.'

Alba let Seven's joke roll off her, relaxing a little.

Kola smiled. 'So you're Seven's girlfriend.'

Beside her, Seven made a sputtering noise. Alba felt her cheeks flush, though partly out of annoyance. Was the idea really so disgusting to him?

'No!' she said quickly. 'We're just friends.'

Kola's eyes glittered. 'Ah,' he said. 'Sorry.' Then his face turned serious once more. 'You were saying something about a report?'

Alba blinked. 'Oh. Yes.' She turned to Seven, reaching for his arm. 'That's why I came. There was a London Guard alert – it said you'd been spotted in South. They know about the tattoo. And they posted a picture, so now everyone knows who you are and what you look like, and what you've done . . .'

His face went so pale she thought he might be sick.

'I'm so sorry,' Alba went on. 'I came as fast as I could. Hans was meant to drive me straight home but I persuaded him to drop me off at a café for a little while. He's waiting there for me. I managed to slip away while there was a crowd of people and then went over Vauxhall Bridge – it's just round the corner from the café. The London Guard let me cross, of course. Northers don't need a licence to enter South. I just hope they didn't realise who I am . . .'

She trailed off, fear flashing through her at the thought of what her parents would do if they were told their daughter had crossed into South.

Seven goggled at her. 'You came through South on your own?'

'Well, it was just a short walk from the bridge –'

'Alba! You could've been killed! Or worse –'

He stopped abruptly, closing his eyes. When he opened them again he was staring at her with such intensity that Alba completely forgot Kola was still in the room with them. The world had shrunk to just her and Seven, the space of their bodies, just centimetres apart. The look in his eyes tethered her to the spot.

'I can't drag you into this,' Seven breathed. 'I just can't.'

'You're not dragging me,' she said firmly. 'I'm here, of my own free will. You haven't asked me to do anything. This was all me. *I* made you bring me here to memory-surf. *I* wanted to see you again. You gave me everything I asked for, Seven, and now I want to do something for you.'

'No,' he said, his eyes hard. 'It's too dangerous. They're gonna come for me, and then they'll give me a fast trial, and once they've found me guilty I'll be dead before you know it.'

Alba shook her head. 'That's not going to happen. I won't let it. There must be *something* we can do.'

Closing the distance between them, Seven took her hand and wound his fingers through hers.

'Alba . . .'

Crash!

A loud noise echoed up into the flat, snapping them alert.

Alba frowned, pulling back. 'What on earth . . .?'

Eyes flashing with fear, Seven turned, meeting Kola's gaze.

The two of them shared a look of understanding. Quickly, Seven started towards the door. Alba hadn't noticed before – she'd been so relieved to see him – but now she saw he was walking stiffly, wincing with each step.

'What's wrong?' she asked, following him. It was clear something was hurting him.

He avoided her eyes. 'A dog decided to have a bit of me for lunch. But don't worry 'bout it. Kola stitched me up.'

'You were attacked by a *dog*?' Alba paled, a disbelieving sound rising in her throat. 'Don't you think that's something you should have told me sooner? You need to go to hospital!'

'Yeah? And can you laser off my tattoo and, oh, you know, just give me a *face transplant* too before I go?'

Kola was watching them, one hand on the front door. 'Stay here,' he said. 'I'll see what's happening.'

After Seven nodded, he opened the door and stepped out. Sounds echoed up from the stairwell: heavy footsteps; things being smashed; voices shouting; the bark of a dog.

Seven pushed Alba behind the door to hide her from view.

'What's going on?' she whispered.

What she really wanted to ask was, *Is it them?* But the words stuck in her throat, too frightening a thought.

Before Seven could answer, Kola strode back inside and slammed the door shut. Even before he spoke Alba knew what he was going to say by the look on his face, and she tightened her grip on Seven's arm, feeling that if she let go the whole world would slip away from her, spiralling so far out of control she'd never get it back.

'It's the London Guard,' Kola said grimly. 'They're here.'

231

51

SEVEN

His first thought was, *Well, we're done for.*

Actually, his first thought was, *Effing Jesus hell. As if this day could get any worse. Some bastard god up there is really having a field day with my life. If I ever die and somehow make it to heaven, it's payback time.*

His second thought was to run.

But run where? It wasn't like they could just stroll down the stairs and out of the lobby. And unless Alba had a private jet he didn't know about, they couldn't exactly jump off the roof either. Not without one hell of an uncomfortable landing.

'Now would be a good time to tell me you *do* have a private jet,' Seven said, turning to Alba.

She was staring at him with wide eyes, her lips fallen open. 'What?' she croaked.

'Never mind.' Letting out a shaky laugh, he backed away. He felt drunk with fear. 'Well, then. It was nice knowing you both.'

Seven's voice was steady, his grin wide, but inside his heart squeezed painfully.

Why did it all have to happen now, just as he was making friends? Just as he was discovering the secrets of his past? Why couldn't the stupid London Guard have saved him the bother and found him out years ago, way before there was anything worth fighting for in his life?

'Listen to me.'

Kola grabbed Seven roughly, snapping him from his thoughts.

'The lift is out. It'll take the guards a few minutes to find out which floor you're on, and then a few more to come up. You've got a bit of time. Go to the roof,' he instructed. 'There are building works round the north side. Climb down the scaffolding. I'll tell them I haven't seen you all day. Hopefully it'll throw them off, and you can get somewhere safe to lie low. If you can, meet me tomorrow night under Waterloo Bridge. Midnight. I'll update you on what happened.'

The sounds of footsteps and shouting and doors banging open rumbled closer.

Kola's eyes narrowed. 'Go!' he urged. 'Now!'

And before Seven could worry if he was going to be able to make the climb down with his injury, before he could even let himself think about all his skids in his memorium – effing hell, he was going to lose *all* of them, his life's collection, everything he owned – he nodded, grabbing Alba's hand and pulling her towards the door.

The noise of heavy boots drumming up the stairwell hit them as they left the flat. The stairwell was dark. A few stuttering neon lights bit back the shadows. Lights pooled as doors opened, residents coming out to see what all the noise was about.

Seven turned to thank Kola, but the door was already swinging shut behind them.

He stared at its peeling red paint, the broken number plate. It was stupid, but he'd never cared about them until this moment. Until he realised he'd probably never see this place ever again. All he wanted to do now was memorise every crack and curl of chipped wood before they too were stolen from him, like everything else in his life.

'Seven?' Alba whispered, and he heard the fear in her voice. Her hand shook in his (or was it his shaking in hers?). 'We need to go.'

Tearing his eyes away from the door, Seven stumbled towards the stairs, and beside him Alba fell in with his strides as they ran hand in hand up to the roof.

52

ALBA

Cold wind rushed at them as they stumbled out onto the rooftop. Behind them, the metal door swung shut with a heavy clang. It was only early afternoon but the sky was so thick with low-hanging clouds it cast the city in a murky twilight.

'I guess', Alba gasped, 'it's probably not the best time to tell you I'm afraid of heights.'

She was panting from all the stairs they'd just run up. Thank the lord she'd worn flats to church this morning. This whole running-for-your-life business would have been impossible in heels.

Seven let out a strangled laugh. 'Not really, no.' But he squeezed her hand a little as he led her towards the edge of the roof where scaffolding hugged the north wall of the building.

Before them, North unfurled in a rush of buildings, pockets of green, and broad, sweeping streets, tiny cars rolling down them like a toy city. Sheets of tarpaulin and tattered bits of fabric strapped to the scaffolding flapped in the wind. The metal rungs reached up past the edge of the rooftop and ran down its side in a narrow, vertical climb.

'Ladies first,' Seven said with a weak grin.

Alba edged towards the side of the building. There was a wooden walkway she could lower herself down onto, but it was narrow, just wide enough for one person. If she slipped . . .

No, she thought firmly. She would *not* slip.

Heart pounding hard in her ears, she crouched down at the edge of the building. She turned her back on the dizzying view and, slowly, limbs shaking, lowered herself towards the walkway. Gusts whipped up her skirt, ballooning her dress around her thighs (how graceful).

Seven knelt down and grasped her hands to steady her. The wind scattered black strands of hair into his eyes.

'How much are you wishing you hadn't worn a dress this morning?' he said, though behind his smirk Alba could see he was in a lot of pain.

Stretching her legs further, she found the wooden slats with her feet. She swung an arm down and clutched one of the poles rising up out of the scaffolding before, in a clumsy, heart-stopping movement, she dropped.

She landed heavily on the walkway. Still clinging to the pole for dear life, Alba shuffled into a more secure position on the ledge.

Seven swung down after her so quickly the wooden planks bounced beneath her feet as he landed. She let out a cry, falling silent as his hand snapped over her mouth. He pressed her back against the cold wall.

'They're here,' he breathed into her ear, and it was enough to make her blood turn to ice.

From above came the slam of the roof door. Heavy footsteps of the London Guardmen; boots crunching across the concrete.

'Check the whole rooftop!' someone shouted.

Alba's stomach churned.

They'll see us! she thought desperately.

As if reading her thoughts, Seven let go and gestured to the end of the scaffolding where a ladder ran down to the walkway beneath them. As quietly as possible, Alba moved towards the ladder, Seven right behind her. The scaffolding was rickety. It creaked under them, the sound only just masked by the moaning of the wind lifting off the rooftop.

'What about the scaffolding?' came a voice just as she reached the ladder. 'He could've climbed down there.'

Stumbling forward in panic, Alba grabbed the ladder and scrambled down. Seven was right behind her. His face was twisted in pain, his skin pale and beaded with sweat, but he made it down, pushing her back when they were at the bottom under the shade of the walkway above, shielding her from view with his own body just seconds, *seconds* before –

Thud.

Someone dropped down above them onto the scaffolding.

It felt as though everything else went silent.

Alba's heart beat so hard it shook her entire body. She held her breath, terrified the sound of it would give them away. Her fingers fumbled until they found Seven's. The whole world seemed to funnel down to this precarious ledge high up on the side of the building, the places where their skin touched, the feel of his heartbeat in his fingertips, his chest heaving against hers.

The walkway above creaked as the boots shifted.

'Don't see anything.'

'He'd have a hard time getting down here in a hurry.'

237

'His flatmate must be telling the truth. The skid-thief's not here.'

'Well, let's station a few men in the flat in case he comes back.'

The planks gave a final shudder as the person above pulled themselves off the ledge, but it was a long time after the sound of the guards' footsteps faded away that Alba finally let out the breath she'd been holding.

Pressed tight against Seven, she picked up his faint, minty scent. 'Why do you smell like that?' she asked suddenly. 'Like mint.'

Alba felt him take a deep breath.

'I – I can't afford toothpaste or soap.' His voice was so quiet it was almost lost under the wind rushing around them. 'I have a mint plant in the flat. I chew it to clean my mouth and rub it on my skin with water.'

Somehow, this felt like the most real thing Seven had ever said to her. It felt as though he'd taken a little piece of his heart and placed it in her hands.

'Oh,' Alba breathed.

When he pulled away, her body felt suddenly cold without him against it. She pressed her hands into the wall behind her to steady herself as the view of South swooped open in front of her. Dear *lords*, they were high up.

'What do we do now?' she asked.

Seven rubbed the back of his neck. '*You* need to go back to North and try and explain why you look like *this* –' he nodded at her dress, which was dirtied and torn, jewels fallen to the floor around them – 'and I need to get some place safe to lie low for a while.'

'But where?'

He hesitated. 'I think I know someone I can trust.'

* * *

238

Alba returned to the car forty minutes later, out of breath and messy-haired, her dress ripped and dirtied.

'Thank you,' she said to Hans as though nothing at all had happened. 'Those honey madeleines were delicious. I feel much better now.'

She met his eyes in the rear-view mirror. The driver stared at her for a long moment before clicking his eyes on the road and growling the engine into life. The screen dividing the front and back seats turned opaque as the car pulled away from the pavement, Hans's face disappearing from view.

'With the utmost respect, Mistress Alba,' he said, voice sounding from behind the tinted glass, 'you will leave me out of this. Whatever *this* is. I took you straight home. Miss,' he added.

Alba felt suddenly angry at his words. *That's all I am to the servants*, she thought. *Little Mistress Alba.* The girl who swung her mother's moods in the wrong direction. The girl they stepped around as she lay broken on the floor, too worried for their own backs to pay her any attention.

Usually, Alba felt she deserved this treatment. But today, after everything she'd just been through, she felt insulted. It wasn't fair. Hans had no idea what had happened to her. She could have been attacked. Raped. It must look like it, from the way her dress was ripped. And he was too worried about being caught up in whatever she'd gotten herself into to even ask if she was all right.

'Oh, this was all me, Hans,' Alba said quietly, though her voice was hard with suppressed anger. 'I did this all by myself.'

53

SEVEN

Loe and Mika lived on a flooded stretch of Bankside near Blackfriars Bridge. A floating community had established itself on the shallows around the abandoned buildings there on the South side of the river. Hunched on mismatched clusters of inflatable objects, the shacks were tied to each other with ropes, their underbellies dug into the riverbed for support. Wooden walkways ran between them.

Twilight was falling by the time Seven made it to Bankside. Diamonds from the lowering sun flecked the water's surface in gold and silver. He'd been sick twice on the way – not that he'd had much to throw up. His insides had already grabbed and digested the battered sausage Kola had given him earlier, probably worried it would be the last thing they'd see for a while – and his chest hurt in a way that made it feel as though his whole *body* was a torn-up dog-toy.

Still, he managed a weak smile as he stepped across the tatty rope-bridge strung between the balustrade lining the riverside and Loe's floating home, imagining Alba's reaction to the structure before him.

'But it's a *bus*!' Seven could practically hear her cry.

And it was: one of London's old double-decker buses, half-submerged beneath the water, its red shell rising out of the river. Long flecks of paint peeled off to reveal rusted metal beneath. Pigeon-stained tarpaulin stretched over the broken windows. Bunches of tyres and gasbags skirted the edge of the bus, steadying it in the shifting riverbed.

Seven rapped his knuckles on the makeshift door cut into its side. He glanced over his shoulder as he waited, the cap he'd stolen off some sleeping drunk's head pulled low over his face. Even though he couldn't spot anyone watching him, it felt as though there were eyes trained on his body, hidden persons silently waiting for the right time to pounce.

'Seven! Seven! Seven!'

A gleeful voice called out from above. He leant back to see Mika waving from one of the windows in the upper floor, beaming down at him. She went to say something else but was drowned out by angry shouting from inside.

'Oops!' she sang, slapping a hand over her mouth and disappearing.

A moment later the door opened. Without a word, Loe grabbed Seven and dragged him inside. She pushed the door shut behind him and ran to one of the windows.

'What are you doing here!' she hissed, peeling back the edge of the tarpaulin pinned over it and peering out. A slice of dusk light streaked in, cutting through the hazy interior of the bus. 'The whole of the London Guard are after you!'

'One time, Loe,' Seven said with a sigh, clutching his aching chest. 'Just *one* time, could you try hello?'

She swerved round. 'What the hell are you playing at, coming here, Seven? You're gonna lead the London Guard straight to us!'

'I was careful. No one followed me.'

'You'd better hope not.' Loe hesitated, seeming to notice for the first time that he was doubled over in pain. 'What's up with you?'

'I was attacked by a dog.'

Her expression softened the tiniest bit. 'Shit. Why? What happened?'

'Seven! Seven! Seven!'

Just then, Mika came bounding down the stairs in a fuzz of black hair and bright red fabric. She would have barrelled straight into him were it not for Loe, who ran forward and scooped the girl up before she could hurt Seven without knowing.

'Mika, for gods' sake!' Loe's voice was hard. She set her down, cuffing her round the ear. 'I told you not to shout out his name. The whole of Bankside will know he's here the way you're going.'

Mika played with the hem of her dress. 'Sorry, Loe.'

'Now go upstairs and stay out of our way.'

'But –'

'*Mika!*'

Sticking her tongue out at Seven, the girl gave him a little wave before dashing back up the stairs.

Loe pointed to the back of the bus. 'Sit down, then, you

idiot – before you faint and throw up on my floor.'

Seven followed her, collapsing gratefully onto a seat. Loe had made a sort of living room at the back of the bus, with a cluster of the original seats arranged into a big L-shape. He leant back, running a hand through his tangled hair.

'Thanks, Loe,' he murmured.

'I haven't done anything yet.'

'Exactly.'

They sat for a while in silence. A tinny patter picked up as it began to rain outside, merging with the sound of the water slapping against the sides of the bus. The shadows deepened, the rain growing heavier. Thick clouds clotted out the light. Loe got up, moving about to light the lanterns strung from the handrails. The bus filled with their amber glow.

It would have been homely, comforting even, if Seven's body didn't feel as though it had been torn apart and stitched badly back together by one very drunk surgeon and a rusty pair of old knitting needles (which was almost what *had* happened).

'So,' Loe said finally. She perched on the edge of a seat, hugging her knees to her chest. 'It's really hit home that Carpenter's dead.'

The flash of a memory, like pain: Carpenter's eyes rolling back, blood gushing from his mouth and the black hole in his neck.

Seven swallowed. 'Yeah.'

'And our jobs are gone.'

'Yeah.'

'And we're wanted by the London Guard.'

'Yeah.'

'And it looks like you've got no home any more 'cause they found out where you were staying. Am I right?'

'Loe,' he groaned, 'you really are just one big shining ball of joy.'

Scowling, she flicked her eyes away. Her shoulder tensed as she lifted an arm to run through her messy crop of hair. She drew a deep breath.

'What am I gonna do?' she said abruptly, speaking in a voice he'd never heard from her before. It was small. Defeated.

'I've got Mika to feed,' Loe went on. 'She might be tiny but damn, does she eat like an overweight North banker after pay day.' She gave a strangled laugh.

Seven knew exactly why she was attempting humour: she was trying to hide just how scared she was.

He'd been doing it for years.

'You'll find a way,' he said.

Loe didn't turn round. The rain drummed harder on the metal skin of the bus. When she finally spoke, there was a hard edge to her voice.

'That's what I'm afraid of.'

54

ALBA

When Alba got home and hurried up to her bedroom, she found Dolly waiting for her.

She was sitting on the edge of the bed, hands folded in her lap. Dolly didn't seem surprised to see Alba looking the way she did. She just tilted her head and said in a quiet voice, 'Your mother called three hours ago to say you were coming home from lunch early.'

'Traffic,' Alba said, closing the door behind her.

Dolly watched her. 'Alba,' she asked gently, 'what are you hiding from me?'

Alba bit her lip. 'Nothing . . .'

'I know you, and this isn't like you. What's the matter?'

Everything! Alba wanted to say. *I'm being forced to marry some pig of a man and become North's leading lady, and my friend from South might get captured any moment now by the London Guard and be executed right in front of my eyes.*

Instead, all she managed in a tiny, broken voice, was, 'Dolly . . . I'm scared.'

At once, Dolly stood up and pulled her into a tight hug. Her arms encircled Alba in the same warm, safe way they had done time and time again since she was young.

'I don't know what to do!' Alba sobbed suddenly. Tears traced wet lines down her cheeks. Her voice spiralled higher and higher, and she felt herself unwinding with each word. 'My whole life has been turned upside down!'

Dolly stroked her hair. 'Tell me what's happened.'

Alba pulled away, her handmaid's arms still around her waist. Blinking back tears, she saw the kindness, the fierceness in Dolly's eyes, and knew then it was time to tell the truth.

'There's . . . there's this boy,' she said.

Dolly's eyes widened, but it was only for a moment.

'He's from South,' Alba went on. 'He's my friend, and he's hurt, and he's wanted by the London Guard.' Her voice shook. 'He's – he's in a lot of trouble.'

Dolly was still, watching her with her wide, soft blue eyes. It felt like hours before she eventually spoke, but whatever Alba had been expecting to hear, whatever words she'd thought might come out, it was certainly not the one simple question that Dolly asked. A question that both broke Alba's heart and mended it again all at once.

'How can I help?'

55

SEVEN

'Who the eff are *you*?'

'I'm a friend of Seven's –'

'Seven doesn't have any friends.'

'Then what are *you*?'

'His fairy-fucking-godmother. Now get lost, before I call the London Guard.'

'You're not going to do that.'

'Oh, yeah?'

'Well, since *you're* wanted for memory-thieving too, Loe, I highly doubt you're going to want London Guardmen coming to your home.'

A pause so tense it could wedge a door open.

'*How in the hell d'you know my name?*'

'As I said, Loe, I'm a friend of Seven's.'

At the sound of voices, Seven stirred blurrily, rubbing his eyes. He pushed himself up in bed. Or rather, he tried to, but pain spiked through his chest and he fell back, cursing.

He was lying on the thin mattress of Loe and Mika's bed on the upper deck at the back of the bus. Over the steady rush of rain outside, the two raised female voices floated up from below. Seven peered around in the darkness. By the lantern-light spilling up the stairs from the lower deck he made out a silhouette with a huge frizz of bushy hair peering down over the top of the stairs.

'Mika?' Seven called.

She looked round, pressing a finger to her lips. 'Shhh!'

The voices picked up again.

'I don't know who the hell you are or how you know my name, but if you don't leave by the time I've counted to ten, I'm gonna break your neck.'

'Please calm down, Loe. I'm here to *help* Seven.'

'One!'

'His wound needs looking at –'

'Two!'

'Could you just tell him his girlfriend sent me?'

'Thr— wait. What did you just say?'

'His girlfriend, Alba.'

'His *girlfriend*?'

Seven slapped a hand to his forehead, letting out a low groan. *Oh, for crying out loud.* Pushing back the blanket covering him, he staggered to the stairs. He winced as he went; each step felt like fire was slicing through his torso.

What the hell was Alba doing sending someone to him? he thought angrily. And why in the eff had she told them she was his *girlfriend*?

'Loe, it's fine,' Seven shouted, starting down the stairs, his next words turning into a shout as he lost his balance and fell.

Someone grabbed him just before his face made contact with the floor. Or rather, *he* grabbed someone, and judging by the sound of their annoyed *oof* as he landed on them, it was Loe.

'Seven!' she hissed, scrambling out from under him.

'Here, let me help you.'

A woman he had never seen before stepped forward. Lantern-light lit her pretty face, all slender cheekbones and large round eyes. She was wearing a long raincoat buttoned up to her neck. Its hood had fallen back to reveal two buns of purple hair twisted on the top of her head.

Smiling, she reached out towards him, but he shrank back.

'Alba said you didn't like people helping you,' she said, a sad look flitting across her eyes.

'Alba doesn't know eff all,' he snapped.

The woman smiled. 'She also said you were rude.'

'That *effing* –'

'And that you like to swear.'

Seven glared. 'Well, that's pretty rich, coming from her. She was banging on my door not long ago, and the language coming from that girl's mouth . . .'

Eyes crinkling, the woman let out a laugh. It was a bright, easy sound, like the pealing of bells. Somehow it made Seven feel as though he could trust her.

'I can't imagine who she learnt that language from.' She tilted her head, expression turning serious. 'Now, let's get you back to bed and I'll see what I can do. Alba told me about your injury. You've lost a lot of blood, and it's possible the wound is infected. And you'll need a tetanus shot.'

Seven grimaced. 'Sounds like fun. But you still haven't said who you are.'

'I'm Dolly,' the woman said. 'Alba's handmaid.'

Then, without waiting for a reply, she leant down and tucked her shoulder under Seven's, helping him up from the floor.

'Oh, just come right in and make yourself at home,' grumbled Loe as they started past her up the stairs.

For a while, Dolly worked in silence, cleaning Seven's wound and injecting him with various medicines. Even though it hurt, Seven didn't cry out or swear even once. He sat topless on the mattress on the upper deck, Dolly beside him. Her fingers worked softly over his skin. From downstairs, the murmur of Loe's and Mika's voices sounded over the metallic patter of the rain.

'You do this a lot, then?' Seven said eventually. 'Come to the rescue of all the poor South boys Alba's made friends with?'

Dolly was smoothing some sort of clear gel over his wound. She glanced up, raising her eyebrows. 'What do *you* think?' Finished with the gel, she pulled a pad of white fabric from her medikit and started taping it over his wound. 'The stitches your friend made are very good,' she said as she worked. 'You're very lucky he was around. If you'd lost any more blood, you might not have made it. Especially in your condition.'

Seven made a scoffing noise. 'My condition? What's that meant to mean?'

'There's nothing to be ashamed of, Seven.'

'Who said I was?'

'I used to live outside London,' Dolly said kindly. 'In the unregulated land to the South. I know what it's like to be hungry.'

Seven watched her warily as she unrolled a length of gauze, pulling him forward so she could wind it round his chest.

'You lived outside the city?' he asked.

Dolly nodded. 'My family owns a small farm in the Sussex countryside. It was hard, without the established trade from the cities, and in the winter almost everything would freeze over.' She paused. 'As I said, I know what it's like to be hungry. What it's like to struggle every day to survive.'

'How did you end up in London?'

'The same reason everyone else comes to the city. In search of a better life, I suppose.'

'And you found it with the *White* family?' Seven said, snorting.

She shot him a hard look. 'There are worse places to be.' She finished bandaging his chest, then began returning the equipment she'd used into the box. 'The Whites have done a lot for me.'

'Like they've done for Alba?' Seven said sarcastically.

He didn't know why he was suddenly so angry. He glared at Dolly, something hot and red rushing through his veins.

The medikit shut with a loud metallic snap. Dolly picked it up, standing. Her pretty face had hardened.

'Seven,' she began in a cool, stern voice, all pretence of niceness gone. 'I don't know what Alba's told you of her life in North, but believe it or not, her parents *do* love her. They might have a funny way of showing it sometimes, and gods know I don't agree with half the things they do, but they do it because they think it's what's best for her. Can you say the same?'

Seven felt as though he'd been slapped.

'I know *I* can,' Dolly continued. 'Which is why I'm asking

251

you to leave Alba alone.' Her eyes flashed. 'I fully understand her need to rebel and, trust me, I'm going to do everything I can to help her out of this arranged marriage. To help her achieve her dreams. But in order to do that, you need to stay away. Whatever the two of you are doing with TMK – it's too dangerous. She can't be involved.'

'You know something about it, don't you?' he said through gritted teeth. He took a shaky breath. 'TMK. You *know* something.'

Dolly looked away. 'Not really. But Alba's father often has business meetings at the house. Over the years, there've been snatches of conversation . . . From the little I've overheard, I know that it's not something *any* of us should be getting involved with.' A kinder tone touched her voice as she turned back to him, eyes softening. 'Alba explained to me about your past, Seven. If you want to continue looking into TMK, then I understand. I cannot stop you. But I *am* responsible for Alba, and so I'm asking you, if you care at all about her – leave Alba out of this.'

She fell silent. Outside, the rain seemed to roar louder, as though the raindrops drumming on the shell of the bus were trying to wash away her words. Seven wished they could be erased from his mind so easily.

Despite himself, Alba had become important to him. He'd let her in. They were friends now. He couldn't imagine never seeing her again. Just earlier that day, he'd held her hand; they'd run from the London Guard together.

How could he just let her go after all that?

But the worst part of it was, Seven knew, even though he hated to admit it, that Dolly was right.

He looked away. 'Fine. I won't see her again.'

'Thank you,' Dolly breathed, sounding relieved. She paused. 'For what it's worth, I can see why Alba is drawn to you.' She leant down and kissed him on the cheek before setting something down beside him. 'Alba wanted me to give you this,' she said, before turning and disappearing down the stairs.

Seven glanced down. It was a small package, wrapped in embossed gold paper and tied with a ribbon. He didn't pick it up. He wasn't going to see Alba again, after all. What was the point? He wouldn't ever get the chance to say thank you.

Letting out an angry growl, Seven grabbed the package and threw it across the bus. A horrible, sick feeling was swinging through his body. Because he saw suddenly what an idiot he'd been.

What exactly did he think would happen between him and Alba? That they'd sneak out at night to see each other for the rest of their lives? That if their friendship was strong enough, somehow nothing else mattered?

Well, they *couldn't* sneak out at night to see each other for the rest of their lives, and their friendship *wasn't* strong enough that nothing else mattered. Seven would never be welcome in Alba's home, or her life, or her family. Let alone her *heart*. His stomach twisted at this last thought. How stupid had he been to hope that the two of them would be the exception?

Some lines could never be crossed. Some things were always going to be divided.

North and South.

Alba and Seven.

What he wanted; and what he got.

56

ALBA

She had fallen asleep by the time Dolly got back to the house, exhaustion finally overtaking her worries about Seven. The next thing she knew she was being shaken awake. Dolly's bright voice sounded from above her.

'Come on, Alba. It's Monday. You need to get ready for school.'

Alba groaned, rubbing her eyes. She pushed back the tangle of hair that had fallen across her face. It was still half dark outside, the sun taking longer to rise in the mornings as winter came creeping closer. Pale amber light washed her bedroom. The sound of birdsong filtered through the closed windows. It was so peaceful . . .

'Wait.'

Alba sat bolt upright as she remembered where Dolly had been that night.

'What happened? Is Seven all right?'

Dolly shook her head. 'We don't have time for that now.

We need to get you ready for school.'

'Of *course* we have time! He was bitten by a dog, Dolly, and chased by the London Guard –'

'Alba! That's *enough*.'

Dolly had never once raised her voice at her. Alba tensed, staring at her handmaid, who was watching her with a hard, unreadable expression in her eyes. Her heart thrummed in her chest. Everything seemed to go quiet, as though a giant hand had curled down around the room.

She licked her lips. 'What happened, Dolly?'

With a heavy sigh, Dolly stepped back. She smoothed a hand down her uniform. 'Seven is well,' she answered. 'You don't need to worry about him. But I don't think you'll be seeing him again.'

Alba blinked. 'What do you mean?'

'I told him . . . I told him to stay away from you.'

It felt as though she'd been punched straight in the gut. Alba sagged forward, mouth falling open. She let out a low hiss of air.

'You told him *what*?'

Dolly shook her head. 'I won't let you see him again,' she said, the usual soft blue of her eyes lit with a hard-edged fierceness. 'It's not safe! Aside from the fact you're crossing into South at night and spending time with a boy you hardly know – all of which is risky enough – the two of you are looking into things you shouldn't be. I don't know exactly what The Memory Keepers is, Alba, or why your father and the London Guard are involved, but I've heard enough to not *want* to know. Anything they're trying so hard to keep quiet is not something to be prying into. Seven is welcome to continue investigating it if he wants, but I'm not going to let you get involved too.'

Alba was shaking. Uncurling her fists – she hadn't even noticed she'd been gripping the bedsheets – she placed her hands flat on either side of her. She was trying to steady herself, because this all felt wrong; *surely* this was wrong, a horrible nightmare she would wake from any second.

'The Memory Keepers,' she breathed.

Dolly's mouth tightened. 'Yes. That's what TMK stands for. And that's plenty more than you need to know.' She reached out an arm. 'Come on. You're going to be late for school.'

But Alba shrank back before she could touch her.

'I expected it from them,' she said quietly. 'My parents. They've always told me what I can and can't do. They've never let me make my own choices. But you, Dolly . . .' Her voice broke. 'I never expected it from you.'

Dolly's face twisted. 'Please, Alba. I'm doing this to *help* you.'

'That's what they always say,' Alba whispered, her voice breaking, and she got up and pushed past Dolly to the bathroom before the first of the tears blurring her eyes could fall.

That night, Alba waited until the house was silent before creeping out of her room and down the servants' staircase. She didn't care what Dolly thought. Seven needed her. He'd lost his home, all his memories, what little safety he'd had . . . She couldn't abandon him now.

That's not what friends did.

A cold, night-time wind on the sloping lawns of the estate met her as she stepped out into the grounds. Her hair twisted and curled in long trails behind her. She buttoned up her coat and pulled her fur cowl tighter round her neck.

It never failed to surprise Alba how quickly the weather changed, even though it had always been this way. There used to be four seasons, the climate in the British Isles steady as it shifted gradually between them. Now, there were just two: summer and winter. The changes were quick and sudden, harshly contrasting. London's high society celebrated their arrivals with the Summer- and Winter-turn Balls. (*Any chance for an extravagant party*, Alba thought wryly.)

Head lowered against the growling wind, Alba made her way to the part of the fence where she and Seven crossed. As she neared, she spotted a finger of light moving slowly through the darkness. Quickly, she darted behind a cluster of nearby bushes. When she was sure she hadn't been seen she edged out, peering over the top of the rustling leaves.

It was one of the Hyde Park Estate guards patrolling the perimeter of the fence.

'Oh, sod it,' she mumbled.

Alba could try and climb the railings before the guard came back. Without Seven's help, however, it would take ages to haul herself over, and she'd rather not be found stuck up the top of the fence, her bottom yet again in someone's face.

But the only other option she had was to go home. Alba didn't know how much longer Seven would be staying with his friend Loe. He'd said he thought he could trust her, but that she was very grumpy and easily annoyed. That wasn't a combination that gave Alba much faith; offensive things came out of Seven's mouth practically every time he opened it. What if he so annoyed Loe that she threw him out? If she didn't go to him tonight, she might never find him again.

'Right,' Alba muttered, nodding to herself. 'Option number one it is, and god help the poor guard who finds my ginormous bottom waving around in the air.'

But just as she stepped out from behind the bushes, readying herself to run, someone moved out of the darkness.

'Alba?' came a familiar voice. 'What are you doing?'

She turned in horror to see a tall figure stepping towards her. It was her father.

57

SEVEN

He was waiting under Waterloo Bridge, back pressed to one of the granite stone arches of its underside. The night was dark and cold. The rumble of lorries passing overhead echoed in the low space. Water whispered as it rushed past the shingly bank. On the other side of the Thames, lights from the Embankment – busy even at this time of night – spilled across the river in melted patterns of yellow and gold.

Seven wasn't alone under the bridge. There were homeless clustered here for shelter, sleeping in cardboard boxes and trawling through washed-up litter. The spot was also popular with the Tube Gangs and the drug dealers they did business with. They knew they were safe to meet here because the London Guard left them alone in exchange for special prices from the dealers.

A few gang members were out tonight, crawled up from their maze-like nest of tunnels beneath the city. They had taken over the disused Tube network years ago after floods rendered most of the tunnels useless, and it was easier for the London Guard to control traffic across North and South via the roads and docks anyway. Seven knew each gang had its own tattoo, just like the skid-thief crews did. One of the gangs, Takeshi's Bakerloo Boys, branded red skulls into their arms, while the Piccadilly Pythons went for winding snakes round their ankles.

Seven watched the gang members and dealers do their trades, their shifting bodies silver-edged in the shadowy moonlight. Lights flickered at the ends of their cigarettes.

He tugged his cap down lower over his face. The gangs were notoriously ruthless, even by South's standards. If they recognised him from the Net broadcasts . . .

'Seven.'

He jumped at the voice. Spinning round, he attempted a karate kick in the direction of the person who'd spoken. But the shadowy figure just moved his leg away easily with the back of one hand and stepped closer.

'It's me,' Kola said, his face coming into view.

Seven's cheeks flushed. 'I knew that. I was just – just easing out some cramp.'

Kola didn't look as though he was listening. His face was tight. The whites of his eyes shone like cuts of silver in the darkness.

'Look,' he said, glancing over his shoulder, 'I can't stay long. The London Guard have got someone tailing me. I think I managed to lose them in the alleys on the way here, but I can't be sure.'

Heart thumping, Seven looked around wildly. He started to speak but Kola interrupted him.

'Seven . . . they took everything.'

He froze.

'The hidden room at the back of the house,' Kola went on, an apologetic tone to his voice. 'They broke into it, found all the memories. There was nothing I could do. They took everything,' he said again, then paused. 'Well, not *quite* everything.'

'What d'you mean?'

Seven's voice was strangled. It felt as though he were very small, looking in on himself from far away.

Kola dug into his pocket. He lifted Seven's hand and pressed something small and metal into his palm: a DSC.

'They missed one,' Seven breathed, closing his fingers round it, carefully, delicately, as though it were a tiny bird (which in a way it was. After all, skids were what gave him wings).

Kola looked round warily. 'I'm sorry, man. I have to go before they find me. Will you be all right?'

'What sorta question is that?'

Seven forced a smile, filling his gaze with as much bravado and confidence as he could muster, though inside he was breaking.

One skid.

That was all he had left.

One tiny effing skid.

Seven cocked his head, cheeks hurting from forcing a grin. 'Course I'll be all right.'

Kola's stare was piercing. Seven knew he could see through his lie.

'Remember,' Kola said quietly after a long pause, 'in the end, all we can do is polish our own patch of the world to make it shine as brightly as possible.' Then he turned and walked briskly away.

Seven waited until he disappeared out of sight before walking out under the bridge into a patch of moonlight. His feet slipped on the pebbly shore. Taking a deep breath to try and calm his skittering heart, he opened his palm.

04.10.2144, H.M., The Manor, Grovewood Close

He stared at the letters scrawled across the label for what felt like an eternity.

'Oh,' he breathed eventually.

Biting back a cry, he pulled off his cap and threw it to the ground. Crumpled to his knees. His fingers squeezed round the DSC until its hard edges dug painfully into his palm.

The skid wasn't even one Seven could remember stealing, let alone surfing. That was what hurt so bad. Now all he had left of his collection, his years of thieving, and a life he'd never be able to get back, was a skid he couldn't even remember stealing in the first place.

He didn't move for a long time. The twanging ache in his chest where the dog had bitten him was rising up again, Alba's handmaid's painkillers finally wearing off. Beyond the shore, the engines of boats and river-taxis purred as they sped across the water. Spray sprinkled his skin.

'OK,' Seven said, raking in a heavy breath. 'One more go.'

He opened his palm, holding the DSC up to the light. He didn't really know what he was expecting; he knew he wouldn't remember anything about the skid. But maybe if he looked again he might find something that jogged his memory. His eyes scanned the label one more time –

And he sat bolt upright, something snapping through him like a tightened band.

Seven's heartbeat raced, a thread of excitement working up through his chest. Because he saw now that the reason he couldn't remember stealing the skid was because he *didn't* steal it.

He couldn't have stolen it, because the date on the label was tomorrow.

58

ALBA

'F-Father,' she stammered. 'I . . . I didn't expect –'

'What in God's name are you doing?' he asked again, striding over and clutching her shoulder. He pulled her towards him, looking over her head at the darkness. 'It's not safe to be out this late on your own, Alba. Even in the Estate. I'm taking you back to the house.'

Not wanting to give him any reason to question her more, Alba let him steer her back across the wind-rushed grounds. His arm was heavy across her shoulder. Once, that weight used to feel safe. It was like a reassurance, a promise that no matter how old she grew, her father would always be there for her, bigger and stronger and ready to protect her from the dangers of the world.

Now, it felt like *he* was the danger.

'I couldn't sleep,' Alba lied. 'I just needed some air. I thought it was safe if I stayed in the Estate. I'm sorry. I shouldn't have.'

Their footsteps were lost under the whistling of the wind

through the grass. All around them, leaves rustled. Shadows pooled deep under the starlight.

Her father sighed. 'No, my dear, you shouldn't have. But I understand. I haven't been sleeping very well lately either.'

'Because of work?'

'Yes.'

From his curt answer, she knew he was warning her not to ask anything more.

They continued on in silence through the dark grounds. Alba felt their secrets walking alongside them, watching from where they hid in the shadows. There were so many questions she wanted to ask her father: what was The Memory Keepers, why was he involved, and why, *why* did he not seem to care that people were dying because of it?

More than anything, she wanted to ask so he could tell her he *did* care. So he could give her an explanation that made him her father again, instead of this horrible stranger he seemed to have become.

'What do you think of Christian's son, Thierry?' her father asked abruptly as they reached the house.

They approached from the front, and gravel crunched underfoot as they stepped onto the drive. A light clicked on above the entrance. Alba squinted as they were flooded in white, her father pulling her to a stop just before the doors. She saw he was still wearing his prosecutor's robes; another late night at work.

'Oh.' She bit her lip and looked away. 'He's all right, I suppose.'

'You don't like him?'

'No,' Alba said. 'I just . . . I don't understand *why*.'

Her father touched her chin, tugging her face up. His eyes softened from their usual cool, steady gaze. 'This is the best path for you, my dear. Your mother and I wouldn't have arranged it if we thought otherwise. We know you will be happy and safe at Thierry's side. Your future will be taken care of. You won't ever have to want for anything.'

(For a flash of a second, Seven's face came to Alba then; his crooked laugh, those grey slanting eyes.

The word *want* danced through her like a current.)

Her father sighed again. 'I know I haven't always been the best father,' he went on, and his voice was softer than she'd ever heard it, golden and warm, full of regret, hidden emotions that curled from his words and hung in the night around them like tiny, glittering fireflies. 'It's been a struggle, often, for me to know how to be with you. How to be a good father for you. But I want you to know that I've tried. I'm *trying*. You are my dear, dear daughter, and I only want the best for you.'

Breathless, Alba stared into her father's eyes, his hand still cupped round her chin.

It was all she'd ever wanted him to say to her.

Her heart soared.

It was all she *wanted*.

And then thoughts of TMK came screaming back. Of her father's mocking laughter over the death of memory-thieves at the raid. Of the coldness, the detachedness in his voice as he talked about Candidates bleeding out and lives being ruined. Of how he never comforted Alba after her mother's outbursts, never told his wife to stop, even though he must have known it was going on. And if he didn't, perhaps that was even worse.

She thought of all the secrets over the years that had built their way between them like a wall, dark and towering and reaching impossibly far into the sky, and her heart plummeted because she knew then that his words had come too late, because even though she believed them, it didn't matter any more.

Alba loved her father, and he loved her. But the things they thought and felt and believed in and wanted were so completely different they might as well have been strangers.

'I know, Father,' she said, then rose up on her tiptoes to kiss him on the cheek.

He gave her a small, tight smile. 'Good. Now back to bed, my dear. Perhaps now you'll sleep better.'

59

SEVEN

The next morning Loe was in an even worse mood than usual. She, Seven and Mika were eating a breakfast of fresh mitten-crabs, which had been caught in a net attached to the underside of the bus. It was just past dawn. Birds cawed noisily as they circled over the water outside, soft pink light from the rising sun filtering through the windows.

Seven wasn't big on seafood, but he was grateful to be eating anything at all. He picked the smelly white flesh out with his fingers, trying to avoid eye contact with Loe, who was glowering at him from the seat opposite.

'So, then, *Seven.*'

He looked up reluctantly. He'd been waiting for this. Yesterday he'd been completely out of it, a combination of exhaustion and Alba's handmaid's medication sedating him to *malnourished zombie* level. Then he'd rushed out for his meeting with Kola. Now he didn't have anywhere to hide from Loe's piercing stare.

She tossed her fringe out of her eyes and forced a smile; a much more frightening expression than her usual scowl. 'That woman the other night. Brolly, or Welly –'

'Dolly.'

'Yes, her. Who was she again?'

Seven hadn't told Loe about Alba when he'd arrived a couple of days ago. He'd just recounted the story of what had happened since the raid at Borough Market without any mention of Alba, her father's memory or TMK. Not only did he not trust her with that information, but after what Mika had said on the night of the raid about Loe . . . about her *fancying* him, he wasn't sure she'd take too kindly to knowing there was a beautiful girl from North in the picture too.

Not that it mattered. Seven's thoughts strayed to Alba's pretty, soft face. The way she'd looked in the bath – *naked* – the cluster of freckles spread across her back like fallen stars. How every time she smiled at him, something ached a little inside. He felt pathetic. Of all the girls he could have fallen for he went for the one he'd never see again.

The one he'd never had a chance with in the first place.

'That woman was from North, Seven,' Loe said into his silence. 'Why would someone from North want anything to do with you? And who's Elbow –'

'*Alba.*'

'Whatever. That woman said she was your *girlfriend*.'

'Why do you care?' Seven snapped.

Loe's cheeks reddened. 'I don't. It's just, I find it hard to believe any girl from North would bother with the likes of *you*.'

He glared at her, noticing Mika, who was crouched in her

seat, staring between the two of them with wide, eager eyes, enjoying this a little *too* much.

'Well, *this* one bothered,' he said, thrusting his head high.

Seven hadn't planned on saying that. He wasn't even going to acknowledge anything about Alba. What was the point? She wasn't a part of his life any more. But he just couldn't stand Loe thinking he wasn't worthy of her (he thought that enough himself).

Loe got to her feet, limbs uncurling like a cat's. 'And how long d'you think that'll last?' she asked scathingly. 'You're probably just an experiment. The dangerous boy from South she can tell all her friends about. How *cool* they'll think she is. How *brave*. Then once she realises you don't actually have anything real to offer her, you'll be thrown aside quicker than you can say *stuck-up North bitch –*'

Whack!

Seven's arm moved of its own accord. He stared in horror at his raised hand, its palm now emptied of the crab shell he'd been holding; the crab shell that he'd just flung through the air, which had smacked Loe straight in the face.

Mika's eyes were so wide now they could have been seen from the moon. 'Oooooh!' she breathed gleefully.

Seven gulped.

Loe's face drained to a cold, expressionless mask. 'I'd chuck you out for that,' she hissed, 'but I know you don't have anywhere else to go. It's not like your precious North girlfriend and her family will welcome you with open arms into *their* house, is it?' Throwing one final look of contempt his way, she strode past to the front of the bus. 'Come on, Mika,' she called over her shoulder. 'Let's go see what we can scrounge up from the rubbish fields at Greenwich. At least there'll be less of a stink than there is in here with *him* around.'

'That was so cool!' Mika whispered as she edged past Seven.

He didn't return her smile. When they were gone, he climbed up the stairs to the upper deck, muttering angrily under his breath. Dolly had been clear enough the other night about him being no good for Alba. He didn't need bloody Loe telling him too.

As Seven got to the top of the stairs, he caught sight of a gold package lying on the floor under the front seat. His breath hitched in his throat. Alba's present.

He crouched down to pick it up. The embossed pattern swirled across the wrapping paper was velvety under his fingertips. He turned it over in his hands. There was something hard-edged inside.

'Well, it'd be rude not to open it,' he mumbled to himself, and before he could change his mind, Seven tore the package open.

Something small and plastic fell out. His heart skipped a beat as he saw what it was: a toothbrush.

60

ALBA

Dolly and Alba walked in silence through Hyde Park Estate. It was a clear morning, bright and cold, though clouds were banking on the horizon. Their feet crunched on the gravel path. Pulled from their trees by the growing wind, golden-brown leaves curled through the air around them, a whirl of winter colours.

'What lessons do you have at school today, then?'

Alba glanced sideways at Dolly, who was watching her with that same tentative look she'd had ever since their argument the night she'd been to visit Seven. Scowling, Alba burrowed deeper into the warmth of her fur cowl that was slung round her neck over her school coat and uniform, and continued on in silence. Their breath billowed out in front of them in soft white clouds.

'You can't ignore me forever, you know,' Dolly pressed.

Want to bet? Alba thought.

'I know you're not happy with what I did,' Dolly went on,

'but I hope you'll realise it was the best thing to do.'

No, I won't.

'Now you can focus on studying to get the grades you need to go to university.'

What's the point? I'm not going, am I?

'Maybe your parents will reconsider your marriage to Thierry if they see how well you're doing at school.'

My parents reconsider something? Hah.

'Soon you'll forget all about Seven –'

'No, I won't!'

Alba's shout rolled through the sleepy morning silence of the grounds, shocking Dolly into stillness. Alba hadn't meant to speak, but she couldn't carry on listening to her handmaid's pointless words.

'He was my friend,' Alba said. 'The only one I've ever had besides you. And you drove him away.'

Dolly's face tightened. 'It wasn't safe for you –'

'That's all everyone seems to care about! Keeping me safe. Well, what's the point of being safe when you're not *free*?'

Dolly opened her mouth to say something, but then her gaze was snagged away from Alba. Surprise flashed in her eyes.

'Seven,' she breathed.

Alba rolled her eyes. 'Oh, what *now*?'

'Seven,' Dolly said again, shaking her head. 'He's here.'

Alba spun around. She let out a gasp as she recognised the tall, gangly figure stumbling across the grounds towards them. He was wearing the same maroon jumper and faded black jeans she'd last seen him in, the wind lifting his messy hair into his eyes. A cap was pulled down low over his head. The long shadows cast by the dawn sun half hid him as he slunk from tree to tree.

As Alba watched him approach, Seven lifted his head and his gaze caught hers, and just like that her heart was racing.

'What on earth . . .?' she breathed.

Dolly strode to meet him. She grabbed his arm and yanked him over to a hedge of blackthorns to one side of the path.

'What are you doing here?' she demanded. 'I told you not to come here again.'

Seven's lips twisted in a grin as he shrugged her off. 'Yeah, well, I've always had a tough time following orders.' He looked past Dolly to Alba, who was frozen to the spot, his eyes travelling down her blue coat and the silk of her school-issue tights. He cocked an eyebrow. 'Hey, Princess. Looking good.'

Alba flushed. Though she wrapped her arms tightly around herself, she couldn't help but smile, a warm rush of pleasure shooting through her. She moved closer, but Dolly held out an arm.

'Seven, this is stupidly dangerous, being here in broad daylight. Anyone could see you.'

He grimaced. 'Trust me, I know. Look, I heard what you said, but something's happened and I need Alba's help.'

Something about the way he said it, so matter of factly, made Alba's stomach spin.

'I told you, Seven. She can't help you any more.'

'Yes, I can,' Alba said quickly. She knew whatever had happened was serious if it had made Seven cross into North in the daytime. She frowned at him. 'What's happened?'

Digging in his trouser pocket, Seven pulled something out.

She recognised it as one of the DSCs he stored his memories on. She reached out and took it, her eyes scanning the label.

'It was the only skid left after the London Guard raided my memorium,' Seven said, voice urgent. 'Kola gave it to me last night. And I didn't think anything of it at first, but then I saw the date and thought –'

'That it's a message,' Alba finished in a whisper.

'What's a message?' Dolly asked.

Alba showed her the label, then turned back to Seven. 'Maybe there's a spy in the London Guard,' she said breathlessly. 'Someone working for the people who are trying to uncover The Memory Keepers' secrets!'

Seven gaped at her. 'The Memory *what*?'

'Oh.' Alba glanced sideways at Dolly. 'That's what TMK stands for, Seven. The Memory Keepers. And this memory . . . someone planted it at your flat somehow.' She gasped. '*Kola* could even be in on it! The date and location on the label are telling us to meet them today!'

He nodded. 'That's what I thought. So I came to see if you would come with me.'

'Absolutely not,' Dolly said sternly before Alba could answer. 'This is far too dangerous. Your reckless behaviour has gone on long enough. It's not safe, the two of you probing into The Memory Keepers. Have you even considered that this message could be a trap?'

Alba felt a flicker of nerves at her words. It *did* all seem rather too convenient. But she pushed the thought away. What other choice did they have but to trust the person who'd sent them the message if they wanted to find out more about TMK?

'Dolly,' she said urgently, 'please. Seven's here now. We can help him.' She bit her lip, voice lowering. 'This isn't some game, or because we're curious. This is about finding out the truth about Seven's life – and mine. I'm fed up of all these secrets. We have to know what's really going on.'

Dolly hesitated. Though she still looked worried, she paused, seeming to consider Alba's words. After a while she said with a sigh, 'All right. We'll go.'

Alba threw her arms round her neck. 'Thank you!' she cried.

'Don't thank me just yet,' Dolly said sternly, untangling herself from Alba. 'Because after today, that's it. No more night-time meet-ups or trips into South. I mean it, Alba, Seven.' Her eyes flashed hard. 'After this, the two of you will be saying goodbye for good and going your separate ways.'

61

SEVEN

They snuck back into the house through the servants' entrance and crossed the empty dormitories to the handmaids' private rooms. Luckily the servants were busy with their morning chores and they didn't run into anyone.

Dolly's room was small but beautifully finished. Draped silk curtains hung either side of the windows. The bed was covered in patterned sheets and blankets. A fluffy fur rug lay across bleached wooden floorboards and strings of lights encased in rose-shaped fabric petals were strung down the wall behind the bed.

'Wait here a minute,' Dolly said after letting them in and shutting the curtains to stop anyone looking through. 'I'll call the school and tell them you're too ill to attend today, Alba. And I need to find Seven something to wear before we go.' A touch of kindness entered her voice as she looked over at him. 'I'll get some food from the kitchen as well. You must be hungry.'

As if answering her, his stomach let out a growl.

Her eyes softened. 'That's a yes, then.' Dolly moved to the door. When she looked back, the tiniest hint of colour pinked her cheeks. 'I hope I don't need to say this, but I expect you both to still be fully clothed by the time I get back.'

'*Dolly!*'

Letting out a little laugh at Alba's horrified expression, she went out and shut the door.

Now they were alone, the room fell into a silence tenser than Seven had ever felt before. There was something electric in the air.

He sat down on the edge of the bed. Rubbing the back of his neck, he looked everywhere but at Alba. Why was he only realising now how pretty she looked today, with her hair tumbling round her shoulders in dark red waves, and the silk of her school-dress clinging to her body?

'I'm glad you came,' Alba said, avoiding his eyes.

Seven coughed. 'Yeah, well, we've discovered all of this TMK stuff together so far . . .' He took a deep breath, then let it out in a puff. 'I – I got your present.'

Her eyes widened. 'I hope you weren't offended,' she said quickly. 'It's just, you know, you told me you didn't have one, so –'

'It's the nicest thing anyone's ever done for me,' Seven interrupted her quietly.

Smiling, Alba moved closer. She perched on the edge of the bed, so close to him he could feel the soft heat unfurling from her, smell the floral scent of her skin.

'That girl – the one you were staying with.' Her eyes grazed his before she blushed and looked away, twisting a strand of hair

278

round her fingers. 'Were you two, um . . . more than friends?'

'Loe and me?' Seven snorted. 'No way! Even saying we're *friends* is weird. We're just tied together by being skid-thieves, you know?'

'What *was* it like?' Alba asked after a pause. 'Living like that, I mean.'

He shrugged. 'Pretty crap. Though the stealing part isn't half bad. It's fun. Sneaking into houses in North, getting to see into their lives . . . it's just a different world.'

'I'm not sure I *want* to be a part of that world any more.'

Alba's voice was a whisper now, skimming across his skin. She moved closer. Her fingertips – pink and polished – were just a breath away from his, and he wondered if she was waiting for him to touch them, wrap his hand round hers.

She looked down. 'Do you think – do you think we could . . .?'

Heart racing, Seven dipped his head towards her. 'What?' he croaked.

Her eyes flicked up to meet his. It was like a shock of electricity, or fire, or like a thousand stars had suddenly fallen and were burning in her eyes.

Their faces moved closer.

Effing hell, she was beautiful, Seven thought. And she smelled like summer and autumn all at once. The way she was looking at him . . . it felt like a beginning, like the start of something unimaginable.

Biting his lip, he lifted a trembling hand towards her cheek –

The door opened.

'I managed to get one of the male servant's spare uniforms and brought you some – oh.'

They jumped apart as Dolly walked into the room carrying a tray loaded with rolls of bread, jams and butter, and a steaming mug of tea. Clothes were tucked under the crook of one arm.

'*Oh*,' she repeated, eyes narrowing.

Alba sprang up. 'Thank you!' she said quickly, brushing down her clothes and rushing to the door. 'Um, I'll just – I'll just go wait in my room now. Come for me when you're ready to go.'

She was blushing a deep, beautiful purple. Seven could feel himself blushing too (though he was pretty sure he wasn't doing it nearly as elegantly). He rubbed the back of his neck, avoiding Dolly's accusatory glare.

When no one said anything, Alba sang, 'Well, bye!' Glancing once more at Seven with that look that made his insides feel like they were being kicked in the best possible way, she backed out of the door and pulled it shut behind her.

Dolly walked over and handed Seven the tray of food. 'I thought you were hungry,' she said coolly.

'Er, yeah. I am.'

'Yes,' she said under her breath as she turned away. 'Hungry for *something*, anyway.'

62

ALBA

Outside Dolly's room, she stopped for breath, clutching a hand to her chest where her heart was beating so hard she worried it would burst through her and fly up and away.

Something had almost happened just then.

The thing –

The *kissing* thing.

Alba didn't know if she was ready. Actually, no, she was quite sure she wasn't ready (how on earth did you kiss someone? Whose lips moved, and when? And – she shuddered – what in god's name did you do with your tongue?). But what she did know was that every time Seven looked at her, something just felt right inside her, like a piece of a puzzle was settling into place.

But that was surely just because they were friends ... wasn't it?

She hurried off to her room, thoughts spinning with her heart.

It didn't help that the only other friend she had to compare her feelings with was Dolly, and even though she loved her very much, Alba knew for certain she didn't want to kiss *her*.

63

SEVEN

He felt completely out of place in the suit. His usually scruffy hair was combed back, a peaked cap pressed low over his forehead. He wore the servants' uniform of white shirt and trousers, both impeccably clean, the White family crest stitched to the breast pocket. There was another crest emblazoned on his long black overcoat.

All of it scratched. And the shirt buttoned up too high. And the blazer was too tight on his shoulders. And it was *all white* for crying out loud; how in the world was he not gonna get it dirty? But because it was keeping him safe, Seven forced himself to bear it.

They'd taken a cab from the house to Holborn Hill. It was a posh residential area near the Glass District, the city's business centre. Modern buildings stood tall on either side of the steep, tree-lined streets.

'We're almost there,' Dolly said as they walked down the sloping road.

Seven looked away quickly every time someone walked past, trying to hide his face. His whole body felt tense and alert, waiting for the second someone would stop him and he'd hear a shout, then the wail of the London Guard sirens.

'It's all right,' Alba said beside him. She seemed to sense his nerves. Before they'd left, she'd changed out of her school clothes into a knitted grey jumper and maroon tights under a thick coat. 'No one's going to notice who you are in that uniform.'

'Well, I guess it's cheaper than plastic surgery,' he said, and she laughed, making him smile.

'Here it is.'

Dolly led them round the corner to a long street at the bottom of the hill. A quiet road ran between the backs of tall buildings. A rust-bitten street-sign read: *GROVEWOOD CLOSE*.

'Last chance to turn back,' Dolly said, in a voice that said, *And I wish you would*.

Alba rolled back her shoulders. Giving Dolly a defiant look, she stalked past, starting down the road. Dolly raised her eyebrows at Seven.

'It's best to let her get her own way,' he muttered, shrugging apologetically. 'That girl's a terror when she's angry.' And he hurried off after Alba, who was already disappearing round a curve in the road.

As he followed her, a house came into view. It was large, set back deep in unkempt grounds, tangles of ivy crawling over worn bricks and cracked window-frames. A set of iron gates hung open as though waiting for them.

'The Manor,' said Alba as Seven stopped beside her outside the gates.

Dolly approached, frowning. 'I don't like this. Something doesn't feel right.'

Even though he got that feeling too, Seven ignored her. They were here now; he didn't want to turn back when they'd come so close. He led them through the gates.

The drive stopped short of the house. They stepped off onto the gravel path, stones crunching underfoot. The air was still. The business of the city felt a million miles away; it was like stepping into a bubble, a pocket of strange silence. Ahead, the house was dark. Curtains were drawn across most of the windows and the ones that weren't covered looked into shadowy, unlit rooms.

Chills pricked across Seven's skin, but he wasn't actually scared until they reached the front doors.

They were open.

Alba froze beside him. They stared at the peeling wood of the doors, swung slightly ajar.

'Something's wrong,' she whispered.

'I know.'

Seven edged closer. Shadows hung in the grand hallway beyond. He pushed open the doors slowly and they gave way with a creak. The back of his neck prickled as he stepped into the hall, treading lightly on the worn wooden floors. Years of skid-thieving had taught him enough to know that his instincts were telling him to get the hell out, and fast.

The house was silent. Shadows moved as Alba and Dolly entered behind him, the pale wash of morning sunlight spilling across the floor. Seven was just about to turn to them when –

A sound.

Thudding, like someone thumping on wood. Then, so distant and quiet he thought he might have imagined it: a cry.

'Someone's here,' Alba breathed. Her eyes were wide and bright in the musky darkness. 'Do you think it's the person on the memory's label? H.M.?'

Dolly moved up behind them. 'Let's go,' she said urgently. 'Now.'

Thud.

Quickly, Seven started towards the stairs at the end of the hall. The sound was coming from somewhere upstairs.

'Seven!'

He ignored Dolly's shout. The stairs sighed under his weight. Each creak sent his heart racing faster. Upstairs, the house was a maze of tall, narrow corridors and closed doors. He spun round, wondering which way to go.

'Help,' came a weak voice.

'I'm coming!' Seven shouted.

He darted off in the direction of the cry, down the hallway to his right, which ran along the outer wall of the house. The windows here were all covered. Muffled golden light filtered in beneath moth-bitten curtains. At the end of the corridor, a figure was slumped against the wall. Seven could see a dark patch of shadow blooming across the ground around them, staining the floorboards.

His stomach dropped.

Blood.

Seven bolted to the end of the hallway. Crouching, he helped the person sit up. It was a man, old and greying, with a tuft of thin hair and thick-rimmed glasses and blood, blood everywhere on his plaid suit and mottled skin.

Seven propped up the man's head, wiping the blood from his lips. The man's milky eyes met his. They fell in and out of focus. His head lolled, and Seven had to grip his neck and shoulders to keep him upright.

'Is it you?' the man asked in a horrible, rasping voice. He coughed, blood splattering Seven's white uniform.

'Who?' he asked.

'Candidate,' croaked the man. 'Candidate Seven.'

64

ALBA

She had never seen that much blood. Even from the end of the hallway, it looked like far too much to be outside of a person's body. Surely he had none left on the *inside*? Her mind swayed as she approached, her footsteps light in the hall. She crouched down beside Seven, who was kneeling in front of the injured man, holding him upright.

The man's eyes were closed. His face was so pale it was as though he was wearing a white mask. Sweat smeared his forehead and temples.

'Candidate,' Seven said, eyes fixed on the man's face. 'You called me Candidate Seven. How d'you know who I am?'

The man's eyes opened. 'I was there – there when you . . .' He dissolved into racking coughs.

Alba's insides were ice. The man was dying. She'd never seen someone die before. It was awful, more horrible than she could have imagined. She didn't realise how you'd actually be able to *see* it happening, see the life draining from a person's eyes.

'Get aside!'

Dolly had reached them. She pushed Seven away with a sweep of her arm and knelt before the man, feeling at his neck for a pulse.

'Who shot you?' she asked.

Alba felt sick. Her heart was spinning up in her throat, dizzyingly fast. The man didn't say anything, but she knew the answer anyway.

The London Guard.

Dolly stood. 'There must be something here I can use.' As she started back down the corridor, she called over her shoulder, 'Use your coat, Seven – for his blood. Alba, keep him talking.'

'Sir?' Alba edged forward. She touched the man's cheek as Seven slid off his coat and wrapped it round him. 'Are you H.M.? Did you send Seven that memory for him to find you?'

The man's eyes flicked to her. 'Dr Harold . . . Harold Merriweather,' he croaked.

The name sounded familiar, but Alba couldn't place it.

Merriweather shifted. A flutter of energy seemed to come to him and his voice grew stronger, his gaze focused again on Seven. 'The memory – Nihail planted it when the London Guard went to your flat. You are the Candidate.'

'*A* Candidate,' corrected Seven.

'No.' The man shook as he coughed heavily. Beads of blood welled at the corners of his lips. '*The* Candidate. The one we freed.'

Alba's eyes widened. She glanced at Seven, but he was still staring at Merriweather.

'We know,' he said. 'I found a memory about it. But why? Why was *I* taken?'

A deep breath rattled through Merriweather's lungs. 'I was Chief Science Co-ordinator. Some of us disagreed with what they were doing. You were chosen to be freed. We tried once, but – but we failed.'

Alba gasped. She reached for Seven's arm. 'The incident involving you as a baby! My father was talking about it to that doctor in his memory.' She gasped again, remembering now. 'Dr Merriweather! That was you!'

Merriweather's eyes fluttered. 'We succeeded the second time. But our member, the one who was looking after you . . . she was found. Murdered. We lost you. Thought you might have also been . . .'

His eyes shut, then snapped open suddenly. They swivelled round to meet Alba. She thought she saw a darkness in them, a shadow approaching.

'Seven,' she whispered. 'I don't think we have much time.'

He nodded. 'Why did you bring me here?' he asked, leaning closer to Merriweather. 'What was so important?'

The man's weak gaze shifted to Seven. His lungs wheezed with each breath. Alba saw him sinking, saw his eyes dimming, heard the emptiness in his voice as he said, so quietly it was just the faintest whisper, 'You, Candidate Seven. You.'

And then he slumped back, falling still.

Tears blurred Alba's vision. Her heart hammered in her throat so hard she could barely breathe. Merriweather's eyes were still open; they stared off to one side, empty and cold.

'No!' she cried suddenly.

Seven went to wrap an arm round her but Alba jerked away. Shaking her head furiously she pushed up off the floor, legs shaking. Her breaths came heavy and hard. She took a step back, but before she could move anywhere a hand closed over her mouth.

So quickly she didn't even have time to think about escaping, arms were locking round her body. Alba saw Seven's eyes widen, saw him stagger to his feet, and then two men had grabbed him too, holding him off the ground as he strained against their grip. From the corner of her eyes, she saw a woman come forward with Dolly, a gun pointed to her temple.

Alba felt hot breath on her ear as the man holding her dipped his head close to hers.

'You're coming with us,' he growled.

There was a sharp bite in the side of her neck, and then everything fell away into blackness.

65

SEVEN

He woke slowly, disorientated, his mind heavy and blurred. For a moment he thought he was back at Loe and Mika's, numbed from Alba's handmaid's medication.

And then everything came back to him in a flash.

Letting out a shout, he jerked bolt upright.

'Calm down, man. The effects of the sedative have still got a few hours before they fully wear off.'

Seven knew that voice. He twisted round and saw Kola sitting against the wall opposite. His long legs were stretched out before him. A newspaper lay open across his knees. He put it aside, lips drawing into a thin, humourless smile.

Seven was so surprised he couldn't even speak. He slumped back on the pillows and blankets under him. Looking round, he saw that almost the entire floor of the large room was covered in them. It seemed to be some sort of sleeping quarters. With a flush of relief, he spotted Alba and Dolly lying asleep nearby. Neither looked hurt. They were curled together, Dolly's arm draped protectively over Alba.

Seven turned back to Kola. 'Where are we?' he asked. He rubbed his forehead; his brain felt foggy.

The room looked as though it were part of a tunnel. Low concrete walls curved in an arch overhead, faded posters tacked across them. To one side was a platform set a foot or so higher than the trenched part they were in. A yellow strip ran along its edge. At both ends of the room sheets of corrugated metal and haphazardly nailed wooden planks blocked it off from the rest of the tunnel. Lanterns were strung from the ceiling and dotted around, lighting the space in a soft, flickering glow.

Seven realised where they were before Kola answered.

'The Underground,' they said at the same time.

Kola nodded. 'This is the Bakerloo Boys' turf.'

'*Takeshi's* Bakerloo Boys?'

Seven's shout echoed off the curved walls. He struggled to his feet, swaying dizzyingly, but forced himself to stay standing, which was hard. The ground felt as though it was tipping beneath his feet.

'Have you gone mad?' he cried. 'Takeshi is a bloody maniac! All the Tube Gang boys are.'

Kola's expression was calm. 'We can trust Takeshi, Seven. He's helping us. Now please sit down before you faint.'

Seven made a strangled sound. Shaking his head in disbelief, he dropped back to the floor. 'I don't have an effing clue what's going on,' he muttered.

'You will know soon enough, I promise,' Kola said calmly. 'But for now you should rest. Let the sedative wear off. Don't worry – you're safe here. When you wake next, I'll explain everything.'

Seven scowled. 'Can't wait.'

Closing his eyes, he lay back on the sea of pillows. In just seconds, the sedative washed back over him and he fell into a restless sleep, filled with dreams of flowers dripping blood and Alba dancing away from him into darkness, her laughter chased by the wind as he ran to catch up with her, always a few moments too slow.

Voices woke him a few hours later.

'Harold's dead?'

'Yes.'

'Fuck. And so close to the finish.'

'I know. But the London Guard have long suspected him. And after the break-in at the lab, it was only a matter of time before they confirmed his involvement.'

A pause. A heavy sigh.

'So. *This* is Candidate Seven.'

'Yes.'

'He doesn't look like much.'

'What does it matter what he looks like, Nihail?'

'Well, if he's going to be the face of this whole charade –'

'His face will do just fine.'

Another pause.

'He really has no idea?'

'No.'

'Fuck, Kola. You could have at least given him some hint all those years you lived with him.'

'I wasn't to tell him anything, remember? I was just there to keep an eye on him. Make sure he was safe. We had to let him discover the truth about TMK for himself. It was only fair. We had – we *have* – to let him decide for himself whether he wants to be a part of this.'

Rubbing his eyes, Seven propped himself up on one elbow. 'Part of what exactly, Kola?' he asked loudly.

The two men looked round at his voice.

'He speaks,' said the man Kola had called Nihail, grinning.

Nihail was heavy set, with thick shoulders and arms, and a square jaw covered in stubble. His skin was a deep mahogany brown. Though he didn't have the red jacket, he wore the grey jumpsuit of the London Guard, and Seven remembered Dr Merriweather mentioning someone called Nihail who worked for them. He'd been the one who'd planted the skid at his flat.

Kola stood. 'Seven, this is Nihail. He works for the London Guard, but he's on our side.'

Seven scowled. 'As if that makes me feel better.'

Nihail's smile widened. 'You know, I like him more when he's conscious.' Sighing, he pushed off the floor, brushing down his clothes. 'Anyway, work calls. Good luck with Takeshi. If he doesn't rip Candidate Seven's head off, I'll know he's a keeper.' He pulled himself up onto the platform and disappeared out through a tunnel set into the wall.

'Seven? Kola? What's going on?'

Seven turned at the sound of Alba's voice.

She and Dolly were sitting up a few metres away in a mess of tangled blankets and pillows. Alba's hair was mussed from sleep. It fell in a bushy auburn sweep down past her shoulders, loose curls sticking to her flushed cheeks. She caught Seven's eye and gave him a small smile.

His stomach tightened. He wondered: would he feel that way every time she smiled at him, no matter where they were and what else was happening? Even in the middle of a hurricane, even as the world was collapsing around them, would her smile make him feel as though he wanted to vault across whatever stood between them and bundle her up in his arms?

Seven clambered to his feet and hurried over. 'You OK?' he asked, crouching beside Alba.

She nodded.

'It's nice to see you again, Alba,' Kola said, who had also come over.

Frowning, she turned to him, her expression icy. She opened her mouth to speak but Dolly interrupted.

'Do you always drug and kidnap people when you want to speak to them?'

Kola's jaw tensed. 'I am sorry for that. But we needed to get the three of you away from there. It wasn't safe.' His eyes settled on Seven. 'You know, of course, who attacked Harold Merriweather?'

'The London Guard.'

He nodded. 'Then you know what they would have done if they'd found you all there, too. Especially you, Seven. And it is of the utmost importance we keep you from them.' He sat down in front of them. 'Let me explain why.'

Alba shifted closer to Seven. Her hand slid easily into his, and he squeezed it gratefully.

This is it, he thought. *This is the moment.*

I'm finally gonna know the truth.

He wasn't sure he was ready. He was only just starting to like who he was becoming, the boy Alba was making him feel like. What if the news he was about to discover broke all of that?

'For over thirty years,' Kola began into the uneasy silence, 'the London Guard have been keeping a secret. They created something called The Memory Keepers. The Memory Keepers – or TMK, as it is often referred to – was established with the Lord Minister at the time, Elson Haverstock. Through a rigorous selection process they recruited a team of scientists, headed by Harold Merriweather. The scientists were offered the highest social privileges and salaries – you saw the house Harold lived in. But in return they had to agree to the strictest of contracts. They understood they were to keep quiet about TMK. That this wasn't a job they could simply quit. Because what TMK was doing broke hundreds of state and national laws.'

Seven listened breathlessly.

'They were experimenting on babies,' Kola said. 'Stolen babies, taken from hospitals and adoption wards. From these experiments, TMK found that by attaching an implanted device they call the Controller to a set of nerves in the cerebral cortex of the babies' brains, those children would grow to be able to . . . manipulate memories.'

There was a gasp from someone. Dolly? Alba? But Seven just felt blank, dizzyingly empty.

'Those babies whose brains accept the Controller implant,' Kola continued, 'grow to be able to physically alter memory-space during surfing. Their thoughts shape memories in the nerve-cells influenced by the Controller and imprint them upon the original memory's recording.'

'No,' Dolly whispered, eyes widening. 'I'd only heard enough to know they were experimenting on stolen babies. That was bad enough. I didn't know it was for *this*.'

Kola was still focused on Seven. 'Have you ever surfed a memory which seemed empty?' he asked. 'A vast black space, devoid of anything? Maybe you could hear voices. Sense something more. But you couldn't ever make any of it out?'

It hit him like a wall.

'R.L.S.,' Seven breathed.

His entire body thrummed as he remembered clearly the skid he'd surfed all those weeks ago, the one from *Fear, Desperation and General Wetting-your-pants Kind of Stuff*. He remembered how he'd felt after surfing it: let down by the vast empty blackness, wordless voices buzzing out of the dark.

'That happens when a memory has been completely wiped,' Kola explained. 'It is another use of the Controller implant. When the London Guard would rather erase an entire recording, the Candidates just distort the memory-space beyond recognition. But more often than not, Candidates are used to alter specific details in memories, falsifying them.'

Alba shook her head. 'But – but *why*?'

Kola turned to her, his eyes dark. 'What does your father do, Alba?'

'He's the city's Lead Prosecutor.'

'And what does he use as evidence in court?'

The air seemed to suck from the room.

Seven's eyes widened, realising what Kola was saying.

'No,' he said. Anger hummed beneath his words. 'They don't. *No*.'

'I'm afraid it's true.' Kola's expression was grave. 'Alastair

White, the London Guard, the Lord Minister – they force the Candidates, their Memory Keepers, to manipulate memories so that they can free criminals they don't want to punish, and find guilty those they *do*.'

66

ALBA

For one long moment, nobody spoke. Then –

'Jesus effing Christ.'

'No.'

'*No.*'

Seven scrambled to his feet.

'Seven, please –'

'Shut it, Kola! I don't give one flying fuck what you have to say. You knew what I could do. What I *am*!'

'We couldn't force you into anything! You needed to find out for yourself.'

'This was my right to know!'

'And now you do.'

'You *effing* –'

'Seven, please calm down.' Dolly stood quickly, laying a hand on his arm. She turned to Kola. 'Why are you telling us this now?' she asked. 'What do you need from Seven?'

'His help,' Kola said.

'Oh, *fuck* that –'

'Seven!'

'What?' he roared, rounding on Dolly. 'You're not my mum! You're not even *Alba's* mum! What do you care what I do? No one ever gave a shit about me, and now all of a sudden I'm wanted?'

Alba watched from the floor, horrified. Seven looked wild and terrifying. His eyes were a storm. She flinched, edging away, scared of him for the first time since that initial meeting back in her parents' memorium, what felt like another lifetime ago. But even then he'd grinned and joked and just been so hopelessly awkward she couldn't feel intimidated by him.

Seven took a step back, his arms shaking. 'Well, you know what? I've managed this long on my own. I don't need any of you.'

Alba scrambled to her feet. 'Seven,' she whispered, voice breaking. She reached for his hand, but he cringed away the moment her fingers brushed his skin.

'I said I don't need *any* of you!'

His shout echoed off the curved ceiling. The words cut Alba, physically *cut* her – how else could she explain the searing pain in her heart, the tears welling in her eyes? – and when Seven spun round and clambered over the ledge of the platform, darting down one of the off-shoot tunnels, she didn't chase him but let him go, knowing that she'd never feel so horrible, so low, as she did in that moment.

Dolly was right, Alba realised with a sinking feeling in her gut. *We should have left all of this alone. We never should have tried to find out more.*

'Let him go,' Dolly said, curling an arm round her shoulder. 'That was a lot to find out. He just needs some time. Are *you* all right?' she added gently.

Alba scowled. She swiped away the tears tracing her cheeks. 'Oh, just fine. I'm only the daughter of a *murderer*.'

Hadn't she always known that, really? Her father executed people all the time. Whether they were guilty or not guilty, what difference did it make? Why should he have the power to take away *anyone's* life?

'I'll talk to Seven,' Kola said, and Alba was glad to see he at least had the decency to look guilty. 'Once the shock has worn off, perhaps he'll be willing to listen to what we are asking of him –'

'Kola!'

The three of them looked up as a sudden voice rang out from the tunnel Seven had run down. A man was standing there, his hands gripping Seven's shoulders as he pushed him into the room. Seven tried to throw him off, but the man kneed him in the back, making him double over.

'Takeshi's ready,' the man called. He laughed, kicking Seven as he struggled again. 'And man, is he impatient to open his little gift.'

67

SEVEN

Takeshi's room was at the end of one of the old Tube tunnels. It looked like some kind of derelict palace. Polished gold vases and worn paintings adorned every surface, set against the grimy backdrop of the tunnel, with its tangles of exposed wires running along the curved walls and dirty floor half hidden by rugs and silk sheets. Gemstone beads dripped from the ceiling. Lantern-light flickered over everything, warped music crackling from a gramophone in the corner. And there, sprawled in a velvet-backed throne on a platform at the back of the room, a crown of what looked like rat-bones set atop his black hair –

Myomato Takeshi himself.

'Welcome,' Takeshi drawled as the man holding Seven shoved him forward. 'Have my Bakerloo Boys been treating you well?'

There were ten or so gang members in the room, slouched against the walls or squatting on the floor. They laughed coldly at his words.

Kola stepped up beside Seven. 'Takeshi. Please remember

our deal. Seven has no obligation to do anything for you.'

Takeshi's lazy grin widened. His slanted eyes were small and glittering. The tips of his tousled black hair brushed the almond-coloured skin of his shoulders. He wore a sleeveless white shirt, unbuttoned down the front, and tight black trousers. He sat up out of his slouch, propping his head on his fist, exposing a red skull branded into one arm.

'But you *will* help me,' he said silkily, 'won't you, Candidate Seven?'

Seven glowered at him. 'What's the magic word?'

It was out before he could stop it.

For one horrible moment, Takeshi just stared. Then he tipped back his head and roared with laughter. The boys joined in, their raucous yells bouncing off the curved walls.

'I like him!' Takeshi announced. 'He's a fighter – I can tell. Which is good, my boys. After all, we've got a fight with North on our hands.'

'A fight with North?'

Seven's heart sank as Alba spoke. For eff's sake! Didn't she realise this was the last place to draw attention to herself? He could practically feel the heat rolling off the boys as their eyes devoured her. Thank gods she was wearing a coat.

Takeshi turned to her, eyes twinkling. 'What a beautiful girl!' He glanced at Kola. 'You brought me a second gift. You are too kind.'

Seven made a growling sound and moved forward, curling his hands into fists. 'You even *think* about touching her –'

Two of the boys grabbed him before he could get any closer. Knuckles cracked into his jaw, then a boot came crushing down on the small of his back, forcing him to his knees.

'Boys, boys.' Takeshi waved his hands apologetically. 'They're a little overeager . . . though I can't say I blame them.'

He slid off the throne and strode over to Alba. Seven caught the scent of his breath – cigarettes and alcohol – as he leant in closer to her face. He traced two fingers across her cheeks.

Alba stiffened, but she didn't look away. Seven could have kissed her for that (he could have kissed her for a million reasons. He wished he had, now. Was it too late?).

'Such a beauty,' Takeshi purred. 'You are wasted on North, my dear.'

'Let go of her.'

This time it was Dolly who spoke. Seven turned just in time to see one of the gang members slap a hand over her mouth, pushing her to the floor.

'Shut it, bitch,' the boy snarled.

Grinning lazily, Takeshi moved over to Dolly. He crouched down. His hand slipped under her chin, a thumb brushing her lips. 'Another beauty,' he murmured.

Seven strained against the boys holding him down. 'Leave. Them. *Alone.*'

Takeshi's eyes crinkled in amusement. 'And why should I want to do that?'

'Because I'll help you,' Seven said quickly. 'I'll do what you want.'

Laughing, Takeshi pushed Dolly back and straightened. 'I knew you would.' He threw an arm out. 'Boys! Get the machine ready.'

From the far corner of the room, two of the boys pulled

a velvet throw off a large shape hunkered there to reveal a memory-machine. Seven recognised it from its logo as a generation six Apple iMemory. Its sleek frame shone silver-white in the dim light of the chamber.

'You want me to surf a skid?' he asked, frowning.

'It's what you do, isn't it? Alter memories?' Takeshi's grin glittered. 'Well, I have one I'd like you to change.'

Kola took a step forward. 'Hang on a minute. Seven hasn't done that yet. He doesn't know how –'

'I'm sure he can figure it out,' Takeshi interjected coolly. He cocked his head. 'Can't you, *Candidate* Seven?'

Seven thought of how he felt during surfing. As though he could move beyond the instincts that were pushing him in a certain direction. As though he could feel the memory-air, shape it under his palms. He'd thought that was just how everyone felt when they surfed, but he realised now he'd been wrong. It was because he was a Memory Keeper.

'I can do it,' Seven said.

Even though he'd never tried it before, he knew he had to give it ago. He didn't have a choice if he wanted to keep Alba and Dolly safe.

68

ALBA

The boys fixed Seven into the memory-machine, yanking off his servant's cap and pushing his head into the indent in the curved back of the seat, strapping him in place. When they turned the machine on, blue lights glowed in its metal curves. It hummed softly under the scratchy music coming from the gramophone.

Takeshi crouched down in front of Seven. 'You'll spot a familiar face in this skid. I want you to replace it with this one instead.'

Alba edged forward to try to see the picture he had pulled out of his trouser pocket to show Seven, but one of the gang members slung an arm across her shoulders.

'You can sit with me, gorgeous,' he sneered.

He pulled her across the room and pushed her down roughly onto the floor. Alba caught Dolly's eyes from where she was kneeling on the ground at the back of the room. One of the boys still had his hand over her mouth. She gave a small, reassuring nod, though her eyes were tense with fear.

Alba's heart broke. This was all her fault.

'Don't be shy.' The boy huddled so close she could smell his cigarette breath. He stroked her arm. 'We're all friends here.'

Some of the other boys jeered.

'Quiet.'

Takeshi's command silenced the room. He held out the picture again to Seven. 'This is Aro Black, leader of the Jubilee Junkers.'

'Jubilee *Jackasses*, more like,' grunted the boy holding Alba, sniggering.

'He has wronged me one too many times,' Takeshi continued smoothly. 'I thought about having him killed or captured to torture. But this way, with a skid as evidence, Aro will be publicly humiliated. His broadcasted execution will destroy his gang's reputation. Do you understand what I'm asking you?'

Alba saw Seven swallow.

'I do.'

Takeshi straightened. 'Wonderful!' he said, his smile widening. 'You're a fast learner, Candidate Seven. I bet you've already realised I'll be surfing the memory afterwards to check you have followed my instructions.'

Seven's glower was answer enough.

'Fantastic!' Takeshi spun round, throwing his arms wide. 'Boys – juice him up!'

As the machine's hum grew louder, some of the gang members punching in instructions on its touch-screen, Kola crouched down beside Alba. His shoulders were tight with tension.

'Do you think he can do it?' he asked quietly.

307

Without hesitation, Alba nodded. The truth was, she had more faith in Seven than anyone else, apart from Dolly of course. He'd survived this long without anyone's help. He'd found the memory about TMK, broken into the houses of the most prominent families in North without ever getting caught (apart from the time they'd met, at least).

Alba had so much faith in Seven, she believed he could move the *planets* if he wanted it enough.

'Good,' Kola said. 'Because if he doesn't, I don't think any of us are getting out of here alive.'

69

SEVEN

He opened his eyes into darkness. There were noises all around him. Gruff voices: low, male, urgent. People shuffling. The sound of something being dragged. Wherever he was, it was hot. He could smell sweat and the acrid stench of alcohol. His own body felt softened by drink, and though the instincts of the memory told him to sway he pushed against them, standing straight, forcing himself to stay alert.

This is what I can do, Seven thought, and felt an illicit thrill of power.

It was soon replaced with disgust. He didn't want this so-called gift. He didn't want something the London Guard and North snobs like Alba's father and the Lord Minister had given him. No, not given him; *made* him. They'd forced this on his body when he was too young to object.

'Here'll do.'

'Turn the light on.'

'Yeah, I wanna see the bitch. You said she's all that?'

'Oh, she's all that.'

More shuffling, then a light clicking on overhead.

Seven squinted. They were in a bare, dirty tunnel. From the thick cluster of wires striping the ceiling and the curved walls, it looked similar to the abandoned underground tracks he'd just come from. Rats scurried away into the darkness to either side where the neon glow didn't reach.

Then Seven noticed the writhing bundle on the floor before him, and his heart clenched.

It was a beautiful young woman. Beautiful even with the dark blush of a bruise touching her right cheek and the filthy rag gagging her mouth. Plastic cords tied her hands and ankles, blood clotting around them. Her simple dress and jacket were dirtied and torn.

She twisted against her binds, veins popping in her neck from the strain. Icy blonde hair fell across her face, and her eyes – a cool, clear blue – swivelled round and met Seven's, and it was as though the ground opened beneath him.

He knew this woman.

The other men were still talking.

'Where'd you find her?'

'By the docks. Looked fresh in from one of the immigrant ships.'

'She's foreign?'

'Oh, yeah. Czech or something. Eastern European. You should hear her accent. It *purrs*.'

'I'll make her purr all right.'

Their throaty laughs made Seven's skin crawl. The men looked like Tube Gang members. They were all grease-stained trousers, bare chests, crude tattoos. He couldn't make out their faces though; they were fuzzy and blurred. The man whose skid Seven was in obviously hadn't been paying that much attention to anything other than the woman on the floor.

The woman who was –

Oxana White.

Alba's mother was younger but there was no mistaking her features, the striking angles of her face. For the first time, he thought he saw Alba in her. This was Oxana before she'd turned cold and hard.

This was her in the *process* of turning cold and hard.

The men around him were jeering and murmuring.

'Who goes first?'

'I found her. You know the rules.'

Seven felt physically ill. His body was sweating, his mind a feverish mess. He'd felt like this a few times before in skids when his own emotions contrasted too strongly with the person whose memory it was. Right now he was fighting the man's feelings with every inch of energy he had.

Oxana's eyes met his a second time. Seven could tell she was terrified – her body was shaking – but he saw a fierceness in her too, a defiance that told him she'd be damned if she wasn't going to give them one hell of a fight.

Just then, footsteps echoed through the tunnel. A cool, shining laugh rang out.

'What's this, boys? You've brought me a gift?'

Seven turned, and there he was.

Myomato Takeshi.

Takeshi was younger but he looked the same: shoulder-length

wavy black hair; glittering eyes; lazy smile. Sweat glistened on the bare muscles of his chest. He tucked one hand into the pocket of his trousers and cocked his head, waiting for an explanation.

One of the men coughed. 'Didn't think she was your type.'

'Is that so?' Takeshi's grin widened. He moved towards Oxana. Crouching down, he brushed the hair back from her face.

She snarled.

He tipped back his head, letting out a laugh. 'She's a fighter. She's most *definitely* my type.'

And as Takeshi started to unbuckle his trousers, Seven strained against the skid, pushing back into its honeyed memory-air with everything he had, clawing, fighting, screaming to get out.

The memory began to darken. Figures elongated, shadows unfurling. Lights popped in front of his eyes. The voices of the men in the tunnel distorted, ringing echoes in his ears. Still he pushed away. He felt as if he were about to explode from the effort, but he didn't stop until there was a sudden flash, a falling feeling –

Seven blinked, Takeshi's room swinging into view.

'Have fun?'

The gang leader sloped off his throne, opening his arms and smiling.

Seven spat at him. 'You *bastard*.'

Some of the boys in the room jumped up but Takeshi waved a hand lazily in their direction, shaking his head. 'Now, now, boys. I'm sure Candidate Seven is just disorientated from his surf.'

312

Straining against the straps of the memory-machine, Seven scanned the room, seeing with relief that Alba and Dolly were unhurt. They were sitting against one of the walls, hands linked.

Alba's eyes caught his. They widened hopefully.

He broke her gaze. *She doesn't have one effing clue what I just saw*, he thought.

'Well?' Takeshi moved closer, his voice lowering to a cold purr. 'Is it done?'

'You fucking bastard,' Seven growled again.

Takeshi cocked his head. 'I'm sorry. You seem to have me confused with Aro Black. Wasn't *he* the one doing the deed?' His voice took on a cutting tone, lips pulling into a smirk. 'The first, I mean. There were *many* after him. And there will be even more with your friends if you don't do what I ask. Do you understand what I'm saying, Candidate Seven?'

Seven forced himself not to look across the room at Alba and Dolly. He couldn't let them see his fear.

Takeshi smiled. 'Good. Now get back in there and do what I said.'

70

ALBA

They were blindfolded and led through the underground tunnels by a group of Takeshi's boys. At one point they rode one of the abandoned trains; the carriage shook as it squealed round corners far too fast. Then the men forced them out of the train and up a flight of steep stairs, and moments later Alba felt cool air on her face. The wind smelled fresh. Raindrops sprinkled her skin. They were pushed into the back seat of a car, and it was only after they'd been driving ten minutes that Kola undid their blindfolds.

'Where are we going?' Dolly asked immediately.

Alba was in the middle seat, Dolly to her right. Their shoulders bumped as the car turned a sharp corner.

'Kensington High Street. Here.' Kola handed Dolly a tablet. 'You should be able to call a cab to take you home from there.'

As she talked into the tablet, Alba turned to her other side and leant in close to Seven. 'Hey,' she said gently. 'Are you all right?'

He was staring out of the car window at the blur of busy streets going by, his cap pulled low over his face. She touched the back of his hand.

He flinched away. 'I'm just great.'

'What was in that memory that's bothering you so much?'

'Look, just drop it, OK?'

Alba drew back. She had no idea what Takeshi had put Seven through with that memory, but it seemed to have really shaken him. Even as Takeshi was clapping him on the back and pushing his servant's cap on (back to front), telling everyone what a wonderful job Candidate Seven had done before ordering their release, Seven had looked utterly miserable.

He'd looked as though he'd failed, Alba thought. But at what, she didn't know.

'We'll be there soon,' Kola said. He was sitting in a seat facing them. He shifted, folding his hands in his lap. 'If you have questions, now is the time to ask.'

Alba glanced at Seven. He didn't seem to be listening. He was still gazing out of the window with glazed eyes that made her chest feel cold and strange. She turned back to Kola.

'You're not doing this all on your own,' she said. 'Who are you working with?'

'A group of people who all want to put a stop to TMK,' he answered. 'We call ourselves the Free Memory Movement. The group was founded by Harold Merriweather and others involved with TMK who wanted to put a stop to their actions. Having people on the inside has benefited us greatly. The Movement has gathered enough information and evidence over the years to use against them now.'

'Which you will do how exactly?' asked Dolly.

'By revealing the facts to the world. There is an event this weekend all the prominent national and international leaders will attend. The Movement will hijack the event and show them the truth about TMK, while also broadcasting our findings across the Net. And now we have, of course, our very own Memory Keeper as proof.'

Dolly leant forward. 'Wait. Are you talking about the Winter-turn Ball?'

Kola nodded.

'No,' she said fiercely, shaking her head. 'No. Alba will be there. It's too dangerous. I will not let you bring her into this any further.' Her eyes flashed. 'What do the Movement's plans for hijacking the event entail exactly? Surely the London Guard and Lord Minister, Alba's father and every other official in North and beyond – not to mention their bodyguards *and* the security at the Ball – are not just going to sit down quietly and listen to you revealing their secrets to the whole world?'

Kola smoothed a hand over his trousers. 'We have our own security. We will be able to restrain them.'

Dolly let out a cry. 'Takeshi and his Bakerloo Boys? You know they were going to –' She stopped abruptly, throwing a worried look in Alba's direction. 'They only let us go because Seven altered that memory. I don't know what deal you and the Movement have struck with Takeshi to get him to help you, but I can assure you, they won't keep their side of the bargain.'

'Then do not go to the Ball if you are afraid,' Kola said. 'Neither of you have to be there.'

Alba gave a wry laugh. 'Oh, I'm going. To be honest, I'm

more afraid of what my *mother* will do if I don't.'

For some reason, Seven jerked round at that. He looked at her – properly *at* her – for the first time since surfing the memory Takeshi had forced him to. There was something uneasy about his gaze.

'Seven?' she whispered.

Wordlessly, he slipped his hand into hers. He stroked the back of her hand with one thumb, his grey eyes anxious.

Still looking at her, he said, 'I'll do it.'

'What?' Alba asked, somewhat distracted by the intense way he was looking at her.

Seven turned to Kola. 'I'll help you. I'll be your proof. If it's what'll put those TMK bastards in jail and stop them altering skids, I'll do it.'

Just then the car pulled to a stop. The engine growled as it sat idly next to the kerb, indicator ticking quietly. The driver – Alba presumed he was another Movement member – twisted round to say something in Kola's ear.

Kola nodded. His eyes were lit up in a way Alba hadn't seen before.

'You'll help us?' he asked Seven eagerly. 'You mean it?'

Seven nodded. 'I don't want anyone being able to change skids ever again.'

Kola slid back against his seat, visibly relieved. 'You made the right choice, man. Really.' He reached into a pocket and handed a small tablet to Seven. 'Take this. Use it only in an emergency. It'd be a good idea to stay with Alba and Dolly from now on – Alastair White's house is the last place they'll be looking for you. If I don't hear from you, the next we'll

317

see of each other will be the night before the Ball. I'll explain then in more detail what we're going to do, but until then . . . stay out of trouble.'

Seven raised his eyebrows, and for once Alba knew exactly what he was thinking.

Fat effing chance.

71

SEVEN

By the time they arrived back at Alba's house it was late afternoon. The air was chilled and grey. Clouds sank low in the sky overhead, their undersides tinged with black; a storm was coming. Dolly ushered them out of the cab and round the side of the house to the servants' entrance before anyone could see, and then into her room at the back of the west wing.

'We need to get you back to your room,' Dolly said to Alba as soon as they were inside, the three of them brushing themselves off from the rain. 'Just in case your mother comes looking. Seven,' she added, 'you'll have to stay here.'

He grinned, though it felt lifeless. 'Crap. I was hoping to crash another one of Alba's baths.'

Dolly's eyebrows shot up. '*Another* one of her baths?'

Alba threw Seven a dark look, her cheeks pinking. 'Ignore him. He's talking nonsense.'

His smile fading, Seven backed over to the bed, sitting down and closing his eyes. He flipped off the servant's cap. Dropping his head into his hands, he ran shaky fingers through his hair. He could sense Alba's enquiring gaze on him.

Seven couldn't bear to look at her. When he met her eyes, it was her mother he saw instead. Oxana, as she had been in the memory, clothes ripped, eyes wide, blood welling around her ankles and wrists from where the plastic cords cut tight.

He heard Alba walk over, then felt the warmth of her hands over his, which were still tangled in his hair.

'I'll come back tonight,' she said. 'As soon as I can.' She leant in close. So close he could smell the sweet sweat on her skin, hear each and every breath. So close he forgot for a moment Dolly was still in the room, because Alba was the only thing in the world. 'You don't owe anyone anything,' she whispered. 'Whatever you want to do, I'll support you. I'll be right here with you.'

Then she kissed the top of his head and was gone.

As soon as the door shut behind them, Seven slid down to the floor, crumpling into a messy heap of limbs and elbows. He scrubbed his palms into his eyes until multi-coloured spots swirled across his vision. No matter how much he tried, no matter how much he wanted to, he couldn't get rid of the image of Takeshi's grinning face as he knelt down in front of Alba's mother, unbuckling his belt.

Even though Seven had twisted, torn at the memory-space, replacing Takeshi with Aro Black, it was still Takeshi's face he saw when he closed his eyes, and his assured, glittering smile.

Seven wished more than anything he could alter his *own* memories. What was the point of being a Memory Keeper if he couldn't at least do that?

72

ALBA

Dolly twisted Alba's hair into curls, fixing them at the nape of her neck with leaf-shaped gold pins, a single crystal set into the centre of each one. Alba sat in silence as her handmaid worked. She didn't know how on earth to talk about everything they'd learnt today. Everything that had happened. It was all just too *big*. She didn't know where to start.

When Alba was five, Dolly had bought her a giant gobstopper at the Hampstead Heath summer fair. Alba had almost choked on it. That's how she felt now: as though there were some huge thing blocking her throat, taking up all of her.

After a few minutes, Dolly stepped back. 'All done.'

Alba looked up at herself in the mirror.

It was like looking at a painting. Her porcelain skin, the soft pink cream blushing her cheeks, the way her hair was pulled back artfully from her head in loose curls . . . it all seemed so fake. It felt wrong getting ready for dinner with her mother and father when just a few hours ago she'd been bruised and dirtied and miles underground. Alba had never felt easy in expensive dresses and jewels, but now it was even worse. Everything about her life in North felt like a lie.

'Your parents don't seem to know about your missed attendance at school today,' Dolly said, touching her shoulder. 'If they ask, just pretend you went.'

Alba raised an eyebrow. 'What a shame. I was *ever* so looking forward to telling them about Takeshi's Bakerloo Boys and Dr Merriweather.'

Her voice caught on Merriweather's name. His face came back to her, ghostly pale, eyes soft and unfocused.

He'd died in front of her eyes.

A sob caught in Alba's throat, and immediately Dolly was crouching down, turning her round in her chair.

'You can do this, Alba,' she said sternly. 'Don't be afraid of them.'

That hadn't been what she was thinking about, but Alba felt herself harden at the mention of her parents. Does Mother *know* what Father did? she wondered. Does she know she goes to bed every night with a murderer?

She pictured her father, smug and distant, echoes of all the deaths he'd been responsible for in those cold, black eyes. If Seven hadn't been rescued would her father have kept forcing him to surf and alter memory after memory until his brain bled to nothing?

Alba bit her lip to stop herself from crying. The idea that she might never even have met Seven, never even known he was somewhere out there in the world, made something inside her physically *hurt*.

322

His grin flashed into her mind, those small grey eyes of his always dancing with some secret or joke. The smell of mint laced in his breath and under his skin. His lopsided, slightly sticky-out ears. How he'd reached for her that morning in Dolly's room, leaning in, their faces moving closer like two planets falling into orbit.

How every single time Alba thought of Seven, she thought of a life she had never even wanted, never dreamed of, but which now seemed like the most precious thing in the world.

Was *this* what falling in love was?

'Are you ready?' Dolly asked, bringing her back to the present.

Steeling herself, Alba stood. She brushed down her dress and pushed back her shoulders, taking a long, deep breath.

'I'm ready,' she said.

And she meant it. Not just about dinner. Not just about facing her parents.

But about facing the world.

73

SEVEN

He was dozing when the door to the room opened and someone came in. Soft footsteps padded towards where he lay on the rug, twisted in sheets and blankets. He smelled her before she reached him – clean, sweet, floral, female, full of *Alba*-ness, whatever that was – and then her warm hands touched his face.

'Come with me.'

'But what about Dolly?'

'She's asleep. Come on.'

Seven pushed back the blankets. He got up and dressed (thank the gods it was dark in here – he was only wearing a pair of boxer shorts), pulling on a thick navy jumper and black trousers Dolly had borrowed for him from one of the male servants. After lacing up his boots he followed Alba out of the room.

She led him through the maze of hidden corridors, one hand curled round his. He tried to ask where they were going, but she hushed him quiet. In the night-time shadows her skin looked as though it were glowing.

It all felt like a dream. Perhaps he *was* dreaming. A beautiful girl waking him in the middle of the night, taking him somewhere private . . .

'Yep,' Seven murmured to himself. 'Definitely a dream.'

Alba stopped by a door. She opened it a fraction, listening through the crack, then pushed it further, pulling Seven through with her into a large room.

It was some sort of glasshouse, the walls and arched ceiling looking out over the dark grounds of Hyde Park Estate. It was filled with rows of plants. The whole place smelled green and fresh, like a summer's night. Outside, rain pattered on the glass, the room alive with its secretive, whispery sound.

'This is the herb-house,' Alba said, leading him into the room. 'No one comes here at night.'

They walked down between the rows of plants at the far side, the glass wall next to them. Faded moonlight, filtered by the thick clouds, touched Alba's outline where she walked slightly in front of Seven, casting her in a glowing silver shell. His heart raced. She was the most beautiful thing he'd ever seen.

Finally, he wasn't afraid to admit it.

When they were deep in the herb-house, Alba stopped, turning to him. She was still holding his hand. She looked down as though only just noticing and let go quickly. Even in the moonlit shadows of the room, he could see her cheeks colour.

Seven's eyes trailed over her long white sweater and leggings. The jumper fell off one shoulder, making his stomach ache at the sight of her pale, curving skin.

He knew what was about to happen. And effing *hell*, did he want it to. But he still felt confused and hurt and angry about everything that had gone on today. More than that, he still felt guilty. Alba deserved to know about her mother; he just didn't know how to tell her.

Seven didn't want her to always think of him as someone who had told her something that made her heart break.

'Alba,' he started, taking a deep breath.

She shook her head. 'I don't want to talk. I don't want to think. I just want you.'

And then she closed the gap between them, slipped her hands up round Seven's neck and kissed him.

74

ALBA

Oh almighty god, we are kissing!

75

SEVEN

Holy effing hell, we're kissing!

76

ALBA

It was both the most natural and the strangest thing she'd ever experienced. But good *lord*, did it feel good. Seven's hands wound round her waist and the back of her head, tugging her closer. His mouth was hot. Their lips parted and their tongues brushed each other's, sending electric shivers down her spine.

So *that's* what you did with your tongue.

Alba sighed. She drew him in like air. Their heartbeats were racing against each other, jumping out of their chests. Her fingers roamed up into his tangled hair, down the ridges of his back. Finding the edge of his jumper, they slipped inside and she traced her fingertips along the skin just above his waistband.

Seven breathed heavier at that, a soft growl in his throat that made her knees weak.

Somehow they lowered themselves to the floor. Still kissing, still curled in each other, they lay on their sides. Alba's shoulder pressed into the cold stone tiles but she didn't notice. She didn't even hear the rain thrumming on the glass walls. All she heard was hers and Seven's breaths, the soft sounds of their kissing.

All she felt was him.

Seven was the one who eventually pulled away.

They had been kissing for what felt like hours. Alba's face felt soft and blurry, and her lips were numb, but her body felt alive. Every inch of her hummed.

Blinking, Seven sat up. His hair was sticking out in every direction, his clothes ruffled. They'd shifted along the floor to the outer edge of the room. He leant back against the glass wall, rubbing his neck.

'Effing hell, Alba,' he muttered.

She laughed softly. Curling under his arm into his lap, she sat with her back to his chest and gazed out at the green shadows of the plants in the room, not really seeing any of it because it felt as though her eyes were still closed, like Seven was still *everywhere*. Why had no one told her kissing was like that, something you felt with every part of you, like surfing the memory of it over and over even as it was happening?

Seven took a deep breath, and Alba moved with the rise and fall of his chest.

'Alba.'

'That is my name.'

She smiled, burrowing deeper into his lap. Tilting her head back on his chest, she looked up at his face. He looked shell-shocked.

'Alba . . .' he started again.

'*Seven.*'

'Oh, come on! I'm trying here. Just – I dunno what to say.'

'Then don't say anything.'

She pushed up, leaning in to kiss him again.

'Alba, stop.'

Seven grabbed her shoulders, yanking her away a little too roughly, and pushed off the floor. He paced along the row of plants opposite. Letting out a sudden growl of frustration, he stopped, shaking his head.

'Fuck!' he cried. 'Fuck, fuck, *fuck*!'

Alba scrambled to her feet. 'Seven, keep your voice down!' She watched him warily. 'What's wrong? Was it – was it the kissing? Was it bad?'

'It was effing *perfect*,' he said firmly, and he sounded so sincere it made her heart feel like bursting. 'It's not that. This is about earlier.'

Alba relaxed, understanding. 'I meant what I said. I'll stand by you, whatever you decide. You don't have to do this for Kola – you don't owe the Movement anything. We could . . . we could run away instead. Maybe Dolly would come. Maybe –'

'No.' Seven's voice was steady. He stared at the ground, hands squeezed into fists. 'I'm going to help. I have to, Alba. TMK is too dangerous. The things it can be used for . . .' He let out a huff of breath. 'That's why I've gotta tell you this.'

Unease twisted Alba's stomach. 'Tell me what?'

'The skid Takeshi made me surf,' Seven began after a long pause. 'It was about your mum.'

And then lights clicked on overhead. Before either of them could say anything, people burst into the room, shouts filling the air, heavy footsteps crunching across the floor, and the last thing Alba saw was the flash of red jackets and Seven's face twisting in fear before some sort of stunning weapon bit into her side.

She fell to her knees, her body locking rigid, her vision blurring to black.

331

77

SEVEN

For the second time that day he woke in an unrecognisable room, this time strapped to a chair. He tried to move but his arms were twisted behind him, and he felt the metallic coldness of handcuffs on his wrists. Plastic ties snapped his ankles to the legs of the chair, which was fixed to the floor with chains. Under his clothes goosebumps shivered across his skin. The air was cool.

Seven twisted his head to look round but there wasn't much to see. The windowless room – more like a cell – was small and bare, the walls painted a dull grey. A strip of white light ran across the ceiling. There was a single door opposite where his chair was set in the middle of the room, and when he craned his neck down he could see a grated drain-cover beneath his feet.

Fear shot up his spine. What did they need a drain for?

He knew what, of course. He just didn't want to acknowledge it because then he would be even more scared, and he couldn't be even more scared because he had to live, had to find a way to escape.

The door to the cell opened.

Alastair White's face was expressionless as he strode inside. The stark light cut the edges of his hard features. He was wearing the black robes and charcoal suit of his office; at the centre of his collarbones, the bulldog clasp glinted gold.

'Well,' he said. 'If it isn't our lost Candidate Seven. We've been looking for you quite a while, you know.'

Seven's heart stuttered. He'd been clinging to the miniscule hope that his captors wouldn't know who he was.

He cleared his throat. 'How d'you know?'

'Blood never lies.'

Seven cast his eyes down and spotted the dot of dried blood at the crook of his elbow. The London Guard must have his DNA profile from when he was first introduced as a Candidate.

'Let me tell you how this works,' White said coolly, moving forward. 'I ask the questions, and you answer them. It's better for us both if you answer me promptly and truthfully.'

Seven scowled. 'Two things I'm pretty crap at, I'm afraid.'

White paused, watching him. 'Well, perhaps this will help you improve.' He reached into his suit pocket and pulled out a toothpick.

'My teeth are clean, thanks,' Seven said, trying for a grin but ending up with a twisted half-smile (he was thinking of all the places on a body sticking a toothpick in would hurt. Surprisingly many).

White's face darkened. He stepped round the chair, out of sight. 'Why do you make jokes when you're scared, Candidate Seven?'

'I make them all the time, really.'

'See? That's what I mean.'

There was a long, heavy pause.

'In case you are wondering, Alba is safe and well at home.' White shifted. His shadow slid across the floor like spilled ink. 'She won't tell anyone what you were doing in my house. She won't say anything. But it doesn't matter – she will eventually.'

Seven snarled. 'If *any* of you touch her –'

'We won't need to,' White interrupted smoothly, 'because we have you.' He moved closer, his shadow falling over Seven. 'We also have Alba's handmaid, Miss Rose. She was rather quick to tell us she was the one involved with you, not Alba. She denied any involvement on Alba's part – though we know she's lying. It's a shame. Miss Rose was a good servant.'

Dolly, thought Seven, feeling sick. She had warned them and they hadn't listened. Now she might be paying for it with her life.

He wanted to rip the handcuffs off his wrists and claw White's eyes out with his fingernails.

'You dare – you effing *dare* –'

'Oh, like I said. We have you. There'll be no need for anyone else to get hurt. You will tell us everything we want to know . . . won't you, *Candidate*?'

'Yes,' Seven forced himself to say, as White stepped out of sight, behind his chair.

The thing was, Alba hadn't been quite right earlier when she'd said he didn't owe anyone anything. There were a few people he owed.

Kola was one. Kola had helped them escape when the London Guard came for Seven at the flat. He'd said, *Do you want to fight them?* on that warm afternoon on the rooftop all those

334

weeks ago, and for the first time in his entire life Seven hadn't felt quite so alone.

Dolly was another person he owed. She loved Alba, and Alba loved her; that was enough of a reason to protect her. But she had also helped Seven after he'd been attacked by the dog, then helped Alba and him find out more about TMK, even though she had asked them not to.

And then, of course, there was Alba.

She had done more than anyone else. Simply by being there, by trusting him. She had given him a reason – *every* reason – to keep fighting.

Seven made up his mind. He would tell White enough to keep him from hurting Dolly, but he would lie about everything else.

A few days. That's all Kola and the Movement needed. A few days until the Winter-turn Ball, and then White would be ruined.

There were footsteps as White's figure came back into view. He stopped in front of Seven, bending slowly and setting down the toothpick. When he straightened, the faintest trace of a smile played on his lips.

'Someone will come by shortly,' he said, before leaving Seven alone in the cold, horrible cell, with nothing to look at except the single toothpick on the floor.

78

ALBA

'You're going to have to speak at some point, Alba.

'Tell me what happened. Explain how that South thief ended up in our house with you. You're lucky your father granted you immunity. You could be in the London Guard's interrogation cells too right now.

'Oh for Christ's sake, Alba. Are you going to ignore me for the rest of your life?'

Alba kept her eyes squeezed shut. She was scared that if she opened them, if she saw her mother and her own bedroom, and the fact that Dolly and Seven weren't here any more, she'd start crying and never stop.

Whatever she did, she would *not* cry in front of her mother.

Oxana had been talking at her for what felt like hours. Alba thought she sounded more tired and resigned than angry now. And she didn't dare believe it, but maybe there was even a hint of fear in her voice. What was her mother afraid of? Of all of North finding out her daughter was involved with a

336

South criminal? Of ruining their marriage arrangement with Thierry's family?

'I'm going to make a call. You're going to talk when I come back. And don't even think about escaping – the house is being protected by the London Guard.'

Alba heard her mother's sharp footsteps click across the floorboards. The door creaked open and there was the rise of voices – her mother and the guards outside exchanging pleasantries – before it slammed shut.

Finally, Alba opened her eyes.

Her mother *had* been here for hours. Outside, the sun was rising. The curtains were half open, and the milky orange light of the wintry morning poured into her room. Birdsong sounded from a distance. There were occasional coughs, staccato bursts of voices, but for the most part the house was quiet.

Alba rubbed her side where the stunning weapon had caught her. It was still stinging. Peeling up her jumper, she saw a bruise staining her skin.

A little wobbly on her feet – she was still weak from the stunner's shock – she got off the bed and went over to the windows. Her stomach dipped at the sight of red-jacketed men moving among the sloping green lawns surrounding the house. So the London Guard *were* keeping watch. She wouldn't have the faintest chance of escaping.

This is it, then, Alba thought. She was trapped, Seven and Dolly were gone, and there was nothing she could do about any of it.

For a second, she broke down. Then, with a gasp and a skip of her heart, she remembered –

The tablet Kola had given them.

Use it only in an emergency.

Breathless, Alba rushed to her bed and pulled up the mattress, snatching the tablet from where she'd hidden it between the slats in the bedframe. She touched the screen. A single glowing word sprung across the black: *CALL*. Beneath it were the symbols for a cross and a tick.

Hoping she was doing the right thing (there wasn't really any more *wrong* she could do now, surely?) Alba pressed the tick.

For a while, there was only silence. Then Kola's voice sounded from the tablet, quiet but clear.

'Seven?'

'Kola! Thank god. It's Alba.' Crouching over the bed and grabbing a fistful of her duvet, she cocooned the tablet, muffling the sound. 'It's an emergency,' she whispered. 'We need your help.'

'What happened?' he asked, voice sharp.

'The London Guard has Seven. Dolly too. I don't know where they've taken them.'

There was a pause. 'I know where. I'm surprised I haven't heard about it from Nihail. He works in Interrogation. He must be busy.'

Alba's stomach flipped.

'If he's *busy* working on Seven and Dolly –'

'He wouldn't hurt them,' Kola reassured her. 'At least, not enough to do permanent damage. He needs to keep up appearances for his own safety. But we will get Seven out of there, Alba. We will help him.'

'And Dolly,' she urged.

'Yes. But we will have to wait until the night of the Winter-turn Ball. If we reveal ourselves too soon our plans will be ruined.'

Alba let out a strangled cry. For a moment she was so angry she forgot all about the London Guardmen outside her door. Images flooded her: Seven and Dolly in cells, being hurt, not given food or water . . . and all the while she was stuck in her bedroom like a pampered Rapunzel.

'But that's four days away! They could be dead by then.' Alba's voice broke. She squeezed her eyes shut, feeling the tears that had threatened to overcome her rush back. 'Please, Kola,' she breathed.

'I'm sorry, Alba. We cannot come any sooner. But the London Guard will not kill Seven – they need him. Too many of the working Candidates are dying from haemorrhages. They will want him alive and well.'

Alba drew a deep breath. 'He's not some toy to be played with, you know. Seven deserves more than that. What you did, bringing him to Takeshi – it was wrong. It was as bad as them, making him alter memories for your own purposes.'

'Forgive us,' Kola replied after a long pause, 'but we didn't see any other way. We cannot let the London Guard continue to murder hundreds of innocents. You saw what happened with Takeshi. That sort of power – the power to change and manipulate memories – is too dangerous to be allowed to exist. In any capacity.'

It took a few moments for his words to sink in. When they did, Alba's breath caught in her throat.

If the power to manipulate memories couldn't be allowed

to exist in any capacity, then what did the Movement plan to do with *Seven*?

'Kola?' Her voice shook. 'What will you do with Seven when you're done? What will happen to the rest of the Candidates?'

But before he could reply, Alba heard the snap of footsteps approaching the door. She had just enough time to stuff the tablet under the duvet before her mother stepped into the room.

'Are you ready to talk now?' Oxana said, one hand on her hip, her long curtain of straight blonde hair rippling in the rising sunlight. She was dressed in a pair of flared silk trousers and a striped Breton knit. As always, she looked impeccable.

Alba got to her feet. 'Yes, *Mother*,' she said, hands clenched at her sides. 'But you're not going to like what I have to say.' Her words came out in a rush. 'I'm not marrying Thierry, and I'm going to get Dolly and Seven back, and then I'm going to leave here forever, and there's nothing you or Father can do to stop me.'

Surprise registered in her mother's eyes for the briefest moment before they narrowed, returning to their usual icy blue.

'You *are* marrying Thierry, Alba.'

'No, I'm not.'

'Because you want to marry this Seven boy instead?'

'Yes.'

Alba blushed as soon as she said it.

'Well,' she amended, 'maybe. I – I don't know. But I *do* know that I want to have the freedom to choose who I marry. And I don't just want to be another North society wife. I want to travel, go to university, learn things . . . I want to experience the world for myself.'

She remembered what it had been like that first time, memory-surfing, jumping off the edge of the cliff into the waterfall, sun like liquid gold on her naked body, the water cool on her skin. How free she'd felt. Then she thought of kissing Seven. Even just his crooked, awkward, beautiful grin made her feel as though anything were possible.

'I just want to be free,' Alba finished.

Oxana stared. Then, something in her eyes softening, she lifted her hand, reaching for her, but Alba shrank back.

Her mother's face clouded over. 'That's not something we can just choose,' she said, and there was something broken in her voice. 'Sometimes others make that choice for us. Your father and I are offering you a safe life, my darling. Wouldn't you rather be safe than free?'

'No,' Alba answered without hesitation.

Her mother looked away. 'One day,' she said softly before she left, 'you won't think that any more.'

After the door clicked shut behind her, Alba stared at the place her mother had been, feeling a new emotion for her then –

Pity.

She was *sad* for her mother. She felt sorry for her, because she couldn't think what had happened to turn her into this cold woman, into someone who thought living a safe, joyless life was better than an uncertain, free one.

To Alba, the choice was clear. Anything else would be like living a lie, living out of sync with your own heartbeat. It would be living as a ghost. And she had felt haunted in her own life long enough.

79

SEVEN

When the door to the cell next opened, Seven was so surprised at who walked in his mouth dropped open.

Dolly.

As she stumbled into the room – her hands were cuffed – a man followed her. Seven's eyes widened with surprise at a second familiar face. It was Nihail, the dark-skinned man he'd met yesterday in the ruins of the Underground, who was secretly a part of the Movement.

'Candidate Seven,' he said, smiling. 'A pleasure to meet you. My name is Nihail.'

His eyes flicked to the ceiling. Seven followed them and spotted a tiny camera tucked in one corner of the room. He looked back and gave the barest of nods to show he understood: they were being watched.

Nihail bent down and picked up the toothpick Alastair White had left, presumably as a reminder for Seven as to what would happen if he didn't comply with them (it had worked – by now, Seven had thought of hundreds of ways pain could be dealt with a single toothpick).

'I shouldn't be needing this,' Nihail said, slipping the toothpick into the pocket of his red jacket, 'because you're going to play nice today, aren't you, Candidate?'

'Yes,' Seven answered dully.

He caught Dolly's gaze and smiled weakly. She smiled back. Or at least, it seemed like a smile. It was hard to tell. Her face was swollen, a dark purple bruise covering her cheekbone and jaw, and her lips were cracked with dried blood. Her hair had come loose from its usual buns; it fell in a straggly purple mess over her shoulders.

I did this, he thought, feeling guilt like a sting. *Whatever happens to her – it's on me.*

Even though Nihail was on their side, Seven knew he wouldn't be able to let them off. Alastair White was no doubt watching through the camera. Nihail would have to act as though Seven and Dolly were any other criminals he was interrogating.

Nihail shoved Dolly forward. 'I thought I'd bring Miss Rose along,' he said, 'just in case you need a reminder of what'll happen if you don't answer our questions. Mr White thought you'd respond better this way. Said South scum like you have so little to lose it'd be more persuasive if someone else was bearing the consequences of your actions.'

Seven scowled. 'That's one thing *Mr White* has got right then.'

Pushing Dolly aside, Nihail went over to Seven, clipping a small device to one of his fingers.

'A lie-detector,' Nihail explained, sitting on a chair he'd dragged in from outside the cell. He pulled out a tablet. 'I'll know if you're trying to fool me, Candidate. For Miss Rose's sake, I hope you save us the bother.'

Seven swallowed. He only had a moment to try and slow his heart – it was skipping along at a thousand miles an hour – before Nihail started firing questions.

'What is your full name?'

'Seven.'

'Seven . . .?'

'Just Seven.'

'Where do you live?'

'Nowhere now, thanks to you lot.'

'Where *did* you live?'

'Flat 23B, Southrise Residences, Vauxhall.'

'Where did all the memories in your flat come from?'

'They were stolen.'

'Who stole them?'

'Me.'

'What for?'

'To surf. Sell on the black market. Don't you guys know all this already?'

'Who do you work for?'

'Carpenter's skid-thief crew. At least, until you shot him.'

Seven saw no point in lying. The tattoo was right there on his chest after all. And Carpenter was dead. There *was* no Carpenter's skid-thief crew any more (his stomach still did a painful flip whenever he thought about it).

'Who else is in Carpenter's crew?'

For the first time, Seven hesitated. 'Dunno. I've never met any of them.'

The tablet in Nihail's palm began to beep. Nihail didn't look down at it, his dark eyes still fixed on Seven.

'I didn't need the detector to tell me you're lying,' he said. Standing, he slipped the tablet into his pocket. 'Come with me. Let me show you why.'

He removed the ties from Seven's ankles and forced him to stand, pushing him towards the door with one hand gripping his neck. Seven stumbled. He'd been sitting so long his legs felt like jelly.

Locking Dolly behind in the cell, Nihail led Seven out into a long corridor. Clinical white walls stretched away into darkness. They passed closed doors, each numbered and marked with the name of the prisoner inside. It was eerily quiet. They stopped near the end of the corridor. Nihail unlocked a door by hitting a code into the panel beside it, and before Seven could even think about who was inside, the door swung heavily open. Still grasping him by the neck, Nihail pushed him forward.

Seven's stomach dropped.

The girl in the cell didn't look anything like the girl he'd known for years. She was slumped low in the chair she was tied to. Blood matted her hair. One eye was swollen shut, and the looped piercing round her bottom lip had been ripped out. Her long-sleeved top and jeans were dirty and torn.

She looked up slowly, then froze.

'Loe,' Seven croaked.

Nihail stepped up beside him. In the briefest moment, shifting as though he were simply adjusting his grip on Seven's neck, he leant in and breathed, 'I'm sorry. They wanted you to know.' Then, in a louder voice: 'I've brought you a visitor, Loe.'

She licked her lips. 'Seven.' Her voice sounded dry and ragged, as though she'd been screaming. All of a sudden she was frantic. 'I'm so sorry,' she cried. 'Please! It was all for Mika! You've got to understand! I'd lost my job – what else could I do? She was hungry! I couldn't bear to see her like that. They told me they'd help Mika and me. They promised not to hurt you!'

Seven's heart thumped hard. 'I don't understand.'

Loe strained against her ties. He saw blood dripping down her feet from where the plastic cords dug into her ankles. There was more blood on the floor beneath her, dried and crusted on the drain-cover.

'I did it for Mika!' She was crying, something Seven had never known her do before, and it shocked him. 'Please. I'm so sorry! But you've got to understand!'

And in one sudden, horrible burst of clarity, he *did* understand.

'You told them about Dolly,' Seven breathed. 'About Alba. That's how they knew I was at her house.'

Loe was shaking. 'Mika was starving, and the reward money for giving them information on you was just *so* much, I couldn't . . . Seven, please! Please, understand! Mika's got a chance now at a life I never could've given her –'

'That's enough,' Nihail interrupted. Ignoring her protests, he twisted Seven round and shoved him back out into the corridor.

The door slammed shut behind them. As they walked back to Seven's cell, Loe's screams and cries followed them down the corridor, muffled but still ringing in his ears until he thought he'd never be rid of their sound, that for the rest of his life all he'd hear were her desperate, ragged screams.

80

ALBA

The next two days went by so slowly she swore she could feel each minute melting into the next. Each tick of the clock on her bedside table felt like the twist of a knife. *One more minute*, Alba thought. *One more minute when Seven and Dolly could be hurting, and I can't do a thing to stop it.* She wished she could be there with them, share some of their pain. Instead, she was trapped in her room with her useless hordes of books and trinkets and jewels.

She hadn't quite believed her mother when she'd said life would continue as normal. It seemed ridiculous to think that life could go on as normal after everything that'd happened. Seven had kissed her. They'd watched a man die. They'd discovered the truth about The Memory Keepers.

The whole world felt different now.

Oxana was talking about Alba returning to school next week after her engagement to Thierry was announced at the Winter-turn Ball.

'All your friends will be jealous,' she'd said.

What friends? Alba thought. *You've taken away the only two I have.*

But she kept quiet. She needed her mother to think everything would return to normal. She couldn't suspect a thing about the Winter-turn Ball, or Alba wouldn't be allowed to go, and she had to go. For Seven. For Dolly.

For herself.

81

SEVEN

After two days in the cell, he forgot what it felt like to have fresh air on his skin. How blue the sky could be. The pattern of stars stitched across it. The smell before rain.

On the nights he wasn't working, Seven used to lie on the rooftop of his block of flats and memorise every cluster and constellation, imagining they formed a secret message from some god in a language no one on earth could understand.

Now he'd never decipher the message. He'd never even see the night sky again.

Seven longed for darkness. The cell was always bright. Sometimes they broadcast noise from hidden speakers just as he fell asleep, so he'd jerk back awake, blinking, straining against his ties, wishing he could cover his ears to block out the violent sound. And yet the times they let him sleep were worse. He'd wake, and it'd be like that first moment all over again, when he'd first opened his eyes and saw the dull grey walls and knew that this time –

This time it truly was over.

After two days, one interrogation blurred into another. It was almost always Nihail, but sometimes they sent someone different, and Seven dreaded seeing the door unlock and an unfamiliar face behind it. They never exactly hurt him because he always answered their questions, but when it wasn't Nihail interrogating him, the fear was worse.

So far they'd only asked about his life as a skid-thief. Then, finally, on the third day –

'Have you heard of TMK?'

It was a new person interrogating him: a Chinese man called Lin with sharp, cutting eyes and a strong, slender body. His black hair was pulled into a ponytail running down the back of his immaculate suit. He sat in a chair opposite Seven, one arm bent across his knees.

At his question, Seven's heart started to beat so fast it sent the tablet in Lin's pocket beeping.

Lin raised an eyebrow, smiling pleasantly. 'I'll take that as a yes. Perhaps you also know what it stands for?'

'Yeah.'

'Which is . . .?'

'The Memory Keepers,' he answered with a scowl. 'Though perhaps it should stand for The Memory Korruptors, given what you bastards use it for.'

Lin's smile was fixed. 'Corruption is spelled with a "C".'

'Just like Candidate, then.'

'Do you know why we call you Candidate?' Lin asked.

'Yes.'

'How?'

Seven glowered at him. 'You've got the skid, haven't you? Your lot took all of them from my flat. You know what I saw.'

There was a pause. Something flickered across Lin's face. 'What skid?'

'Don't tell me you haven't gone through all of them already.' Seven looked for recognition in his eyes but saw nothing. Instead, he saw something else.

Fear.

Lin leant back. 'Whose memory are we talking about, Candidate Seven?'

'Alastair White's.'

Lin blinked. Standing, he turned to the door. 'One moment.'

As soon as he was gone, Seven's mind began to race.

He's actually worried, he thought. *They don't know. They didn't find White's skid in my collection.*

Who hid it – Kola? Nihail?

He drew in a sharp breath.

Seven knew the Movement had needed him as proof of TMK's experiments. He knew they'd been counting on showing him at the Winter-turn Ball. And he also knew that was unlikely now the London Guard had caught him. But this skid; it was enough. Along with the other information they'd gathered on TMK, it would at least force an enquiry into what Alastair White, the Lord Minister and London Guard had been doing.

Excitement whirred through him at the realisation.

Lin took a long time to come back. He looked calm again as he sat down in front of Seven, though he couldn't hide the flicker of unease in his eyes.

'Who else has seen that memory?' Lin asked.

351

'No one.'

'Who have you *told* about what you saw in that memory?'

'No one.'

And the lie came easily, the detector not giving Seven away, because for the first time since he'd been brought here he felt the golden, winning force of hope.

The Movement had Alba's father's skid, and soon the whole world would know what was hidden inside it.

82

ALBA

The day before the Winter-turn Ball – the third day since Seven and Dolly had been taken away – her father finally came to see her.

Alba looked round at the sound of the door opening from where she was lying on top of her bed. She'd drifted in and out of a restless sleep all night. It was now almost midday. The sky was a clear, pearly blue outside: a beautiful winter's morning. Under the sun, frost glistened on the lawns of the estate.

Her father was wearing a polished suit in a dark, charcoal colour over a silver-white shirt. A golden bulldog clasp sat at the base of his throat.

He spread his arms and gave her a smile. 'What do you think? Is this suit grand enough for the Ball tomorrow? I've just had the last-minute adjustments done.'

Alba stared. 'Looks just *great*,' she said coldly, turning back to the wall.

Her father sighed. She heard footsteps as he crossed the

room, then the mattress dipped under his weight. He laid a hand on her shoulder.

'My dear. Please – talk to me. It pains me to see you like this.'

Well, it pains me to know you're a lying murderer, Alba thought, but she bit her lip, staying silent.

'I can't help you if I don't know what's wrong.'

'Do you really want to know?' she murmured.

'Of *course*, my dear.' He squeezed her shoulder. 'You can tell me anything.'

Alba snorted. *Let's see about that.*

Pushing herself up, she brushed her hair back from her face. Her father's hand dropped to her back. His gaze met hers as she looked up at him, and even though she despised him, even though she hated what he'd done, she found herself memorising the look in his eyes then, because it was kind, and loving, and for the briefest of seconds she could pretend that he was just her father and she was just his daughter, and that was all there was in the world.

Then she said, 'I know about The Memory Keepers.'

To his credit, he had the decency to look guilty.

'What?' he breathed.

'I know everything.' Alba's voice broke as tears rushed suddenly from nowhere. 'I know what you make the Candidates do, and what you use the altered memories for. I know about it all!'

Perhaps she'd been hoping he'd try and tell her none of it was true. Or perhaps she'd just wanted him to apologise. To wrap his arms round her and say sorry, because he should be, he was her father and he *should be sorry*.

Instead, he stood stiffly, staring down at her with eyes that closed her out even as she looked into them, a tiny flame of hope still fluttering in her heart.

'I expect you to keep this quiet,' he said, before turning and striding out the room.

Alba doubled over as the door clicked shut. She let out a cry that choked away into sobs. Up until that moment, she hadn't realised she'd still been holding onto the idea of her father as he was before all of this happened – before Seven, before TMK, before anything – and it was only now that she knew she'd lost that part of him forever.

83

SEVEN

One day. That's what he kept telling himself. One more day until the Winter-turn Ball. If he could just make it until then, maybe the next person to open his cell door would be someone from the Movement coming to free him. Maybe it would be Kola. Maybe Alba would be there too, and she'd smile and throw her arms round his neck and bury him in kisses.

What a way to die.

Or maybe their plan would fail and Seven would be buried another way; in the prisoners' cemetery, his body lost among thousands of anonymous others.

He shook his head. 'Don't think like that,' he muttered fiercely.

The Movement's plan would work. It had to. He went over all the things they had going in their favour; the element of surprise, insider information and evidence, Alastair White's skid. And, of course, the truth.

Though, Seven thought, that didn't seem to be something London valued very much any more.

84

ALBA

Preparations for the ball had been underway since sunrise, clattering and hammering and shouted instructions filling her room with noise. Alba was curled on a chair by the windows, watching the grounds around their house being transformed. There were marquees, fountains, seating areas with velvet sofas and chairs, lights with star-shaped casings draped from the trees, elegant statues, stages for performers. Underneath it all, a soft covering of fake snow turned the ground white and glittering in the low, wintry sun.

It was beautiful.

'Seven would *hate* this,' she said with a small laugh, then fell silent, biting her lip.

Alba didn't know what she'd do if he didn't turn up with the Movement that evening. Everything she wanted, everything she was hoping for now, was tied inextricably to Seven. His lopsided grin and sharp grey eyes were in each and every one of her thoughts of the future. When she touched her lips she imagined she could still feel him on them, that she was still holding onto the taste of him.

Was this love? she wondered. The way her heart beat fast every time she pictured him? The way she could hear his laughter when she closed her eyes?

The way the world became ever more unbearable each moment he wasn't in it?

A knock on the door brought Alba back to the present. A small woman with short mousey hair stepped in.

'Malinda, ma'am. I'm your new handmaid, ma'am. Mrs White has sent me to get you ready for the Ball.'

Alba glanced at the clock. 'Already? It's only four in the afternoon.'

'Mrs White thinks three hours is just about enough time, ma'am.'

It turned out three hours *was* only just about enough time for Malinda to prepare Alba for the Ball. She was steamed, plucked, pruned and primped, and her hair (some wispy half-up, half-down style threaded with small white flowers) and make-up (dusty, shimmering skin and pale pink lips) alone took over an hour. It was already darkening outside by the time Malinda fitted Alba into her dress. It was a sparkling, jewelled creation, all silver and white, strapless, with a fitted bodice and long hem that swirled round her ankles.

Alba stared at herself in the mirror when Malinda had finished clipping a heavy necklace of shining white diamonds round her neck.

'You look beautiful, ma'am,' Malinda gushed. 'Mrs White will be so proud.'

No, Alba wanted to say, *Dolly and Seven* would be proud. Well, Seven's jaw would fall open and he'd mostly just be a stuttering wreck, but she'd know what he meant when he muttered, 'Effing hell, Alba.' She'd know, because she knew *him*, and yes, yes of course this was love, what else could it be? And if the gods were kind enough to let her see him again, she would tell him, she would tell him she loved him.

I love him, Alba thought, feeling breathless.

'It's time, ma'am. The guests will be arriving soon.'

Malinda led Alba from the room, leaving her alone once they were outside the house to help with the guests' arrival. Alba spotted London Guardmen stationed around the grounds, their uniforms swapped for black suits and silver waistcoats, the outline of a bulldog stitched onto their breast pockets.

A lantern-lined path led round to the back of the house. Alba's heels clicked as she followed it. Even though it was a clear November night it wasn't cold, the tall, light-strung heaters blasting warmth, making the air – spun with orchestral music from the live band on the main stage – sugary and soft.

It all felt so dreamlike. *This is what North has gotten used to*, she thought. *A beautiful, fake world.*

No wonder they thought nothing of fabricating memories, too.

'Alba.'

She turned at the sound of her name and saw her mother walking towards her on the path. Oxana looked beautiful in a tight-fitting gold gown, slit high on one leg. Her hair was tied in a sleek ponytail, tiny beads and diamonds threaded through it. Deep plum lipstick coloured her lips.

359

'Am I going to have to worry about you tonight?' Oxana asked, moving closer until Alba could smell her too-sweet perfume. Her eyes were dark and glossy.

'No, Mother,' Alba answered dully, not missing the threat in her words.

'Good. Your engagement to Thierry will be announced tonight during your father's speech. You'll be expected to join him on stage for photos.'

'I can't wait.'

Her mother's eyes hardened. 'None of this petulance any more, Alba,' she said sternly. 'You are marrying Thierry, whether you like it or not. You should be grateful for this opportunity. You are just sixteen. What can you know of what you want in life? Everything you believe in, your hopes and dreams – they could be torn from you at any moment. Your father and I are offering you safety.' Her voice softened. 'Please take it.'

When Alba didn't reply, her mother took a long breath. She reached out, her polished fingertips touching Alba's cheek.

'You look beautiful, my darling,' she said gently.

After a long, searching look, the hint of something soft turning behind those iced-over blue eyes, she turned and swept down the path back towards the front of the house, her dress rippling silkily along the ground behind her.

85

SEVEN

The door swung open for the first time that day. Seven had lost track of time in the eternally lit cell. Was it night yet? Had the Ball started? Lin entered, holding a tray of food that smelled so good it made Seven's stomach curl. All he'd been given so far was stale water and crusty bread, stuffed into his mouth because his own hands were in cuffs.

'Dinner,' said Lin with a smile. He set the tray down on the spare chair and moved behind Seven. There was a click as the handcuffs sprang open.

Immediately, Seven grasped his hands. They were covered in dried blood. He flexed them, trying to ease off the constant cramp that had settled in his wrists and arms.

'Here.' Lin handed him the plate of food. 'As a thank-you for complying with us so far.'

Seven let out a snort. 'Poisoning me as a way of saying thank you? No thanks.'

'It's not poisoned.'

'Well, I don't want it.'

His belly let out a growl.

Lin's smile edged wider. 'Are you sure about that?' He sat back in the chair, resting his hands on his knees. 'We're not heartless, Candidate. We know to reward loyalty.'

'I'm not loyal to you,' Seven spat.

'Well, we're hoping we can change that. Now, please – eat. You'll need your energy for what I am about to ask of you.'

Just for a second, Seven considered throwing the plate of food in Lin's face. Then (telling himself that it would be an insult to the animal that had died for this meal) he began stuffing the tender slices of roast beef, rosemary potatoes, garlic beans and fried onions into his mouth. Juices dripped down his fingers. Of course they hadn't given him any cutlery. They were aware of how much could be done with a toothpick; gods forbid he ever got hold of a *spoon*.

Lin smiled when he'd finished. 'Good, isn't it?'

Seven licked his lips. *Only the best effing meal I've had in my entire life*, he thought.

Instead, he shrugged. 'Needed more salt.'

Lin laughed. 'Well, Candidate Seven.' He stood, brushing down his sleek grey suit. 'Now you've got your energy back, I've got a little exercise for you.'

He took the empty plate and set it down on his chair. Pulling something out of his suit pocket, he bent and crouched beside Seven, cutting the plastic cords round his ankles. Then he moved to the door and waited for Seven to follow.

But Seven stayed put. 'Damn,' he said, yawning theatrically. 'Still knackered. Think it'll take at least two more plates before

I can go anywhere.'

Lin's glare was cold. 'Come with me, Candidate. You can eat again after.'

'After what?'

'Come with me, and you'll find out.'

Knowing he didn't have any choice, Seven got to his feet. He moved shakily, his ankles feeling swollen and bruised, and it hurt to stretch out his legs after all this time. Lin led him down the corridor in the opposite direction to Loe's cell. He didn't put Seven's handcuffs back on or guide him by the neck like Nihail had done, but when Seven glanced over his shoulder he saw a burly London Guardman following them as they walked, and knew better than to try anything. Besides, one thing he did know for certain: his fighting skills (or rather, lack of) weren't going to help him one bit here.

They came to the end of the corridor and turned into a lobby area with a set of lifts. A desk ran along the opposite wall, two guards sat behind it. Moving over to the lifts, Lin swiped his access card over the panel to call for one.

'Since you know all about The Memory Keepers,' he said, 'including the fact that you *are* one, we thought it was time you had a go for yourself.'

Seven tensed. He thought of the skid Takeshi had made him alter; the overpowering scent of male sweat, Oxana's ripped clothes, the metallic snap as Takeshi lowered down, unbuckling his belt . . .

Seven used to love skid-surfing. Now, he didn't think he wanted to look inside some else's mind ever again.

When the lift arrived, Lin, Seven and the guard who'd been

tailing them all got in and the doors slid shut.

It happened so fast Seven didn't even have time to react.

Just as the lift began to glide down, the guard jerked forward and grabbed Lin, locking an arm round his neck and jabbing something into the side of his neck. Lin's shout died in his throat. He slumped down and the guard dropped him, kicking his body to the back of the lift.

'I'm Axel,' grunted the man, turning to Seven. He had a stony face and deep-set blue eyes. 'Welcome to the Movement, Candidate Seven.'

'Er . . . hi.'

Axel jabbed a different floor on the lift's display. Crouching beside Lin, he took an access card and a tablet from his pockets before gagging him and tying his arms and legs with plastic cords.

'Wh-where are we going?' Seven stuttered, gaping at him.

Axel grinned. 'Why, to the Ball, of course, Cinderella. The others are waiting in the car park. We need to get going quick before anyone raises the alarm.' Flipping the back of Lin's suit jacket over, he pulled out the gun that was tucked there and held it out to Seven. 'Have you ever used one before?'

Seven shook his head. He took it with shaking hands: it was cold and heavy.

Axel finished running him through how to use it just as the lift slid to a stop. But before the doors could open fully, Seven jammed his finger on the *close* option on the controls, then the number of the floor they'd come from. The lift began to move back up.

Axel turned, frowning. 'What the hell?'

'My friends,' Seven said. He swallowed, trying to calm his spinning heart. 'I can't leave them here.'

Axel's mouth tightened. 'Yes, you bloody *can*.'

He took a step towards the control panel but Seven blocked it, his face hard.

'Two of my friends are up there. I'm not leaving them behind. After everything I've done for you guys, the least you can do is help me free my friends.'

'It's too dangerous. The whole building'll know that we're here.'

'I don't care!' Seven shouted. 'If I don't try, I'll spend the rest of my life hating myself.' *And I've done enough of that already*, he added in his head.

They were three floors away now.

Axel was glaring at him. Seven glared back.

Two floors away.

One floor.

'Oh, fuck this.'

Axel grabbed him by the scruff of his neck and pushed him in front of the doors.

'Bastard attacked Lin in the lift!' Axel yelled at the guards behind the desk as the doors opened. He shoved Seven forward. 'I'm locking him back up. Gonna teach him what a mistake that was.'

The guards scrambled up. As they rushed past towards Lin's unconscious body in the lift, Axel turned, pulled a gun from his holster, and shot them in the backs of their heads.

Seven's mouth dropped open in horror, but Axel was already wheeling him away, leading him quickly down the corridor to the cells.

'Where are they?' Axel growled.

'W-who?'

'Your friends! Which cells are they in?'

Seven swallowed. 'I – I don't know where Dolly is. But Loe's at the end of the hall.'

'Isn't that the girl that gave you up to the London Guard?' Axel threw him a sharp look. 'Still think she's your friend?'

Without hesitation, Seven nodded.

He'd had plenty of time to think about what Loe had done over the last three days, and what he realised was that he *did* understand. He knew how desperate she'd been. She had given him up to protect Mika. Seven would have done the exact same thing for Alba, because that's what you did when you loved someone, wasn't it?

And he'd realised that he *did* love Alba. That he'd fight the whole world just to keep her safe. Just to see those pretty green eyes one more time, feel her kiss him that way she had the other night, as though she'd die if she didn't, as though she needed his lips against her to breathe.

Seven needed her to breathe.

They stopped outside Loe's cell. Axel punched in the code to release the door and they went in.

Seven couldn't help it; he recoiled at the smell. Loe was in an even worse condition than when he'd last seen her. Blood caked the skin around her jaw. Both eyes were swollen and bloodshot. She looked up as they entered, but her movements were slow and difficult.

Anger twisted like a knife in Seven's gut. What did the London Guard want with Loe? Couldn't they tell she was just a frightened girl trying to survive in a world that was doing everything it could to bring her down? How could they hurt her, knowing what they were doing themselves to innocent people?

Bending down, Axel cut Loe's bindings free with a thick pair of metal clippers and unlocked her handcuffs. She didn't seem to understand what was going on. She looked down at her uncuffed hands as though she'd never seen them before.

'Who was the other one?' Axel asked, getting back up.

'Dolly Rose.'

He nodded. 'I know where she is.'

As he left the room, Seven went over to Loe and swung an arm round her waist. Her eyes focused in and out as she looked at him. Her throat strained as she tried to croak something, but he cut her off.

'It's OK,' he said gently. 'We're getting you out of here.'

Half carrying Loe, Seven left the cell. He spotted Axel, back the way they'd come at the far end of the corridor, disappearing into another cell. By the time they reached it, he was leading someone out.

'Dolly!' Seven cried.

She turned, her eyes flashing as they met his, and the barest hint of a smile touched her lips.

Then shouts echoed from the lobby. The lights overhead switched in an instant to red, flooding the corridor with a deep, bloody colour, and a siren started to wail.

86

ALBA

'I've been looking for you everywhere, Alba. Why are you hiding away?'

Alba's stomach knotted at the sound of Thierry's voice. Twisting round, she forced a smile. 'I just wanted a few moments alone.'

He didn't take the hint. He moved closer, swaying slightly as he set down the drinks he was holding and lowered himself to where Alba was sitting on a fur rug, laid out under the low-hanging branches of a tall beech tree. The tree was on the very edge of the grounds, hidden behind a stage where performers were twisting down through the air on long silk ropes.

Alba felt annoyed Thierry had found her. She'd come here to escape the Ball, with its whirl of glittering dresses and jewels, bubbling champagne, waiters in white serving canapés on silver platters and endless laughter and inane chatter and gossip, gossamer strains of orchestral music sweeping over everything.

She couldn't think straight in the midst of it all, and it was important she keep a straight head.

The Movement could show up any minute. Alba needed to be ready.

'This is intimate,' Thierry purred, brushing her back.

He gazed up at the lanterns and fake snowflakes adorning the branches of the tree. They lit the space underneath in a warm, golden glow. Beyond, away from the party, the lawns disappeared into frosty darkness.

'Come here.' Thierry wrapped an arm round Alba's shoulder, tugging her closer. His breath reeked of alcohol. Leaning in, he whispered, 'I want to kiss my wife-to-be.'

She pushed him away. 'I'm not your *anything* yet,' she snapped. (*And good lord, I hope I never will be.*)

Thierry flushed. Against his dusky pink suit and white shirt, his coloured cheeks looked a sickly red. Watching her with narrowed eyes, he smoothed a hand over his hair.

'Let's change that, then, hmm?'

Alba glared at him. 'You're drunk.'

'And you're a prude.'

He leant in again, reaching for her, but she pushed him away. 'I said *no*!'

Thierry glowered, and it was like thunder rolling down on her, his usual easy smile replaced by hardness.

'That's not a word I like to hear.'

All of a sudden, Alba felt cold. Gathering up the skirts of her dress she went to stand, but had only half risen to her feet when Thierry grabbed her arm and pulled her back down. Before she could do anything, he twisted her onto her back and pressed his lips hard against hers, forcing them apart with his tongue.

'Get *off*!' she gasped, throwing her head to one side.

Alba dug her fingers into his shirt and pushed hard, but Thierry was heavy. He shifted his body on top of her, pinning her to the ground.

She writhed and squirmed and kicked and bucked, but his weight held her down. Her hands were trapped between their chests. She screamed, and he shoved his arm up under her chin, forcing her mouth to snap shut.

No one could hear her anyway, Alba realised desperately, heart pounding. The music was too loud. They were too far away.

Thierry grunted. His lips and tongue were all over the bare skin of her shoulders and chest, each touch making her feel more sick. Drawing his free hand down, he began tugging at her dress. She felt fresh air on her legs, then her hips.

Alba tried to scream out loud again (she'd never stopped).

When Thierry's fingers reached between her thighs, she felt a part of herself break. Tears streamed down her cheeks. She tried to twist her neck out from under his arm, thinking she'd bite his hand off if she had to, anything, *anything* to stop this nightmare –

'Get off her!'

A shout rang out.

Thierry's weight lifted suddenly from her. Alba gasped. Air rushed back into her lungs. Through blurry eyes she saw him scrambling to his feet, turning angrily to face the figure cutting across the grounds towards them.

It was her mother.

There was a look of pure hatred on Oxana's face. She flew at him, grabbing the lapels of Thierry's shirt to shove him away.

'She wanted it!' he shouted, staggering back. His face was a red, twisted mess. 'Ask her. She wanted it!'

'Leave,' Oxana snarled. 'Now.'

Throwing Alba a disgusted look, Thierry backed away, brushing down his rumpled clothes and smoothing a hand over his slicked hair before disappearing back into the lights and noise of the party, leaving Alba and her mother alone.

87

SEVEN

The alarm howled.

'Get back!' Axel yelled.

He pushed Seven, Dolly and Loe behind the cell's open door just as two guards rounded the corner, shots ringing out. He fired back.

Seven drew his own gun, holding it with shaking hands, but before he could do anything Axel had moved out.

'Follow me!'

Still half carrying Loe, Seven ran after him down the corridor, Dolly beside them. They stumbled over the bodies on the floor.

It was like being submerged in bloody water. The disorientating red light made it difficult to see: he guessed that was the point. They rushed through red-lit halls to the lobby. The two men Axel had shot earlier were still lying by the lifts, legs sprawled, necks twisted. Blood pooled across the floor.

One of the lift doors opened. A guard moved out with his gun raised.

'Drop your weapons! I said drop –'

Axel silenced him with a single shot, and the lift doors slid shut. Running forward, he swiped Lin's access card over the control panel.

Nothing happened.

'Shit! They must've locked the lifts from leaving this floor.' He spun round and moved to a door to the side of the lifts. He yanked it, but it didn't open.

'The stairs?' asked Seven, panting for breath. He was trying not to look at the bodies at their feet, the bloody footprints smearing the floor.

Axel didn't answer. He backed away from the door to the stairs and fired three shots at the lock. Then he lunged, crashing into the door shoulder first. It burst open with a loud *crack*.

'Come on!'

He disappeared into the shadowy red darkness of the stairwell.

'Here,' said Dolly at Seven's side. She swung an arm round Loe's waist and pulled her close. 'I've got her.'

Seven shook his head. 'I'm fine.'

'Not with your injury.'

She threw him a look that said, *Don't you dare argue with me*. Not wanting to waste any time (besides, she was right – his chest was starting to feel like ripped meat again where the dog had bitten him), Seven went into the stairwell, Dolly following behind with Loe.

They went down and down. Axel moved quickly, gun held out. He kept swinging round checking for guards, but it wasn't until they'd reached the twentieth floor that a door flew open above them and shots rang out.

Dolly let out a cry.

Seven whirled round. He saw her falling just in time and jumped the few steps between them, reaching out to grab her and Loe. Bullets spun through the air. He helped them to their feet, biting back a groan of pain as he felt the stitches in his wound snap open. He barely noticed Axel run past, gunshots ringing out as he took the guards down one by one.

'Are you hurt?' Seven asked breathlessly, looking over at Dolly. He couldn't see any fresh blood, but she was more bloodied and bruised than the last time he'd seen her.

She gritted her teeth. 'I'm fine. They just – they surprised me.'

'Hurry!'

Axel was off again now the guards were down, taking three steps at a time as he ran into the dark red shadows. One arm looped round Loe's waist, Seven started back down the stairs, Dolly behind him.

They staggered on, passing floor after floor. When they finally reached the basement level, they burst out through the wide double doors into an underground car park, stumbling straight into the car waiting for them.

They crammed into the back seat. Axel clambered into the front as the car sped off, tyres squealing loudly in the sudden silence of the echoing concrete basement. He launched into a tense conversation with the driver while changing out of his London Guard uniform.

The car swerved wildly round a pillar. Seven flung out an arm to steady himself. Loe slipped in the middle seat, sliding into Dolly and crushing her against the window.

Dragging Loe back into her seat, Seven pushed the straggly,

374

matted hair out of her eyes. She looked half dead.

'Wake up,' he grunted, shaking her. 'It's me. Seven. Your favourite person in the world. Come on, Loe. Don't you wanna shout at me? At least throw *one* punch?'

Her throat squeezed. A little colour seemed to seep back into her cheeks.

'Why?' she breathed finally, her voice rough.

He flashed her a grin. 'Why should you punch me? Ah, come on. I'm sure you can think of a million reasons.'

Loe gave a tiny shake of her head. Her bleary eyes focusing on him, she licked her lips. 'Why . . . help.'

Her words cut through Seven like a knife.

'Because I understand,' he said, grabbing her hand and squeezing it.

Then the car gave a great swerve and they were thrown in their seats.

'Fuck!' yelled the driver.

'Just get to the exit, Jacob!' Axel ordered him.

Seven turned to the window and saw three huge black cars – the London Guard's bulldog seal painted in white on their sides – speeding after them.

'They're shutting the grilles!' Jacob cried.

'You can make it!'

Through the windshield, Seven saw a metal grate lowering across the car-park exit. It was halfway down already.

Jacob swore loudly. 'Hold on!'

Seven threw his arm out and gripped the back of the chair in front just as the car reached the exit.

Screech!

His ears shattered. The awful grinding sound of metal against metal filled the air, deafeningly loud. The car shuddered. It slowed, but it didn't stop, and even though it sounded like the grille was tearing it in two it managed to drag itself through.

Everything fell quiet again as the car cleared the exit. They wound quickly up a long, twisting tunnel. Seconds later, they were out.

Axel looked back from the front passenger seat. He had changed into a black T-shirt and jeans. He grinned, dark eyes flashing as he met Seven's gaze.

'Ready for the Ball, Cinderella?'

88

ALBA

She felt a hand on her back.

'My darling. Are you – are you all right?'

Alba was kneeling in a ball on the ground. She wasn't sure how she'd got there; she just felt frosted earth beneath her, the smooth texture of her dress where she was doubled over, hugging herself. Her eyes were squeezed shut, but that didn't stop the tears running down her cheeks. She wanted Dolly. She wanted Seven. The last person on earth she wanted was her mother. It felt all the more humiliating that she had been the one to find her like this.

'Go away,' Alba breathed, her voice muffled. 'Please. Go away.'

'Alba –'

'Please, Mother! Just leave me alone!'

She wrenched her head up, crying hopelessly as she turned to face Oxana. She hated the pity she saw on her mother's face, the worry in her eyes.

'*Now* you choose to care?' Alba shouted. Anger ripped through her. Her chest heaved as she dragged in heavy, stuttering breaths. 'What about all those times it was *you* hurting me? Didn't you care then? Didn't you care at *all*?'

Oxana looked as though the world was falling around her. For the first time, Alba saw real emotion etched on her mother's face.

'Of course I care,' her mother said, her voice breaking.

Alba threw her arms out. 'Then why do you treat me like you wish I'd never been born!'

'Because sometimes I wish you *hadn't*!'

Everything fell silent.

Alba stared through blurred eyes at her mother, and her mother stared back. It was as though a switch had gone off. The soundtrack of the world turned to mute, the sounds of the Ball fading away, and all she could hear was her own ragged breaths and her heart, beat beat beating in her chest.

After what felt like an eternity, Oxana shook her head. 'I – I didn't mean that,' she said shakily.'

'Please. No more lies.'

For some reason, Alba felt strangely calm now. A sense of peace enveloped her. Her breaths slowing, she stood, smoothing down her mussed and dirtied dress.

Her mother drew a heavy breath. 'I think,' she said, 'it's time I told you the truth.'

She took her hands. Alba could see the soft tracks of tears running down her mother's face, and she stared at them in disbelief.

Her mother, the Ice Queen, was crying.

'When I left Ukraine,' Oxana began, her voice even, despite the tremor running through it, 'I was only seventeen years old. I came to London hoping for a better future. One of the girls I knew from my district had left a few months before. She told me that the streets were paved with gold. That women had as many rights as men, and there was more for us than marriage and hard factory work. She told me there was no crime. We didn't need to be scared of walking through the city alone. London was safe. It sounded like heaven.'

Oxana looked away. When she turned back, there was a hardness in her eyes.

'It was only an hour after I had arrived at the port. I'd just left the Immigrations Office. They attacked me near the river, beating me before tying me up and blindfolding me, and taking me away on a boat.'

Alba could feel her mother's hand shaking in hers.

'They took me somewhere underground,' Oxana continued. 'I know now, of course, that they were Tube Gang members and they'd taken me to the maze of disused tunnels beneath the city. I thought I'd die there. That I'd never see the sky again. And I thought how wrong my friend was – London was *not* safe. It was not heaven.'

She took a deep, shuddering breath, her gaze drifting away. 'But I didn't die there. They let me go. I suppose they didn't think they needed to worry about me telling anyone because I was new in the city. Two men from the London Guard took me to hospital when they found me walking the streets later that night, bloodied and dirty.' Her eyes clicked back to Alba. 'That's where I met Alastair. He came to ask me for details on my attackers. At the time, he was working on a big case involving one of the Tube Gangs and was hoping I might have some useful information.' She smiled tentatively. 'He proposed after a month. And eight months later, you were born.'

The shock of her mother's words snapped through Alba like a current. Every inch of her seemed to scream alert.

'Eight – *eight* months later?' she croaked.

No.

No.

Oxana's eyes were imploring. 'Please, my darling,' she said desperately. 'You have to know that your father loves you every bit as much as he would if you were his own. That even though I know I might not show it all the time, because sometimes the memory of it all just gets too much and something inside me breaks, *I* love you too, Alba. I love you so, *so much –*'

BOOM.

The world let out a giant shudder.

Alba dropped her mother's hand as the ground shook. The air snapped, breaking apart with a horrible, groaning roar that seemed to rip everything in two. All of a sudden the November night felt hot and burning, and as she stumbled back she saw flames dancing where the Ball was taking place, fiery tongues licking high into the sky.

Her mother's eyes were wide. 'What on *earth* . . .?'

'The Movement,' breathed Alba.

They were here.

She looked back at her mother. Her beautiful face was lit by the glow of the flames. Alba knew they only had minutes, that this was very possibly the last time she'd ever see her, and she felt desperate because of what she'd just learnt. How strange and sad it was that knowing the truth about how she'd been brought into the world only made her feel closer to her mother than she'd ever felt before, because now –

Now she understood.

Before she could think about what she was doing, Alba threw her arms wide and pulled her mother against her so tightly their hearts raced alongside each other.

'I love you,' she whispered.

Then she let go, running in the direction of the Ball, forcing herself not to look back, even though every step that took her further away from her mother broke her heart into another tiny piece.

89

SEVEN

The car sped through the night-time streets. They heard the wail of sirens in the distance; the London Guard were chasing them. Over the growl of the engine Jacob and Axel discussed the Movement's plans in low voices. They cut off as the beeping of a tablet sounded.

'It's them,' Axel said, then fell quiet; Seven guessed he was reading a message. A moment later, he let out a shout. 'They've done it! Detonated the bomb! They had to go ahead early as the guards at the Ball just got the message about our break-out – they didn't want people to start leaving.'

Seven's heart skipped a beat. 'Bomb? No one said anything about *bombs*.'

'Kola told you, Candidate. He said it would be dangerous.'

'I don't care what he said! Alba's there. If she's hurt –'

Axel cut him off. 'Look, we're almost there. Just keep a hold of the gun I gave you and be ready to go.'

'It's all right, Seven,' Dolly said, reaching across Loe to take his hand in hers as Axel fell back into conversation with Jacob. She gave him a small smile. 'Alba will be fine. I know it. She's strong, you know. Stronger than anyone gives her credit for.'

Seven's glower dropped away. 'I know,' he said. 'It's just . . .' He trailed off, frowning, a sickening feeling twisting in his stomach.

Something was wrong.

Gazing down, he let go of Dolly's hand –

And his palm came away slicked with blood.

'No,' he breathed. He looked back up, feeling as though he'd just been winded. His voice flew higher. 'No! You said you weren't hurt!'

Dolly drew back her hand. She slid it behind her, holding it low on her back. Seven leant over and saw the dark, blooming stain that had spread across the bottom of her pinafore and white of her tights.

'No!' he cried again. He jerked forward, grabbing Axel's shoulder. 'Stop the car! We need a doctor!'

'Seven,' Dolly said gently.

'Axel, stop the car!'

'Seven, please.'

Slowly, reluctantly, he turned to face her. Her eyes were filled with tears. Under the cuts and bruises and swollen mess of her face, he saw her then the way Alba saw her: a woman who was more of a family to Alba than her own flesh and blood.

Tears filled Seven's eyes, too.

'You're gonna be just fine,' he croaked.

But she shook her head. She reached for his hands again. 'Listen to me. Alba – she is a treasure. She deserves the world. If I find out you've hurt her in any way, I'll be coming for you.

Even if it's from my grave.'

Seven's face twisted. 'Don't say that.'

'Just promise me.' Dolly's hands were grasping his with such a fierceness he could feel her fingernails marking his skin. 'You'll keep her safe.'

It wasn't a question, but he answered anyway.

'Yes. I promise.'

And it wasn't like promises Seven had made in the past. This promise was different. It was real and true, and Seven knew the moment he made it that he'd spend his life doing everything he could to keep it.

Dolly let go of his hands just as the car growled to a stop. Without Seven noticing, they'd entered the grounds of Hyde Park Estate and pulled up to the Whites' house. Gold flames flickered in the distance. He heard shouts and screams piercing the night. Figures rushed about in the shivering darkness. The sirens that had been tailing them wailed louder.

'We've got to go,' said Axel, turning round in the front seat.

Seven shook his head. 'Dolly and Loe –'

'Jacob'll drive them to our getaway spot by the lake. They'll be safe. Come on.'

Axel opened the door. Sounds that had been muffled now flooded in, sharp and clear. Gunshots rang out. He got up, the car shifting as his weight was lifted, then slammed the door. A moment later, he yanked Seven's door open.

'Come on!' he barked again. 'Now!'

Seven looked back at Dolly. He was about to tell her he'd see her soon, that he'd find Alba and keep her safe, but then he saw Loe's expression and how still Dolly had gone, how her eyes were glazed and blank.

The words died in his throat.

'Seven, go,' Loe said, looking at him with tear-streaked cheeks.

What else could he do? Biting back his own tears, he turned and stumbled out of the car.

The night was a mess of gunshots and screams. Bursts of light studded the darkness. The glow of the fire at the heart of the Ball made everything look as though it were trembling, like the world was melting away. Or maybe it was because Seven was shaking so hard he was throwing off his own vision.

As the car squealed off behind them, Axel grabbed his hand and led him towards a line of people. Seven thought for a second they were London Guardmen, and his gut swooped. *You bastards.* Then he saw their ragged clothes and realised they were Takeshi's Bakerloo Boys.

'I've got Candidate Seven!' shouted Axel over the roar of noise.

The gang lowered their guns, letting them past. Seven guessed they were here to stop anyone entering or leaving the party.

Slowing a little, Axel steered him into the main throng of the Ball. It was chaos. There were people everywhere. Women whose expensive dresses were ripped, men with singed hair, waiters and guests and performers alike all crushing together, straining to leave but beaten back by the studs of the gang's gunfire. Seven stumbled over a body on the ground. He tried to look back to see who it was but Axel was moving too fast. He pulled him down a narrow path between the back of a bombed-out stage and a line of melting ice statues.

'Kola!'

Seven looked ahead at Axel's shout and saw the tall outline of his flatmate crouched next to something on the ground. As they neared, he saw what it was –

A girl.

His heart flew into his mouth. Then he realised the girl had blonde hair and was older than Alba. He sagged with relief but immediately felt sick at himself.

This was still someone. Someone else's Alba.

As Axel hurried to the girl, Kola stood and turned to Seven. His face was tight.

'We need you. Now.'

'Not until I find Alba.'

Frustration flashed across Kola's face. 'There's no time for that! It's about to begin.'

But Seven was already backing away. 'I promised!' he shouted. Then, quieter, 'I promised Dolly.'

And before Kola could stop him, he span on his heels and ran back into the flame-lit crowds.

90

ALBA

She didn't know where to go. What to do. Everywhere she turned there seemed to be something that made her want to turn back, get away: bodies flung across the ground; a woman whose dress was on fire; a man in a purple suit sitting calmly on the edge of a stage, holding the bloody stump of his leg, looking down as though wondering where on earth his foot had got to.

Alba was shunted aside as a man carrying a young child shouldered past her. She only caught the girl's limp wrist, how one of her little sparkly shoes had fallen off. She stared hopelessly after them, confused about how this had happened, how in a few minutes the whole world had been torn apart, when –

A voice cut through the night air.

A voice she had never quite believed she'd hear again, and yet had never quite believed she wouldn't.

A voice that put her world back together with one shout.

'Alba!'

Seven was on her at once. Slamming into her, they staggered back against a broken statue. His arms clung tight around her. She squeezed back, imagining that if they held each other hard enough they could disappear into each other, dissolve away from here. His heartbeat raced under her cheek where her face was pressed to his chest.

When Seven eventually drew back, Alba stood on her toes to kiss him.

'I was so worried,' she breathed.

She pulled back to look over him. Though he looked haggard and haunted, Seven didn't appear to be hurt. His clothes were scuffed but there was nothing that indicated he'd been tortured by the London Guard.

Alba's mind flicked to her handmaid. 'Where's Dolly?' she asked.

Her heart skipped as she noticed for the first time the red slicking one of Seven's palms. She glanced down at her dress. Dazed, she saw dark patches smeared where he'd touched her.

She looked back up, something wild dashing through her. 'Is that . . . blood?'

'I love you,' Seven said suddenly.

Alba blinked.

'I'm sorry, and I love you, and you have to know –'

But before he could go on, a great, booming voice blasted through the fire-torn night.

'LADIES AND GENTLEMAN, WELCOME TO THIS YEAR'S WINTER-TURN BALL!'

The noise of the ruined party fell at once. It wasn't silent;

there were still sobs, murmurs, cries, the crackle of flames. Gunfire cracked in the distance as the London Guard fought Takeshi's boys on the edge of the Whites' grounds. Shouts drifted across on the burnt air. But a chilling hush spread through the crowds at the sudden announcement.

It took Alba a few moments to find the source of the voice. She was still dazed from Seven's words; had he just told her that he loved her? But why was he sorry about it? Everyone was turning to the main stage, a large platform backed by a screen that had earlier been drifting with glittering silver snow, but now was a deep blood red. Written across it in bold black print were the words:

THE MEMORY KEEPERS IS MURDER

Alba let out a gasp.

'Let's give a round of applause to the White family. They have been such welcoming hosts, have they not?'

No one clapped, apart from the speaker on the stage. He was a tall, slim man, an oriental slant to his elegant features. Dark hair fell to his cheeks. Unlike the rest of the ball-goers' clothes, his were still immaculate: metallic black suit and white shirt loosened at the top, with a red bow-tie open and slung round his neck. A microphone was clipped round one ear. Though his smile was warm there was an edge to it. Alba could sense the tension thrumming underneath. He was flanked by a group of people; she spotted Kola and Nihail among them.

The Movement.

She wondered why no one was shooting at them. Where

were the security guards? The London Guard? Surely they couldn't all have been killed.

Her stomach flipped at the thought. All those men, all those people who'd just been doing their jobs . . .

Seven shifted closer. He didn't hold Alba, but there was something protective in the way he stood with his chest pressed to her back, as though ready to shield her at any moment.

'I love you too,' she whispered, though she knew he couldn't hear.

'I'm sorry for the nature of our entrance,' the speaker on the stage went on, holding his hands out in an apologetic gesture. His smile vanished. 'There was no other way to guarantee you would stay to hear us out, to see the things we have to show you. And they must be seen, ladies and gentlemen. It's finally time for you all to know the truth.'

There were murmurs among the crowd. Alba noticed several people shoving their way through to the stage. She froze, recognising the tall, striding figure of the man who had raised her.

Alastair White's face was murderous. He was shouting something, but Movement members surged forward, cutting him off as they grabbed him and dragged him on stage along with Christian Burton-Lyon, Rossmund Pearson and a few others Alba didn't recognise.

Christian Burton-Lyon and Pearson were fighting and shouting, trying to throw off the men holding them, but her father had fallen still. He stood tall and quiet, staring at the speaker at the centre of the stage with such a dark, intense gaze Alba was amazed the man hadn't keeled over and died.

Something twisted in her heart as she watched him now with the knowledge of what her mother had told her.

Alastair White wasn't her father.

And at the same time, he was.

Ignoring the struggle going on at the back of the stage, the speaker continued to address the crowd. 'My name is Kite Sung. I am the leader of the Free Memory Movement, a group dedicated to revealing the despicable practices of these men behind me, among others, and the project they call TMK – The Memory Keepers.'

A ripple ran through the crowd. Alba caught snatches of conversations whirling through the air around her.

'. . . Memory Keepers . . . ?'

'. . . someone from Intelligence once mentioned something about a TMK . . .'

'. . . don't believe it . . .'

'. . . where the bloody hell is security . . .'

On stage, Kite Sung's expression was stormy. The dark red of the screen backlit his figure in a glowing halo, casting shadows across his face. He opened his mouth to speak and the crowds fell quiet once more.

'I have worked on TMK since the very beginning as part of their Science team, led by Harold Merriweather. Some of you knew him, I am sure. A brilliant scientist, but more than that – a brilliant man. When he understood what the results of TMK's experiments were being used for, he knew he could not continue to stand idly by. Along with me and a few others who knew of the cruel, dark secret of the Memory Keepers, Harold Merriweather formed the Free Memory Movement.'

Sung took a deep breath. For the first time, there was a crack in his façade. His voice shook slightly when he continued.

'Harold Merriweather would have been here today, addressing you all instead of me, the true leader of the Movement, if he had not been murdered by the London Guard five days ago in a bid to silence him.'

Gasps of shock threaded through the ball-goers. It felt like the air had suddenly thinned, making the night feel even tenser, even more taut.

'But what', continued Sung in a low, dangerous voice, 'is one more murder to men like Alastair White and Rossmund Pearson? Even our very own Lord Minister? What is one more murder to those who kill innocents in cold blood every day?'

He strode to the side of the stage. The other Movement members also shifted to clear the space in front of the screen.

'Ladies and gentlemen,' Sung announced, spreading out an arm, 'let me present to you the truth about The Memory Keepers!'

The screen turned white. A second later, a face flashed onto it, Alba's heart flying as she took in its tangled flop of hair, those sharp, grey eyes, and that beautiful, beautiful grin, lopsided and messy and just about the best thing in the world.

It was Seven.

91

SEVEN

The crowd gasped as one. Well, all except for one. *The* one.
Seven, standing there in the middle of the ball-goers, staring
with them all at his ugly mug splashed across the screen, could
only let out a half-hearted, 'Effing hell.'

Alba reached back for his hand as whispers filled the air.

'He's that memory-thief, isn't he?'

'The one from the London Guard News Net broadcast?'

'His name was something like Eight. Or Six . . .'

Then, a louder voice, cutting over them all –

'Look! He's here!'

Alba squeezed Seven's hand so hard he could feel her
fingernails digging into his skin. Faces were turning their way.
With a rising panic, he stumbled back into someone who pushed
him roughly away. A space opened in the crowd around him
and Alba.

'Come with me,' said a kind voice.

Kola had come down from the stage. He curled an arm round

Seven and, Alba in tow, led him to the front of the crowd. They climbed up to join Sung.

Sung gave him a quick, tense smile before taking his hand and pulling him forward.

'This boy', he announced to the crowds, 'is Candidate Seven. Due to operations on his brain when he was a baby, Candidate Seven is able to manipulate the physical properties of memories – just like all the Candidates involved in TMK's experiments. All of the Candidates, that is, who don't die from the operations forced upon them by these men standing behind us.'

'Lies!' hissed Pearson, who had managed to free his mouth from the hand of the Movement member restraining him. 'You'll be executed for treason, all of you!'

His shouts were muffled as his mouth was covered again.

'Execution,' said Sung slowly, and the word seemed to carry the weight of a physical object. It hung heavy in the air. Still gripping Seven, he turned back to the crowd, sweeping his gaze over them. 'Lies. Mr Pearson has aptly hit upon the two things TMK is founded upon. Creating lies in the very things we trust the most – our own memories. And using those lies to execute innocents.'

Seven saw the expressions on the ball-goers' faces. Doubt flickered in their eyes, along with confusion, anger, fear. There was no belief yet . . . but there was the space for it.

Maybe, he thought, a flush of hope spreading through him, *this is actually gonna work!*

And then the roar of a second explosion ripped through the night air.

The next things happened so quickly they all seemed to

bleed into one long, terrible moment. Screams. The shuddering ground. Sung's hand dropping from his. Thuds of gunfire rising, drawing nearer. People scattering, the crowd turning once more into a crushing throng of chaos as men in red jackets – the London Guard – charged round the side of the house, guns aimed at the stage.

They'd cleared through Takeshi's defence, Seven realised. They'd bombed them, all those boys.

'We have to get out of here!'

A small, warm hand slipped into his and then he and Alba were off, running to the edge of the stage, stumbling down and careening wildly through the panicked crowd, not looking back, not waiting to see if they were being followed, just running as fast as they could, getting as far the eff away as possible from this hell of a night.

92

ALBA

They charged into the flame-cut darkness of the outer edges of the Ball, slipping on the frosty lawn, feet pounding in time with their heartbeats. Screams and gunfire beat against their backs. Alba chanced a quick look over her shoulder but could only see a mess of fire-lit figures, the silhouettes of fighting bodies.

And then it hit her.

'Dolly!'

She dragged Seven to a stop. Panting, she doubled over, clutching the stitch in her side.

'We have to go back,' she gasped between gulps of breaths. 'We have to find her!'

'Alba . . .'

She tugged him in the direction of the Ball. 'She was with you and the Movement, yes? She might still be back there! She might be hurt!'

Alba pulled harder but Seven was rooted to the spot. She felt like screaming at him. *What's* wrong *with you?* she thought desperately. *Don't you understand? Dolly's my family! I can't leave her!*

'Alba,' Seven repeated, firmer this time, and it was only then that she heard it in his voice.

Dolly was dead.

She dropped his hand as though it had burned her.

No.

Seven took a step towards her but she backed away, stumbling on the icy grass.

No!

Alba couldn't breathe. She felt as though she were dying. Her chest was cleaving in two, her heart shattering into tiny pieces of glass that were digging into her insides.

A few people ran past them across the shadowy grounds, but they were like ghosts, echoes, distant and untouchable.

'No,' Alba breathed, and it came out like a question.

A beg.

Seven answered softly, 'Yes.'

She stared at him through blurred eyes. 'When?' she croaked. 'How?'

'She was shot when we were escaping. She – she died in the car on the way here. When we arrived.'

Alba felt sick. Dolly had been *here*. She'd been so close, and she hadn't got to see her, talk to her one last time. Hold her in her arms and tell her that she loved her, that she couldn't have ever asked for a better friend. That Alba thought of her as a sister and it didn't matter what their blood said, *she* was her family.

Seven moved closer. He took both of her hands in his. 'Do

you want to see her?' he asked.

Alba closed her eyes and nodded.

They moved slower now, partly because it felt safer in the dark, moonlit grounds of the estate, far from the fight raging back at the Ball. But they were also slower because Alba couldn't run. She was having a hard enough time just walking, staying upright, *breathing*. It took every inch of her energy to keep from dropping to the ground and screaming her lungs apart.

When they reached the lake, the Serpentine's surface was still and silvered in the starlight. Shadows of willows dipped their long leaves into the water at the edges of the lake. The soft rush of the water filled the air like a lullaby.

Alba saw blurrily that there was a car waiting on the bank beside the lake.

'I thought there'd be more,' Seven muttered. 'This was their getaway spot. Where're the rest of the cars?'

'They went to help.'

A voice sounded from the car. A few seconds later, a girl's thin silhouette came out from behind it.

'Loe,' Seven said, sounding relieved.

The girl stepped closer, moonlight washing over her to reveal a face so torn and swollen she looked disfigured.

'Who's with you?' she asked.

'Alba.'

There was a pause.

'Your *girlfriend*?'

The girl's voice took on a mocking tone, and suddenly Seven moved forward to wrap his arms around her.

'You're back,' he croaked.

She flashed a crooked smile. 'Barely.' When they broke apart, she took a heavy breath. 'They explained everything to me while we were waiting. But they left when they got an SOS message from the others at the Ball. Took the cars. They're hoping to get away straight after the fight – said we could have this one.'

'I can't drive,' Seven said.

'Well, learn.'

Alba listened to their conversation as though she were far away; their voices reached her thickly through her tears. When she couldn't bear it any longer, she asked, 'Can I see Dolly now?'

The girl's eyes met hers. Understanding darted between them, and she nodded. Silently, she led Alba and Seven to a willow at the edge of the lake and brushed back its leaves, stepping aside to let Alba through.

But before she went in, Alba stopped. Suddenly, panic gripped her. Dolly was dead. If Alba saw her, saw her body, then she would know it was real, and forever she'd have the image to haunt her, to replace the memories of her laughing, smiling handmaid with the darker, still, shadow version.

Alba turned back to Seven. Tears flowed fast down her cheeks. 'I don't think I can,' she said, voice breaking.

He was by her side at once. He pulled her against him, wrapping his arms tenderly around her.

'Yes, you can. You can do this, Alba.'

She shook her head, face still pressed into the warm fabric of his jumper. 'I don't think I can.'

'Well, I know you can.'

'She's dead, Seven,' Alba breathed. 'Dolly's dead.'

'I know. But nothing can bring her back now. And you'll never forgive yourself if you leave without saying goodbye.'

It was that which finally made her realise what she had to do. Sniffing, Alba pulled away. She met Seven's eyes and nodded, then took a deep breath and stepped through the willow's curtain of leaves into the hushed darkness below.

Dolly was lying at the base of the tree. Her silhouette was small. Still. Alba's heart skipped at the sight of her, and her tears flowed faster, warm as they traced down her face, but she forced herself on. She crouched down beside Dolly. Reaching out, she cupped her handmaid's cold cheek as gently as she could.

'I'm so sorry,' Alba whispered. 'I'm sorry you were dragged into this. And I'm sorry I can't drag you back out.'

Her voice broke. Letting out a soft cry she collapsed, holding Dolly tight, wishing she'd been able to see her one last time, just to tell her what she'd never told her enough.

That Alba loved her.

That she loved her more than sunshine and moonbeams. That she loved her to the ends of the earth and back. That she had loved her – and *would* love her – every day, every night, every single moment of her life.

THREE WEEKS LATER

4.40 p.m., West Gloucestershire countryside

Seven had been out fishing at the river all afternoon. Sometimes Alba came with him. Not that she joined in; she just sat beside him, wrapped in a thick coat he'd stolen for her from the farmhouse, staring out in silence at the water rushing by. But today she'd stayed back.

The river was starting to ice over. December was just around the corner, and he could feel winter in the air. There was a cold, bitter wind that made his nose run. The ground was covered in frost. It glittered in the misty grey light like a field of crushed diamonds.

Seven wished it *were* diamonds. They could do with more money at the moment (could do with *any* money at the moment).

The walk back to the barn from the river took over an hour. Seven's fingers were freezing by the time he arrived. He fumbled with the latch bolted across the barn doors, easing it up, then slipped inside. He still worried each time he went in. But the farmhouse was a good distance away, and from what he'd observed this was the least used of their two barns, and they'd not been caught yet.

Seven felt a touch of pride. 'Still got it,' he muttered.

'Got what? Your charm? Your looks? Trust me, you never had any in the first place.'

'A pleasure as always to see you too, Loe.'

She moved out from her lookout spot by the door, throwing him a mocking smile. Three weeks on and she was looking much better, though her face was still shadowed with bruises and her right ankle was twisted oddly, making her walk with a limp. She was dressed in a big black hunting jacket and a pair of men's trousers. Her hair hung messily around her face.

Seven handed Loe the newspaper he'd wrapped the fish in and wiped his hands on his trousers. 'How was she today?' he asked.

Loe shrugged. 'Better, I think. Moving about a bit more. She's telling Mika a story right now.'

He followed her gaze up past the space of the barn's lower level – cluttered with bales of hay and broken tractor parts, the concrete ground hidden beneath mussed straw – to the upper floor covering the back half of the building. It was just an open ledge with a ladder running up to it, but they'd piled some of the haystacks along it to create their own private space. It was where they slept and spent most of their time when they were in the barn, just in case anyone came in and they needed to hide.

A hushed voice drifted down.

Nodding a thanks to Loe, Seven crossed to the ladder, climbing effortlessly up the wooden rungs (if only skid-thieving had been this easy). Squeezing through a gap in the haystacks at the top, he put on his widest grin and shouted –

'Boo!'

Alba and Mika were at the far end of the balcony. Mika was wrapped in a puffy coat, lying on her elbows and gazing up at Alba, who was wearing a khaki farmer's coat and a tartan scarf. Her hair was loose and long. It hung in thick auburn waves past her shoulders, golden strands shining in the dim light of the barn.

'Seven! Seven! Seven!'

Mika pounced on him at once. Her little arms squeezed round his neck. He laughed, picking her up round the waist, and walked over to Alba. He had to crouch to avoid hitting his head on the sloping roof of the barn.

Alba's eyes lifted to meet his. They were red, and her skin was still a little sallow, but her cheeks were fuller now, almost like they were before.

She managed a tiny smile, and Seven's heart flipped. It still did that every time she smiled at him, which unfortunately wasn't a lot lately.

'What story has Alba been telling you, huh?' he asked, sitting down. He peeled Mika off him and set her back on her feet.

Mika snuggled in his lap. 'One about her friend Dolly! She was a naughty maid. She showed Alba how to trap frogs by the lake and then put them in the servants' beds!' She squirmed, looking wide-eyed at Alba. 'Can you teach me? Please! I want to try it on Loe!'

Alba glanced away. 'Soon,' she promised.

Seven pinched Mika's cheeks. 'Go help Loe with dinner – otherwise you know she'll probably end up poisoning us.'

Giggling, Mika ran off and swung down the ladder, leaving Seven and Alba alone.

'Any more news?' Alba asked quietly.

He nodded. 'I caught a little on the way back.' Shifting closer, he took one of her hands and cradled it in his lap with both of his. 'There've been more uprisings in South. Sounds like the new stand-in Lord Minister is doing his best to deal with it, trying to create a better relationship between North and South. Seems like there's good progress on the investigation into TMK now, too. More evidence coming through. And . . .' Seven hesitated, watching her carefully. 'Those involved with TMK have been charged with murder. Their trails will start in a few weeks.'

'Good,' Alba said. Her voice was hard. She took a deep breath. 'I mean, as long as the trials are fair and just. The nationwide ban on executions *is* still in place, isn't it?'

She avoided Seven's eyes, and he knew she was thinking of her father.

'Yeah, it is.'

Alba relaxed a little at his answer. Seven moved closer so he was sitting at her side, his back propped against the wall. He tucked an arm round her shoulders. She leant in, pressing her face into his chest. She smelled of straw – what *didn't* now? – and of that soft, floral scent of hers.

He thought of how broken she'd been after the Winter-turn Ball. How stepping into the shadow of that willow had transformed her somehow. She'd left something behind there; something more than Dolly's body.

Seven didn't know if she'd ever get it back.

Alba hadn't said a word the whole journey from Hyde Park Estate, Seven driving wildly out of the break in the fence

406

that the Movement had cut for their getaway, then through the moonlit streets of North to the river. Nobody had chased them. The entire London Guard must have been at the Ball, fighting the Movement.

She'd continued to be silent as they'd crossed the river on a water-taxi – illegally paid for with Alba's necklace – to pick up Mika from Loe's home at Bankside. Because of course the London Guard hadn't given Loe the reward they'd promised for her giving up information on Seven. After that, they'd travelled for hours up the Thames, far out of the city and deep into unregulated country land.

Alba still hadn't spoken when they made camp in a forest near the river, lost in endless countryside, moving every day, Seven having to steal food and other supplies from farmhouses and local villages.

It was only when they'd come across this unused barn that she finally, finally spoke.

'I'm tired. Can we stop here for a little while?'

Everyone had seemed glad she'd suggested it. They were all tired, all craving a place to stop and call home, even if it was only temporary.

They'd been in the barn now for a week. Each day, Seven and Loe – they were the two thieves of the group after all – went to steal the things they needed: warm clothes, food, blankets. They only took the essentials to survive. Seven had had enough of stealing for a lifetime, but until they figured out where they were going to go and how they could earn money legitimately, it would have to do.

They tried to catch the news on Net programmes when

they passed houses or shops. This was how they'd learnt about the impact of the Movement's actions at the Ball. Despite its abrupt ending, the Movement's suggestions on the night and the broadcast they'd sent out over the Net had been enough for an official national inquiry to be launched into TMK. Sung, Kola, Axel, Nihail and the rest of the Movement members were aiding the investigation, though they themselves were awaiting trial for what happened at the Ball. Seven was hoping all charges against them would be dropped once their allegations about The Memory Keepers were proved to be true.

And a few days ago, Seven and Loe had overheard a broadcast mentioning that Oxana had divorced Alastair White and left the country. They'd decided not to tell Alba. At least, not yet. Seven hadn't told her about what he'd seen in the memory Takeshi had made him alter either. He was pretty sure he never would. Why cause her more pain?

If there was anything he and Alba had learnt from what had happened, it was that memories were sometimes best left well alone.

Before he'd left the river that afternoon, Seven had stood looking out at the rushing water. There was something he'd been wanting to do for a while and it finally felt like the right time. Bowing his head, he pulled off the long chain hanging round his neck.

The key to his memorium.

He could have thrown it away weeks ago. Before the Ball, even. As soon as his flat had been taken over by the London Guard. But something had held him back. The key represented everything it used to unlock –

New worlds.

New experiences.

Freedom.

But Seven didn't need a key for those things any more. He didn't need a memory-machine or skids. He didn't need to steal parts of other people's lives, because he finally had his own life, his own memories to make. And when he'd thrown the key into the river, watching it disappear under the churning water, he knew he could finally let go of his past and move forward into his future.

Alba gave a soft sigh, shifting under his arm, bringing him back to the barn where they were tucked up in a corner under the sloping roof. He smoothed the hair away from her cheeks and kissed her forehead.

The truth was, Seven didn't have an effing clue about any of it. Not one. He didn't know how long they'd be able to stay here. Where they'd go after, what they'd do, how they'd live. But he did know one thing for certain: they'd be doing it together. Alba, Loe, Mika and him.

All right, he'd be the first to admit it was a weird little family. And half the time he wondered how on earth they'd not alerted the people in the farmhouse nearby with all their squabbling. But he had a feeling they'd be OK. Because for the first time in Seven's life, *his life* felt like enough. He had Alba by his side. He had someone – three someones – to love . . . and to love him.

Loe's voice reached them from below.

'Could you have caught any more puny little lumps of fish, Seven? I'll do it myself if you're always gonna be this rubbish.'

Well, perhaps the word love was a *bit* strong when it came to Loe.

'Feel free,' he shouted back down, grinning. 'I'd like to see *you* try.'

And, though he might just have been imagining it, because it was so quiet a sound and her face was turned into his chest, buried in the fabric of his jumper, Seven thought he heard Alba let out a little snort of laughter.